Unknown Border

by

Jason Spencer

Acknowledgements

I would like to express my gratitude to the many people who saw me through this book; to all my friends who provided support, talked things over, offered comments.

I would like to thank my sons; Gavin, Kole and Ryan for the constant Bigfoot calls throughout the house and the hours and hours of watching and researching Bigfoot with Dad.

Stephanie Young… Your patience and professionalism are second to none. Without your continued efforts and support, I would have not been able to bring my dream into a reality.

Finally… Tim Levick for countless hours discussing ideas and listening to campfire stories.

First Edition - December 2015

Note for Librarians: A cataloguing record for this book is available from Library and Archives Canada at www.collectionscanada.ca/amicus/index-e.html

ISBN – 978-1-77084-583-1

Printed in Canada

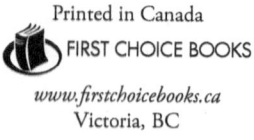

FIRST CHOICE BOOKS

www.firstchoicebooks.ca
Victoria, BC

10 9 8 7 6 5 4 3

Prologue

Washington State, 1975

*J*eff made a wild leap over a stray fallen log, his foot snagging in the grasp of the spindly branches, and fell with an uncoordinated thud to the moist ground. Brenda was at his side a moment later, hauling him to his feet.

"Get up, Jeff, get up."

A long, reverberating howl echoed through the dark woods as if to reinforce her urging, and Jeff vaulted to his feet as if he'd been hit by an electric current. Brenda was already ahead of him, and he took off hot on her heels. He could not afford to be left behind, not now. They wove a jagged path through the forest, shoving through spare, scratchy branches and shrub which seemed intent upon hindering their progress. The undergrowth was thick at the height of summer, and they had only the waning light of the shadowed moon to guide them, which left them little room for mishaps. Jeff kept his eyes solely on Brenda's back, ignoring the sweat beading down the side of his head as he strained to keep her pace.

Suddenly, she veered off to the right and disappeared into the night. Jeff followed her erratic movement, crashing through a thick wall of sharp sticks and thorns to find himself face to face with Brenda's tearful eyes.

She held a quivering finger to her lips, the whites of her eyes wide.

Jeff nodded and looked around to get a bearing on their surroundings. Somehow, in the midst of her spastic sprinting, Brenda had managed to spot a thicket concealed on all four sides. It made a perfect hiding spot.

They crouched down together in the dirt, Jeff's knees popping, holding their breath. The seconds passed in what seemed an eternity.

"Do you think it's—?"

A great roar of rage shook their tiny refuge. Jeff covered his ears to shut it out, wincing.

It was close.

A horrible, deafening silence followed the roar, punctuated only by nearly imperceptible footsteps. The silence, it seemed, was worse than the sounds. The silence was, in fact, deafening. The thing was coming.

The footsteps stopped right outside the thicket. Jeff kept his hands clamped over his ears and shut his eyes, reverting to his childhood, to a mantra he hadn't thought of in years. If he couldn't see it or hear it, it wasn't there. But he realized, with increasing agony, his mantra was not true. He could hear the slow, thick, humid breathing. He moved one hand to cover his mouth in order to keep from gagging on the musty odor of the beast's fur.

But then, after an impossibly long minute, the footsteps thudded away into the distance, and fresh air flooded Jeff's lungs again as he took a deep gasp. He opened his eyes and peered out of their hiding place, surveying the surrounding cover of trees for a few long moments before he dared to speak.

"It's gone," he finally whispered. "I think it's gone."

Brenda's eyes were still squeezed shut, and she rocked back and forth in a slow, quivering pattern.

Jeff laid a supportive hand on her shoulder, squeezing and leaning down to her ear, whispering comfortingly. "It's all right, we're safe now."

"All right?" She smacked his hand away and glared at him, her voice hoarse. "How can you say that? Don't say that to me, Jeff. They're dead, they're all dead."

She was right, of course. But there was no time to think about the grim truth, not when they were exposed out in the open of the woods. "Brenda, we have to get out of here."

"You don't even care, do you?" Freed tears glinted in her eyes and left shiny trails on her cheeks, catching the light of the moon.

Jeff's temper flared and he hissed. "Of course I care, but we can't just sit here crying; we have to move. It's still out there somewhere."

Brenda was silent for a long time, as if taking her own private moment to mourn, and Jeff tried to be patient as a pastor may be at the funeral, but he knew they didn't have time to wait much longer.

"What is that thing?" she finally rasped.

Jeff looked over his shoulder as if to make sure it wasn't eavesdropping and dropped his gaze momentarily. "I don't know." They had no time to try and give it a name. They had to leave. Now.

"What do you mean, you don't know? I thought you were the big outdoor expert," Brenda snapped, her hands still shaking despite her fretting with them.

"I've never seen anything like that before. It's huge and what it did to Terry, it just—" Jeff rubbed his mouth with his hand and tried to forget the sudden thunderclap of horrifying images he remembered. There were no words to describe what it had done to Terry. "I don't know what it is, okay? But, Brenda, we have to go."

She finally nodded and stood up carefully in the midst of the thorns. "Do you even know where we are?"

"Good question," Jeff admitted. He looked around once more. They'd been running uphill, that much he knew. That should mean they were heading away from their campsite, which had been nestled in a lower part of the woods to avoid wind chill. If they went back the way they'd come, they should reach the camp before too long and then, not far from that, run into the trail that led to the road where their Jeep was parked.

"We need to go this way." He pointed downhill, sparing her further details, and started walking before Brenda had a chance to object. God knows the thing would find them for sure if he gave her enough time to start questioning him again.

Finding the trail should have been easy enough, but he had to make absolutely sure they went through the camp first. His gun was there, and he wanted to have it with him in case that monster showed up again. It may be his saving grace if worse came to worse.

As they walked in silence, Jeff struggled to identify the creature in his mind. He hadn't gotten a good look at it in the darkness, of course. It was fast enough to catch up to them at their top speeds and really tall, at least eight feet, maybe more. A bear would have gotten tired of the chase and dropped off long ago. The sounds it made were like nothing he'd ever heard before, a guttural, hoarse breathing made from an animal with intent to kill anything in its path.

And it was stronger than any bear, too. The way it had snapped Terry in half without any resistance, like a twig...

Jeff shook his head with a grunt to force the memory out once more.

Focus, he told himself silently. If he was going to find the camp, he'd have to concentrate. They should have reached it by now, but it was hard to know how far they'd run in their moment of panic. It would be all too easy to walk past it in the darkest part of the night. It could be fifty yards to the right even now, and he'd never even know if he wasn't ever vigilant.

"There!" Brenda suddenly hissed, snagging his arm and pointing.

He followed her extended finger and saw their distant tents to the left. Brenda had proven her usefulness. They'd found the camp. He breathed a sigh of relief.

"Come on," Jeff said, grabbing Brenda's hand and pulling her toward the tents, focused only on the thought of his gun and how better it would feel to have his finger resting on the trigger.

Just outside of camp, Brenda stopped and screamed. Jeff plastered his hand over her mouth to cut off the sound, pulling her close. She violently pushed him off, twisted to her left, and promptly threw up into the leaves.

Jeff stared at what had triggered such a reaction; the sight of Mary's body, stomach slashed open, one arm missing entirely, brought bile to his throat as well. He coughed a few times to hold it back, turning away.

To distract himself from the grisly murder scene, he knelt down next to Brenda and waited for her to finish, helping hold her hair out of the way. When she finally lifted her head, her body quivering, wiping her mouth on her sleeve, he took her hand again and helped her stand. Her legs were shaking like jelly, but she let him lead her away.

They walked all the way into the campsite and stopped in front of Jeff's tent. He put a hand on each of Brenda's shoulders and turned her to face him. "I need you to wait out here, okay?"

She grabbed at his shirt frantically, her fingernails almost scratching him through the material of his clothes in earnest. "No, Jeff, don't leave me, don't leave me."

"It's okay. I'm not leaving you, I promise." He nodded at the tent. "I'll be right in there. I'm just going to get the gun, okay?"

Brenda nodded but didn't let go of his shirt, her hands clenching the cotton.

"I need you to watch. If you see anything, if you hear anything, scream."

Another nod.

Jeff grabbed her hands and gently pried them from his chest, covering them with his own hands and an added powerful squeeze. "I'll be right back." He dropped to his knees, dove into his tent, and scrambled blindly for the gun inside his pack. He yanked it out of his bag and checked the chamber by running his fingers over the spaces, his heart racing. Empty.

He dug through the bag again and pulled out a hand full of shells. Jeff frantically fed two into the gun when he heard Brenda gasp. He dropped the shells still in his hand and rushed outside, hand feeling slick on the metal from his sweat.

What he saw stopped him cold.

Brenda's feet dangled in front of his face. He looked up to see her throat in the grip of an enormous hand. Beyond that hand were two sharp eyes, red and glowing with fiery fury.

There was something else in those eyes, something almost human, but Jeff ignored that, brought the rifle to his shoulder to brace it, and pulled the trigger with a squeeze.

The explosion of his gun firing filled his ears, but the roar of pain he expected from the bullet piercing fur and flesh didn't follow. Instead, there was the sound of the grotesque snapping of human bone.

Brenda didn't even have time to scream. Her body crumpled to the ground in a heap as Jeff chambered another round.

Before he could take aim again, the rifle was yanked from his hands, and a crushing pressure enveloped his chest.

Blood bubbled out of his lips in place of breath, and he looked down to see the giant hands wrapped around his chest. He stared wide-eyed into the creature's red eyes a final time before the hands tightened. His vision ebbed away as the world went dark.

Chapter One

Present Day

Hank Tomkins stood at the crest of the ridge and thoughtfully stared down into the valley below. He took a deep breath, inhaling the essence of the open outdoors air, letting it soak into his soul. Nowhere on Earth was he more at home than here, in the wild.

After a few more lingering moments enjoying the view, he walked down into the valley and concentrated on the reason he had come to the forest in the first place – to hunt.

Hank dropped into a crouch at the edge of the valley and closed his eyes, letting the sounds of the forest overtake his human senses. At first, his human instincts prevailed, and he heard nothing but dull silence, but Hank had hunted far too long to give up that easily. The longer he listened, the quieter his own thoughts became and the more the world of man faded away until he was able to hear the opening notes composing the symphony of the woods. He listened longer. The sounds grew stronger, painted a picture filled with details his eyes could never capture. A bird high in a nearby tree called to another, possibly a mate. Within seconds, a second bird answered the call, this one farther away from Hank.

He turned his head, listening for sounds the forest masked; animals, birds, the wind in the trees. A stream gurgled through the woods, probably a home for salmon, and Hank pictured the animals that would come to the water's edge for a drink.

A series of rustles in the leaves told him a squirrel was nearby. The scraping of its tiny claws on bark as it scampered up the tree told him it had found the nuts it was looking for. A faint buzzing announced the presence of a bee close to him. It faded away, and he knew it had gone in search of flowers elsewhere.

Hank remained frozen in place, waiting and listening to all the sounds. He sorted the noises and identified the cause of each, in awe of being audience to such a true score from nature's concert. Finally, he heard what he had been waiting for, the sound of hooves striking the soft dirt near the stream. A pair of deer approached the bubbling stream for their morning drink. He opened his eyes and saw them--a tall buck and a doe, only slightly smaller, next to him, hesitant, sniffing the air for predators. He took a moment to appreciate the beauty and grace of the creatures, the smooth ripples of their muscled flanks, and the majestic antlers of the buck.

Hank could see in their eyes that they were considering darting away. Every step was slow and calculated. Their eyes never stopped moving, alert for even the smallest sign of danger, ears flickering at the slightest movement around them. A single unnecessary movement or the slightest sound would cost him the kill.

He had no desire to kill both the doe and the buck. He didn't need that much meat, and he didn't want to take the time to dress and haul back two deer. He would shoot the buck and let the doe run.

With a hand steadied by years of experience, Hank lined up the sights on his rifle. He waited until the buck leaned down to drink from the bubbling water of the stream, tilting the rifle to aim for the heart, and pulled the trigger.

The shot echoed through the valley and scattered any other nearby animals. The doe bolted from the riverbed, leaving a splash and the flash of her white tail as she disappeared into the canopy with a bound. There was no need for a second shot. The buck lay dead on the ground in a small pool of blood.

Hank shouldered his rifle and walked to the buck. He took a knee next to it and inspected his kill.

It wasn't the largest prize Hank had claimed by any means, but it was a respectable six points. Hank pulled it up over his shoulders with a grunt of effort, spreading his legs as he balanced the weight.

"I don't know how many more years I'm going to be able to pull this off," Hank remarked to the forest as casually as if it were an old friend. His fifty-five year old body was struggling under the weight of the hundred pound buck on his shoulders. It was a painful, truthful reminder that he wasn't in his twenties anymore.

As he approached his old truck, the phone on his hip buzzed. Time to get to work--real work.

He dumped the buck in the truck bed and walked around to the driver's door. It was unlocked as usual, and not just because it was parked in the middle of the woods. The power locks only worked with the heater running full blast, so using them wasn't very practical. Such was the life of a truck which was probably feeling its age as much as he was.

He hopped behind the wheel, turned the key, and kicked the radio without a thought. That was the only way he knew to get the thing working. Not that it was much use once it was running. It could only pick up AM frequencies, so his music choices were limited. And he hated talk radio. There was a tape deck, too, but after years of leaving the truck windows down overnight in the forest, all of his tapes were chewed far beyond the point of being useful. Today the radio settled on a faint country song speckled in occasional static.

But even if the aged truck was three decades old, it still started without a hitch every morning, even in the middle of winter. It faithfully took him where he needed to go, which was no small feat, considering he drove all over the often rugged terrain of the Cascade Mountains. Sure, it would have to be replaced someday, but until it left him stranded on the side of a mountain, he wouldn't be abandoning it. It seemed an injustice to repay such loyalty with anything other than the same in return.

Hank worked his foot on the accelerator and pointed the truck back down the mountain. Time to start the day.

*

Hank pushed the door to the Warden's Office shut to keep the chill of fall from following him in. It was a chilly evening, so he would only be partially successful, but partially meant he might not have to sleep with his socks on tonight. With the door shut behind him, he pulled off his muddy work boots and stretched his stocky frame. Something about releasing his feet from the confines of his boots and offering them fresh air brought him unexplainable joy after a long day.

He walked through the main part of the Warden's Office to his own private area behind it. A glance around the room reminded him that he needed to do a little cleaning the next day. All his clothes were put away and his gear well organized, but piles of old, outdated papers and useless artifacts from the outdoors had accumulated along the walls. His mother would have wasted no time in serving him a light scolding. With any luck, he wouldn't have much on his agenda tomorrow and could spend some time going through the piles and throwing away the junk.

He shut off the lights in the front office and closed the door to his private quarters. It wasn't much of a living space, but in any case, it was his and that meant something. It had a bed to sleep on, a kitchen to cook in, and a small sitting area in front of a fireplace. What more could a man ask for?

Hank thought about the home he had down the mountain closer to town. He paid someone who actually lived in town a pretty penny to take care of it and keep everything in working order. But living there would mean driving up the mountain every morning and driving back at night, and his truck surely couldn't handle the commute over the spare crags. It was simply easier to stay in the small space he had made at the back of the Warden's Office. Besides, the house he owned contained too many memories that Hank didn't want to face on a daily basis. It was easier to stay up here and leave whatever remnants of what had been lingering there. He had the mountains, and that was enough.

Hank let his weight sink into the handmade rocking chair as he settled in front of his fireplace. He thought about starting a fire but decided against it. It had been a long day, and making a fire meant he'd have to gather the wood, stoke the blaze, and put it out before he went to bed. He'd just rely on gas heat for tonight. He laid his head against the soft chair cover's back and let his mind mull over the day's events to the rhythm of the gentle creak of the chair.

He had spent the majority of the day helping people. Though it hadn't left him much time for taking care of his other responsibilities or cleaning out his nook, he didn't mind it. Helping people was part of his job, and he liked helping people most of the time. Besides, most of those other responsibilities were just paperwork, anyway, and that could be put off a few days without endangering anyone.

After hunting early in the morning and finishing cleaning the majority of his kill, he'd received a call from a couple stranded in the woods with a car that wouldn't start. They'd been out camping the night before and found themselves unable to leave when they woke up. Turned out the overly paranoid city girlfriend had left the GPS plugged in, which had drained their battery overnight. Luckily for them, Hank knew his way around cars and got them jumped as well as on their way without too much trouble.

As the couple, who were bickering with one another, was pulling away, Hank received a second phone call about a family who had lost their pet while hiking. Looking for a lost dog wasn't particularly part of his job, but Hank knew that he'd have a much easier time navigating through the forest and finding it than they would. And the last thing he needed was a lost family wandering through the woods looking for their equally lost pet. Together, they'd managed to find the dog near a stream with his paw stuck in a broken log. They got him out, checked for preliminary injuries of which there were none, and the family blissfully went on with their day's adventure.

By then, it was past noon and Hank was ready to go and get some work done in his office, including starting that pesky paperwork. He'd gone inside and sat down at his desk to start filing reports, but, just as he'd picked up his pen, a frantic father came careening through the front door carrying a sick child.

According to the father, the little girl had vomited several times already and was continuing to dry heave every few minutes. As Hank felt her forehead, he could tell she was burning up and weak, probably from dehydration. As a Game Warden, Hank was trained in basic first aid; he knew right away that the child was experiencing heat stroke. Drilling the father with instructions as the phone rang, he called Search and Rescue to assist in getting the child to the local hospital.

While they waited for help to arrive, Hank and the father persuaded the little girl to drink water and cooled her down with a steady breeze from a few fans. By the time her ride arrived, she was feeling much better and chattering about a squirrel she'd seen outside the window, but Hank still recommended the girl be taken down the mountain to the hospital. The father thanked him at least a dozen times and even went so far as to call him a hero.

Hank smiled, shaking his head. He honestly liked being there to help people when the unexpected happened. He was the type to keep his calm, and his vast knowledge of the forest made him valuable help. Helping others was probably his favorite part of the job. Yes, it had been a long day, but a good one, too.

Despite being so tired he could hardly move, Hank knew he had to rouse himself to find something to eat. He'd had no time for a real lunch and breakfast was long gone. If he didn't eat something before he went to sleep, he was sure to be up in the middle of the night, starving. He sighed and pushed himself up from the chair to rummage through the refrigerator for some sustenance. He quickly found a left over deer steak he'd grilled a few nights ago among the various bits of ripening fruit and browning vegetables and praised his foresight in cooking an extra for a night like this one.

Hank haphazardly threw the steak in the microwave and grimaced as he set the time. Steak is never as good re-heated as fresh off the grill, and he hated to eat it this way. But as exhausted as he was, he wasn't going to be cooking anything else, either, so a microwaved steak was the best he would get.

He sat by the empty fireplace and ate the steak slowly so as to enjoy the taste more. He stared up above the mantle of the fireplace and admired the ten-point deer head mounted to the wall. A few of his other prize kills adorned the Warden's Office, from birds he'd shot with past buddies to some other deer, including his first, and he was proud of every single piece individually.

But that buck above the fireplace was really something special. It represented more than just a kill. It was a reminder of Sarah, and there were few he would have shown to the outer world, much less himself, as anything more than a seldom reminder of her presence.

Back when Hank had been a young man, in his early twenties, he'd taken his wife, Sarah, out for her first real hunting trip. She'd grown up in Washington but had never been exposed to the outdoors beyond watching Animal Planet on television. Naturally, Hank took it upon himself to rectify that sad situation.

Even though Sarah wasn't a real outdoorsy girl, she wasn't afraid to get her hands dirty or do some heavy lifting if she felt inclined. Everyone who knew Hank's priorities on the outdoors had been skeptical when he announced he was going to marry a city girl. But once they'd had a chance to get to know Sarah, everyone had admitted that she was the perfect wife for Hank.

All of their friends made fun of Sarah for the girly butterfly tattoo she had just above her left ankle. It was so out character for her. She and a girlfriend had stumbled upon the ingenious idea to have matching tattoos after getting carelessly drunk one night while celebrating their eighteenth birthdays. It wasn't the most intelligent thing she had ever done, and she'd admitted that with a laugh every time someone mentioned it, but it provided her a story, and Sarah was all about sharing her stories. She and Hank often talked about getting tattoos of their own, and this time Sarah insisted they would not be butterflies, but they'd never found the time to have the procedure done. She had died before they had the chance.

Hank had boasted for months after they'd gotten married about his hunting skills, but Sarah had yet to see any proof. He had been out hunting at least half a dozen times and, as cruel fate would have it, hadn't brought anything home to prove his point.

Hank tried to explain that even though he'd had plenty of opportunities to make a kill, he was waiting for the perfect animal. Sarah didn't understand why he would wait when he had opportunity, but she would nod her head anyway if for no other reason than to make him happy.

Eventually, Sarah started joking that Hank wasn't even out hunting, spending his days down at the bar instead. Of course, Hank had taken offense to that remark. He knew he was a great huntsman, and even jokes otherwise made him prickle in defense. To prove it, he challenged her to come with him the next time he went out. She hadn't really wanted to, but similar to Hank, her pride wouldn't let her turn down a challenge.

Before the grand expedition, Hank took the time to teach Sarah how to shoot. They shot various targets behind the house; empty soda cans, clay pigeons, and any other things Hank could think of to shoot. Sarah got to be a pretty good shot with only a little work, proving she had some natural talent in handling a gun. She wasn't perfect by any means, but she wasn't bad for a beginner. She figured she could probably hit something as long as it wasn't running and she maintained her focus.

With Sarah properly prepared for their hunt and excited to prove her own skills in the midst of her husband, they took the plunge. The day started out normally, with no real surprises. Hank took Sarah to his favorite hunting spot, with the beautiful view of the valleys and hillsides, well before dawn when the dew formed on the meadow and the deer would be coming out to feed. Sarah, judging by her grumbling, didn't want to be up so early; she'd always had more of a night owl persona. Hank had explained that dawn was the best time to hunt and she was satisfied.

There had been another reason he wanted to be there before sunrise, one that he didn't explain. He wanted her to see the beauty of the mountains as the sun broke through the trees. That view had made Hank fall in love with the forest in the first place, and he knew it would have the same effect on Sarah.

It had worked perfectly according to his plan. Hank and Sarah sat crouched in a hidden grove and watched the sun's first rays shine through the trees and dance gracefully on the ground around them. Drops of beaded dew glistened like diamonds in the morning's light and as if by magic, everything came alive all at once. The grass and flowers seemed to extend themselves as high as possible, reaching for the warmth of the sun. Small rodents and insects emerged from nowhere, scampering under the leaves and through the branches as the day called to wake them.

The forest came to life before their eyes, and Hank watched Sarah come alive with it. Her wheat blonde hair glistened in the morning sunlight, and her blue eyes widened with the blooming flowers. Hank smiled to himself as he realized that she was falling in love with the forest just as he had years before.

And that's when Hank saw him. Walking through the trees under the streaming sunlight, cautiously emerging from the forest boundaries, was a ten-point buck. Hank reached out to touch Sarah's arm and pointed to the creature. There was almost nothing he wanted more than to shoot the buck himself. He could have taken the shot at a moment's notice. The only thing he wanted more than the victory was for Sarah to have the chance to shoot it on her own. He nodded, and she raised her rifle to her shoulder. Hank almost reached out to help her, but any extra movement would startle the buck for sure. She was on her own.

Sarah lined up her shot with its vital organs, keeping both eyes open just like he'd told her. She took a breath, held it, and waited. Hank looked from her to the buck, then back at her. He was braced for a shot, but it didn't come. Why was she hesitating? Was she scared?

Just when he thought she wasn't going to pull the trigger, her shot rang through the trees. They both watched as the buck fled off into the woods, leaving behind nothing but a few hoof prints.

She had missed. Sarah wasn't one to swear, but a slew of curse words came out of her mouth that made Hank chuckle.

Had Hank been paying more attention, he could have shot the buck on the run, but it really didn't matter in light of the shared moment. There would be other times, other hunts. This was Sarah's first, and he wanted to remember every moment of it, including her disappointed face when she realized she had missed.

He reached over to console her with a pat on the back, but that wasn't what she wanted. Her pride couldn't be consoled by petty encouragement. She shrugged away from him, glowering at him as he tried to stop chuckling. Swiping his hat off his head, she pushed it back into his hands and knocked him onto his back with a pout. "Don't laugh at me." What she really wanted, Hank knew, was to get better, practice harder, and become a better shot. For a long time they joked about that buck as "the one that got away."

Sarah worked hard after that day so that she would never let another buck get away. She practiced until she became an excellent marksman. And the buck that sat above the fireplace was hers.

It was a ten-point buck. They had joked, after the shot, that it was the same buck from that first trip to the mountains together. Whenever Hank looked at the buck, he couldn't help but miss those trips with Sarah. They were special memories.

Hank tried not to be sad when memories of his wife visited him, but it was never an easy task. They had only spent four years together before she had been taken unfairly from him. When he remembered things, he focused on the good times. He didn't want the memories he had left of her to be tainted by sadness.

Sarah had always been one to take good care of herself, which was why everyone was shocked to hear that she had bone cancer, but no one was more shocked than her. It started as a few aches and pains at odd times, nothing major, so she didn't take anything to stall it but over the counter painkillers, making up playful excuses such as too much housework or too much cooking. But her excuses and stalling caused the cancer to spread until it was untreatable. They had tried to treat it with any remedy they could find, whether by Google or books, even friends or rumors, but every doctor told them the same thing — it was too late. Finally they were left with no options or advice but to cherish the time they had left together as a family.

The day she died was one that Hank would never forget, no matter how much he wanted to erase that memory of Sarah laying on their bed in the country house. She was quiet. Quieter than normal. Her breathing slowed, and her words were softer. In her final moments, Hank and the girls sat beside her, Hank holding her hand, all of them gathered on her bed, doing their best to make Sarah feel comfortable and loved. She pulled them all close, knowing she was leaving soon, but still afraid.

She spoke to the girls first, and Hank knew right away it was time. There was something in her voice, a resignation to give them her final words. She told them to mind their father. She told them how much she loved them and that she would watch over them forever. Then she asked them to leave the room for a few minutes so she could speak with Hank alone.

After the two of them sat in silence for a moment, she told Hank that no matter what happened, she would always be there for him. She would always be watching him through the wind in the trees, the clouds in the sky, and the rain from the heavens, and if he ever found himself missing her, he could turn to those things to find her waiting for him. She started to cry and turned away from him to hide her tears, but he turned her face back to his, for tears were in his eyes, too. They shared the tears just as they'd shared everything else in life, from their sicknesses, to their health, and now, their love. They looked out the window together at the mountains they both knew so well. Then she took Hank's face in one hand and looked into his eyes again. She smiled at him, squeezed his hand, bestowed it a gentle kiss, and closed her eyes, settling back onto her pillow and sighing for the last time.

Everyone had encouraged Hank to move on with his life and find someone new after a few months had passed. After all, he was so young, and he had the girls to worry about. But Hank knew that he had only three loves in this world —Sarah, their twin daughters, Heidi and Sage, and the mountains. His heart couldn't handle anyone else, and despite all their encouragement to try, there was one problem.

He didn't want to try.

A few weeks after Sarah's death, he started staying at the station rather than the house. His mother helped raise the girls there, and Hank went to the mountains every day for work. As the years passed, Assistant Game Wardens came and went, but Hank stayed on. Where else would he go? It was a given that he would take over as Head Game Warden when Alan Morrison retired.

All of that seemed so long ago. Hank frowned. It all was so long ago.

He stared at the empty fireplace, truthfully wishing for dancing flames but still too tired to bring them to life. To stall himself, he thought back over his life and all the things that had led him to where he was now. He had grown up in the area, and working in the mountains felt natural to him after all the time he had spent outdoors as a kid. He couldn't possibly see himself working anywhere else.

His grandparents had owned a cabin only a few miles from the ranger station. It had been neglected for decades now. The porch was rotting through thanks to termite damage and the humid season, half the windows were broken by random kids or harsh storms, and there were a few holes in the roof. But when Hank had been a young kid, he had spent most of his summer vacations in that cabin. It was there he had first learned to shoot a gun. He would wander the woods, first with a BB gun, later with a .22, shooting at anything that moved like any young kid would. He learned from his grandmother what to do with the animals that his father and grandfather brought home. She knew what to do with almost every part of every animal.

Hank smiled at the memories, also part of the distant past, but pleasant ones. His grandparents had long since passed away. His mother, too. His father was still alive, living in a nursing home in town and probably driving the staff crazy on a daily basis. Hank knew he didn't make enough time for his father, and the thought of him now brought the usual pang of guilt. But his job took so much time, it was hard to find any time for a private life. It truly demanded twenty-four-hour-a-day devotion from him. There were some occasional days when things moved at a more relaxed pace, but someone always had to be in the office, just in case the need should arise, and that meant taking a whole day off to himself was next to impossible.

When it was, on the very rare occasion, possible, Hank would leave an assistant in charge of things and go down into town to see his father. But it wasn't often that he felt he could entrust things to an assistant. His father said he understood why Hank didn't make it down more often, but that sounded more like something any father would say to a son and didn't make it any easier or change the fact that he should be making more time for his family.

His girls were both off at college now, and Hank had only been to visit them on their campus once. They came home for holidays and breaks, but they never wanted to stay up in the mountains, so reunions were a little strained. On the obvious side, there wasn't enough room for all three of them at the Warden's Office, and the girls weren't comfortable staying alone in one of the cabins close by. They usually stayed at the country house where they'd lived as a family or his parents' old house where they'd spent most of their childhood. Regardless, they didn't see one another as much as they should have during their holiday breaks.

Heidi was going into law, and she was so busy with school and studying for the bar exam that she didn't make it home very often anymore. When she did, it was rare to see her without one of her many books with so many terms and legal jargon Hank had never bothered to look at it after the first time he'd scanned a few pages. Breaks never seemed to be real breaks with her schedule. Hank suspected there was a boy she wanted to stick close to that contributed to the infrequency of her visits, which never really bothered him too much. She was growing up, and their bond was spread thin. To push her about something risked her putting him on the silent treatment, and there was no telling how long that might last. She'd never mentioned the boy to him outright, but Sage let some things slip now and then when she was home without Heidi.

Sage was an environmental major, an odd choice considering the upbringing she'd had in Redwood. Whenever she came home, she was always critical of Hank's lifestyle. She didn't approve of the way he used the land or killed animals. Or didn't recycle. She was always trying to help him learn new ways to be more environmentally friendly, and she was open about it, as annoying as it could be. For the sake of being a good dad, he would try to take her advice while she was around, but the recycling bins and compost piles would go unused as soon as she left to go back to school, only for her to scold him when she came back.

Hank smiled when he thought about his girls, all three of them. The memories were painful in some ways, but he treasured them. Every single one of them.

Hank stretched his arms high toward the ceiling and decided to turn in for the night. He never knew what a new day might bring, so he had to get to sleep early to be prepared for the next emergency to barge in his door. He lifted himself from the chair and ambled to the cot on the far side of the room, dropping his clothes on the floor as he went. There was one good thing about living alone; no one cared how good of a housekeeper you were. He stretched his body out on the bed, closed his eyes, and let his thoughts drift from Sarah to his girls to fishing trips with his grandpa to hunting with his father until sleep finally overtook them completely.

Chapter Two

Scott

Scott Huntington smiled at the little girl who stumbled out of the green one-man tent he'd erected the night before. She rubbed her eyes with her fists and smiled when she saw Scott, revealing a large gap where her front teeth should have been. She took a big step toward him.

"Watch out for the—"

The girl's foot caught on a tent peg. She fell on her face with a squeal of surprise.

Scott failed to suppress a small laugh as he hurried over to help the girl up to her feet. He usually remembered the names of everyone in his tour groups, but this girl's name eluded him. That was the good thing about forgetting a child's name. They were never bothered when you reverted to "kid" or "squirt" while you tried to figure out what it was.

"Got to be careful about those pegs." Scott scooped her up into his arms and headed for the fire he'd just started.

The girl giggled and shrugged as she leaned against his shoulder. "I always forget."

What was her name? It would bug him all day if he didn't get it soon. Her parents were Joe and Melanie, and her older brother's name was Ryan. Why couldn't he get her name? Was it Susie? No, it started with an 'r' or maybe a 'p.' Patricia?

Scott set the adorable little girl down in the green chair that had come with the tent she'd slept in. She kicked her legs and hummed one of those tunes that little girls always seemed to pull out of nowhere, so he returned his attention to the fire and started making breakfast while she entertained herself.

He rubbed the light blond stubble on his face that matched the mop on his head. One of his favorite parts about his job was that he didn't have to shave unless he felt like it. Hygiene be damned; today, he didn't feel like it.

He'd spent more time in these mountains growing up than in his parents' home. It only made sense for him to make his living out here. Tourists were always looking for a good guide for a decent price, and no one knew the mountains better than Scott. His parents had been a little upset when he'd ditched his plans for college to start his own wilderness guide business at nineteen, but he'd proven it to be a good choice over the past fifteen years with a steady rise in tourism, especially recently. After some early struggles to get his name out there, word of his expertise and kind demeanor had spread, and now business was thriving. He'd had to turn people away after getting too many requests during the same timeframe. Even his father had admitted that his son's crazy idea wasn't so crazy after all.

"Did you sleep okay?" Scott asked the Jane Doe girl. He still couldn't remember her name. Rachel? Or Bella?

"Yep." All hints of sleepiness were gone from her voice and it was a typical cheery little girl tone. Like most kids, she seemed to wake in a snap and fall asleep in the same fashion, since she was young enough.

"The scary noises of the forest didn't bother you, huh?" Scott teased her with a wink as he stoked the crackling fire.

"I'm brave." She sat up taller in her chair as if to emphasize this point. "I don't get scared from noises at night anymore."

Scott smiled at her, amused by her expression of vigilance. "I bet you don't. You're too tough. Someone's got to protect Ryan and your parents, right?"

"That's right." She gave a stern nod and scanned the campsite for signs of danger, holding her hands over her eyes as if they were binoculars.

Faint laughter came from the yellow tent where her parents had spent the night.

"What would we do without you to protect us, Becca?" Joe said, his head poking out of the tent to check on his daughter.

That's it! Rebecca, of course. Scott repeated it to himself over and over to make sure the name was ingrained in his mind. He wasn't going to forget it again.

"So, Mr. Scott," Rebecca said, "what are you cooking right now?"

Scott managed not to laugh at the serious tone she had assumed. She was taking her role of protector quite seriously.

"Right now I'm just boiling some water so we can have hot chocolate and oatmeal." He turned to look at her. "That sound good to you?"

Rebecca smiled that disarming little girl smile, showing off her missing teeth again. "I love hot chocolate. But..." The smile faded and she wrinkled her nose. "...oatmeal isn't my favorite. Mommy always buys the brown sugar kind, but I think it tastes like cardboard." She leaned in closer to Scott and lowered her voice to a whisper, a hand helping shield her voice. "Don't tell her this secret, but Daddy thinks so too, he just won't tell her."

Unfortunately for Joe, Rebecca's loud whisper carried to her parents' tent, and Scott heard a muffled thud and grunt of mock pain from the yellow tent.

Scott smiled at the show of family interaction. He was still young, too young to have a family of his own, so seeing families in action was as close as he got to it. His childhood hadn't been quite like Rebecca's. Not that he hadn't had a great childhood; it was just different somehow. He was looking forward to having a wife and kids of his own someday, when he got the chance to settle down into that kind of life. But he wasn't married yet, so that dream was still that, just a dream visiting him in the dead of night.

Joe and Melanie emerged from their tent a few moments later, Mel going to check on her daughter and beginning to run a soft bristled brush through her mussed hair. "Morning," Joe said, approaching Scott with a rested look on his face.

"Good morning." Scott stood to shake hands with both parents, starting with Joe and then Melanie once the mother had finished tying two quick pigtails in her daughter's willowy hair. "Sleep okay?" he asked. He felt like a giant standing next to them, his shadow washing over their bodies halfway. They were both no more than five foot six, and he was just over six two.

"Yeah, slept great," Mel replied, "thanks to our little guard dog here." She looked down at Rebecca and gently ran her fingers through the ends of her brown hair.

Rebecca smiled, closing her eyes as her mother stroked her but didn't say anything.

"Heard from Ryan yet this morning?" Joe asked, looking back at his son's tent.

Scott glanced over at the teenager's tent as well--another one-man set up identical to Rebecca's--and shook his head.

"Well, it's time he got up," Melanie said. "This is a family vacation and we didn't come all the way out here in the lovely outdoors to sleep." She took a step toward his tent, but Joe waved her back.

"I'll get him," he said, approaching the tent.

Melanie took a seat next to her daughter instead, and Scott checked on the water. It was boiling, so he went to work on the rest of breakfast.

The family had asked Scott to take them on a short camping trip in the mountains, nothing too hard. He'd offered to provide main meals as part of the package, and they'd readily accepted. They had moved into the area just a few weeks ago, and Scott could tell Joe was anxious to get to know all the best spots for hiking and camping. Joe was a big outdoorsman and fisherman, and he was hoping to pass his passion on to Ryan.

Scott knew before the trip even began that Ryan wasn't on board with the idea. The teen's jaw had dropped nearly clean off him when he learned that cell reception was unavailable in the mountains. Like most teenagers, the thought of being forced to spend time with his family was about as appealing as a session of water boarding.

Ryan had checked a few more times to be sure his texts weren't going through, tossed his phone back in the car and mumbled something about having at least a hundred texts from people who would think he was dead by the time they got back.

Scott smiled at the memory of the boy's grumpy face as he stirred the oatmeal. Of course, he had a phone that worked up here in case of a real emergency--a satellite phone that each employee of his company took when they went out with a client, but it wouldn't be playing games or asking advice from a virtual personal assistant for the nearest pizza place. Safety was something that Scott didn't mess with. The mountains could be dangerous.

Each of the guides had used one of the phones on a handful of occasions, but Scott's homemade company had never had a "real" emergency. They'd had their share of broken bones, heat exhaustion, and broken down equipment, but nothing had happened in his fifteen years as a guide that he would classify as life-threatening, which was great for his guide rating for those who might do research before picking one. He credited his stellar safety record to the meticulous precautions he and his staff took every time they went out on an excursion.

Ryan rolled out of his tent after his father's third call and trudged over to the fire half-heartedly. His cheek had a huge crease from a wrinkled pillow case and his eyes were only half open. He sat down in the last remaining camp chair, yawning audibly. Ryan was obviously not an early riser.

"Breakfast is ready," Scott encouraged, putting the oatmeal and hot chocolate where everyone could get to it and passing around cups, bowls, and spoons. He waited while the parents poured the hot water for the kids and themselves before serving himself. Chalk up another star for a polite guide.

While they were eating, Scott ran through the plan for the day. "So, there is a stream that has great fishing that isn't too far from here. I thought we'd take the time to visit there first. It leads to a waterfall that is beautiful as well, so we can hike there before making our way back for the day. How does that sound?"

"I think that sounds great," Joe said between spoonfuls of oatmeal.

"How long is the hike?" Ryan asked.

Scott was amazed to hear the boy speak. He swallowed the bite of oatmeal he'd just taken. "Oh, it's not too far, maybe a couple miles."

Ryan positioned a skeptical stare at him, mind working behind his leveled stare. "A couple miles round trip or a couple miles each way?"

"Total," Scott answered, returning the pointed stare with one of his own.

"That's probably too far for Becca to walk, don't you think, Mom?" Ryan turned to look at his mother, putting on his best syrupy sweet voice of pity.

"I think she'll be just fine. We'll walk slower if we need to," Melanie replied with a knowing smile.

You never could fool mothers, Scott reasoned. He took another bite of oatmeal to cover his own smile. It was obvious to all of them that it wasn't Becca's endurance Ryan was worried about.

"How far did we walk yesterday?" Joe asked Scott.

Scott did a quick mental calculation and guessed the rest of the way. "About three miles."

"Becca did great with that. I think she'll do even better today," Joe said.

"Yeah, Ryan," Becca said with a know-it-all tone, pointing to herself with her thumb. "I'll be fine. You're the lazy one, anyway. We'll see if you make it."

Ryan stuck his tongue out at her when their parents weren't looking.

They finished breakfast a few minutes later and cleaned the camp. Scott directed them as they packed what they'd need for the day's hike. Bug spray, some trail mix and sandwiches for lunch, and plenty of water bottles. Scott carried a few extra items, his sat phone and a first aid kit, just in case. But it would be a light hike. On a last minute whim, he tossed in his rappelling ropes. It was probably ridiculous to take them in the first place, but they weren't too heavy, and you never could know. If the rocks weren't looking too slick, maybe they could do a bit of rappelling. Even Ryan might get excited about that. Scott was pretty determined to get the boy excited about something on this trip.

Once everything was gathered and ready to go, they stood at the edge of camp for Scott's pre-hike briefing, which was another tradition he upheld no matter where they went. "After we spend a little time at the stream, we'll be approaching the waterfall from the top," Scott said. "Then there will be a trail that we'll take down to the bottom. We should make it to the bottom by lunch, eat there at the waterfall, do some fishing, and be back here by dinner."

"All right, let's get going." Joe took a step toward the trail, the typical father figure eager to take the lead of his family.

"I'll be leading, but please don't hesitate to speak up if you need a break or want us to slow down," Scott said, stepping out in front of Joe; then they were off.

Scott had hiked with enough different age groups to know how to set a good pace by their standards – especially with young children tagging along. The parents might be able to hike a little faster, but he didn't want to risk pushing Becca's limits.

They took regular breaks to make sure everyone stayed hydrated since, by far, one of the biggest problems was caused by others not drinking enough water. Scott didn't want to take any chances with heat stroke or dehydration. At each stop, he would talk about the terrain, local plants, and animal life to keep the down time productive and educational. Chalk up another star for his rating.

On one break as they approached the stream, they were lucky enough to see a few deer run past the trail. Joe, Melanie, and Becca were all fascinated by the graceful sight, but Ryan didn't even look up from his bag of trail mix.

Scott walked over to him and attempted to bridge whatever gap that kept them so far apart. "Hey, why don't you take a look around? Lots to see. You won't find anything in that trail bag but peanuts, raisins, and a rare piece of chocolate."

Ryan only grunted and grabbed some more trail mix, set on not being consoled. Scott frowned and walked away. Getting the teenager interested in the great outdoors was proving to be quite a challenge, but he wasn't giving up yet.

A few minutes after spotting the deer, they finally reached the stream. They paused on the bank so Scott could tell them about the area, where he stepped up on a flat piece of granite as if it were his podium.

"This particular stream is a little hidden treasure up here. It runs with great trout the majority of the year and isn't known to most people – only the locals, really. It's a great spot to fish for those who know it's here. We call it 'Heavenly Stream.' The flow is always heavier in the spring during the run-off, but it never dries up, at least not enough to scare the fish off completely. We'll follow it all the way to the top of the waterfall."

After resuming the hike towards the waterfall, Scott dropped back to try and start a conversation with Ryan again. His mother always said he was stubborn, and he would prove it by making the boy say more than two words.

"You like sports, Ryan?"

The boy shrugged. Strike one.

"What's your favorite team?"

Ryan glanced at Scott as if he were an annoying fly, only begrudgingly answering if for no other reason than to swat him away. "Patriots." There was one word, time to push him for two.

"A football fan, very nice. Ever been to a game?"

Ryan shook his head in stubborn silence. There was strike two.

"Maybe your dad will take you someday."

Another shrug. Strike three, you're out.

The only time this kid spoke more than one word at a time was when he was complaining, and he had failed to change that record. Oh well, live and learn. Scott gave Ryan a pat on the back and went back to his place at the front of the group.

One hour and two more quick breaks later, they reached the top of the waterfall. It was a high fall, at least fifty feet straight down to the bottom, and as lovely as Scott remembered. Large rocks flanked the water here, providing stunning but dangerous places to stand and look down on the falls. Scott saw right away that the higher winds had sprayed the rocks all around the area with water. He gathered them into a group small enough to hear him easily, warned them of the slippery conditions and decided today was not the day for rappelling.

"It's beautiful," Mel said, surveying the view around them.

Scott nodded in agreement, emphasizing the danger it carried too. "Yes. Yes, it is. But you have to be very careful of the water here. The current is stronger than it looks. It could pull any one of us right over the edge before we know what's happening, and believe me, you don't want to go for a ride over those falls."

"So what now?" Ryan asked, already looking back in the direction of their camp wistfully.

"We hike to the bottom, right, Mr. Scott?" Becca said, her voice filled with excitement.

"Exactly," Scott said, charmed by the formal use for his name. "The trail is just to the right of the waterfall." He pointed to the massive boulder that sat by the edge of the drop. Secretly, Scott wished he could stay there longer, because from the top of the waterfall viewing area, he could spot the valley below them. On clear days, he also had a view of the reclusive restricted areas higher above them.

Nearly halfway to the trail heading down, Scott noticed they were one person short. There was Becca, by her mother, and Joe was leading the pack again. Where was—?

His head whipped around when a sudden, high-pitched scream echoed on the rocks. Ryan disappeared over the edge of the boulders at the water's edge.

Scott sprinted back up the hill at full speed. When he reached the spot where Ryan had fallen, he felt his own boots slide over the slick rocks, and he steadied himself. He dropped to his hands and knees, crawled to the edge, and yelled over the side, "Ryan!"

"I'm here." The voice almost didn't reach him over the noise of the rushing water.

Scott leaned over the edge, keeping his body weight on his back heels so he didn't go over himself, and saw Ryan clinging to a ledge about fifteen feet below him. He was out of the main flow of water, luckily, or he would have been dashed against the rocks below, but he was still getting subsequent splashes by the water churning against the rocks. He was soaked from the spray residue but looked mostly uninjured.

Adrenaline kicked in and his body moved into overdrive. If he didn't move fast, the boy would be dragged over the waterfall and die. Scott thrust his hand into his pack and pulled the rappelling equipment from it. The equipment wasn't designed for these slick conditions, but it would have to do because a life hung in the balance. He found the best anchor he could and tied his ropes around the rock, knotting it three times to be sure it held tightly.

The rest of the family had reached him by now, and Joe ran forward, always the first of his family anywhere. "Ryan! Hold on!"

Scott held up a hand to halt him, thrusting it back. "Stop. Don't come any closer; it's not safe."

Joe's feet skidded for a brief moment on the wet rocks in his haste, but he steadied himself and nodded at Scott before easing back to Melanie and Becca, who could only watch and wait.

Scott looked down at Ryan one last time to confirm his position before starting his descent, shouting to be heard over the angry roar of the falls. "Ryan, I'm coming down to get you. Hang on for just a few more minutes, okay?"

"Okay," Ryan said through chattering teeth, shaking visibly.

Scott knew he had to get to him quickly or Ryan might lose his grip. He gave the rope a firm tug then pushed himself out over the edge. The spray from the waterfall blinded him temporarily, and he had to pause to wipe the water from his eyes.

"I don't think I can hold on much longer," Ryan called in panic, his voice shaking as much as his grip.

Scott looked down. He was just a few feet above the boy now. It was imperative he remain calm to keep the boy focused. "I'm almost there. Keep holding on."

Scott descended the few final feet and grabbed Ryan around the waist the instant he had the opportunity. He was soaked and shivering so hard, Scott was surprised he'd held on this long. Surprised, but grateful. He wrapped his rope around Ryan to give him something to rest his weight on for a moment.

"I've got you, Ryan. Okay, we're going to use the rope to walk back up the rocks. We'll walk together, one step at a time. Do you understand?" Scott had to yell so Ryan could hear him over the roar of the waterfall.

Ryan nodded.

Scott leaned back into the ropes, guiding Ryan to do the same. When their bodies were perpendicular to the wall, he took a step. Ryan matched him exactly. After a few steps, Scott began to relax his pace; Ryan picked up Scott's rhythm quickly. They were sure to make it to the top unscathed if they kept up this pace.

Ryan suddenly slipped, and his weight jerked the ropes. He cried out in fear, but Scott grabbed him and kept them steady.

"It's all right, you're doing fine, it's only a little slip, just keep going. One step at a time," he coaxed gently.

A few steps later Ryan slipped again. The rocks were worse the closer to the top they got, and Ryan's strength was quickly failing. Scott still had his right arm behind the boy and braced him for extra support. But Ryan's body went limp, and Scott wasn't ready to hold the teenager's full body weight without warning. Scott lost his footing and slammed into the hard rock wall. Ryan's body followed suit, slamming into the rock as well, and Scott felt at least two of his ribs snap as the dead weight collided with him.

Scott groaned and doubled over, releasing Ryan's body for a moment. The boy was tied to the rope and swung out over the falls before sweeping back toward Scott again. This time he was ready and blocked him.

Ryan had passed out, but Scott wasn't sure exactly why. It could have been the cold or the pain of holding onto the ledge, but either way, Scott was going to have to carry him to the top now. With two broken ribs.

Scott pulled Ryan's body back toward him and winced at the pain in his ribs. He looked up to measure distance. They weren't more than seven or eight feet from the top of the cliff, but it was going to be a long eight feet with the pain he was currently feeling.

He hauled himself and Ryan up. One step at a time. Every step sent a shaft of pain through his side.

Three feet from the edge, the rope jerked. Scott couldn't suppress a cry of pain as his broken ribs were jolted by his and Ryan's combined weight.

It hadn't been a big jerk. He didn't lose even a foot of wall, but if the rope was starting to slip there was no way to tell when it would come loose and send them both plummeting to certain death.

"Joe!" Scott yelled as loud as he could, bracing himself. Even the breath he had to take to shout sent a shockwave of pain through his chest. He had to hope that Joe's outdoors experience included at least a little knowledge of ropes and rappelling. "Secure the rope!"

He didn't know if Joe had heard him or not, and he couldn't wait for confirmation with a loose rope. He could only hope. He climbed on.

The rope was giving with every tug now, hopefully because Joe was straining to support their weight and not because the anchor was slipping even further. There was no way to tell, nothing to do but pray and pull.

Scott's head cleared the ledge and he saw Joe leaning back with the rope to hold it as steady as possible, straining to support the two bodies. Scott shouted for him to pull, and he pushed up on Ryan's body with every ounce of strength he had left.

The boy slid over the edge to safety, and Scott sagged into the ropes in relief, grunting. Joe pulled again and Scott was back on level ground, where he revelled in how good it felt to have solid ground beneath his feet once more. He managed to stand long enough to help Joe get Ryan clear of the fall's edge before collapsing again, exhausted and in agony. His ribs rippled with pain.

Melanie ran to Ryan, but Joe had already confirmed that their son was fine, reassuring his wife before hysteria set in.

Scott looked at Rebecca, standing next to his backpack with wide eyes. He motioned with a small wave of his fingers. "Can you bring me my bag, Rebecca?"

The girl nodded and walked over to him, bag extended in her small hands.

He smiled at her to help reassure the young girl. "Your brother's going to be just fine. Thank you."

She nodded and sat down next to him while he pulled out the satellite phone to arrange for an early extraction. He asked the office to send three jeeps. Two to pick them up at the falls, another to gather all the equipment back at the campsite.

Ryan woke up a few minutes later, confused and disoriented, asking about when they were going on the hike and then if they were already back. Scott worried that he had hit his head and suffered a concussion, but after a short talk he was satisfied that the boy would have no lasting damage from the incident. Other than maybe his pride.

Once Ryan remembered everything that had happened, he wouldn't even look Scott in the eye. He seemed especially ashamed of the fact that Scott had broken his ribs while saving him. Scott reassured him with a pat on the shoulder and get well soon wishes.

A half hour after Scott and Ryan had reached safety, the two jeeps pulled up. Scott walked to the one that would be taking him to the hospital, but Joe grabbed him and pulled him aside, careful to be gentle but firm.

"I don't know what we would've done if you hadn't been here," Joe said.

"Hey," Scott said amiably, "don't worry about it. That's why I'm here – to keep everyone safe and make sure you all make it home."

"I'm just not sure how to express my gratitude. It could have been so much worse." He shook his head. "It would have been so much worse if I had tried to take the family out on my own, much less if Ryan hadn't... I just want you to know how grateful I am." He handed Scott a wad of bills, too thick to feel out, but Scott estimated it was far more than his usual fee and their trip wasn't even halfway done.

Scott, who had always made a conscious effort to be fair, shifted his weight back, waving the money away. "That's not necessary."

"I know it's not," Joe said, "but it would make me feel better if you would accept it. It's the only way I can show my appreciation for what you did today. And know that we will definitely be back to have you take us out again once we've all healed up properly. You've been great."

"Your continued business is appreciation enough," Scott said with a smile and a wince.

Joe hesitated, and after being sure Scott would not take the offered money, he nodded and put the bills back in his pocket, then joined the rest of his family in the jeep that would take them back to town.

As a visit to the hospital would be a waste of time because he already knew his own diagnosis, Scott decided against going to the ER and stopped by the doctor's office instead. The doctor was a friend of his. They'd grown up together, and Scott knew he would understand everything. Instead of waiting for hours to see an ER doctor, go through X-rays, and be told what he already knew, Scott was able to confirm his suspicions quickly. He did indeed have two fractured ribs, which would heal on their own in time after some stiff wrapping and lots of rest. His friend gave him a prescription for some pain medication if he wanted it, and Scott headed home.

Scott shoved open his front door and trudged inside, exhausted. Even the weight of the door was almost too much for him to handle after all he'd been through today. He was looking forward to a nice long shower and then sleep. Lots of sleep.

Even though this particular trip had been a little more stressful than most, he didn't feel that much more drained than usual. Working in a field that required him to take care of people and their needs was admittedly stressful, both emotionally and physically, and he felt the weight of responsibility almost as a physical burden every time he led an excursion. Coming home always felt great because that weight was lifted from his shoulders.

"You're home early."

Scott jumped at the voice, but he recognized it. "Dad?"

"I heard there was a little trouble on your excursion today." Scott's father, Ace, rose from a stool at the bar and walked over to the entryway.

"Yeah, a little, but you didn't have to sneak into my house and scare the hell out of me to ask about it. You could have just called if you were that worried." Scott walked past him into the kitchen, grabbed an apple, and started eating, taking his time with swallowing because the motion caused him pain. He offered one to his father, but he waved it off.

"I didn't sneak into your house. I have the garage code, remember? I could have called, sure, but I wanted to make sure everything was okay and you weren't just telling me you were okay to keep me from worrying. I knew you weren't in the hospital, but I didn't know anything else. Is it a crime for a dad to worry a little about his son?" He smiled at Scott as he examined him.

"All right, all right, you win." Scott returned the smile with open hands. "I just didn't get a chance to stuff all the unwashed clothes in a closet and hide the dirty dishes."

Ace laughed. "Remember you're talking to me, not to your mother. And here I thought you'd matured into someone that wanted to keep a clean house."

"Well, yeah, most of the time. But there is still that little part of me that feels the need to tidy up before my parents are over," Scott said with a laugh.

Ace rerouted the topic to the blighted excursion. "So what happened?"

"You mind if we sit down first before I start talking? I'm beat." Scott was already making his way to the living room and his favorite recliner.

Ace followed. Scott explained what had happened with Ryan on the way, settling down with a low sigh. "It wasn't really a big deal in the end. I'm glad things worked out the way they did. We were lucky the kid didn't die."

"So the parents decided to cancel the trip early then?" Ace asked.

"Yeah, they said they would come back and do another trek some other time, but none of them were in the mood to continue the trek today. And I don't blame them. Tough to have a good time after all of that. And I probably couldn't have continued with them anyway." Scott finished his apple and started on a banana from the fruit bowl.

"Well I'm glad everything worked out okay. And I'm glad you're okay, too. I always worry about you up there alone," Ace said.

"I don't know why you worry. I was born to be in those mountains. I know them like the back of my hand," Scott smiled reassuringly at his father. "So how did you hear about the trouble?"

"Oh, I just hear things," Ace said distractingly, looking around the room.

"You always just hear things."

Ace was in a place to hear lots of things. He was one of the most powerful men in the city. He ran a construction business in town, and other than a few little mom & pop places, he was pretty much it. Scott didn't know how much his father was worth, but it was a lot. When he was little, he loved the idea of working in the construction industry.

What little boy wouldn't be drawn to all the big trucks and tractors? But as he got older and saw that his father sat behind a desk all day instead of getting his hands dirty on construction sites, he knew he wouldn't be going into the family business. That lifestyle just wouldn't work for Scott. He was made to be outside, breathing fresh air in his lungs and feeling the sunshine on his face.

"So you got a free day, what are you going to do?" Ace asked.

"What?" Scott turned his head sideways, blinking.

"You were supposed to be working tonight and tomorrow. Now you aren't, you're home instead. So what are you going to do with your time off?"

Scott shrugged. He often didn't have immediate answers. He preferred to take things as they came, but his father was a planner. "I don't know. I really haven't given it much thought. I just want to shower and sleep right now, but after that, who knows. I need to call Beth. She doesn't know I'm back early."

"I'm sure she'll want to know you're okay. Does she know about this?"

"Not that I know. Did you call her?" Scott asked, hoping he hadn't.

Ace shook his head to ease his son's worries. "Nope."

"Okay, well, I'll call her." Scott stood up to go get his phone.

"Yeah, it's probably a good idea. Fiancés like to know that kind of stuff." Ace cuffed him on the arm as he walked past. Scott laughed, turned and grunted to himself. His father's punches wouldn't have bothered him if he didn't have a few cracked ribs.

"Well, I need to be off," Ace said as he headed for the front door, "but I'm glad you're okay and that everything worked out with the trek. Hopefully they come back, good for business. I'm scheduled for a golf tee time tomorrow at nine if you want to join me. It'd be fun to play eighteen. We haven't played in a while."

"Yeah, that would be nice, apart from the fact that I have broken ribs. Funny how you invite me out to play when you know I can't swing. Sometimes I think you're just scared of being beat." Scott mimicked a botched swing and the sound of a golf ball plopping into the water.

Ace snorted a laugh. "Well, in any case, you can always come by and be my caddie."

"Now you're really starting to talk crazy. I'll be checking you into a nursing home soon," Scott commented with a teasing smile.

"Well, if you change your mind, let me know." Ace chuckled and gave his son a quick hug, making Scott wince at the pain. He walked out through the garage door with a wave. "I can always use a good caddie!"

Chapter Three

Beth

"Scott?" Beth's voice called out in worry as she ran into the house. "Scott, where are you?"

"I'm in here, Beth," Scott said from the family room. He tried to lift himself up from the leather couch to greet her, moving slowly.

"Don't move. I'm sure it hurts. Are you okay? What did the doctors say? How are you? What the hell happened?" She stopped in front of him, arms folded, forehead lines hard with worry.

Scott smiled up at her beautiful face. The worried look and the concern in her voice made him feel better if only to know someone else cared besides immediate family. "I'm going to be fine now that you're here."

Her expression softened when she heard that. In the fading afternoon light, Scott could see the glowing red of her hair that hung over her shoulders. He reached up and brushed it out of her eyes, fighting the urge to wince from the pain in his broken ribs.

Her green eyes met his, and she leaned down to kiss him. "Thank God you're okay."

"Tis merely a scratch." Scott winked and tried to laugh, forcing her good sense of humor, but a sharp pain in his side told him that wasn't a good idea.

"Oh, don't try and make me laugh." Beth moved her five foot frame onto the sofa next to Scott and put his head in her lap. She twirled his hair in her fingers. "Tell me what happened."

Scott told her all about Ryan's fall and his daring rescue. He was beginning to alter the story a little depending on who heard it. He left out the part about his fear that the rope might slip free and send them both plummeting to their deaths. She was already worried enough over a couple broken ribs.

"So what did the doctors say about your injuries?" Beth asked when he was finished with the stories.

"Nothing I didn't already know. I have two broken ribs from when Ryan smashed me against the rocks. Doctor said there's nothing to do but rest and let them heal on their own." He frowned. "Means I won't be able to trek for a while, of course."

"How long?"

"I'm on bed rest until Dr. Knight clears me. Probably a month or so. Not the best timing, that's for sure. We have three clients next week, and I was scheduled to take one of them rock climbing." Scott looked up at Beth. "We were going to do Petrified Peak."

"Oh well. That's not happening now," Beth said sternly. Her tone reminded him of the way she talked to her second graders when they were in trouble. Firm but not harsh. "You have plenty of qualified employees that can handle the jobs."

"I know, I know," Scott said with disappointment. "I was just looking forward to it. I always love doing the rock climbing expeditions. You know that. And Petrified Peak is an advanced climb."

Beth nodded. "Do you remember the first time we went rock climbing together?"

A smile crept across Scott's face. "How could I forget? We weren't even dating yet."

"Nope, but I was hoping we would be soon. I'd been flirting with you forever, trying to get you to notice me. You were about the only guy in high school who didn't notice me. At least, not until I got above you and you weren't interested in the view of the surroundings anymore."

Scott grinned at that, but managed not to laugh. His ribs were grateful.

Beth had been homecoming queen junior year. She was popular, smart, participated in all the clubs, and played sports. She was the most beautiful girl in school. The typical homecoming queen, getting everything she could out of the high school experience.

Scott, on the other hand, saw high school as just another hoop to jump through on his way to starting his own business. He wouldn't have even bothered finishing, but his father made it very clear that no one would take a high school drop-out seriously as a business owner. So he'd stuck it out, keeping to himself. Of course, everyone had known who Scott was because of his father, but he'd stayed out of the social spotlight and focused on getting through his classes.

He still had no idea why Beth had even developed an interest in him.

"We had that class together, remember? Psychology with Mrs. Feldman." Beth smiled and brought her hands up to mimic the look of glasses on her face. "She had those glasses with the rhinestones on the corners."

"Oh yeah." Scott struggled harder not to laugh at the memory. "They were probably from the 80s, and we made so much fun of them. They'd be cool now!"

Beth laughed, then reached out to hold Scott in place on the couch. "Oh, baby, I'm sorry...don't laugh."

"I know," Scott said through a grimace. The pain subsided, and Scott went on. "You sat next to me on the first day of class. It was kind of awkward, because we were good friends when we were little, but we hadn't talked in years. It was like we were introducing ourselves all over again." He looked at her with a sideways grin. "I didn't understand why you wanted to sit next to me."

"Yeah, I remember." A soft smile slid onto her face. "I had a plan all along."

"It started with passing notes back and forth every day like we were in junior high. Mostly making fun of Mrs. Feldman," Scott said.

"I don't even remember what they were about. Was she really that bad?" Beth said.

"I don't remember either," Scott said. "All I remember is that most of my scribbles were chicken scratch, and I used to keep your notes to analyze after school."

"Really? I didn't know that."

"Yeah, I never told you that?"

"Nope," Beth said. "Guess we still have things to learn about each other."

"Yep, I guess so." Scott looked at her and put on a serious face. "Well, I think now is as opportune time as ever to tell you. Beth, you could have used your penmanship for so much more. Now I know how you skipped all those gym classes. Your ability to pass as an adult's signature is unparalleled."

Beth laughed in response. "Thanks."

"It was after a month or two of talking that we started ditching class thanks to your notes. Does that sound about right?" Scott asked.

"Yeah, I think so," Beth said. "Because it was early fall when we went rock climbing. The leaves were just changing colors."

"I'm surprised you remember that." Scott looked at the ceiling and thought for a moment. "It would have been probably early October. That would have been the best time to show you the colors. Of course I was more impressed with you than the leaves."

"Yeah, when you weren't trying to show off by beating me to the top," Beth replied, crossing her arms and serving him a disapproving look.

"Just a friendly competition. An opportunity to show you what you were getting in a boyfriend." He took the opportunity to flex his bicep, doing his best not to wince.

Beth raised an eyebrow and wryly smiled. "Ok, ok, whatever, you can impress me for years to come, but for right now just impress me with your memory, not your muscles. How about that? Now where were we?"

Scott looked at the ceiling again, concentrating. He'd been challenged, and he never turned down a challenge. "So we had talked about ditching class to go rock climbing for a few days, and then finally we decided to do it. You were the good student, probably never ditched class until you started hanging out with me. Guess you could say that I was a bad influence on you, huh?" Scott commented with a sly smile.

"I had ditched class before," Beth said in defense. "There were times when I had to set up for assemblies and stuff for student government, so I didn't make it to class. Or there were plenty of classes that I missed for sports."

Scott held back another laugh. Barely. "That's not ditching, Beth. Nice try. Those absences were all excused because you were doing school-sponsored stuff. Ditching is when you don't go to class because you just don't want to." Beth's fists clenched and her jaw set, her lips turning into a pouty frown. Scott enjoyed ruffling her feathers, but he knew when to quit. "Oh well, it doesn't matter now, it was like ten years ago."

"Anyway," Beth said, taking over the story, her cheeks looking a little ruddy, "we decided not to go to class and instead went rock climbing, which was a very productive activity, I might add. Much more productive than whatever was going on in that stupid psychology class, anyway. So we were really learning more than we would have in school."

"Easy, Beth, you don't have to defend your perfect record...that's definitely true," Scott agreed. "So I took you up the canyon and we climbed, and you were a natural little climber, as swift as a squirrel. I was really impressed with you, but that didn't mean I wasn't still able to show off all my climbing skills and the power of the mountains."

"Yes, it was beautiful." Beth sighed at the memory.

"And those skills. Don't forget to mention the skills."

Beth chuckled and nodded. "Yes, your skills. As long as you don't go breaking any more bones. I see no reason why we can't go again this year, maybe not to climb, but maybe fishing, a little hunting. It's getting to be near the time when the deer frequent the open spaces."

"You really think you could shoot straight enough to get one this time?" Scott joked, winking at Beth to remind her of her last hunting trip and her wayward arrows.

"I'm certain," replied Beth with a little smack to his arm. "I've been practicing a little."

"I knew right away you would grow to love it," Scott replied, rubbing his arm playfully. "Ever since I took you the first time. Same thing happened like I grew to love you."

Beth slapped his shoulder lightly again. "You just said you didn't even know why I sat next to you. Now you want me to believe you saw our whole future after you barely knew me?"

Scott shrugged, resting a hand on hers. "I didn't know why you wanted to sit next to me, but I knew what would happen once you did." He smiled and spread his hands, the gesture encompassing them both. "This."

"And what is this?" Beth asked, raising an eyebrow.

"Just being together," Scott said, resting his arm behind her shoulders and drawing her close. "Like we'll always be. After all, you deserve the best, and you got it."

"Uh-huh," she murmured, unwrapping his arm and meeting his eyes. "You just remember you're lucky to have me, too. You can be replaced, you know." She replaced his arm, entwining it about her shoulder and giving his hand a little, puckered kiss. "But I don't see it happening... yet."

Chapter Four

The Denied Request

Three months after Scott's injury, he decided it was long past time to get out of puttering around the house and return to the mountains. He only hoped the first trip would be with buddies as a warm welcome back. He had a few major obstacles to climb over on the way, though. One being the Warden...

Scott killed the engine to his car and reached over to the passenger's seat to grab the six pack of Diamond Knot IPA he'd placed there. His dad had suggested he bring it along for his talk with Hank. It had been expensive, more so than he'd regularly be willing to pay, but the bribe was worth it. It would have to be, for where he was planning on going.

He climbed out of the truck and walked up to the Warden's home, admiring the view of the wilderness as he went. This was one of his favorite parts of the forest. He was about to knock on the door when it swung open to reveal Hank.

"Scott, good to see you." Hank held out his hand for a shake.

Scott took the hand and shook it, making every effort to be polite. It probably wouldn't sway Hank, but it never hurt. "You, too." Hank had a firm grip for a man his age.

"Why don't we just sit out here on the porch and drink those," Hank said with a nod to the beer. "I assume you brought 'em to share." He winked playfully.

Scott laughed in response. "Of course. Dad said this is your favorite."

"Oh, did he?" Hank questioned. "Well, the man has a good memory. I don't get Diamond Knot much anymore. Too expensive. Just about any brand of beer that's on sale is what makes it in my fridge these days." He offered Scott a slightly dusty outdoors chair with a plaid cushion helping comfort the seat, and they both took their own seat, a small wicker table between them. Scott suspected it'd seen better days, but he wisely kept his mouth shut.

Scott placed the pack of beer on the table and offered one to Hank, snapping it out of the elastic. "You have an incredible view from here." The trees were cleared out just enough to reveal a sweeping view of the valley and the rest of the mountain range beyond it.

"Yes, it was planned that way when we built the house." Hank popped the tab of his beer and took a sip. "There are some things that stay the same, no matter how much time passes. Like this beer."

Scott liked Hank. Always had. Of course his trekking business meant he worked with Hank on a regular basis, and those dealings had always been reasonable and fair. Scott was counting on some of that reasonableness today more than ever before.

"So how is the ol' man?" Hank said after a few moments of silence spent enjoying his beer and looking off into the distance of the valley.

"He's good, working hard – you know him. He works every day like it's going to be his last day in the office." Scott laughed and popped the cap off his own beer.

Ace and Hank had been good friends years ago, when Scott was younger. Work, families, and life had driven them apart over time, demoting their status from great friends who spent a few days a week talking to simply friends who spoke a few times a year, but that was no bother to them. They were the kind of friends who could go months or even years without seeing each other and pick up without missing a beat the next time they met.

"He's always been a hard worker, your dad," Hank said knowingly. "When he sets his mind to get something done, it'll get done, and nothing in the world can stop him."

"Except maybe my mom," Scott said with a smile.

"Yeah, except maybe your mom." Hank laughed. "Laura did carry a little weight with Ace. She was the only one that could talk some sense into him when he got his mind set on something stupid. Women have that effect on their husbands."

Scott knew that was true. His dad was never one to care about who he hurt or made angry in the process of getting things done, but Mom could always slow him down and make him see things more clearly. Beth often did the same for him.

"Did your dad ever tell you about the time we went cliff jumping out at the lake?" Hank asked.

Scott thought for a moment. The question had come out of nowhere, but it was best to humor Hank if he was planning on asking such a large favor of him during the visit. Even if he couldn't remember, he could fudge it. "Maybe. But if it involved him doing something stupid, I'm sure he left that part out."

Hank set his beer on the table between them and clapped his hands together. "Yeah, I don't expect this is a story he would share. We were out at the lake; it was hot, too, probably July. Your parents were engaged, and I'm pretty sure your dad was out to impress your mom."

Scott nodded. He knew what that was like. He liked to impress Beth when he had the chance.

"So he challenged me to go cliff jumping with him. And, of course, I was young and stupid, just like him, so I wasn't about to back down from a challenge. So we started jumping off the cliffs into the water." Hank shook his head as he told the story. "It started out pretty innocent. Probably ten foot cliffs, fifteen at the most, nothing more extreme than a high dive. But then testosterone or adrenaline or stupidity or maybe a combination of all three kicked in and we started challenging each other to go for the higher cliffs."

Scott leaned back in his chair and sipped his beer. He could see why Hank liked this brand so much, and he wondered why he'd never tried it before.

"We jumped a few times, and I could see right away that Laura wasn't impressed by the macho men showing off before her. She was plain out pissed. She screamed at us and told us not to go any higher. She reminded us that we didn't even know how deep the water was where we were jumping and either one of us could hit the bottom at any time, so we should come back down to the beach while we were still in one piece."

"All valid points," Scott interjected.

"All extremely valid points," Hank said with a nod and a chuckle. "But remember we're talking about your old man here. Ace has never been one to listen to valid reasoning. Not even when Laura was speaking it." Hank laughed loudly, and Scott joined him. "I was hesitant to go any higher after Laura's warnings. I hadn't thought of all that yet, but once she'd said it, it sure made a lot of sense to me. So I tried to talk a little sense into your father, thinking maybe a fellow man could do more good, but he just insulted my manhood."

Scott laughed, almost spewing a mouthful of beer all over the porch. In the end he just coughed and choked it down with a pat on his chest. "That sounds like him."

Hank smiled. "Yeah, I think he called me a pansy or a wuss or whatever the insult of the day was. But I decided I'd rather listen to his dumb insults all day long than end up dead or with a bunch of broken limbs. I told him that he could be the stupid one and I was heading back down."

"Let me guess, he jumped anyway?" Scott sighed.

"Not exactly. So he ignored me and decided to climb higher and jump from probably forty or so feet. That's when your mom stepped in. I'd never heard her yell like that before, and I haven't heard it since. She was standing on the beach, one hand on her hip, the other waving a finger at him up there on those cliffs, her face red as if she'd been sunburned."

Scott could see that in his mind. He knew Mom's classic lecturing pose well. "What did she say to talk him down?"

"Oh, all kinds of things. Things like she wasn't about to marry a cripple and she did not want to be widowed before she was even married." Hank waved his own finger to punctuate. "Those are the phrases I remember." The memory growing fresher the longer he thought on it, he laughed and picked up his beer. "I was glad that I was already halfway down the rocky crags so I could laugh quietly and neither of them would know. It was the funniest thing to watch. Ace backed right away from that cliff's edge as if it would kill him on contact. He took off like a shot, beat me down to the beach, and was apologizing to her by the time I got there."

"That's one I'll have to give Dad a hard time about," Scott said with a grin. "That's a good one."

"We had some good times back then," Hank said. "We were young and stupid, but everyone has to be young and stupid at some point, I think. It gives the best stories."

"Yeah," Scott agreed. "I've done my fair share of stupid things."

For a moment, he thought Hank might ask about these times, but the man seemed content to reminisce on his own past. They sat in comfortable silence for a few minutes, drinking beer and watching the night creatures as they came out of their daytime hiding spots. This was one of Scott's favorite times of day, if he had to choose a period. Just after the sun went below the veil of the mountain range, before it was too dark, the edge of heat gone, leaving a pleasant warmth that lingered for a few minutes before the evening chill settled in.

Hank finished his first beer and traded the empty bottle for a full one to start in on his second. "How's business these days for you?"

"Things are going great," Scott replied, purposely leaving off the rib break that had happened recently. "We had to hire a few extra employees for the busy summer season this year, so that's always a good thing for us and them."

"Yeah, can't complain about too much business on either end. Seems like we had more people in the mountains this year than last," Hank said with a swig. "Maybe I'm just getting older and can't keep track from year to year anymore, but if I had to guess, I would think we had twice or three times as many campers."

"Don't you keep track of those numbers?" Scott asked, driven by a bit of curiosity.

"Well yeah, but we won't tally this year's final numbers until the parks officially close for the winter, and that's a ways off. Then I will know for sure, but until then, there's no way to know. I guess I could compare the numbers to years past if I really wanted to get a good idea."

Scott nodded his head in agreement. "It wouldn't surprise me if the numbers are that high. We've seen a huge boost this year. I haven't run our numbers in a month or so, but I'd guess we've easily had twice as many people wanting to go up on different kinds of trips."

"Yeah, the tourism department is really doing their job getting people to come visit the area. Maybe we're finally on the map as a major tourist destination. Next thing you know we'll be besting Yellowstone." Hank shook his head, smiling.

Scott smiled. That wasn't likely to happen anytime soon. "I don't know what it is, but whatever they're doing, I hope they don't stop, because it's working in my favor."

Hank shrugged, making the beer inside his bottle swish a little. "I get paid the same, busy or not, but it's nice to see people are enjoying the area. I would rather see the parks and forests around here used than unused." He raised his beer towards Scott. "To tourists."

Scott laughed and clinked his own glass with Hank's. "To tourists."

Hank swigged his beer. His tone was serious when next he spoke. "Son, now I've sat here and talked and enjoyed my beer, but I assume you didn't come over tonight just to sit out on my porch and drink with me. Not that I'm trying to kick you out or anything, but do you have a particular reason for coming over and sweet talking me with this case of Diamond Knot?"

"I'm enjoying the porch and the beer, too, but yes, I do have a reason. And you can't tell me that the beer didn't sweeten the pot a little." He looked over at Hank and winked.

"Oh, I won't deny that. It still might not get you what you want, but we'll see how big of a demand it is."

Scott took a deep breath. Here it came, the big moment. He just hoped the beer and the company would be enough leverage after the series of accidents that had recently occurred there. "I'm hoping to get your permission to go up into the back country, to Spider Lake – the area that's restricted for everyone."

Hank's body tensed up instantly at the mention of the words. Scott knew he had to act quickly if he wanted to convince Hank, especially with the history both of them had recently shared.

"Now before you think too much about the past and shut me down completely, hear me out a little. I'm an expert outdoorsman, Hank. I've been in these mountains my whole life, you know that. There's no one that knows these mountains better than I do, except maybe you. I know there are safety concerns up there with the rock slides and unstable ground and all, but I know how to stay clear of stuff like that. I know how to watch for trouble and how to anticipate it. That's part of my job." He held his breath while he waited for Hank to reply. He didn't have to wait long.

Hank had listened patiently, but he began by setting his beer down and leaning forward on his knees. "Now you know as well as I do what happened up there recently has nothing to do with it. I can't start making exceptions to the rules, Scott. Even if you are able to handle yourself up there, which I believe, by the way, I couldn't let you go. If I let you go, then others with less experience would want to go, too. It's just not something that needs to happen."

Hank wouldn't make eye contact with Scott. He wasn't sure if the Warden was uncomfortable with having to deny his request or if there was something more, something he was trying to hide. He had to look for any kind of wiggle room, anything which might change his mind. It was like his father always said when you're trying to convince someone of something - no isn't no until it's no.

"But Hank, you've got to appreciate my love for the outdoors and my desire to go up there to solve the mystery of what happened. I've heard that area has the best fishing for hundreds of miles, better than anywhere I'd find here. It hasn't been touched in decades, it's got to be incredible. You of all people can relate to how free that feels." Scott poured his passion into his voice, doing everything he could to sway his friend.

"I can, and I do, Scott," Hank said, pointing to himself. "But do you see me running up there to fish on my time off, to figure out what happened?"

Scott had no reply to that. He couldn't dare question Hank's choices. He raised his bottle for another sip to make more time to think but found it empty. It was true, he'd been planning on investigating what happened with some friends of his disappearing up there recently, but he didn't want to mention it.

Hank bent down and rubbed his hands on his legs as if trying to smooth out some wrinkles, a nervous gesture. "There are safety concerns and rules that you don't bend even for expert outdoorsmen like you and me. I don't think you quite understand the risks of going up that way, no matter what the reasons."

"I've already heard all the myths and old wives tales about the area, but you can't honestly tell me that you believe any of that stuff, can you? They didn't shut down that area because of a bunch of stories, did they?" Scott asked.

"No, no of course not." Hank brushed off the question with a scoff. "You know the reasons it's restricted. The rockslides and unstable ground up there are too unpredictable for anyone to navigate. The slides killed a couple of young people back when I was a new ranger, and for all we know it could have killed those friends of yours a while ago, too."

"Yeah, I remember Dad telling me about those. But if someone doesn't go up there, Hank," Scott leaned forward to emphasize his point, "how will we ever know if the rockslides have stopped or if the ground has stabilized? Maybe things have improved – did you ever think of that? Maybe we could open it up again." He did his best to sound positive rather than desperate.

"I don't think you understand what I'm telling you, Scott." There was an edge in Hank's voice that hadn't been there earlier. He was getting tired of arguing. "It doesn't matter what kind of argument you present, I won't change my mind on this one. When you spend as much time in the outdoors as we do, you just learn to sense things. And I know that area, Scott. It's not an area that anybody needs to be fishing or hunting in — trust me."

"Alright, then, what if I don't fish or hunt the first time I'm up there? It'll just be a scouting trip to begin with, a learning experience. I'll go up there to get a feel for the place, see if it's safe to open back up to tourists, like a research trip. You're welcome to come, too, if you'd like." The moment he made that offer, he wanted to take it back, but it was already out of his mouth. Hank's face had paled at the mention of going.

"After talking to your friend, you couldn't get me up there if I were at gunpoint. I have no desire to ever see that place. Sorry, Scott, you are pleading with the wrong guy on this one. Appealing to the outdoorsman in me isn't going to help your cause any more than bringing me my favorite beer." Hank paused. "I have no desire to go up there and die in a tragic, unforeseen rock slide where no one but God Himself will ever find the body. Why would I want to end my life that way? No, thank you."

Scott fell silent. He'd heard the no not once, not twice, but three times in that last statement. He wasn't ready to give up, but he didn't know what else to say to get through to Hank after what they'd both seen. There was nothing left to bargain with, and his mind was as empty as his beer bottle.

"And honestly, Scott, you shouldn't want to, either – die up there, I mean. Didn't you just get engaged to a pretty little thing in town? Don't mess that up by running off into a restricted area and getting yourself injured or killed just to solve a mystery." Hank shook his head. "Don't be like your father. Listen to me, Scott."

Scott's sense of pride was pricked by the comparison, though he couldn't say why. Normally he would have been glad to be compared to his father. "I consider myself a pretty skilled outdoorsman, Hank. I don't think I'd find myself in a situation where I'd be killed or even seriously injured up there."

"Scott." Hank's voice was stern, though tired. "You don't know what's up there like I do. It's not a safe place. The rules and restrictions are there for a reason. I would never forgive myself if something happened to you up there." Hank looked over and made eye contact with Scott for the first time since they'd started the conversation, and his stare was a solid wall against argument. "It's just better this way, trust me on this one."

The silence that followed was no longer comfortable for either of them. Scott couldn't think of any other argument to convince Hank to let him go. And he knew better than to expect any bending of the rules because Ace and Hank were friends, so he didn't bother pulling that card.

Hank put his second empty bottle on the table next to Scott's, and Scott took that as his cue to leave.

"It was good to see you, Hank," Scott said, standing up and extending his hand. It was nothing but a formal gesture because he was too disappointed to make it friendly.

Hank stood and took the offered hand, and Scott thought the grip a bit looser than normal, a bit more apologetic. "I'm sorry about your request."

"Don't be." Scott shrugged as if it didn't matter. "I knew it was a long shot, anyway, after Kole snuck up there with the guys. I enjoyed catching up and hearing a good story about my dad."

"You tell that ol' man he better come by and say hi one of these days," Hank said. "A visit with him is long overdue. Tell him to bring more beer, too."

"I'll tell him," Scott said, smiling. "I'm sure he would enjoy stopping by."

"You gonna take the rest of it?" Hank raised his eyebrows, gesturing to the bottles left beside the table.

"Nah, you keep it," Scott said as he hopped off the porch and towards his car. "Enjoy."

Scott drove home, contemplating his conversation with Hank and running over the ideas in his mind. He was frustrated, not because Hank had said no, because a part of him had expected that. What bugged him was why he'd said no.

Hank had questioned Scott's abilities as an outdoorsman. He treated him like the son of his friend rather than an equal in a common field, and that was unacceptable. The more he thought about it, the more he felt the heat of anger rolling through him. No one else in the area could match Scott's knowledge or expertise in the outdoors, except Hank. That should have made them equals. It was just outright wrong for Hank to dismiss his request without even considering it only because there were unforeseen rockslides and a scare with one of Scott's friends after the man's trip up there. Scott had been working in these mountains for a decade; how much more experience did he need before he'd be qualified to go up into the restricted area? Who could say he'd even live long enough to have that much experience?

To make it even worse, Scott was sure that Hank was holding back information about Spider Lake and why it was really off limits, and this jilting idea only made the situation worse. Scott could feel Hank had held back information, and the sense he'd been cheated of the real reason for his denial gave the beer a bad aftertaste. He didn't know what it was or why Hank hadn't been honest, but it burned him up to feel lied to and manipulated. Especially by Hank, who he'd always considered, until now, his equal.

But what else could he do? Hank had said no, and no meant no. It didn't make any difference that he was upset by the decision. It didn't change the fact that Hank wasn't going to let him or anyone else go up there after Kole.

Scott pulled into his driveway and sat in his truck, rolling his shoulders once to loosen them up a bit. He was looking forward to a good night's sleep after his unproductive discussion with Hank, but he couldn't shake the feeling that the man had a point. Scott was meeting his dad in the morning so they could spend the day together. They always tried to spend Sundays together. Maybe he would have an idea about how to change Hank's mind after talking with his dad. His dad always had good ideas, but at the moment all Scott could think of was the memory of Kole's trek and witnessing the frightening aftermath.

Chapter Five

Kole

"Hey," Stafford called to the others, pausing his trek, "this looks like a good place to set up camp."

"Looks pretty flat," Mike agreed, catching his breath, his pale eyes appraising the spot.

Kole and Gavin dropped their packs without ceremony and brought out their sleeping bags.

Each of them took in their surroundings as they unpacked. Fir trees towered stoically above, their branches rustling in the evening breeze, as if trading secrets while dusk crept in on either side. Emerald mosses blanketed their trunks, and lush ferns posed in delicate bunches all around.

They were accustomed to the mountains just outside Vancouver, which were beautiful in their own way, but Kole felt that Washington was different. The strange thing was, he couldn't say why. Being so near to each other, their forests shared many of the same plants and animals, yet some instinctive part of him sensed something else here. It was a subtle insinuation that both fascinated and nagged at him.

"It's been too long since we've done this," Gavin said, drinking in a deep breath of fresh forest air and sweeping his shaggy auburn hair from his eyes. "Smell that air!"

"It was two weeks ago!" Mike chuckled as he set up his tent.

"Like I said, too long," Gavin grinned.

A silence fell over them as they took their time getting set up for the night ahead. Alert as always, Stafford's dark keen eyes scanned the area for possible dangers. He decided they had chosen a good location. The nearby stream would provide them with clean water, and it burbled its invitation for them to drink freely. They had a healthy share of rations to keep them fed, and now a good place to sleep. That left them free to spend the rest of their four-day trip hunting, fishing, or rock climbing away from the demanding tedium of civilization.

"So are we in the area that Scott told you about?" he asked, taking a refreshing swig of cool water from his bottle.

"Yeah, this should be it," Kole answered, stretching his muscular frame and pausing to think. "He told me about it ages ago...when we went on that river rafting expedition with Julie. I swear, Scott knows Washington better than anyone. It was a fun time."

"Fun for you, maybe," Mike jibed, his commentary as quick as his lean frame.

"So nature wasn't Julie's thing. That didn't mean I couldn't have a good time."

"And if I remember clearly, you also had a good time with some river guide chick on that same trip," Gavin added with a theatrical waggling of his eyebrows.

"Hey, you swore you'd never bring that up again! In my defense, I didn't hook up with her until after Julie and I broke things off," Kole pointed out, proud of his restraint.

They laughed anyway.

"And if you'll remember clearly," he added, "I dated Stephanie, the river guide, for at least a few months. I can't help it if long distance relationships are hard. We didn't see enough of each other."

"'Get enough' is more like it," Stafford chimed in.

"At least I can maintain a relationship for more than one night," Kole shot back mischievously, knowing how easy it was for Stafford to get away with one-night-stands. Tall, dark and handsome seemed to work out well for him and the women who had previous commitments of their own.

The others paused only for a second before all of them laughed together at their own ridiculous relationship challenges. If this were a competition, the match would undeniably be declared a tie.

"Anyway," Kole went on after they quieted down, "Scott told me about this place when we were on the river. He said there were rumors about it, like urban legends and stuff. But we didn't get into too much about that beyond joking. I mostly remember the fact that it's been untouched for years, so it's great for hunting and fishing. Then there's the rock climbing and the hiking. I mean, really, it's an outdoorsman's paradise, right?"

"And you're sure this is the spot?" Stafford asked, a hint of reservation in his tone.

"Well, it's the best I could do with the directions he gave me, but it seems close enough to me. I emailed him about a week ago and asked for more info. He said he would have met us up here if we'd given him more notice, but he was already booked with another group heading up to see the falls, a parent and kids one, too tame to tag along. It's too bad. He's really a cool guy; it would have been fun to have him around. The best he could do was send me GPS coordinates. Sadly, the state doesn't provide maps for this specific area, since it's restricted, but that's what makes this place special." He gestured to the pristine forest around them.

"Restricted?" Mike echoed, raising his sandy blond eyebrows. "You never mentioned that when we were making the climb."

"What's 'restricted' supposed to mean anyway?" Gavin scoffed. "I didn't even see signs or warnings posted or anything to stop us. It's probably just another way for the U.S. government to control its citizens, and the more control they have, the more zombie-like the people down here will be." He stood up and shambled around groaning in a perfect blend of obnoxiousness and accuracy until everyone was cracking up. He had a gift for entertainment, that much was obvious. No wonder he was always the most social of the group.

When they finally recovered some of their composure, Kole went on. "Yeah, Scott said it wasn't a problem, since the park rangers don't even come up here anymore. We shouldn't have any trouble from authorities."

"Well then, let's have a good time!" Gavin urged, his brown eyes bright with enthusiasm. "I mean, who knows when we'll be down in the good US of A next? Let's live it up and enjoy ourselves." He pulled a bottle of whiskey out of his bag and waved it around for emphasis.

"That's what I'm talking about," Mike said, plopping down on a flat rock next to Gavin and pawing for the bottle.

"I'll get some firewood for the night," Stafford volunteered, "as it appears somebody needs to be responsible in this group." His voice dripped with feigned weariness as he sauntered off.

"Hurry up if you want any whiskey, pretty boy," Gavin called after him. "Can't guarantee we'll save any while you're gone."

The sound of their chatter grew distant as Stafford worked his way out of the campsite. The forest floor was damp, so finding dry fuel was a fun challenge. Stafford always loved a good challenge. He listened to the trees and birds, in tune with the nature around him as he searched in the growing dimness. The quiet and peaceful feeling of the outdoors was soothing.

Then, like the flame of a candle extinguishing, it suddenly wasn't soothing at all. Everything had gone quiet…too quiet. He noticed it in an instant and stopped to look around the wooded glade. The birds had ceased their evening calls too suddenly and too soon. Even the bugs, who had been impossible to ignore earlier, had gone silent. He held perfectly still, his whole body on alert. The only sound was that of his friends laughing in the distance, until the leaves rustled with a fresh breeze as if conspiring to distract him. The hair on the back of his neck stood up, prickling and making him desperately want to scratch. He refused to let fear overwhelm his powerful senses, but every facet of his awareness unified for one dominating conclusion; he was being watched.

His eyes dissected every shape in his field of vision to find nothing, so he turned in fluid silence to face the opposite direction with the same result.

The rare temptation to ignore his perceptions fluttered through his mind as the shadows deepened, but Stafford was not a fool, not out here in the wild. He was being hunted, and movement meant death.

A twig snapped behind him and he spun to face it, dropping the firewood in his arms with a clatter. Nothing moved. In a split second decision, he sprung away toward the camp, but before his foot could return to the ground, an unstoppable force caught his middle and lifted him bodily into the air. The impact was so forceful, the air went out of his lungs. Held by what felt like a huge arm, he sucked in a choking gasp, unable to scream as the ground spun far below.

Adrenaline shot through his veins like lightning, only to slow his sense of time as he was slammed against the trunk of the tree like a ragdoll. A sickening crunch drowned his ears as the bones inside him were crushed into splinters. Stafford felt his head ricochet against the wood and his vision blurred. Then he was falling, the forest floor racing toward him. He readied himself for the final impact, but what felt like a giant hand caught his ankle, pulling him back up to face the monster. His swimming vision revealed only a hateful pair of blazing red eyes that seemed to burn through him with rage and madness.

Stafford tried to find his voice, to plead for his life in hopes the creature would understand him, but no words formed and nothing but an agonized groan escaped his mouth.

The beast threw him against the trunk again and everything went black.

"Stafford's sure been gone awhile," Kole said, his light brown eyes scanning the forest where his friend had gone. "It's getting dark."

"He's probably taking a shit somewhere," Mike suggested, smirking. "He takes forever and he's picky as a girl when it comes to what he calls 'the right spot'."

"We're out in the middle of nowhere, asshole," Gavin said, rising to his feet. "He's not going to take a half an hour."

"Idiot's probably lost then. He'll find his way back eventually."

"It's going to be dark soon. We need to not only find him, but also get some firewood."

"Alright, alright, no need to get all upset," Mike grumbled, trying to keep up with Gavin's mercurial moods.

"Let's split up and look around," Kole suggested. "Gather some wood, too, while we look."

They nodded and walked off in separate directions, calling their friend. Kole threaded through the trees to the west, picking up dry pieces of wood here and there as he called out for Stafford until his arms were comfortably full. He shouted again, louder. A voice answered, but it wasn't Stafford's.

"Guys! Guys, hurry! Come here quick!" Mike screamed out into the night, the edge of panic in his voice.

Fear spiked in Kole's chest, and he dropped the firewood he had collected, running to his friend. He couldn't imagine why Mike would scream like that, and feared the worst. Darting around a tree, he nearly crashed into both of them where they stood staring up into the branches of a tree.

"What's the deal? Did you find him?" Kole asked panting as he shouldered his way around them to look up.

They answered with silence as Gavin pointed.

Kole's eyes drifted from Gavin's finger to the lifeless body draped over the branches above like a shirt hung out to be dried in the breeze.

Bile rose in his throat and he struggled to swallow it back, bitterly tasting the acid as it returned to his stomach. "Are you sure it's…" his voice trailed off, unable to finish his thought. Between the distance, the darkness, and the blood, it was hard to distinguish the features of the limp man above them.

"His hair… his clothes," Gavin's trembling voice rasped.

It was Stafford, and no one could doubt it. They all stood frozen in shock and fear at the scene before them. The moments that ticked by felt like hours to them.

"What did that to him?" Mike whispered, whirling around to check their surroundings. His frightened eyes darted to every shaking leaf, his voice dropping into a whisper. "What could do that to him?"

"I d-don't know. Mountain lion maybe?" Gavin suggested half-heartedly. It was clear by the tone in his voice even he did not believe it.

It couldn't even be a valid suggestion, and Kole knew why. "Mountain lions don't stash their food in trees. They hide their kills on the ground...bury them, if anything. They don't hang them like that..."

They all stood silently, their imaginations racing with explanations from nightmares.

"This can't be real," Mike whispered when logic failed to help them. "This doesn't happen in real life. It only happens in horror movies."

"There were rumors about this place, weren't there?" Gavin asked, his voice rising in pitch. "I mean, wasn't something supposed to be up here?"

"Well, yeah, but Scott just said they were myths, old wives' tales," Kole said aware of the panic rising between them. "There can't really be something up here hunting people, can there?"

He hadn't even finished his question before all three of them backed up in tandem and stared out into the darkness. Something could be hunting them this very moment. Kole stared down at his hands, defenseless without a weapon against whatever was out there. He was one strange sound away from running the hell out of here, but to where? It would be hours before he reached any kind of civilization, and that was only a guess.

"We've got to go," Mike said anxiously. "We need to get back to camp and make some sort of plan."

"What about Stafford? We should get him down," Gavin said, still staring up, his eyes filled with a haunted look.

"You can climb that high?" Mike asked.

"He's— he was our friend," Gavin argued. "We should try and get his body back to camp. Not to mention the authorities will want to look at his injuries and figure out what the hell did this. In any case, we can't just leave him there like that."

"I'm not saying I want to leave him there either," Mike argued through clenched teeth, "but I'm not going to break my neck trying to get up there and lower his two-hundred-pound body to the ground. We should just get back to camp and figure out what the rest of us are going to do to get out of here alive."

Kole interrupted before Gavin could reply. "Hey, we're not going to fight among ourselves. Whatever's out there could be back. Mike is right, we need to get back to camp and figure out what we're going to do."

Gavin didn't argue, but his frustration was obvious.

They hurried back, each listening for any sign of danger. When they arrived, they dug their phones from their packs.

"I don't have service," Kole announced, waving his phone about to check in different directions.

"Damn it!" Gavin cursed at his glowing screen, the antenna blinking with a line drawn through it.

"Mike?"

"Hang on," he answered. "Come on, come on. Shit! There's no coverage here. Of course there's not. Okay, let's get a fire going."

They had a messy one burning in short order. It may have been smoky with green fuel, but light was light.

"We should leave now," Gavin said. "Make for town while we can. It can't be too far from here. Ten or so miles, right?"

"I'm not sure exactly how far, but it's a good hike," Kole said, rubbing his temples and trying to get his head on straight. Every time he closed his eyes, even to think, he saw images of Stafford's body, bloody and ripped open from side to side.

"I agree with Gavin," Mike said. "We should pack up the essentials and leave now. We can bring the bare minimum gear with us. Let's travel light and get the hell out of here. This place," he looked out into the darkness, "is evil."

"I don't know this area," Kole said, trying to be rational though his mind was in a whirl. "None of us do. If we leave now in the dark, we could end up wandering around the mountains and get ourselves completely lost. This isn't like camping back home where we know the mountains and where the rangers have outposts spotted around in case they hear of trouble. These ranges go on for hundreds of miles. And don't forget that no one knows exactly where we are. By the time they sent a search party, they wouldn't even know where to start looking." He paced around the campfire, trying to ignore the dancing shadows it flung against the forest. Its mysterious beauty had suddenly turned sinister. Would they really be better off blundering around in that blackness? "We need to wait it out until the morning when we'll have a better idea where to go."

"Wait?" Gavin shouted, not bothering to keep his voice down by now. "Wait for whatever killed Stafford to get hungry again? Whatever it is, it already knows where we are and I'm sure as hell not sitting here waiting for it to come after me!"

Mike's eyes were everywhere, and he shuffled his feet uncomfortably against the forest floor as they argued.

"I'll take my chances with the mountains any day and any time over whatever is out in these woods," Gavin continued, this time remaining unchallenged.

"Fine," Kole surrendered, tired of arguing. Gavin was probably going to leave on his own whether they went with him or not, and separation was the worst possible choice they could make at a time like this. "You two pack what we need, and I'll study the paper map as best I can so hopefully we can at least start in the right direction."

For the next ten minutes, all was quiet aside from their shuffling as they prepared to leave. Kole sat by the fire with a flashlight and studied every inch of the map. He tried using his compass and the stars to determine what direction they should start hiking. He hoped that after five, maybe seven miles of hiking they would come across a trail that wouldn't be overgrown and would lead them the rest of the way to town. It was a shot in the dark, literally, but it was all they had at this point.

"We should fill up all the water bottles we have before we start," Gavin said. "We don't know when we'll see water again, and we may not want to stop once we get going. Once we get moving, we want to put as much distance between us and this place as possible."

"Agreed," said Mike quickly.

"Speaking of distance, I don't want to take water from that stream. It's too close to here, keeps us all too open. I know it's cleaner, but I'd rather make a dash for the lake," Kole told them. They didn't argue.

Shouldering their packs, they stamped out the remains of the fire, switched on their flashlights, and jogged to the lake. The trek took five grueling minutes. They dropped their packs in the grass beside the water's edge. Their hearts pounded, more because of their fear than their exertion. They couldn't escape the darkness or any danger it might conceal. The moon was full, but it did not feel comforting, rather eerie, casting a silver, ghostly glow on the wilderness around them. Now that they were free of the trees, they could switch off their flashlights. They crouched at the edge of the lake to fill their bottles.

The moon reflected off the rippling water, and it didn't seem to be the only witness tonight. Kole was about to suggest they leave with whatever water they'd collected when two red eyes appeared just below the surface.

"Oh shit!" he leapt back from the edge of the lake, but not fast enough. The lake's surface was shattered with froth as a massive creature exploded from its depths. With one blinding sweep of its great arms, it caught all three of them and dragged them into the shocking cold murk below.

Kole's eyes were wide open as the water swirled around him, but he could only see bubbles and vague shapes as he felt the creature pulling them further from shore, deeper into the abyss. His lungs burned for air as he battled the deadly urge to scream. He fought against the beast's strength, trying to pry himself free, but it was futile. He felt Mike and Gavin on either side of him, fighting for their lives in similar fashion.

One of them must have struck the creature into slackening its grip. It was just enough for Kole to kick his way free. He launched himself from the creature's chest with a springing of his knees, kicking upward and away from the struggle with only thoughts of air and survival in his desperate mind.

His head hit the surface of the lake, and he gulped long gasps of air, choking on the water that had gotten into his lungs. With long, frantic strokes, he swam as fast as he could away from the center of the lake and toward the shore. His lungs afire, his mind reeled with the thought of his friends still in the clutches of the creature beneath the surface.

He was still swimming when he heard them emerge behind him. For a split second he thought that maybe they had also sprung free, but in the same moment, he knew it couldn't be. He knew the beast was coming for him. His friends were as good as dead if they weren't already.

Kole made it to shore, but didn't stop to catch his breath even though every muscle in his body screamed in pain. He ran into the forest, hoping he had enough sense to go in the right direction.

Screams shattered the night air behind him. Even in his frantic flight, Kole could tell it was Mike's voice, babbling unconscious words. The screams turned to gurgles as his friend begged for mercy from a monster with no conscience. Kole hesitated for only a moment, but knew there was nothing he could do and forced himself to continue moving in what he hoped was the direction of town.

A second blood-curdling scream filled the night, prompting Kole to pause again. This time, it was Gavin. Mike was gone, and now Gavin was being savaged by this thing that lived in the mountains and killed without remorse. His screams were distant and much further away. Kole felt burning tears fill his eyes for the unspeakable horrors inflicted on his friends in their last moments of life, knowing that he couldn't stop and couldn't help, even if he desperately wanted to save them. He had to get to town. If he wanted to survive this, he had to keep moving. The beast would be after him now. It was only a matter of time until it closed the gap.

Kole didn't know how long he had been running. The minutes and hours all seemed to blend together in his mind, and all he could think about were the screams, the harrowing experiences of the night blending in one long reel. He had long since lost all sense of direction, driven by the maddening fear of what was behind him.

He couldn't stop. Any rest he took would be his last. His energy reserves propelled him on and on, his body strained almost to the breaking point, where all he could think about was the pain. He crashed through the trees and underbrush, branches and tree trunks scraping his sweat-soaked skin. Dehydration and exhaustion drained him with every step.

He fell to the forest floor, his legs refusing to listen to his brain's insistence any longer. Crawling to his feet, he stumbled on, only to fall again with a choked sob of defeat. In the silent moments that followed, he lay sprawled in the fallen pine needles, certain that he was hearing the haggard breath of the beast approaching. Then he realized the breathing he heard was his own. Shaking violently, he forced himself onto his knees until a wave of nausea and dizziness overtook him, and he had to brace himself against a tree trunk to quell his body's revolt.

His body was shutting down and forcing him to stop. He couldn't continue. Every sound around him sent jolts of fear and paranoia through his tormented mind. After several minutes, he realized he had to get help. He wasn't going to get any better, and he obviously couldn't continue onward. His best option was going to be to light a fire and hope that someone close by would see the smoke and come to check on him, a ranger or fellow camper perhaps, if there was anyone else up here.

The paranoid side of him also knew that setting a fire could bring the monster to him, but he didn't have a choice, not when he couldn't move. Death was imminent if he didn't get help soon. Digging in his pockets, he found a book of matches that he didn't even remember putting there. It was one spot of luck in this unending nightmare, if only they weren't wet. Kole stared down at them until his vision blurred with sensory overload or tears, he couldn't tell which. The matches were like a small reminder of the normal life he had left behind, including his friends.

Luckily there were enough branches and bits of kindling close by that he didn't have to stand, but could crawl around to gather what he needed to start a small fire. The morning was just beginning to dawn by now, but it held no warmth or new sense of hope for Kole. Fires would be harder to notice in the daytime.

He struck one, but the water had ruined it. He tore off another and desperately raked it across the box's rough edge. A tiny flame sputtered to life but fizzed out before he could light it to the scraps of wood and pine. "Please, God..." he rasped, taking the whole pile and squeezing them in his hand, striking all at once. An orange glow took hold, giving him enough time to transfer the fire to the pile of branches.

Once the fire was started, he sat next to it with his knees pulled tightly to his chest. This time, he tried to put as much green material on the flames as he could. The more smoke the better. He stared into the fire, hoping and praying for help to arrive, turning his head away from the plume of gray that rose into the sky. Now the sounds around him inspired both hope and terror at once. Would the creature find him and finish him off, or would another human being rescue him from this hell?

The world swirled around him and even sitting was too hard. He didn't want to sleep, but it was becoming harder and harder to keep his eyes open after so much exhaustion. His tongue was so dry and seemed to stick to the roof of his mouth. He daydreamed of cool water quenching his torturous thirst until his eyes closed and the world went black.

"I just found him out there by the fire after I followed the smoke," Hank spoke in low tones to a junior ranger at the station. "He was practically dead. Barely had a pulse when I found him."

"Where was he?" she asked quietly, her pure blue eyes full of concern. Jennifer wasn't just junior, she had only been at the job for a few weeks.

"About six or so miles north of here, toward the restricted area but not quite in it," he replied, his gravelly voice low. "Kid had the smarts to light a fire before he passed out. Probably trying to signal for help, but he could have lit up the whole forest. I think he'd have gone up with it, if it got out of control. Luckily I was up that way checking for poachers and saw the smoke and found him before it got too big." He shook his head and glanced toward the back room where Kole was laying. "The only people who take that chance are either really stupid, or really desperate."

"And no idea who he is?" Jennifer asked, letting his words sink into her mind.

"None. He's got nothing on him. He didn't have a pack, a wallet, nothing. He'll come around soon and we'll get the full story about what happened."

"Weird though. A guy just up hiking by himself without any gear, especially that far from roads," she murmured.

"Yeah," Hank agreed.

Kole heard their voices and gently started to sit up from the bed he was laying in, turning his head to the side. At first he couldn't figure out where he was or why he was lying in a bed that wasn't his own. He rubbed the back of his neck and tried to piece together the last memories he had.

It didn't take long before everything came rushing. It was like waking up from a nightmare and finding out it was real. How could all of that have been true? Did all his friends die at the hands of that thing? He tried to stand, but his legs were weak and he immediately felt dizzy. Sitting back down on the edge of the bed, he tried to calm himself, but the memories were overwhelming. His mind spun with images of red eyes, a monster covered with hair, and the sounds of his friends screaming for help.

Was he safe? Or would the monster hunt him down just because he'd survived and gotten away? The panic and fear came rushing back and he struggled to breathe as his heart pounded in his ears.

The rustling and movement brought Hank back into the room.

As the door opened, Kole tried to reassure himself that the creature wasn't on the other side, while his body argued strenuously. He didn't have the energy to fight back but couldn't let himself go down without a fight. He lunged from the bed, trying to escape from the terror his frenzied mind ensured was coming, but instead a ranger emerged to catch him mid-fall and carefully laid him back on the bed, his hands supportive and strong. His eyes were surrounded with both laugh and frown lines. Silver ran through his thin hair at the temples, and his mouth was thin but not unkind. He must have been in his early fifties.

"Kid," the ranger said, "I don't know what you've been through, but it's obviously been quite the ordeal. I'm Hank, the Game Warden hereabouts. I'm here to help you, but the best way I can do that is if you talk to me about what happened to you. Are you feeling alright?"

A Game Warden. Kole tried to listen, but he was still staving off spikes of fear, and his body was shaking uncontrollably from his shock and exertion. He looked up at Hank again and tried to concentrate, but the images that flashed before his eyes were not the Game Warden's office, but images of Stafford's dead body and the feel of the creature's hand around his throat. He couldn't move past the grip of fear that held him firmly in place.

When Kole didn't respond, Hank spoke again, "Son, what happened out there?"

He didn't know how to respond. He didn't even know where to start. His friends were dead. He was almost killed by the same beast that destroyed them. And then he nearly ran himself to death. He cradled his head in his hands and tried to sort out the tangle of his thoughts. This ranger was going to think he was crazy if he told him the truth. Who was going to believe him when he said there was a creature – a monster killing people in the mountains? Was he crazy? No, it was all too real.

"I'm sure you're thirsty," Hank sighed and turned to a small fridge in the room. "Here, drink." He handed Kole a bottle of water.

The bottle felt foreign in his hand, like it came from a different, more pleasant, humble world – one that didn't include monsters and murdered friends. Kole sipped slowly from the bottle and spoke quietly. "Are we close to Redwood?" he mumbled.

Hank nodded.

"I need to see Scott." His voice was rough and raspy. "Scott Huntington. He lives there."

"You know Scott?"

Kole just nodded and continued to sip his water, imagining his story. If anyone was going to believe the truth, he knew Scott would. But even as he thought about it, it occurred to him – what was his story? Images of bodies and red eyes swam across his memory. The creature's roar and the cries for help from his friends.

His heartbeat quickened and just thinking about it made him begin to sweat all over again. His breathing came in short, shallow breaths and he suddenly didn't feel like he could get enough oxygen into his lungs. He felt confined, like he needed to run and no place was safe from the monster. Even at this very second he expected the creature to come crashing through the door to kill them all.

Noticing the man's shaking spell returning full throttle, Hank decided to keep him grounded where he was. "Now, come on, kid," Hank said a little more sternly, "I rescued you out there. Saved your life, probably. The least you could do is tell me what you were doing up here and what's going on. Are there others besides you that need help? I'm the ranger around here and that's my job to know."

"I need to see Scott," Kole managed again as a harsh whisper between breaths and turned away from the ranger. He pulled his knees to his chest again and shut his eyes, trying to force the memories away. Fear encompassed him, and he curled into the fetal position on the bed, blocking everything from his mind.

Hank turned to Jennifer and nodded briefly. "Call Scott," he growled with frustration, recognizing the signs of a panic attack. He debated taking the kid down to the hospital but knew that if there were more people in trouble it would be faster to get the information here and then transport him down to the hospital.

Scott showed up at the ranger's station a little less than half an hour after the call from Hank, which meant he must have sped a little to get there. Luckily he had been in town to begin with, since his tour group for the day had rescheduled for tomorrow.

He walked into the ranger's station, confused as to what he was going to find. He hadn't got a lot of information from the junior ranger, just that he was needed at the station immediately and that lives could be at stake.

"Scott, thanks for coming," Hank said extending his hand when he walked in the door.

"Sure, it sounded urgent," he said, shaking Hank's hand. "So what can I do?"

"Well, we're not exactly sure what it is," Hank admitted, "but it might be…"

For the next few minutes, the ranger filled him in on what little information they had.

"And he refuses to talk to anyone but me?" Scott asked, glancing at the closed door of the room where Kole was waiting.

"Yeah," Hank said. "I'll warn you, he may not be real coherent with you. He seems to be in and out of shock. I thought about taking him to the hospital until he asked for you. He could be suffering from dehydration, exhaustion, or something more. That's what you're here to find out, if he'll talk to you. First, you've got to ask if anyone else needs help out there. I can't get anything out of him and that's the first thing we need to know."

"All right," Scott said, feeling the gravity of the situation. "I'll do my best."

He walked to the door and went inside the room. The man inside sat up, and for a second, Scott almost couldn't recognize him. "Kole?" he said, bewildered. "Kole, you look like hell!" he regretted the words as soon as he uttered them, but it was as if he hadn't spoken at all with the way Kole reacted.

"Shut the door," Kole gasped, trying to control his breathing.

Scott let the door click as he shut it behind him and sat down on a chair next to the bed. "What's going on? What happened to you? I thought you and some friends were going to go fishing and rock climbing up in the mountains this weekend?" he asked, settling down in his office chair.

"We were," Kole replied. "I-I mean, we did."

Scott waited for him to continue.

Kole couldn't speak for a minute as the images rushed through his mind like a torturous picture reel, replaying everything for him to relive over and over.

"We were having a good time at first. We hiked to the place you suggested. It wasn't too bad of a hike. It was beautiful, peaceful, just like you said it would be. We set up camp and everything. But that's when everything went to hell. We lost Stafford first."

"He got lost?" Scott asked, apprehensively. "Like he left the group and never came back?"

Kole shook his head wildly back and forth, fighting back the emotion that was building in his throat, teetering on the edge of hysteria. "We found him up in the tree, dead, just like that. He was hanging like a piece of laundry on a clothesline, Scott. So we decided we had to try and make it to town before the same thing happened to us. We went down to the lake to fill up our water bottles, and that's when it got Mike and Gavin. It almost had me, but I got away. I still don't know how, but I did."

"What are you talking about?" Scott asked, utterly confused by the whole thing. "What's it?"

"There's something up there, man," he repeated, rocking back and forth where he sat, burying his head in his hands. "Something killed my friends," he whispered.

*

Scott peered out of the truck window, the engine still running as his mind reeled from the memory of Kole's whisper. "What happened to you up there, man?" he muttered, shutting his engine into silence. His eyes rested on the distant mountains, the restricted area looming in the far distance. It was unknown territory, and could be dangerous at that. Though his mind was already picturing the horrors that awaited him, a small part of him, almost unknown to himself, began to plan a trip. Because not knowing what had really caused Kole's panic was just as bad as knowing and never finding out.

Chapter Six

Other Options

Sundays were Scott's favorite day of the week. He didn't get a chance to see his dad much during weekdays. Both of them were busy with work and their social lives during the other days, but they always made time for each other on Sundays. Scott couldn't remember how the tradition started, but as far as he was concerned it was a good one that he intended to keep going for years to come.

He grabbed his phone off the dresser, unplugging it from the charging cord as he did, and stuffed it in his pocket before leaning over to brush his lips against Beth's forehead. It was the best way he could say goodbye to her without waking her up.

Scott practically danced across the room, careful not to hit any of the squeaky floorboards on his way out. After living with Beth for a few years, he had learned a few things about her. One of the most important things he'd learned was never to wake her up before she was ready to wake up on her own. Never. She was an angel if she got her beauty sleep each day, but Scott knew better than to mess with her while she slept, or he may have a devil on his hands

The events of the previous night played in his mind during the drive to his parents' house. Remembering Hank's blatant refusal to even discuss the area around Spider Lake sent his blood boiling all over again. He turned on some smooth jazz music to drown out the anger, which worked for the time being. He would tell his dad about the conversation later.

Once he arrived at his dad's place, Scott jogged up the front steps, knocked on the door and pushed it open without waiting for an answer. It wasn't as if he needed permission, being the son. The door was never locked, anyway. The house was huge, two stories, all brick, with a wrap-around porch and dormer windows. It was, without question, the most expensive house in town, but his parents trusted people and crime was always less of a problem in smaller towns. So locking the doors never even occurred to them.

And it wasn't like anyone would want to steal from them, anyway. Scott couldn't think of a single person that didn't like Ace and Laura. Ace was a close friend to almost everybody in town. And the few people he didn't know personally loved him, too. A few years ago, he had rebuilt the town rec center, donating the materials and labor. Scott couldn't remember what the rec center had been like before the remodel because he'd never been there. No one went there. But after Ace was done with it, it was the highlight of the community. With bowling lanes, an ice rink, and even an indoor aquatic center, it was crowded all the time. Every weekend was booked for birthdays, school events, and family parties, and people talked. Word spread, although Ace never deliberately tried to be the center of attention, so people soon knew of Ace's good deeds.

Ace was a hit with the kids, too. Halloween and Christmas were major events at their house. On Halloween, the house would be decorated with decaying tombstones scattered in the yard, wispy spider webs over the windows, and realistic zombies on the porch. The variety and scale of decorations were popular with both adults and kids, but what really drew the kids in were the huge gift bags Ace handed out after they knocked on the door. They had something different in them every year. Sometimes it was just lots of candy, the good kind of candy, but one year Scott heard there were MP3 players in them, though Ace denied it to everyone. Yes, his father was the kind of man who had so many stories told about him, it was hard to tell which were true and which people made up just because they liked him so much.

Christmas was an even bigger event for them. Ace hosted a big party for his neighbors and friends and gave gifts to every kid that showed up. They used to host it at the house, but after so many years and so many more people invited each year, they started having it at the rec center. It also became more of a festival with games and prizes for the kids. People pitched in and brought their own food and invented new activities every year. The important thing to Ace was that every kid went home with something, and everyone had a good time.

Scott could smell sausage, eggs, hash browns, and waffles wafting from the kitchen and smiled. As he rounded the corner to the hallway, he could hear the sizzling pops of the oil in the pan. Another great thing about spending Sundays with Dad was getting Mom's home-cooked breakfast, of which he'd never seen the equal to since moving out of home.

He was about to walk into the kitchen when he remembered he still had his shoes on and froze. He backed up slowly, removed them, and set them down by the door. He was lucky he remembered in time.

Safely shoe free, he returned to the kitchen. "Morning," he said as he walked in, swallowing to keep his mouth from watering.

"Good morning, son," his mother answered pleasantly from her place at the stove where she was flipping sausage. "I hope you remembered to take off your shoes. I don't want you tracking in all that dirt and mud from your treks up in the mountains."

"They're off, Mom," Scott said. He leaned in to give her a quick kiss on the cheek. "But thanks for the reminder, just in case I forgot." He winked at her.

"Hey, you try cleaning up after your father's mess for forty-two years. He brings mud and dirt, sawdust and grit from those construction sites of his and drags it all through the house. You would think if I could train you to take off your shoes in thirty some odd years, I would have been able to train him after forty-two, but it would be easier just to coat the house in plastic wrap." She smiled and shrugged her shoulders.

"Are you talking bad about me again, sweetheart?" Ace walked into the kitchen and sneaked a quick kiss to his wife's ear. "Don't you be telling our son stories, now!" A big smile split his face and lit up his blue grey eyes with a warm light. His hair, a thick brown when Scott was younger, was almost totally silver now and starting to thin out, but it added refinement to him more than anything else.

"Lies? Oh, I never tell lies. Only the truth, isn't that right?" She turned and winked at Scott.

Scott laughed at their familiar exchange. "Dad, how was your week?" They clasped arms then slapped each other on the back as a father and son might greet one another.

"Oh, it was all right, I suppose." Ace sat at the bar on the edge of the kitchen and shrugged a shoulder. "Building new buildings and tearing down old ones. All part of the business model."

"Just business as usual?" Scott joined him at the bar.

"Yeah, can't really think of anything new." Ace rubbed his scruffy jawline.

"What about your new bid?" Laura interjected from the oven as she sprinkled something over the eggs. "I'm sure Scott would love to hear about that."

"Oh, yeah," Ace said with vague affirmation, "you're right honey. I bet he would." He swiveled to face Scott. "The School Board commissioned me to rebuild the high school. How about that?"

"What? Really?" Scott said. "My high school?"

Ace laughed. "Well, it's the only high school in town, son, so yes, you could say it's your high school."

"Wow." Scott shook his head, picturing the old building. "Are you remodeling it completely or tearing it down and rebuilding from the ground up?"

"From the ground up," Ace said as Laura poured him a cup of coffee and brought him cream. "It's easier than trying to run new electrical and plumbing through the old walls. Plus, the existing walls probably aren't built to code anymore anyway, so getting them up to standard would probably be more work than it's worth. Not to mention all the work it is to get everything technology-savvy these days. Schools want all top of the line equipment, and installing those kinds of systems in ancient structures is next to impossible. Needless to say, it's more cost effective and much easier to just start from scratch."

"Wow, so it'll be completely gone." Scott looked away, thinking over all the memories attached to that building. The thought of it all being torn down was sad.

"You okay?" Laura asked, her attention focused on her son's forlorn expression.

"Yeah," Scott said. "It's just, that's where Beth and I first met and dated. It'll be kind of hard to part with the building." He paused and shook his head. "I know that probably sounds stupid. It's just a building, not like it's going to destroy our relationship if it goes down and all."

"But it's not just a building, Scott." Ace reached over and patted Scott on the back. "I create buildings for a living – it's what I do. And with every building I create, I ask myself, what is this building going to be used for? But more importantly, how will this building be remembered by those who use it? What kind of memories will be made in it? Questions like those guide me through the whole creation process for my buildings. Buildings aren't just buildings. They house our experiences, and with those experiences come our feelings. Without the building and everything in it, the experience wouldn't be the same, couldn't be the same. I understand why it might make you feel a bit sad to see it go after all you've been through in it."

"This conversation is too deep for me on a Sunday morning, Ace," Laura announced. "I remember when we were kids in the same high school. I was just a freshman when you were a senior, but I can remember you and all your friends putting firecrackers in the garbage cans and starting them on fire. Do you remember those good ol' days?" She threw another wink at Scott, and he suppressed a laugh.

"Me, light the school garbage cans on fire with fire crackers? Must have been your other high school boyfriend, Laura," Ace said, smiling behind his cup of coffee.

Laura rolled her eyes. "Yeah, I suppose it must have been, since I had so many." Scott smiled. He knew his mom hadn't dated anyone in high school except his dad. "Let's have some breakfast, shall we? Before I start remembering other things my many boyfriends have done." Laura turned from the stove and began preparing plates.

Ace and Scott moved to the table, and a few seconds later, Laura was setting plates stacked high with sausages and scrambled eggs in the center of the table. A moment later, she was back with the hash browns and waffles, still giving off a little steam with warmth. The waffles were covered in fresh strawberries and whipped cream, which was beginning to melt a little over the crevices of the golden waffles. Of course.

Although Laura didn't make the same thing every Sunday for breakfast, this particular meal was a common one to expect. Probably because she knew it was one of Scott's favorites, and she always tried to please her son even now. He couldn't remember the first time he'd had Belgian waffles, but he could remember the first time he had a Belgian waffle with fresh strawberries and whipped cream.

He'd been eight years old and Ace had been away on business. He'd only been gone for two weeks, but that had felt like an eternity to his eight year old brain. His mom explained to him that when his dad came home, they would have some special family time together, but that didn't help matters much.

He had no idea what this special time was going to be. No matter how many times he pleaded with his mom to tell him, she wouldn't do it. He spent every day doing nothing but waiting for the big family surprise. All he could do was imagine. The night before his dad came home, he'd gone to bed but couldn't sleep. No matter how hard he tried, his eyes would not stay closed. Visions of new toys and special vacations danced in his head, visions he'd seen before, but never this real. Laura came in to check on him before she went to bed and found him wide awake.

When she asked him why he was awake, questioning him further to be sure he wasn't frightened or waiting for his father to come home, he'd told her that he was too excited to sleep. Then he asked one more time what the special family time was going to be. She just smiled, gave him a goodnight kiss on the cheek, and shut his door, leaving him more excited and lost in anticipation than ever. At some point during the night, like any child, he'd managed to fall asleep.

When he woke up the next morning, the most delicious aroma he'd ever smelled filled the house. He flew out of bed, certain that this smell, whatever it was, had something to do with the big surprise. He launched himself down the stairs, almost tumbling down them in the process, and found his dad in the kitchen, cooking breakfast.

He had brought a new Belgian waffle maker home from his trip. But that was only part of the big surprise. He was making Belgian waffles and serving them just like he'd had them while he was away – with fresh strawberries and whipped cream. Scott could hardly believe it was supposed to be breakfast. How could something so delicious and so sweet be something for your first meal of the day? It tasted more like dessert, but of course he didn't point that out to his parents for fear they would realize their obvious mistake and take it away.

After breakfast, Ace gave him a new bicycle, which was almost too much for Scott, and they'd gone on a family bike ride beside the river trail. It was the best day of his life up to that point and he talked about it for years to come. Scott had never forgotten that day, and Belgian waffles with fresh strawberries and whipped cream had since become his favorite thing to eat for breakfast, which it seemed his mother had never forgotten as well.

"This looks great, Mom," Scott said as he filled his plate. "Thanks."

"Of course," she replied. "You're welcome."

"I'm just glad you come around every once in a while," Ace said, a crooked grin on his face. "It's the only time she cooks breakfast anymore."

Laura threw her napkin at his face, but he caught it and tossed it back. His parents remained playful even in older age. "You aren't ever around in the mornings to cook breakfast for," she scolded to defend herself. "Your father," she turned to Scott, "gets up before dawn and comes home after sun down." She turned her head back to face her husband. "And yet he blames me for not cooking."

Ace didn't say anything. He just put his head down and kept eating.

"Speaking of cooking breakfast," Laura turned her full attention to Scott. "I think it's high time that Beth started coming to these Sunday breakfasts. I want to spend more time with her."

Scott's mouth was full, but he nodded his head. As long as they didn't interrupt Beth's beauty sleep, he was fine with that.

"She's always welcome, so make sure she doesn't think this tradition is something she shouldn't impose upon. I would love to have another girl around. You two boys can go off and do whatever it is you do, and she can stay here and have girl time with me if she wants. But during breakfast, the four of us can have some family time. I'd like that."

Scott swallowed his food before replying. "I'll let her know."

"You just make sure that girl knows that she isn't breaking up some tradition between you and your father, all right? This isn't the boy's club anymore, and she's a part of this family. You make sure she understands all that."

"I think he gets it, Laura. Give the boy a break," Ace interrupted her before she could continue her tirade.

Scott laughed at his parents' back and forth banter. He knew it was all in good fun. They had been married forty-two years last summer, and Scott had never seen them happier, a testament to true marriage. He hoped that after he and Beth had been married forty-two years, they'd still be as happy as his parents. At least they were the best example they could have.

For their wedding anniversary last year, his parents had gone on a cruise to Europe. They had been gone for three weeks, sailing to points all over the Mediterranean. They'd stopped in Spain, France, Italy, Greece, and a few small islands that Scott had never heard of. It had killed Ace to leave his business for that long, but Laura had been begging for years to spend time in Europe. She knew that he wouldn't say no forever, and after dropping a few clever hints about how much longer they'd have the chance, she'd finally gotten him to cave. Scott had wondered how much of the trip Ace had spent on his tablet or computer, working and sending emails. He had never seen the man go more than a day without doing some kind of work.

But Laura had come home raving about the trip, the sights of Europe, and how much fun she'd had, so even if he had snuck a little work time in here and there, Ace had done everything just right in her eyes.

"So Scott, how's business for you?" Ace asked between big mouthfuls of waffle and sausage. Despite the refined look he derived from his graying hair, he was a notoriously messy eater.

"It's great," Scott said. "We just finished our busiest season yet. I don't know what it is, but something providential is bringing the tourists here and keeping us on our toes. I've had to hire more help to keep up with all my clients."

"That's great to hear." Ace took another bite of his breakfast, then leaned back in his chair to chew.

Scott saw Laura open her mouth to tell him to lean forward and drop his crumbs on his plate instead of his lap, but then she must have decided against it, because she filled her mouth with a bite of eggs with a resigned roll of her eyes.

Scott used to worry that his father would be upset that he wasn't going into the family business, especially after he graduated high school. Since before Scott was born, Ace had started lining everything up for his son to take over the construction business. But Scott wasn't interested in construction or building, not enough to make it his career. He'd given it a fair shot, back in high school, but he didn't have a passion for it.

The only thing that had saved their relationship was that Ace had realized Scott wasn't going to stay in the family business long before he announced his decision to start a wilderness touring company. Scott had always wondered if his mother's gentle, or not so gentle, prodding had helped that realization along. Either way, that had to be why it had gone so well when Scott finally did build up the courage to tell his dad.

Scott's decision not to take over the business, and Ace's reaction to it, were probably the best things that had ever happened to their relationship. That conversation had taught Scott that his dad would always support him, no matter what decisions he made. And that had increased the tremendous respect Scott already had for him.

"And it seems like we're not the only ones to see an influx of tourists. I was visiting with Hank last night and he told me it's the same way in the park. They've seen more traffic this year than ever before, too. Hank said it's a little early to calculate the numbers, but he thought they were significantly higher than any other year he's worked at the station. Crazy, isn't it?"

"You talked with Hank last night?" Ace asked, perking.

"Oh yeah, he said to tell you hi," Scott said. "You too, Mom." He looked over at Laura. She smiled as she took a bite of waffle and nodded to return the sentiment.

Ace laughed the deep, rich laugh he seemed to save for interactions with old friends like Hank. "Why didn't you say so? How is the ol' man? What's he up to?"

"Funny you should call him that," Scott said with a smirk. "He called you the same thing. And he told me that you better go visit him one of these days. I think he said something about a visit being 'long overdue.'"

"Yeah." Ace turned his head to the left to stare out a window. "It probably is. You know, I can't remember the last time I spoke with him. Sad how time moves so fast these days. I'll have to make some time to go up and see him."

"He'd like that," Scott said. "He didn't say it, but I could tell he's pretty lonely up there on his own most days. He seemed to really enjoy having me up there to talk to as we thought about old days. Like he wanted somebody to sit and talk with him a while."

Ace nodded, still looking out the window. "Well, it probably does get pretty lonely up there, being by yourself all day."

"Yeah," Scott said. He could have brought up Hank's decision now, but he decided it wasn't time yet. He paused for a moment, and then shifted to a more pleasant subject. "Hank told me a story about the two of you from when you were first engaged."

"Oh really?" Ace turned back to Scott. "And what story was that?"

"About the time the three of you went cliff jumping out at the lake," Scott said.

"Oh yeah, that was a good time. You remember that, Laura?" Ace looked over at her.

The subtle glare in her eye made it clear she did remember it, and with a little less fondness than Ace, but she didn't say anything, just nodded.

Scott suppressed another chuckle and retold the story as best as he could remember from the details.

"Now, that's not exactly how I remember the day going," Ace said.

"Well, how do you remember it?" Scott wasn't surprised at all that his dad remembered it differently. Or that he'd take some objection to the way Hank told the story. In fact, he'd expected it.

"I didn't jump off the highest ledge that day, and Hank got that part right, but it wasn't because of anything your mother said. We were too high up to hear if she was shouting at us. No, I didn't jump because I was smart enough not to. I was only up there because I was trying to convince Hank it was a bad idea. He was bound, set, and determined to jump, no matter what I said. I practically had to drag him back down the cliff to make sure he didn't break a bone. Or worse."

Scott nodded as his dad told his side of the story, managing to keep a straight face the whole time. He doubted he'd ever know the real story of that day, not unless he asked the third party. Maybe his mom knew the truth. But if it was really true that they were so high that she couldn't talk to them, she might not even know herself. It was Ace's word against Hank's. And Scott had no idea who to believe.

"That's how you remember it, right Laura?" Ace looked over to her for support.

"I'm sure if that's how you remember it, Ace, that must be how it happened." Laura shook her head and rolled her eyes, then winked at Scott when Ace wasn't looking.

"I assume you didn't go up there just to visit Hank and hear him tell these little lies about me." Ace's face grew more serious. "Why did you go up there?"

"Well, I was curious," Scott said. "You know about the restricted area up near Spider Lake? The area that got shut down and closed off like thirty years ago? No one I know has been up there. I want to go up and check it out."

Laura jumped back into the conversation before Ace could reply. "Why on Earth would you want to do that? It's restricted for a reason, Scott. It's not safe."

"Mom—"

"The government says no one should be up there, and you shouldn't try to act like you're above those rules and regulations." Her fork was waving at him the whole time, because his mother had always spoken with her hands as much as her mouth. Her movements were so erratic, he wondered if he should be ready in case the fork flew out of her hand.

"Mom, it's okay, calm down."

She lowered her fork and let out a breath, but her eyes still had the protective mother edge in them. "Tell me this, why would you want to go up there, anyway, if the people in charge say it's unsafe?"

"I'm just trying to learn more about the area. It's closed because of rockslides and stuff like that. I wanted to know if Hank knew more about why it was restricted and if there was any way I could have access to check it out since I'm an expert outdoorsman. That's all."

Laura opened her mouth, but Ace beat her to the punch. "And what did Hank say?"

It was time to reveal the results. "He said no." Scott sighed and set down his fork, abandoning the last bit of his waffles to elaborate to his parents, who doubled as his therapists. "I admit that I was a little offended by his refusal, Dad. I mean, I know he's a friend and all, but I don't think he understands my experience and understanding of the outdoors. He was pretty firm about it, almost harsh. I don't think there is any way he's going to bend."

"Rockslides, huh?" Ace asked, taking a drink of his coffee. "Is that all they're worried about?"

"That's what's listed under the restrictions on the county records, and Hank didn't tell me anything else. There's also a mention of unstable ground, which would contribute to the rock slides, avalanches, and mudslides, depending on the time of year you're up there."

"Sounds dangerous," Laura said in approval. Good old Mom, ever trying to keep him safe and sound.

"All I know is that I hear the best fishing for a hundred miles is up there. I want a part of that. And I want to see the landscape for myself. Can you imagine going up there one weekend and seeing it? Land that hasn't been touched by man for decades? No trash, no residue from people, just real, raw, nature as God intended." He could hear the passion in his voice mounting as he spoke.

Ace leaned forward, obviously moved by his son's desire. "And Hank didn't understand that?"

"I tried to explain it to him, exactly like I'm explaining it to you, but like I said, I don't think he understands the kind of experience I have in the outdoor field, or maybe he just doesn't like me." Scott crossed his arms, the same frustration he'd felt last night mounting again. "I don't know why he's denying me access, Dad, but whatever his reasons, he isn't bending the rules for me, not even for beer. I don't think there's anything else we can do about it at this point."

"I wouldn't be so sure about that." Ace scratched the scruff on his jawline, setting his coffee down on the table.

"What do you mean?" Scott tilted his head.

"I might know a few guys that could pull some strings, make some things happen for us." Ace got a twinkle in his eye as he spoke.

"You'd do that?" Scott said. He didn't doubt his father had the connections, and his hopes were dredged back into existence.

"You are the best outdoorsman I know," Ace said. "If anyone deserves to go up there, it's you. And besides, you can handle yourself on a little wobbly ground."

Chapter Seven

Permission Granted

Ace woke up while it was still dark outside, the black and blue edge just beginning to dim, giving way to the lighter orange of the sun's imminent arrival.

He looked at the clock and shook his head. 6 A.M. Since when did he wake up at 6 A.M. without an alarm or a reason? He rolled out of bed and groaned when he felt the stiffness in his back. Then he remembered, he was old. The older he got, the less sleep he seemed to need and the more he needed to take it easy in the morning. He sat on the edge of the bed and stretched his arms, a ripple of popping sounds coming from his shoulder.

"Are you going to talk to Hank this morning?" Laura asked, her voice slow and thick from sleep. He wouldn't have even known she was awake unless he heard her voice from the way she was still lying down, her side facing away from him.

"Sorry, did I wake you up?" Ace twisted around to look at her.

"It's all right, I was already starting to wake up."

"Yeah, I'm going to talk with him." Ace stood and stretched his legs next, first the right, then the left. "It's been too long since we've visited, and I'd like to hear what he has to say about Scott going up to Spider Lake. Seems like a pretty innocent request to me. The boy just wants to go fishing. He's not looking to cause any trouble; I don't see what the problem is."

"Well, you and I both know Hank. Don't go and get upset without giving him a fair chance to explain himself." Laura eased herself up to sit in the bed, leaning against the head post. "He wouldn't say no without a very good reason."

"Maybe." Ace walked across the room and stopped in front of the window overlooking the street below, dotted with only the earliest of risers at this hour. "But we also both know that Hank can be a stubborn idiot sometimes all on his own. I have a feeling he may just be stuck in his ways and not willing to listen to reason."

Laura smiled. "Sounds like another old man I know."

Ace turned around, hand over his heart. "You ain't talking about me, are you? Old?"

Laura laughed and threw a pillow at him, but she'd never been a great shot. "And stubborn."

Ace caught the pillow and tossed it back towards her, the pillow plopping down over her head.

"Me? Stubborn?" Ace turned toward the bathroom to start freshening up for his trip. "Never."

*

Hank jumped a little bit at the sound of a knock on his door. He looked at the old clock hanging on the wall, making sure it was still ticking.

Who was knocking on his door at 6:50 A.M.?

He hadn't received any distress calls from the assistant rangers. There must be trouble up on the mountain for someone to come by unannounced this early. His work was truly never done.

Hank yanked the door open only to find Ace standing on his porch. He sighed with relief and exasperation. "I should have known to expect you, just didn't think it would be this early."

"I don't even get a good morning?" Ace asked, raising an eyebrow.

Hank laughed and opened the screen door. "Come on in." He saw Ace was holding two steaming cups of coffee in his hands and a small box of donuts under one arm. "I sure hope those are for us to share."

"Of course they are. You're not too old for doughnuts, are you?"

"I'm not if you're not. Let's go sit in the kitchen."

"How have you been?" Ace said as they walked through the house.

"Been good. How 'bout yourself?"

"Can't complain. Things are good. Business is good, Laura's good, Scott's good. My health is good. I guess that makes everything good."

Hank chuckled at that statement, gestured to a chair for Ace and took a seat opposite. Ace handed him a cup of coffee and put the box of doughnuts on the table between them.

They sat in silence for a few moments, attention too focused on the doughnuts and coffee to talk quite yet.

Hank lowered his second doughnut to the lid of the box when it was half gone. "It's been awhile."

"Been too long," Ace said, his mouth still full. "Laura's been on my case about sugar more and more often the older I get."

Hank laughed. "We're getting to be old men."

Ace jutted his chin out at Hank and purposely finished his doughnut in one bite. "Not too old. We've still got some good years left in us."

"Yeah, but I think our better years are behind us." Hank leaned back in his chair, stared out the window, and took another bite of his own doughnut, sprinkles dotting his shirt.

"You're probably right, but that doesn't mean we can't have good times ahead, either." He raised his coffee cup in a toast. "To the good years ahead of us!"

"I'll drink to that." Hank raised his own cup of still-steaming coffee, and then took a long sip. "How's Laura been doing lately?"

"She's the same as she always is." Ace smiled. "A little fireball that keeps me on my toes."

Hank smiled back. "She always was. That gal is good for you."

The conversation faded away between the two men, so Hank finished his doughnut in peace. If Ace was here to talk about Scott and his crazy request, Hank made sure he'd have to bring it up himself.

Ace finished his own doughnut, took a deep breath, and set down his coffee.

Here it comes.

"So I visited with Scott yesterday," Ace said. "He came over to the house like he always does on Sundays. He mentioned that he'd been over here to talk with you."

"Yeah." Hank affirmed. "I saw him Saturday night."

"And he said that the two of you talked about him going up to Spider Lake."

"That's right." Hank took another doughnut, the box quickly growing low between the two of them.

"But Scott said there are some regulations keeping him from going up there?"

"Again, that's right." Hank bit into the doughnut to keep the impatience from showing on his face. If Ace was going to try and convince him otherwise, he'd have been better off not coming at all.

"Now, Hank, you know Scott." Ace leaned forward, over the table. "He's probably the best outdoorsman around here, other than yourself. He'd do just fine up there with the research he's bound to do. Aren't the regulations thirty years old or something like that?" Ace spread his hands and leaned back. "When was the last time somebody was up there to check on the area, anyway? What are the restrictions for? Mudslides, unstable ground? Who's to say that the area isn't safe now? Why not let him see for himself?"

"Who's to say it isn't worse?"

Ace blinked, cut short.

"Ace, let's not waste this time arguing. I know that you want me to bend the rules for Scott, but I'm not going to bend them. I told Scott the very same thing on Saturday. I'm not going to bend them for you either. We're friends, and I appreciate you stopping by to say hi, but that doesn't change anything about what I said before to your boy. Scott's not going up there." Hank popped the last bite of doughnut into his mouth. "Period."

"Hank, really?" Ace put both palms on the table, clearly irritated. "You're really going to be like this with our relationship the way it is? It's just a rule, a stupid rule. Scott's safe and competent. You know that. He can handle himself up there. He'll be just fine."

"If Scott was truly a competent and safe outdoorsman, Ace, he wouldn't want to go to a place as dangerous as Spider Lake in the first place. He'd know to respect the rules." Hank stood. "I've said no. I won't bend on this. You don't understand the risks of allowing him to go up to Spider Lake. I do. I was around when those regulations were put in place. It's not safe up there. I remember. You just need to trust me on this."

Ace pushed himself to his feet, heaving a deep sigh. "You always were a stickler for the rules."

"It's not just about following the rules." Hank took a deep breath. When he continued, his voice was softer. "It's about staying safe and being smart." He glanced at the old clock again. "I'm due up the mountain soon. I need to get going."

"It was good to see you. We should go fishing sometime together. Soon." He pointed at Hank. "I mean that. Let's find a weekend and go up, just the guys."

"That'd be fun. I could use some relaxation." Hank shook his friend's hand. "I'll bring the beer this time."

"Great." Ace walked out the front door and stopped on the porch. "I'll call you maybe later in the week, and we'll set up a weekend."

"Sounds good," Hank said.

Ace walked down the steps of the front porch.

"Tell Laura hi for me," Hank called after him.

"I will," Ace called back as he climbed in the cab of his truck.

Ace called Scott as he pulled out of Hank's driveway to give him the bad news. If he postponed it, it would only be worse later. "I'm sorry, son. I really thought I would have more pull with him."

"It's all right, Dad," Scott said. "There are plenty of other places to fish in the mountains. We'll find somewhere else." Disappointment was thick in his voice.

"I know there are plenty of places to fish, son. I've been to most of them with you when you were younger. It would be awfully nice to see what this Spider Lake has to offer, after all this time." He switched the phone to his other hand. "I'm not giving up on getting you up there just yet. I have a few other strings I can pull before we're stuck up a creek without a paddle."

Scott chuckled, confident his chances were low, but he was willing to give his dad a chance to try. "Alright, Dad, but don't stress too much about it, okay?"

"Hey, you're my only son. It's my job to do stuff like this to help you out."

"Thanks, Dad."

"I'll call you when I know something." Ace hung up the phone as he pulled into his office.

Ace pushed Spider Lake out of his mind for now, as he had business that needed attending to regarding the school and the rest of his work. He spent the next two hours calling clients, dealing with suppliers and relaying instructions to his foremen out on projects. He even set a date for the school demolition, though he doubted it would happen just as planned. He often had to re-plan these dates several times until they took place. He accomplished a lot that morning, but he could have done more if half his attention hadn't been taken up by ideas to get Scott into that restricted area.

When he finally had time to take a break, he had taken time to think about Scott's dilemma, and by then, he had a plan to help make Scott's trip happen. Having built many buildings for the city, county, and even the state, Ace had more than a few friends in high places. And plenty of favors he could call in from these friends when necessary.

Ace carried a lot of weight in Redwood after all these years. He had money, power, and lots of friends. Politicians at all levels were always quick to help people like him if he asked. He could find someone to step up if he chose the right people to call.

He decided to start with the Sheriff. He placed the call and got through quickly to the man's office. He explained the situation briefly before being denied by the man. Strike one.

"Sorry, Ace, I can't do anything for you."

"Come on, there must be something you can do for me. Big, important guy like you, you must have some connections."

The Sheriff chuckled. "I'd help you if I could, Ace, but there's simply nothing I can do for you. That's Hank's territory, and all that stuff has to go through his channels."

Ace thanked the Sheriff and hung up. It didn't help that everyone respected Hank so much. If they saw waiving the regulation as an action against Hank, no one would do it. He tried the county commissioner next, feeling hopeful this attempt would work better.

"Commissioner, good afternoon, Ace Huntington here. How are you?" Ace used his friendliest tone. "No, everything's fine, just wanted to call and catch up a little if I caught you in a free moment."

After the requisite banter about family members and mutual friends, Ace got down to business.

"Commissioner, there is one thing I wanted to ask you about. As you know, my son, Scott, is an expert outdoorsman. He's owned his own outdoor recreation and sporting company for fifteen years. I think you even took the wife up to the falls yourself with Scott a couple years back for a date, didn't you? Yeah, so you know he practically lived in the mountains as a kid. He wants clearance to backpack up to Spider Lake. Unfortunately, the area is currently restricted to all citizens, but I'm looking to get him special permission to go up there for a couple days for a fishing trip. I'm not sure who I need to talk to about that."

Ace could hear the Commissioner breathing on the other end of the phone, but he didn't respond right away. It was a good time to push for permission now that the Commissioner was hesitating.

"After thinking it over, I decided you might have the authority, since it's in the county of Jennings and it's under your jurisdiction and all. That's why I called you first." It was a small lie, but it played to the Commissioner's pride.

"And you were right to call me first," the Commissioner said, his ego stroked sufficiently. "We can make that happen. I'll need a few days to get all the paperwork straight for the rights, but I'm sure it'll be fine. Let me call you back first thing tomorrow morning so I can make sure I got it all straight. I'll get my staff working on the clearance right away."

"Thank you so much, Commissioner, for all your help. I knew you were the right man to call on this. I can't thank you enough. My son will be thrilled to hear the news."

"Of course, Ace. Anything for you. I'm just glad we are able to help each other out."

"Always." Ace disconnected and dialed Scott's number without setting the phone down.

"Scott, good news. I've got your clearance." Ace tried to keep his voice calm, but he knew he was failing as it wavered with excitement.

"What? Really?"

"Yep, the County Commissioner is working on making it happen right now. He said it might take a few days for the paperwork to be drawn up right, but he'll make it happen." Ace was beyond proud to be able to put this special trip together for his son with his connections.

"Dad, that's awesome. I can't believe you actually got permission to do it."

"Hey, anything for my boy. So you better start figuring out your route and what you plan to do up there, because this clearance will only last so long."

"This is great news, Dad. Amazing. I've gotta call the guys together. They're going to be so excited to hear it. Thanks."

"Of course. That's what dads are for." Ace had a huge smile on his face as he hung the phone back up.

Chapter Eight

Permission from Beth

Beth heard Scott lift the covers off himself and swing his legs over the edge of the bed before she was fully awake. It wasn't the first time he'd gotten up before her, but she was puzzled by how often it happened. She cracked open an eye just enough to see the clock on her bedside table. Her eye closed again, and she reached out to touch Scott's back.

"Scott, it's 7 A.M. Can't we sleep in for just one single morning? You big goof, the day isn't going to go by without you if you sleep in a little." She ran her hand across his back, clenched the cloth of his pajama shirt and gently pulled him back down close to her.

He smiled, turned around, and leaned over to kiss her on the forehead in response. "But that's why you love me, isn't it? I'm always ready to go!"

It wasn't the response she was looking for, but it satisfied her, so she released him, let out a sharp laugh, then grabbed the covers and pulled them up over her head.

Scott laughed too and stood from the bed, feeling better than he'd felt in a long time. "I'm going to get breakfast going, babe."

"You'd better be making your famous pancakes for me," she grumbled without removing the covers from her head.

She heard him groan and knew he was stretching his arms high over his lean, muscular body. She almost stuck her head out for a peek at his outline, but decided against it. The blankets were too warm, and she had all her life to see his body.

"I sure am!" His voice was bright and chirpy. She liked hearing him like that, but it was far too unusual for a normal morning.

Beth knew what that cheeriness meant today. She yanked the covers down and sat straight up in the bed, drilling Scott with her well-practiced, suspicious stare. "Oh, really? Well then that tells me one of two things. Either you are about to tell me something important, or you're going to ask me something that you know I'm not going to like. I hope it's the former."

Scott smiled at her and leaned across the bed to kiss her again. "Relax, my dear. Be downstairs in twenty."

Beth flopped back down on the bed, pouting. She knew she wouldn't go back to sleep, but she'd need the twenty minutes to finish waking up. Not everyone could bounce out of bed wide awake at the crack of dawn like Scott. At least, no one normal could.

They'd been together for twelve years now and had known each other for well over twenty. Beth smiled at the thought. It was a miracle she lasted some days without sending him to sleep on the couch for being so reckless. Ten minutes after Scott went downstairs, Beth sat up again. She was as awake as she was going to be without getting some food in her belly, and sitting there wasn't doing anything to help.

She sat on the edge of the bed and ran a hand through her thick, red hair in a vain effort to tame it. She knew many women in Redwood lusted after her hair, and a few brave ones had even tried to copy her color at the salon by mixing up a few different shades. But nothing could compare to a natural redhead.

Beth got up, feeling the lure of pancakes as their aroma drifted up to the bedroom. She stretched her arms out in front of her and groaned. Her eyes fell on the tattoo on the inside of her right wrist. It read 'ICE' in flowing letters. Its meaning was something only she knew, and it was a secret that she would always hold dear to her heart, no matter how many people asked her what it meant.

She threw on one of Scott's T-shirts for the moment, the hem falling just below her knees. Beth smiled in anticipation of the reaction she would get from Scott when he saw her, crossed her arms over her chest and walked out of the bedroom. The stairs creaked under her feet, and her stomach grumbled as the smell of Scott's pancakes got stronger. She hadn't realized how hungry she was.

Scott looked up at her when she walked into the kitchen, looked back at the stove, then back at her, eyes wide by the second double take. Beth made sure to walk close enough to the window to let the morning sun gleam in her hair, holding Scott's eyes as she crossed the room. She didn't realize the sun was also shining through the thin cotton of her fiancé's shirt.

She couldn't keep a small smile from her face when she noticed that the hands that had been busily flipping pancakes a moment before were now frozen over the pan. It was amazing that she could still shock him into speechlessness like this after knowing him for over twenty years.

His T-shirt clung to her frame in all the right places. She knew he loved the girl-next-door look, and she could pull it off perfectly every time. He smirked at her.

"What are you staring at?" Beth smirked right back at him.

Scott left his station at the stove and strode towards her, his eyes fixed on the curves of her body. He bent close to her ear. "If your pancakes burn, don't blame me." He met her lips and began mouthing at her, his hand trailing along her waist.

Beth was torn, her body shivering at his touch, but her stomach aching for a taste of the breakfast. "Scott," she whispered, trying to voice her conflict. His fingers began to slip further down, toying with her navel, trailing along the rim of her panties. "Scott, wait." Her fingers took his, halting them. "After."

Resolved disappointment filled his features, but he sufficed for a single long kiss. "Alright."

She laughed harder and he released her, a huge smile on his face.

Beth crossed the room to sit at their antique kitchen table and left Scott to finish up the pancakes, unable to keep from smiling herself. Her stomach growled again, and she considered going back to the stove to see exactly how much longer those pancakes were going to take. But if she did, Scott would only get distracted again and they'd take even longer to finish. Better to wait here and let him focus on their food.

After what felt like an eternity but was probably less than a minute, Scott scooped the last of the pancakes onto a plate and turned around.

"Hungry?" he asked with a strained smile, his eyes trained on her chest. He was purposely withholding, just to let her know what she was missing. "I sure am."

Guess she wasn't hiding her impatience as well as she thought. She nodded her head up and down, smiling in anticipation of the meal.

Scott placed breakfast in front of her--the pancakes piled high in the center of the table, with sugar, maple syrup and a glass of orange juice to complete the delicious ensemble. With everything in place, he sat down next to her.

She reached for the partially full jar of maple syrup. "Hmm. We're running a little low on syrup."

"I'll check the cupboard for more." Scott jumped up and headed to the cupboard to tell her what their remaining supply was. He raised the glass jar for her to see. "We only have one more jar."

Beth glanced behind her out the back window at the group of sugar maple trees in the yard.

Her mother had taught her years ago how to take sap from the trees and make homemade syrup, which was incredibly cheaper than buying the fructose loaded stuff from the supermarket. The result tasted a million times better than anything they could have gotten themselves. She had always enjoyed the process, and it was even more special now that her mother had Alzheimer's. Making the syrup reminded Beth of the good times she'd had with her.

Whenever Beth made a batch, she took some over to her parents' home and shared it with her mother. Sometimes she swore her mother's eyes had a twinkle in them that she hadn't seen for years when she tasted the syrup.

Beth turned away from the window and back to Scott. "I'll make some more this weekend. We should be able to squeeze two or three more jars if the trees are still generous."

"That sounds like a great idea," Scott agreed cheerfully.

Something about the way he said it sounded almost relieved, and Beth jabbed her fork at him after she filled her mouth with a bite of pancake. "Your pancakes are as amazing as usual," she said with a full mouth. She swallowed before continuing. "But don't think that gets you out of talking about whatever is wrong. I know you, Scott." She laid down her fork. "I know there's something on your mind. Tell me what it is."

Scott rubbed a hand over his jaw, thinking about how he was going to break it to her. She'd never been supportive of him going in the first place. "You do know me too well." He set down his own fork without taking a bite. "Well, it's nothing to be alarmed about, or anything to get upset about. The boys and I were planning a little impromptu get-away this weekend."

Beth nodded and looked up. She picked up her fork again and cut into a pancake. "That's awesome! Where are we going?" She slipped the end of the fork into her mouth. Why was he acting like he had some kind of bad news? A trip up into the woods was a fantastic idea, and she loved to go on trips with the guys.

"Well." Scott squirmed in his seat. "That's just the thing, sweetie..."

Beth stopped chewing, her fork frozen over the plate. She leveled a hard stare at Scott, eyebrow raised, and waited for him to go on.

He cleared his throat and glanced up at her, but couldn't maintain eye contact. "Please don't be upset, you know it's not a slight against you, nothing personal. I love having you come along. The boys do, too. But this time we're hiking up to a place that we've never been before. I don't know the terrain well—no one does—and it just isn't safe for you to come along."

Her eyes narrowed, hardening, her arms crossing. She dropped her fork against the plate with a clatter and leaned back in her chair, her nose wrinkling and her mouth dropping open in a short chuff of disbelief. "Wow."

Scott reached out and put a hand on Beth's arm, but she jerked it away instantly, as if his touch were hot enough to burn. "Beth, please. Don't be like this. I promise you'll come along next time. I only just found it on an old map; no one's been up there in years. It really isn't safe."

"Oh, that's bullshit, Scott, and you know it." Beth motioned at his chest. "What, you think just because you're a tour guide that you can't get hurt like this on a whim? You can break your ribs and it's okay for you to suddenly decide to go on an adventure? You can go up on this wild adventure in the middle of nowhere and I can't go with you because it's dangerous?" Beth glowered at him, her eyes spitting venom. "Seriously?"

Scott sat back and bit his lip.

"You know I can handle myself just as well as any of those guys. Just as well as you so you'd better come up with something better than that."

"Beth—"

"If you want to have a boy's weekend, you can just say so, you know." She folded her arms and refused to look at him, pouting. "Go to some bar, go hiking, but don't make excuses about it not being safe, because I'm too weak to handle it." Now she hit him with another stare. "I don't want to hear that crap from you."

"Beth—"

"Don't 'Beth' me, Scott," she snapped. "Tell me the truth. Why don't you want me to come?"

"Beth, sometimes I just need some time alone with the boys. You think I broke my ribs on purpose? I'm not trying to make this hard, but you're making it harder." Scott reached across the table for her hand, but Beth yanked it away. He sighed and ran his hand though his hair.

Beth knew he wasn't trying to be insulting, but that didn't mean she was going to let him brush her off so easily without giving her a little leeway on her end.

She put her hands on the table to emphasize herself. "Scott, just admit that I am as good as any of those guys. Say that you just want a trip with guys for your little boy time, and this argument can be finished."

Scott looked up and met her eyes. "Fine Beth, fine. You would handle it just as well as any of the other guys. I've got an idea to make both of us walk away from this happy. How does this sound? I'll go and have a guy's weekend and check this place out, make sure there's no big danger and scope out the most romantic spots there, and then you and I can go up and explore after I come back. Just the two of us this time, Beth. Wouldn't you like it better like that?"

He moved to kiss her smooth, supple, cheek, and she couldn't keep a small smile from curling up her lips. "You and me, out exploring the woods together, without the other guys harassing us? I know that's what I'd prefer."

He kissed her ear, and she giggled, so he kissed it again.

"Okay, okay, stop it!" Beth said, pushing him away. "You're free to go. But..." She took hold of his face between her hands. "...you have to follow a few rules. One, no more broken ribs. No more broken anything. You come back just like you are now. Two, you keep in contact with me whenever you can. I have to know when you're getting back so you don't overstay that welcome."

Scott scoffed lightly, but she pinched his cheeks to emphasize her point, hard enough to get his attention. "Listen to me, Scott! I know you think you're an expert and you know what you're doing as a macho man tour guide. But I've been with you long enough to know your vices. You're careless, Scott. You get to thinking your invincible and you can't think that. Because when you start to think that, you're challenging everything up there to get the better of you." She took a slow breath. "Just promise me you'll remember I'm here, and I'm waiting for you."

He chuckled and pulled her close to his chest to cradle her there. "You can be such a worry-wart sometimes, my dear." He pulled back and looked into her eyes. "Dry your eyes, now. You spend the weekend making syrup and enjoying some time with your mother without even thinking about me. I'll be fine. I'll come back all in one piece, I promise, and before you even know it, we'll be hiking up there together."

He pulled her close again, and she rested her head against his chest listening to the steady, rhythmic thump of his heart and counting them.

They stayed like that so long that Beth lost track of how many beats she'd counted, and the pancakes were soon forgotten, having grown cold on their plates.

Chapter Nine

The Confrontation

"You went behind my back, Ace." Hank paced back and forth in the sunroom of Ace's house, his fiery gaze moving from Scott to Ace and smoldering them both as it flashed between them.

The room glowed with the orange light from the setting sun, but the tension in the air made it feel hot and uncomfortable rather than warm and pleasant.

"You underestimate my son's abilities, Hank." Ace's voice was louder than usual but still under control.

Ace had called Scott after getting an angry phone call from Hank and asked him to come over; Ace had never liked leaving something unresolved. Beth had been with Scott, so now they were all gathered to hear what Hank had to say.

So far, it was nothing new.

"It's not that I underestimate Scott." Hank waved his arm and turned away from the table where Scott and Beth sat. "Apparently I underestimated you," he accused Ace. "I can't believe that you went behind my back like that after I gave you both an answer."

"I didn't want to go over your head, Hank. I tried talking to you." Ace took a step towards Hank and gestured back at Scott. "Scott tried talking to you. You were being ridiculous, not willing to budge about a restriction that's thirty years old, even in the face of all the reason we tried to talk into you."

"The rules are in place for a good reason." Hank put his head in his hand, kneading the bridge of his nose, then turned back to Ace and Scott. "I told you both the very same thing when you asked me. There's no need to rehash it now. You should have listened to me before. This is only going to get uglier now, and I didn't want it that way."

Scott shifted in his chair. If they were going to talk about him, he was at least going to be a part of the conversation.

"Hank, you have to believe I can handle myself up there. There is nothing, I repeat, nothing, up in those mountains that I'm not prepared for," Scott said. "My father knows that. And he understands my desire to see the area, explore it, and discover what it has to offer. I just don't see why you can't."

Hank shook his head, letting his hand drop to his side, and when he spoke, his voice was calmer, steadier. "How about your friend Kole, Scott. I am sure he was an expert too. You don't understand the dangers you might find up there, son. None of you do. I know that you fancy yourself experienced, and you are a very experienced outdoorsman. I don't doubt that for a second, so don't take this as a personal slight. The dangers that could await you, or anyone, up there are beyond what any of us could handle." He took a deep breath. "We just don't know."

"What are you implying and who is Kole?" Ace asked, his voice sharp.

"I'm not implying anything, and you can ask Scott about Kole and his friends. All I'm saying is that area was closed off for a reason years ago, and all of us should respect that decision." His gaze shifted to Scott. "Regardless of who we are or how experienced we think we are. I haven't been up there since it was closed, and I would weigh my own experience against any outdoorsman around."

No one spoke after the revelation because no one dared challenge Hank's experience.

Scott still wasn't satisfied with Hank's simple repetitive answers, though. He knew he could handle himself on a little unstable ground or whatever else might be up there. These vague and unnamed dangers Hank kept going on about meant nothing.

"What did you mean when you said things would get uglier now? And as for Kole and his friends, they were not as experienced as me and had an unfortunate encounter with a bear," Scott barked at Hank.

The old warden sighed, and the fading sunlight deepened the wrinkles on his weathered face. "Really, an encounter with a bear? Yeah, let's go with that explanation."

"Scott, what in the hell is Hank talking about?" Beth demanded.

"Nothing relevant, Beth," Scott answered her dismissively. "Kole's group were not even in the same area. They simply were not experienced enough, and it cost them. I am done discussing this moot point."

"Are you going to try to get the permission revoked?" Ace asked Hank with a half laugh.

"No," Hank replied with a slow shake of his head. "I know how your world works, Ace. It all turns on favors you call in from your Internet of friends. You make promises – political promises – and in return you get what you need from each other. I can't compete on your level because I can't offer what I know you can, but I will simply state my case as best I can. I need to make myself heard and let them know I'm against you going up there, even if I can't call in favors."

Ace huffed and turned away.

"Why, Hank?" Scott said, more puzzled than flustered. Any normal person would have given up long before now. "It's done now; why make it into something bigger than it has to be?"

"Because he doesn't like having the power taken out of his hands," Ace announced with narrowed eyes. "The big warden needs to be in control."

Ace's back was turned so he didn't see it, but Scott saw the look of pain on Hank's face at those words.

"It's not about that at all." Hank's voice was soft. "You just don't know what's up there."

"And you do?" Ace argued. "Because if you do, I have yet to hear anything my son can't handle."

Hank didn't respond, and the conversation stalled.

"Scott," Beth said after a moment of silence between them, "maybe Hank is right about this. I mean, he knows the mountains better than anyone, even better than you."

Scott gaped at her, so Beth grabbed his hand.

"Maybe this area isn't safe. How much do we really know about it? Have you done any research about the area? Real research? Do you know why the area was restricted in the first place? Is it still something that you need to be worried about?"

"Beth--"

"No," Beth snapped. "You can't just dismiss my concerns like they don't matter." Beth's eyes were on fire now. "What precautions have you taken to prepare for this trip, Scott?"

Scott didn't answer. He hadn't done much of anything other than find the place on the map.

"Scott," Beth continued, "I'm serious. You know I love adventure as much as you do, and I understand better than anyone how much you want to explore a new area. But I'll feel better about you going on this adventure if I know that you've done your research and you're prepared. Just like any other expedition."

He stared down at the table, and she squeezed his hand to make him look at her again.

"If there are wild animals, what kind? And what have you done to prepare for them? If its rockslides, earthquakes or floods, how are you prepared? I'm not going to stand by and let you go on a boys' weekend just to die up there in a rockslide because you were ill-prepared."

Ace and Hank kept their eyes diverted, and Scott found himself a bit embarrassed by Beth's tone. But he couldn't deny that she had a point.

"Beth, I swear to you I will not go up to Spider Lake without being prepared." He put his free hand over hers. "I've always been prepared in the past, and this trip will be no different than those. Have I ever been one to make poor decisions, rash decisions, in the past? You know me better than that, I know you do."

Beth held his gaze for a heartbeat. She nodded. But there was still something in her eyes that told Scott she wasn't totally convinced. They'd have to talk more later when they were alone and he could properly deal with whatever was bothering her.

"Beth's right, Scott," Hank said. "No one's been up there in decades. Who knows what's up there now? It could be wild. The animals aren't accustomed like they are down here. The animals here are used to people, but up there things could be very different. Bears, wolves, any manner of beasts might be up there. They won't have seen a human in years, if ever. They will be unpredictable when faced with a person."

Scott covered up a laugh with a cough. Was Hank really warning him about bears and wolves? But Beth had brought it up first, and he wasn't going to throw her under the bus; he knew better than that.

"I'll be cautious of the animals," he said to Beth and to Hank. "And if there are other things like rockslides, I'll be prepared for those, too. I can do research on it, bring supplies in case of emergencies."

"But you haven't done the research yet," Beth said, a hint of accusation in her voice.

"He still has time," Ace commented. "Scott is capable of doing the research and applying it when needed. He can, and will, do just fine. He'll be ready by the time he leaves."

Scott was thankful for the assistance and gave his dad a look of gratitude.

Hank took a few steps away from the other three and rubbed the back of his neck. "I know you've already made up your mind, Scott." He turned and met Scott's eyes. "I know nothing I say is going to change your mind at this point, but I'm speaking to you as a friend." His eyes were pleading, almost desperate, and his voice was tight with emotion. "You shouldn't do this. This isn't something you really want to do. You have to trust me, as a man who knows what it's like up there, as an expert outdoorsman…as a friend of your family."

A flash of indecision shot through Scott. Should he really be doing this? Spider Lake was unknown territory, and Hank was legendary for his knowledge and experience of the outdoors. If he was afraid of Spider Lake, maybe Scott should be too.

Ace stepped between Scott and Hank. "We appreciate your concern, Hank." He clapped Hank on the shoulder. A friendly gesture that failed to lighten the mood. "We are friends and always will be. I'm sorry I went behind your back. No hard feelings, I hope. We'll have to have you over for dinner soon. Maybe Scott and Beth can join us, too – after Scott gets back from his trip to Spider Lake."

Hank nodded, his face sagging with defeat. "I'd like that, Ace. I really would."

He walked to the front door and paused there. He turned around, and Scott thought he was about to say something else. Hank's eyes searched the room, as if looking for a final argument that would convince Scott to cancel the trip.

A small part of Scott wanted him to say something. His pride wouldn't let him back out now, but if Hank gave just one more reason, one new reason, he might take the opportunity to call the whole thing off.

Hank opened his mouth; Scott held his breath. But after staring at Scott for a long moment, Hank's mouth closed again, and he pushed the door open.

Ace followed him out, leaving Scott alone with Beth in the sunroom. He turned to speak to her, but she rose to her feet.

"I'm going to the bathroom." She was gone before Scott could say anything, and he was alone with his thoughts.

*

Beth went through the kitchen and outside through the back door. She had to catch Hank before he left. She wanted to talk with him one more time. She didn't know why, she just did. Call it woman's intuition. And she couldn't do it in front of Scott and Ace, not in the frame of mind they were in now. Any word against Scott's trip was an attack that would be shot down immediately.

She reached the corner of the house and pulled up just as Ace and Hank were saying good bye on the front porch. She couldn't hear their conversation, but she could tell it was awkward.

Ace tried to offer a friendly hug, but Hank extended a hand. When Hank saw Ace's intention, he tried to spread his arms, but by then, Ace was already shifting to receive the handshake and their hands missed each other. Hank ran a hand through his hair and Ace scratched at his jaw, both vain attempts to disguise the botched gestures with forced awkward chuckles.

Beth felt a pang of guilt.

These men had been friends for decades. It hurt to see their relationship strained like this because of Scott. She hoped their friendship was strong enough to overcome the wedge this situation was driving between them.

Once everything blew over in a week or two, they'd be fine. True or not, she had to believe it.

Ace went back inside, and Hank headed down the front steps. As soon as the door shut, she slipped from her place at the corner and ran up behind Hank.

"Hank?" she said in a whisper.

"Good god, sweetheart." Hank grabbed his chest. "You nearly gave me a heart attack."

"Sorry." Beth looked down at the ground and tucked her hands behind her.

"I'm an old man; you can't just come up on old men like that. You'll kill us dead on the spot." He chuckled half-heartedly. "What can I do for you?"

"Sorry to startle you, but I had to talk to you, and I really didn't want to speak up in front of Scott and Ace again. Sometimes they can be a little intimidating," she confessed, looking at Hank.

"A little?" Hank laughed. They continued walking toward Hank's pickup. "You'd think if you went against Ace the town itself would ride you out on a rail."

Might as well get straight to the point. "Hank, why don't you want Scott to go up to Spider Lake?"

Hank didn't respond right away. He stopped by his truck and stared off into the trees. He finally turned to look at her. "I already explained myself inside, Beth. I don't think we need to get into it all over again."

"I know what you said inside, but I think there's more to it than that."

Hank looked away again.

"Isn't there?" It had just been a feeling before, but now she was sure of it. Hank was hiding something.

"Now, you don't need to go poking your nose where it don't belong, Beth." His voice was surprisingly harsh. "I said my piece back inside, and you heard it as well as Scott and Ace. No need to repeat it again."

"I love him, Hank. I love him more than anything in this world. I don't want to lose him because of some stupid macho decision he makes when I could stop him if I knew the truth. Please." Beth grabbed his hand and looked into his eyes.

Hank sighed and took his hand back from her grasp. "Beth, if you love Scott, love him as much as you say, then you have to help him understand that going up to Spider Lake is a bad idea, a terrible idea, probably the worst one he'll have in his life."

She opened her mouth to ask why again, but he cut her off by holding up a hand to silence her.

"The reasons I've already told you are enough. You don't need me to make up other stories to get him to stay home." Hank grabbed the door handle to his truck and opened the door, having to pull extra hard to get it to open without resistance.

Beth reached out and stopped him from getting inside by putting her arm across the space.

"There's something else up there, isn't there, Hank? Something you're not telling us? You're hiding something. I can see it in your eyes." Beth held his stare. "I wish you would tell me what it is."

"Beth, nothing is certain in these mountains. If it's restricted, it's restricted for a reason, expert or not. You'd do well to keep him here, where it's safe." Hank pushed his way up into his truck by gently moving her arm away, turned the ignition, and drove away without another word.

Beth stared after his tail lights, feeling alone and unsure. What could she do to keep Scott from going? She wasn't sure if she could do anything.

Chapter Ten

The Iron Pub

Without a doubt the most imposing structure on Main Street, The Iron Pub was as statuesque as an ancient Greek ruin and nearly as old as far as the people of Redwood were concerned.

It was more than any other building lining the street. It was an appendage of Redwood as old as the town itself. Etched into the thick iron bars that covered the heavy wooden front doors was the date 1913, the year the town was founded. From the first time a cartographer marked Redwood, Washington, on a map, the Iron Pub had been there. It should have been declared a historical wonder for being still in the working condition it was since then.

Decades later, the pub remained the one unchanging constant in the town. Old buildings collapsed or were torn down; new ones were built in their places. There were plenty taller than the Iron Pub, plenty larger, plenty more modern. But none more solid. At the Iron Pub, time stood still.

William Mason stood outside and looked over the building during the post-lunch lull. The window pane on the front door had just been replaced after another late night brawl recently, and he wanted to get a good look at it to be sure the repair work was decent. His wife, Grace, always made sure to pick something that mimicked the original stained glass. She loved the way it let in the light using different shades and softening techniques.

And that was fine by William. He'd run the pub since inheriting it from his father, and he considered it his responsibility to keep it as much the same as possible. He would be letting the people of Redwood down if he did any less.

Williams's father, who may have been one of the first to become part of the town, had come into money when he found silver on his land. It wasn't a lot, certainly not enough to buy a mansion or retire early, but it was enough to make sure that his son wouldn't be forced into logging or mining to make a living. He poured almost all of his new-found fortune into the pub, raised young William around it, and taught his son the ins and outs of the business. William and Grace had instilled that same work ethic in their four boys. He'd taught his sons the discipline and grit needed to run a business and have it stand the test of time. Grace had always wished for a daughter, but their family business wasn't particularly a proper place for a young lady, and her dreams of a baby girl dissipated after the birth of their fourth and final baby boy.

William gave a satisfactory nod to his wife's choice of window. It was time to go inside and get ready for the afternoon rush. He swung open the wrought iron bars and ran his fingers along the mahogany doors underneath. They were covered with hand carved scenes from the Washington countryside and were one of William's favorite parts about the building. Everything on the exterior but that window was from the original building. The rustic wooden planks paid homage to the booming twenties and provided a glimpse into the town's glory days.

He stepped inside and scanned the interior.

The floor was planked wood. It was chipped and battered by years of wear and discolored by the bleach water that Grace insisted they use to clean it. After all, there wasn't anything better than bleach for cleaning up the blood left over from Saturday night brawls, which often happened after too many drinks and one misheard word. Despite the damage from smashed beer bottles and the heavy boots the loggers stomped around in, the floor was all original. Every now and then, a patron was crazy enough to suggest that they replace it with something nicer. When that happened with William around, everyone at the bar groaned. He would inevitably break into his speech on the history of the Iron Pub, what it meant to Redwood, and why it would be sacrilege to get rid of a perfectly good floor just because it was a little old.

He smiled at the memory of driving all over the state to replace a board that had been busted a few years back. Even Grace was ready to find a cheap replacement and paint over it to make it blend in. It was just a small piece, after all. But William would have none of that. He'd spent over a week tracking down a board that would be a suitable match for his venerable old flooring. He'd finally found one in an abandoned warehouse an hour's drive east of Seattle that had been built only a few years after the Iron Pub itself. As soon as William saw it, he knew it would match perfectly. He took the time to drive down to the warehouse, pry up the board and load it, then bring it back and cut it to measure in on the floor of the pub. As he looked over the pub now, he couldn't even spot the replacement, and he'd installed it himself.

That floor was covered in sawdust at the moment from the loggers who'd been in for their short lunch, chowing down on the house special – beef stew. The recipe was one Grace had learned from her mother. All she would tell anyone about it was that it required the freshest ingredients and the perfect cooking time. They made it with beef from the Millers' farm, and carrots, potatoes, and celery from old widow Stevens. That beef stew made the best lunch for at least a hundred miles, and everyone knew it.

William walked over and grabbed a broom to sweep at least some of the sawdust away while the place was empty. He knew it wouldn't be empty much longer.

The logging mill let the workers off early on Fridays now, and word had spread about the great prices and good beer at the Iron Pub. It felt like every logger in the region packed into the place on Friday afternoons. The two dollar draft beers would be flowing nonstop from 3:30 to close, and the keg would need to be switched out every few hours. Friday was a good day for business. Even with the beer selling at a dollar less than the other taverns in town, they were making a killing with the constant flow of business. Plus, they could barely make enough of the famous Iron Pub Stew to keep up with the demand. Loggers made hungry men.

Once the logging crews made their way into town, this dusty, empty room would transform into a speakeasy from the prohibition days. There would be billows of cigar smoke floating over the heads of elderly locals nursing their beers. There would be guys throwing darts in the back to the sound of music and boasting about who got the best shot. Nothing loud and obnoxious like in your average bar. William only played the classy stuff in his place.

The main focal point of the tiny pub, like many other pubs in history, was the pool table, and it would be surrounded by tired loggers within a couple hours. Built of solid oak from local timber, it might be nothing special to anyone who frequented big pool halls, but it was something all the locals loved. The table was regulation size, lined in green felt that was peeling from old cigarette burns and warped from years of drinks being spilled on it, despite several clearly posted signs forbidding drinks in the vicinity. It was an old table, no coin slots, its sides lined with busted blue chalk squares. William and Grace didn't allow gambling, at least not with money. They weren't fond of the habit, and drunk loggers tossing cash around was a sure fire way to have a pub-wide brawl. They'd been lucky to only have to replace one window so far, and they intended to keep it that way. The only bets allowed were rounds of drinks.

Top all that off with the smell of Iron Pub Stew drifting out of the kitchen, and you had a pub with real character, not a cheap Hooters knock-off like the other bars lining the street a few blocks over.

William was halfway done sweeping the floors and collecting the stray cigarette buds from under tables when the door opened. He glanced over, but the light streaming through the opening was so bright, he could only see a man's silhouette entering. He turned back to his sweeping and left the early afternoon customer to Grace.

Scott crossed the floor of the Iron Pub to William without making a sound and laid a hand on the old man's shoulder. "Good afternoon, Mr. Mason."

"Jesus Christ," William yelped, jumping a little at the sudden touch. "Does anybody work in this town anymore? I remember the days when———"

"Yes, Dad." Frank Mason, William's oldest son, walked out of the kitchen, wiping his hands on a bar towel. "We know how hard your generation worked and how we were all born with silver spoons in our mouths and them fancy Nike tennis shoes covering our feet."

All three men laughed. It was a running joke between them to make fun of William whenever he broke out into one of his lectures, and he did a good job of playing along.

"You boys don't ever listen to me anymore," William muttered when the laughter died. "I don't know why I bother trying to teach you anything about how it used to be."

"That's because we all listened to you enough when we were little," Scott teased. "It's ingrained in our minds."

William opened his mouth, probably to make another retort, but Grace rushed over to hug Scott before he could get it out.

"Oh my Scottie boy. Such a handsome young man." She squeezed him tightly.

"Frank, I didn't know you had a sister. What a fox! Is she single?" Scott declared as she pulled back. She swiped at his shoulder gently, and he kissed her cheek. "Missed you too, Mom. You have any of that stew left? I'm starving."

"Coming right up." Grace disappeared back into the kitchen.

Scott took a seat at the bar and leaned back in the tractor seat bar stool to stretch his back. "You know what, Pops, as many places as I have traveled, I've yet to find a pub as awesome as this one."

"You won't find one like ours much as you look, silly boy," William said. "This is the Iron Pub, only one like it, and we aim to keep it that way."

Grace came back out with a steaming bowl of stew and set it in front of Scott.

He inhaled the rich, meaty aroma. "Thanks! Smells great."

Grace smiled in return and went back to sorting things behind the bar.

Scott turned back to William. "I didn't say I expected to find a better one. Can't you just take a compliment when you hear one?"

William mumbled something about disrespectful young men these days and went to the other side of the room to finish sweeping.

Scott shook his head and turned to Frank. "He hasn't changed much, has he?"

Frank laughed and sat down next to Scott. "Not a bit. He's that same stubborn old badger who used to take us out on those fishing trips."

"We did learn a lot from him, though," Scott said between mouthfuls. "I don't know if I'd have my business today if it wasn't for him."

Frank leaned over and held a finger to his lips. "Don't let him hear you say that." They laughed loud enough for William to hear them.

"You boys best straighten up," he said without looking up from his sweeping.

Scott smiled. Coming here and being around the Mason family was always just like being a teenager again. "Speaking of those old trips, wait until you hear what I've—"

The door opened again and Scott stopped, turning to squint into the sunlight.

"Marcus, you prick devil, how the hell have you been?" Scott jumped off the barstool and ran over to greet his friend. He wrapped his arms around Marcus' short, slender frame and hoisted him a few inches into the air, putting him down and giving him the once over. "Shit man, you look horrible."

"Eh, a little worse for wear maybe, but not too shabby. The ladies still love me, so there's always a ray of sunshine." Marcus dropped into a sumo squat and flexed his arms to show off his muscles.

Scott laughed and raised his eyebrows. "Looks like you've beefed up even more. You using steroids?"

Marcus punched him in the arm. "This is all natural muscle, man. Maybe if you had a real job, you'd have some muscle, too."

"If working in that mill is a real job, I'd rather have a fake one," Frank said from the bar, tracing a pair of initials carved into the wood with a finger.

Marcus walked past Scott with his head held high. "That's because you're not a real man, Frankie boy."

"Big words from a man the size of a garden gnome," Frank shot back, ever the quick thinker. He hopped down to give him a hug, lifting the man off the ground for the second time that day, punctuated by a slap on the back.

"Mom, I'll have a bowl of that famous stew, please," Marcus shouted toward the kitchen as he and Scott took seats next to one another at the bar. "And lots of that hot sauce you make, too."

Grace emerged a moment later, bowl in hand, the contents still steaming. "Already added it in, Marcus. Still had a bottle from the last time you were here."

Marcus smiled and rubbed his hands together as the bowl was set before him, his expression making him look like the villain in some cheesy eighties movie. "Excellent."

Scott returned to his original seat. "I was just getting ready to fill Frank in on some of the details of the trip, so it's timely you came in when you did."

"Well, don't let me stop you," Marcus managed between huge spoonfuls of stew. "I'm dying to hear about it. Anything that'll get me out of the house for a few days, I'm down." He looked at Frank, then Scott, going back to his soup and remarking under his breath. "Even if it does mean I have to put up with you clowns."

"Married life treating you that well?" Frank said.

Marcus paused between swigs of the soup to reply. "Don't get me wrong, I love my family. But I'm pretty sure my wife will look better after I don't see her for a few days, and that girl of ours. Let's just say I could use a break from that hellion. Hell, that hellion could probably use a break from me. All around better for everyone."

They all laughed.

Marcus was right, Scott thought. Good life or bad life, a break from the routine was always welcome after so much repetition. Especially when that break involved old friends.

"When was the last time we all got together?" Scott asked, trying to think back. "Wasn't it when you got your ass beat on the dart board two years back, Frank?"

"Pops, I'm off the clock," Frank said to his dad, not bothering to answer. He walked behind the bar, grabbed a few pint glasses, and filled them up with beer. "Once your Nancy ass is finished eating, we'll see who beats who on the dart board," he remarked.

Frank snatched up the house darts on his way back around the bar and headed to the infamous Iron Pub dart board to the right of the hallway, right before the bathrooms. Many lives and wives alike were ruined by this famed dart board, or so it was said. Though Scott didn't actually know of anything getting ruined but Frank's pride, the saying was still mysterious and witty, so it stuck.

The board was made of rusty metal and old cork and had been in exactly the same spot since William's dad bought the bar. Like everything else in the place, William was hell-bent on keeping it just like it was.

A few years back, some of the locals pooled money together to get the pub a new board for a specific anniversary present of its existence. Scott had heard about it second-hand and started laughing before the story was even finished. He knew there was no way William would hang a fancy new dart board with LED lights and electronic score keeping on his wall. Scott wasn't sure exactly where the board did end up afterwards, but he guessed it probably got stuck in the supply closet with the rest of the new items people had so graciously donated to the Iron Pub over the years, probably right next to the neon shop sign and the little box of velvet coasters with the name on them.

"Right there, there's your tip," Frank told Scott, pointing at the plastic dart tip still embedded in the board from the last time they'd played each other.

"Tip, I got your tip right here," Tim said, grabbing his crotch as he walked into the bar.

"Timothy, watch it," Grace scolded sharply, scowling at her son.

"Sorry, Mom, didn't see you there," Tim apologized, approaching her and sheepishly shrugging his shoulders. "You know how I get around the brothers." He gave her a hug, then walked over to sit with the rest of the guys.

Everyone greeted Tim as he arrived, and Grace brought out another bowl of stew for him without being asked, flashing him a motherly smile.

"Where's Pete?" Marcus asked as he finished off his bowl. "I thought he was closing the shop early today to come meet us."

"Pete Sandercock, shut down early?" Frank said. "Are you insane, man? That guy wouldn't leave before closing unless he sliced his arm off, and even then, he'd probably just put up the sign that said he'd be back in half an hour. Remember that time he was smashing those cars for scrap and pinned his arm under one? Instead of stopping, he pulled it out and left half of—"

"Left half of what, you story-telling jackass?" Pete hollered from the doorway.

The four guys at the bar stood as one and rushed Pete all at once. It was a tradition to try to knock him over every time they saw him. It only stood to reason to try all together.

So far, they'd been unsuccessful.

Scott reached Pete first. Scott himself wasn't a small guy, but Pete outweighed him by a hundred pounds, easy, and that kind of weight gave a man a big advantage. Scott feigned high and then dropped low to drive a shoulder into Pete's gut. But the massive man batted him aside like a fly. Scott regained his balance with a shaky laugh and watched as the others met similar fates. Frank bounced off a shoulder without doing any more damage than Scott had. They both laughed when Pete hoisted Marcus two feet off the ground and used him as a shield to fend off Tim. After all was said and done, Pete was still on his feet. As usual. He feigned a yawn and shrugged his shoulders.

"All right, kids, settle down," he said as he wandered towards the bar. He ran a hand over his smooth head. He would deny it if asked, but the buzz cut was his way of hiding his premature baldness, and for the time being, it worked pretty well.

"What's that smell?" Scott said, wrinkling his nose. "Is that you, Pete? Couldn't you have at least taken a shower first?"

Pete looked at his grease-stained fingers and wiped them on his pants. "How important do you think you kids are? Why would I waste perfectly good water getting cleaned up for you?" He grabbed a barstool and sat down, leaning over and smelling the scent of the stew in the back.

"Now that everyone's here," Scott said, "let me tell you about the—"

"Shut up, Scott," Kirstie, the bartender, came out from the kitchen. "Now that everyone's here, less talk, more drinks." She slid a beer to Pete, and he snatched it up swiftly. "You guys will have plenty of time for talking about whatever you talk about when the tables are full and I'm busy. Now we drink." She tossed her long dirty blond hair over her shoulder and threw back a shot of Jack Daniels, the empty glass clattering as she clapped it down on the counter.

"Darts, my good men, now we play darts," Frank called from across the room. "And in the process, we find out who the better man is."

Still exchanging little jabs with one another, they walked over to join Frank for a few rounds of darts. Even Kirstie joined in for a round before more customers started coming in and she had to slip back behind the bar. Secretly, the brothers were glad, because at the time she had to go back to work, Kirstie was winning.

After five or six rounds, the place was starting to fill up, so they settled down in a corner booth before the seats were entirely gone.

"So, Scottie boy, what is this big trip you have planned for us?" Marcus asked. He punctuated the question with a shot of whiskey.

"Damn great question, Marcus." Frank looked at Scott. "So spill it."

Scott looked around the table and confirmed that everyone was listening. He didn't want to have to explain it more than once. "Okay guys, you know the land up on the other side of the cliffs, the land that's been deserted for years, up there near Spider Lake? Well, I will be hiring a private bush plane to take us up there day after tomorrow, drop us off for a few days of fishing, and then pick us up on Monday."

"You're taking us into bear country, where the witches and goblins dance naked at night," Tim said, his words punctuated with disbelief. "Are you out of your mind?" He looked around at the others. "Who the hell is crazy enough to want to—?"

"Even if someone wanted to go up there, you couldn't," Pete said, snorting and swiping Marcus' second shot for himself. "That place has been fenced off for years as far as the public is concerned. Remember hearing those stories when we were kids? Once you go in, you never get back out type shit, people vanishing, bam, just like that. And you want us all to go up there with you for a happy fun time in the woods? You're nuts, brother. I love you, but you are fucking nuts? Have you even talked to the warden about it?"

"As a matter of fact, smart ass, I have spoken to the warden and he said it was fine," Scott lied, his cheeks going red.

The whole table erupted in laughter.

"Scott, God as my witness, I know the old warden did not say it was okay, no fucking way man," Tim barked, attempting to control his laughter. "Your face is a dead giveaway."

"I know, I know, guys." Marcus waved for silence. "Your Dad paid his ass off, didn't he?"

More laughter followed.

Scott was getting ticked off. They could laugh and poke fun at him all they wanted, but when they brought his father into the picture, it was another story. "No, Marcus," he snapped, staring the man down across the table. "My father did not pay him off. He just paid him a visit."

"Last one buys the next round!" Tim picked up his beer and started hammering it down. Somehow he had the uncanny ability to settle down tension, smooth over rough situations. The other guys followed suit with their own mugs, and the tension dissolved with their beers.

Marcus' glass hit the table last, a split second after Frank's.

Frank pointed at Marcus, swallowed his last gulp, and said with a gasp, "It was you, man, it was you."

"No way, you were way after me," Marcus debated. He was called out by the rest of the table and gave up with a great sigh. "Fine, fine, fine. Kirstie, you sexy babe, another round for me and my brothers, if you don't mind." Marcus had to yell across the pub to be heard.

Kirstie didn't even look up from her work. She just lifted a middle finger in their direction and kept pouring drinks, her hands moving in a flurry.

"She's busy, you ass." Scott held out his hand across the table. "Give me the money. I'll get it."

"I'll help you carry 'em," Pete said as he scooted out of the booth with Scott. "And when we get back, I'm sitting on the outside. I'm the biggest and I'm not a sardine in this tin can."

Scott and Pete walked up to the bar and ordered another round for the table. Scott laid the money on the bar and looked over at Pete. The large man was shifting his weight from one foot to the other and glancing around the bar, his lips pressed together in an expression of thought.

Scott punched him in the arm to get his attention. "What's the deal, man?"

Pete met Scott's eyes for a moment before looking away again. "Sorry, man, I don't know. I'm just kind of nervous about this trip, I guess. Are you sure it's safe?"

"Would I take you guys someplace if I didn't believe it was safe? This is what I do, man. Trust me, I've looked into everything we might run into up there."

Pete shifted his weight again and looked away. "There was that one time."

Scott cocked his head. "What are you talking about?"

"Don't tell me you don't remember," Pete said. "That summer up at Aunt Missy's place."

Scott scratched his chin as his mind ruminated on the name, then the memory hit him. "That? That was nothing, man."

"Nothing? What do you mean nothing? We were running for our lives."

Scott almost doubled over laughing. After all these years, Pete was still hung up on that. "I didn't even see anything. Could've been a squirrel for all we know."

Pete shook his head. "Or it could've been a bear. Or who knows what else. It freaked me out, man. I haven't been in the woods since. Now you want me to come with you in this place that's been forbidden to people for who knows how long."

Kirstie put their drinks on the bar and Scott grabbed two, leaving the other three for Pete, but the big man didn't move a muscle, just stared at the glasses.

Scott controlled his laughter. This really did seem to be bothering Pete.

"I'm always up for your crazy adventures, you know that, but this one is a little different. I mean, people go up there and never come back. That freaks me out a bit." Pete looked at Scott. "Doesn't that freak you out just a little?"

"Freak me out? Jesus, Pete, this is the shit I live for. I thought it would be perfect for us all. The fishing up there is unlike anything you've ever seen."

"And you know this because you've been there." Pete stated flatly, as if to remind Scott of his reservations. "That's what you told me about that fishing hole at Aunt Missy's," Pete reminded him.

"Forget about Aunt Missy's. This is untouched, virgin territory."

"Aren't no virgins round here, hot stuff," Patty, the town drunk, said as she staggered behind them.

They laughed as she tried to seat herself and nearly fell off her chair. Pete picked up his share of the drinks before heading back to the table.

"Look, Pete, this is what I do for a living. If it wasn't safe, I wouldn't take you guys up there. I've done my research about the mudslides, the animals, everything. Plus, my dad already talked it over with the warden and we're golden. The plans have been made; it's too late to back out. Just relax, big man; let's get hammered tonight and soon we will be off on our adventure."

"Okay, okay," Pete said, loosening up a little. He stopped just out of earshot of the others and nudged Scott in the shoulder to stop him as well. "One last question. What did Beth say about it?"

Scott bit his lower lip. "She's okay with it."

"Bullshit," Pete said out loud, gaze darkening a little.

"Lay off me, man. We'll be fine, and she knows that I'll be safe." Scott started for the table again. "Let's drink," he said, setting the beers down on the table.

"I want everyone to trust me. We are going to have the adventure of a lifetime. The warden gave me our permits, everything is squared away, so let's drink and be merry and pray that tomorrow's hangover is bearable." Scott raised his mug in the air. "Here's to more fish than we can fry, hearing Pete's bullshit campfire stories, pissing in the wind, and raising hell in the woods. When they next tell rumors about this place, they'll be about the wild men and their unforgettable weekend!"

"Here, Here!" the group replied in unison and clanked their mugs together. Pete hesitated, the last to join in on the toast and the last to finish his drink.

Chapter Eleven

The Hire

The kitchen table was covered in maps and pamphlets from one end to the other, most of them with papers over them or little messages scribbled in pencil. Scott had gathered every scrap of information on Spider Lake and the surrounding areas he could possibly find in the last two days, and the culmination of it lay strewn over his table.

It didn't take long for him to realize that a quick weekend trip wasn't going to be enough. He'd need more time with all the traveling they'd have to do. So he'd revised the plan to make it a four-day trip. One more day, what harm could that do? Even two or three couldn't hurt, if it became necessary. That way they'd have enough time to fly up, hike to the area they wanted to camp in, spend a few days there, and then hike out to meet their plane without having to panic at any point.

Planning was exhilarating. Planning the trip was nearly, just nearly, as exciting as the trip itself. It had been years since Scott had planned a trip to an unknown area.

After spending his entire life in the mountains around Redwood, there weren't many places he hadn't been at least once. All the treks he took customers on were based on plans he'd first made after high school and updated over the years, and although it was nice to see their expressions when they saw the sights for the first time, it had become routine for him. Every now and then, he had a request for something that required a bit of new planning, and those times were definitely appreciated, but nothing that required breaking out the maps had been done before now. He knew every square foot of the Redwood area and only took maps with him as a matter of habit.

This trip, he knew, was different. He'd be dependent on the maps this time, and he needed to commit them to memory as much as possible before they left. It would be difficult because likely many of the maps would have needed updating after this long, but he had no choice.

The new adventure was a little bit frightening, but the rush of exploring the unknown and trekking out into territories he had never been in filled him with a burst of adrenaline and joy he hadn't felt in years. Scott traced various routes with different colored pencils to compare them and decide which would serve best, making little marks in black for the areas they would have to avoid.

It was mostly guesswork. The maps he had were all either outdated or lacking useful details. But that was to be expected, given that no one had been up there in over thirty years. All the more reason to correct the maps while he was there.

How was he supposed to know where the best fishing would be? Or what the best approach was? Maps couldn't tell him that when he had no experience in the area.

There was one person who would know, who had been there before. Hank.

At least a dozen times, Scott had thought about calling Hank to ask his advice about what trails and routes they should take, but his pride wouldn't let him. He had burned that bridge. At least for now. He was truly on his own.

After the trip, he hoped he could sit down with Hank and talk about everything, maybe share what he'd seen and what he'd done to mark the area. The excitement of a successful trek would, Scott hoped, be enough to get Hank to open up, and maybe they could mend fences. But for the time being, he would have to depend on his own experience and outdated maps. Fabulous.

His computer filled the only space on the table not taken up by old maps. He had a Word document open with a running list of the supplies they'd need and a vague timeline of where they should be each day. That was something else he hadn't needed to do in a long time. His usual equipment list was so ingrained in his memory that he didn't waste the time or the paper. This trip would require all the normal gear, but Scott wanted to make sure they were prepared for the unexpected, and that meant bringing along a few extras, so he prepped the Word document just in case.

A sound from the kitchen door snapped Scott out of his focused concentration, and he turned around to see Beth, realizing he held a pencil between his teeth. He removed it and tucked it behind an ear.

"Beth, didn't know you were there." He glanced back at the table. "How long have you been there?"

"Sorry, baby. I should have said something. I could tell you were caught up in your work and didn't want to distract you."

"It's okay." He stood and walked over to her. "I could use a break for a minute or two."

She smiled at him, but something was missing from the smile. The radiance he was used to seeing behind her smile was gone, and there was something hiding behind her eyes, an uncertainty, a secret of sorts.

"What's the matter?" he asked, eyebrows furrowing.

"Oh, nothing. It's nothing." Her eyes went to the ceiling, the floor, the walls, anywhere but his face. She couldn't meet his gaze.

"Beth, sweetheart." He took her hands in his, suspecting she was bothered by the idea now that the time had arrived for his departure. "I don't want you to worry about this trip. I'm going to be fine. You've seen how I am in the mountains. I'm like a different person out there. My brain processes problems faster, sees new options. I can always find the way out. There's nothing up there that I haven't seen a hundred times before. Nothing I'm not prepared for. Nothing."

Beth still wouldn't look at him, her eyes focused down toward the floor. "You don't know that, Scott."

"Of course I can."

She shook her head, and her auburn hair bounced around her shoulders. "You said it yourself, this is all new territory. If you knew exactly what was up there, it wouldn't be so exciting. You don't know."

Scott opened his mouth to object, but then closed it again. She was right. This was exciting because it was unknown, new, even a little frightening. He couldn't say truthfully he was prepared for anything it could throw his way if he'd never been there.

Her eyes found his, and there was an intensity in them he didn't often see. "You know it's true, Scott. You don't know."

He took a deep breath and nodded. "Okay, you're right. We don't know everything about what we're getting into." Scott squeezed her hands to reassure her. "But part of my training is to know how to deal with the unexpected. Just trust that I know how to be ready for anything. I know it's hard because it's so close to when I leave."

Beth looked away and sighed.

"That's what all this is about." He waved a hand at the maps scattered over the table. "I'm getting ready for every possible situation. You don't have to worry."

She met his eyes again and managed a weak smile. "I know I shouldn't worry about you." She kissed him on the nose. "It's my job to worry about you, though. Somebody has to...because we know you won't."

Scott laughed. "I suppose you're right about that."

"I'll let you get back to your planning. I'm sure you have a lot more to get done."

There was still something in her voice that told Scott she hadn't relaxed yet. "I'll welcome interruptions from you anytime." He kissed her on the cheek and gave her a light pat on the butt as she left the room.

Scott watched her go and considered calling the trip off for the briefest of moments. He didn't want to dismiss Beth's concerns. She had a way of knowing things sometimes that couldn't be explained, and when she worried about something, she was more than often right.

But he shook it off.

Spider Lake might be a new area for him, but it wasn't another world. It was still in the mountains he'd grown up in, and there were no challenges it could present that would be completely foreign to him, he was sure.

Everything was going to be fine. Beth would see.

Scott reached for his phone and sent the guys a group text. It saved him time from having to search them out one by one, and he wanted to get the ball rolling to keep himself from backing out.

I think I have some things planned out for the trek. Let's meet at my house tomorrow night to go over the routes and campsites, just so we're all on the same page. Seven work for everyone?

Within a few minutes, Scott had confirmations from all of them, and Tim volunteered to bring the beer.

The biggest thing left on Scott's to-do list was arranging their transportation up to the area.

Earlier that day, Ace had given him the name of a local pilot who might be willing to fly them up to the remote area. Scott dug through the mound of papers and found the scrap he'd written the name and phone number on, examining the number for the third time that day.

Scott punched the number into his phone and waited while it rang three times.

"'Ello?"

"Hi, I'm looking for Jake?" Scott asked.

"You're talking to 'im."

"Great. Jake, this is Scott," he said. "My Dad, Ace Huntington, gave me your contact information. I'm looking for a pilot to fly me and some friends up somewhere soon."

"You Ace's boy?" Jake asked.

"Yeah," Scott replied.

"Ah, that's great. Ace, he's a good man. A good man." There was a hint of reverence in Jake's voice. Once again Scott had to thank his father for having such an influence. "Well, let's get together tomorrow and talk details. I don't commit to nothing over the phone but who I'm talking to. Got myself into a few bad contracts that way, if ya know what I mean. Not that I'm sayin' you're asking me to do anything illegal, just want to make sure we're on the up and up and that's easiest in person. So why don't we meet at the Country Bear, tomorrow morning at nine?"

Scott almost laughed out loud at how quickly things had progressed but was able to hold it back. "That would be great."

"Sounds grand. I look forward to breakfast then." The phone clicked, and the connection was broken.

Scott put his phone down and chuckled. It was by far one of the strangest conversations he'd had in a while, but Jake sounded like a decent guy, and Scott was optimistic that he'd found their pilot.

*

Scott walked into the Country Bear at five minutes to nine. It wasn't like him to be late, and he wanted to make a good impression on their pilot.

He hadn't eaten breakfast here in years, not since his grandpa used to bring him. When he was a kid, the place had seemed like a great adventure, with wild game mounted on the walls, music always playing, and a row of locals lining the bar.

Now it appeared to be a place for the older crowd to gather and get away from the young people. It still held a certain charm, but he doubted it would become a regular destination for him any time soon.

Scott stood in the doorway for a few moments, feeling a bit out of place. Did he sit or wait for a waitress to show him a table? There was no way he could recall just from past memories.

He decided to grab a barstool for himself, and once he was seated, realized he didn't have a clue what Jake looked like. How was he supposed to find the man?

A waitress approached him. She was younger than most of the patrons, but still a good twenty years older than him.

"What can I get ya, sweetheart?" she asked, her hair bobbing in its bun as she did, finger poised with a pencil in case he was a specific customer.

"A coffee, please?" he asked, watching her put away her pad and pencil in her apron. Scott wondered if they even had a menu.

"Comin' right up." She turned and disappeared into the kitchen.

Scott looked around the room. The waitress returned seconds later, sliding a steaming cup of coffee to him. She pushed the rack of sugar and creamer over and walked away, all without a word.

"You must be Scott."

Scott turned to see a man he didn't know sitting on the stool next to him.

"I'm Jake."

The first thing Scott noticed was that Jake had a few years under his belt. The portions of his face that weren't covered with deep, craggy wrinkles were wrapped in a thick red beard peppered with grey.

"I am." Scott shook the calloused hand Jake offered, putting on a polite smile as he did. "Nice to meet you, Jake. How did you know who I was?"

Jake laughed. "Well, I…hey, Jeremiah." He waved at a man across the room. "I'm here often enough to know who doesn't belong and you're the only one I didn't recognize. Pretty easy when you show up every day to tell who belongs and who doesn't."

Scott laughed and conceded a nod. "Fair enough."

Jake slapped him on the back, and Scott realized just how big of a guy he was. It was hard to be sure with him sitting down, but Scott guessed he was easily over six feet tall.

"So, my boy, let's talk about where you want me to fly ya."

"Morning, Jake." The waitress had reappeared. "The usual?"

"Yeah, Maria, that'd be great." His smile revealed a row of straight white teeth that seemed out of place among the pilot's rough features.

He looked back toward Scott with a raised, expectant eyebrow.

"Oh, right." Scott pulled the map from his backpack and smoothed it out in front of him on the bar. "My friends and I are looking to travel up here, to Spider Lake, and the only access is--"

"Spider Lake?" Jake shifted on his stool and looked like he was about to get up and walk out right then, squinting one eye at the map as if it were diseased. "Whoa, whoa, son, that area is restricted. Off limits. What're you pulling me into an illegal expedition for?"

"Oh, I'm not." Scott held up his hands and shook his head to emphasize the point. "We've got the permits to go up there. I know it's restricted, but we've gone through the proper channels to get permission, and believe me, it's been a long road. So now I'm trying to find the right or best way to get up there, and I need your advice."

"Proper channels?" Jake's eyes narrowed like he was trying to stare into Scott's mind and see the truth.

"Yeah, I promise this is legitimate. I wouldn't ask you to do this if we didn't have permission. Believe me, we've done our homework."

"Okay, but before we even turn on the props I wanna see those permits for myself," Jake said.

"Fair enough." Scott nodded.

The waitress came back and slid a plate piled high with still sizzling bacon, lightly browned sausage, sunny side up eggs and toast in front of Jake.

"Looks great, as always; thanks, Maria," Jake said before diving in.

Scott sipped his coffee as he watched. He wasn't sure if he'd officially secured Jake's services or not. Did the arrival of the meal mean the conversation was over? If so, was Jake going to fly them out to Spider Lake or not?

"Permits or not, I still don't know about headin' up that way," Jake said between a mouthful of food. "I've heard all sorts of stories about that place."

"They're just stories," Scott muttered dismissively. He wasn't about to let some old superstitions hold them back from this trip.

"Stories or not," Jake said. "I don't know that I want to get messed up in something like that."

Scott realized his heart was beating faster at this point; he took a deep breath to slow it down. All the work he'd put into this trip was on the verge of being for nothing. If Jake wouldn't fly them, no one would. And if they didn't get a pilot, they weren't going to get up there at all.

"What if we double your fee?" Scott spit it out before he really thought it through. But the guys wouldn't mind, he was sure. And if they did, he'd pay the extra himself. He'd come this far, and he wasn't giving up now.

Jake stopped with a fork halfway to his mouth. His face showed nothing, but the fork slowly lowered back to the plate. The old pilot pulled at his beard for what felt like an eternity to Scott before he picked his fork back up and ate the bite.

"All right, I'll do it for double," Jake said finally, going back to his eggs.

"That's great," Scott said before Jake had an opportunity to back out again. He turned his attention back to the map and pointed to the area up by the lake. "I think this is going to be the best area to drop us off and pick us up. What do you think?"

Jake leaned over the map as well, following some of the pencil routes Scott had traced upon it with a finger and a few low, unintelligible mumbles. "Yeah, well, looking at what you got here, I'm probably going to agree with you. It looks like you've done your homework. I'll look into it a little further and make sure. I've got some charts back at home that'll give me a better idea."

"Okay," Scott replied, trying to keep the excitement from his voice.

Another checkmark on his list of preparations. They had a pilot.

*

The doorbell rang, and Scott got up from his place on the sofa to answer it. "That's got to be Tim."

All the boys were over to discuss the plans for the trip and make sure they were ready.

Tim walked in with two twelve packs as Scott was still swinging the door open.

"It's about time you showed up," Scott said. "Everyone else is already here. We thought you were chugging the beers yourself."

Tim walked into the living room and dropped the beers onto the floor. "Well, I had to stop by the store on the way here after work." He gestured at the load he'd just put down. "How can we go on a trip without beer? And no, this isn't all for right now."

Scott chuckled and shook his head. "Whatever, you're here now, let's get started."

Marcus leaned over one of the old maps stretched out on the coffee table. "I don't know what we're doing, besides drinking beer, anyway. Why do we need to know all the trails for if Scott knows them?"

"What happens if we get split up?" Scott asked him.

"Split up?" Tim ripped open the first twelve-pack and started distributing beer, one to each man. "What kind of trip are you planning?"

"I'm planning a great guys' trip with awesome fishing, incredible hiking, and lots of drinking around a camp fire." Scott accepted a beer from Tim and cracked it open. "That's what I'm anticipating, but we have to be prepared for the worst, just in case."

"Sounds like somebody who owns some kind of outdoor rec company or something," Pete teased.

"Or somebody with a fiancé who doesn't like where he's going," Tim joined in on the joking, a wide grin on his face.

Scott grabbed a pillow and chucked it at Tim's head, but he ducked. "You guys can joke all you want. I'm just trying to be prepared here. We can see who's laughing when one of you gets left behind in the woods."

Frank waved for attention from his brothers and gestured to Scott, "Okay you guys, let's listen to the expert."

The joking died away after that, and Scott went through his plans with the guys. The drop-off point at the lake, their route into the woods, the various campsites they'd stop at, and the places where they were likely to find the best fishing.

"No one's been up there in thirty years, so the trails on these maps probably don't exist anymore," Scott said, passing some of his maps around so everyone could see what he was talking about, gesturing to his pencil marks. "So we'll have to blaze our own for the most part. Also, I'm only guessing about these fishing spots, so we may have to adjust that on the fly."

"That's no big deal," Marcus said with a friendly shrug. "But I'm not worried about fish jumping out of the river and attacking us. What about the real dangers? What could go wrong that we need to know about?"

"Honestly, I don't really know." Scott looked around at all of them as he spoke. "We have to be prepared for anything and everything that might come along unexpectedly. I'm talking anything from rockslides to wild bears with no fear of humans to something as ridiculous as rabid squirrels. Guess the last one's okay, 'cause we can just sacrifice someone's nuts." He laughed at his own joke, and then shrugged. "It's hard to predict when I've never been there before, so we have to stay alert and know the area as best we can while having fun."

They all nodded in response, but Scott knew his declaration of danger, though somewhat lightened with a dash of humor, had cast a gloom over the meeting. He raised his beer. "To adventure!"

Eyes brightened, jaws squared, and beers lifted into the air. "To adventure!" they shouted together.

Chapter Twelve

The Goodbye

Beth walked in the front door and her nostrils filled with an incredible smell. Not just any incredible smell, but Scott's famous home-made spaghetti. Her favorite.

And one of the only things other than breakfast that Scott was capable of cooking; it was his specialty.

"What's the occasion?" she said as she walked into the kitchen. Her eyes swept the room and took in the expensive bottle of wine waiting to be uncorked on the table. Yes, it was definitely suspicious.

"No occasion." He wrapped his arms around her when she walked to the stove for a peek at dinner. "Can't I cook a romantic dinner for my fiancé every now and then?"

"Yeah, if only it happened more than once a year on that mythical date called an anniversary." She reached around him to dip her finger into the pot of simmering sauce. "I know you can cook for me like this. You just don't. I've just never known you to do it without some kind of reason, and I don't think this is any exception." She licked the sauce from her finger and her eyes widened in pleasure, the spices leaving her mouth tingling. "Mmm, this is delicious, even better than usual, I'd say." Her fingers swept the pot again. "Here. You taste." Whirling around, she smeared some on his cheek, and made a show of slowly licking her fingers.

Scott's spaghetti was always good, but it somehow miraculously got better when he really wanted to impress her or to make up for something a man inevitably did. So the fantastic taste only naturally had her a bit suspicious.

"Hey." Scott raised the spoon in his hand with a sheepish look. "I know I'm not the best chef in the world, but there are a few things I can cook well, and this is one of them."

He jabbed at her with the spoon playfully as if it were a sword, and Beth jumped out of reach to avoid the sauce still on it.

"I told you it was delicious, all right? And I meant it. Plus, I'm excited not to have to cook as I'm sure any fiancée would be." With the spoon safely occupied stirring the sauce, she moved back in for a quick kiss.

While Scott drained the noodles, Beth set the table and opened the bottle of wine.

Scott served up the food, and they ate in comfortable silence. Beth knew there was something on Scott's mind, but she didn't rush him to bring it up to her. It was something important if the taste of the spaghetti was any indication. And it always was. It probably had to do with the trip. Maybe it was a last ditch effort to try and obtain her blessing. But this wasn't any old regular trip with the guys.

This was the trip she didn't want him to go on.

The thought made the spaghetti taste bland. She had a bad feeling about the trip, but she didn't know how to change Scott's mind, and there wasn't any time left.

"Are you excited about your trip?" Beth leaned back and sipped her wine to disguise her concern.

"You know, I really am." Scott looked up from his plate. "It's been a long time since I felt this kind of anticipation about something. This is personal, not business like all my usual expeditions. I think that's what makes it so much more exciting. I planned this whole thing because I wanted to go, not because someone else paid me to do it, and it feels good to do something for myself...to be selfish once in a while."

There was a passion in his eyes that Beth had to admit she hadn't seen in years. Maybe this was a good thing for him in the end. Maybe her worry was herself being selfish. If it made him happy, was it really so wrong to let him go?

"Not at all nervous?" she asked.

"Well, I'd be lying if I said I wasn't a little nervous with all the mystery surrounding it." He shrugged. "But it's not like I think there's going to be something up there we can't handle. I get nervous before every expedition."

"But this one is different," Beth commented.

Scott looked at her, and she thought for a moment that she'd given away her purpose.

"Well, yes, this one is different," he said. "But that doesn't mean I'm any different myself." He gave her a goofy smile. "I'm still the same old Scott that goes into every expedition boy-scout-prepared. I'm ready for this. The nerves are just part of the excitement and the anticipation."

Beth forced herself to smile back at him. He was so excited, so eager for adventure, she couldn't bring herself to ask him to stay home. She dropped her gaze to her half-full glass of wine.

"I'm sure you guys are going to have a great time."

They lapsed into silence again, and Beth focused on the taste of her wine, strong and dry. Not something she wanted to drink all the time, but Scott insisted on getting the "good stuff," as he called it, for special occasions. This special occasion left her feeling more dread than anticipation.

"There's one thing I haven't told you yet about the trip." Scott's voice had the slightest quaver in it as he helped himself to more spaghetti.

A fresh wave of worry flooded Beth, but she kept it hidden. "What's that?"

"I won't have any way to communicate with you during the trip." He refused to make eye contact while he said it, instead focusing on adding sauce to his meal.

"What?" Beth shouted, half rising from her seat.

"Beth, there's nothing I can do about it. There's nothing for a phone to connect to up there. No towers, no electricity. Nothing."

"What about a sat phone? You can always get a signal on a sat phone."

"That's what I thought, it's why I didn't say anything sooner. But apparently there are dead zones for sat phones, too, and up there is one of them," Scott said.

That was the end of it for Beth. No more being subtle.

"This is just getting worse and worse. I don't like it, Scott." Beth rubbed her temples. "Is it too late to just call the whole thing off? This place just seems like a disaster waiting to happen."

Scott reached across the table and took her hands. "It's not, Beth, I swear. I'm trained for this. I'm an expert. We'll be fine. There's no real reason that we would need the sat phone except for me to be able to call and wish you a good night. Everything is going to be just fine."

She gaped and recoiled. "Good night? What, am I a little girl to you? You're going to call to wish me goodnight and that's it? What do you mean there's no other reason to call? No call to let me know you're alright?"

"I promise, Beth."

"You promise? You promise what? You promise that I shouldn't get worried when I don't hear from you?" She was stuck. There was no way she was going to talk Scott out of going on the expedition; that was obvious now. Part of her wanted to keep trying to change his mind, but she didn't want to spend the last night before he left fighting about it if it meant neither of them won.

If only he had listened to Hank in the first place.

"Beth." Scott reached for her hands again, and she gave them to him. "I know you're worried about this trip. We've already talked about that. I don't want you to worry. I want you to have a great weekend with your mom, make some syrup, and forget about where I am and what I'm doing. I'll be back before you know it and I'll tell you all about it."

"That's easy to say."

"I know this is hard for you, believe me, I do." Scott lifted her chin with his hand. "But I really mean it. It's only four days. I know it was hard for you to give up going with me, too. And I love having you with me on trips. So I'll make it up to you just as soon as we get back."

Beth forced another smile. He still didn't get it. She didn't care that he was going without her; that was so insignificant in the grand scheme of things. She didn't want him to go at all. But she was tired of fighting this fight.

"Oh, you better." The playful tone she injected into her voice made her feel a little better.

"I will, I promise."

"Don't worry, I won't let you forget."

"I know you won't."

Scott laughed, and Beth allowed herself to laugh with him. If only for tonight, she'd let her worry go, but when he got back, he'd hear about it again.

*

The next morning, Beth rode with Scott to see him off and say good bye properly. When they drove up to the dock, the rest of the group was already gathered and getting ready to leave.

Beth wasn't surprised to see that Ace and Laura were there as well. They didn't always come to see Scott off on his expeditions, but, like Scott had said last night, this one was different.

Ace moved among the guys on the dock, talking, shaking hands, and patting backs like the finest of politicians. She allowed herself a faint smile. In another life, in another place, that man could have run for president, and he might have even won it. But she knew he'd laugh it off if she ever suggested it.

Laura was next to Ace with a bag of bagels in one hand and a tray of coffee in the other, always a servant towards her husband with a love for him that could not be rivaled.

Scott went around to unload some gear from the truck, calling to the guys. Beth walked over to his parents.

"We didn't know we'd be seeing you guys this morning," she said. "You should have said something earlier. I would have brought something."

Laura smiled. "We wanted to come. This is a big trip for Scott."

Scott walked up behind Beth with a backpack on each shoulder.

"Hi, Mom." He hugged Laura, then slung the bags onto the dock. "Get over there and grab some stuff," he said to the guys. "You can come, but you can't be a freeloader with me."

"Get yourself a bagel, dear." Laura held out the bag to Scott. "Don't go off somewhere wild without a full stomach."

"Thanks. I'm glad you guys could make it." He took a bite of the bagel. "Especially with breakfast."

"We knew how much this trip meant to you," Ace said. "And we wanted to be here to celebrate the momentous occasion. And we had to head downtown for a meeting this morning with a few politicians, boring stuff, really. So we thought we'd just leave a little early and swing by to see you guys off while we were close."

Beth stood to the side, watching them talk. Her worries about the trip had been pushed from her mind last night and even when she woke this morning. But now, standing on the dock while the guys threw bags into the plane, all her worries came crashing back. The feeling that she would never see Scott again after this moment kept rising up no matter how forcefully she pushed it down, ready to erupt like a geyser.

Marcus walked up and grabbed the final bagel from the bag.

"Thanks, Mom!" he said in a muffled tone, his mouth still full.

Laura laughed. "I did bring the extra for you, Marcus. Somebody's got to take care of you boys. It doesn't matter how old you guys get, you always need your moms to take care of you."

Marcus stuffed the rest of the bagel in his mouth, smiled, and walked off with a wave behind him.

"Have a great trip," Ace said. He gave Scott a hearty slap on the back. "I can't wait to hear all about the wild things you see while you're up there when you get back. I'm sure you'll have some crazy stories to tell. Maybe they'll even name something after you." He leaned in close like he was telling Scott a secret, but Beth could still hear him. "Some of those tales you might not want to tell in front of your mother or your fiancée, but I'll be happy to hear them all, you just keep that in mind."

Ace's not-so-secretive joke brought the fear back up in Beth's gut, but she ignored it.

Scott laughed and patted his father on the shoulder. "I'll be glad to share them all with you when we get back next week."

"I can't wait!" Beth exclaimed, unable to keep quiet any longer.

Laura looked at Beth and rolled her eyes. "Call us when you get back on Monday."

"I'll call as soon as I can," Scott said. "I promise." He hugged them both one last time, then turned to Beth.

"Love you," he said, a bright smile on his face.

Beth both loved and hated those words as much as she loved and hated that smile. That smile, so excited and happy, killed the words forming in Beth's throat like poison, the words begging him to stay with her instead of going on this trip. So instead of pleading with him to abandon the journey one last time, she smiled back.

"I know you do, Scott," she said. "And I love you, too. You know that. Please be careful up there. Don't let the other jackasses' rope you in to doing something stupid that gets you all killed, no matter how cool you think it is." She took his face in her hands. "Please come back to me in one piece."

Scott leaned down and kissed her softly on the forehead, brushing her hair back behind her ear. "Don't worry, Beth. I won't let anyone or anything get in the way of our safety. We're going to have a good time but still be safe. I'll be back on Monday, you'll see, and all your worrying will have been for nothing."

Scott pulled her in close and wrapped his arms around her with a squeeze. He suddenly felt a quick punch to his shoulder, her fiery hair flying around her. Her lips parting, she hissed. "I hope you don't catch anything and come home hungry."

Regardless of her hit, he held her, his arms sliding along her back. She hated to admit how good it felt and even more, how much she would miss it. Far too soon for Beth, Scott's arms loosened, and he started to pull away from her. Beth reached up and pulled his face down for one final kiss. Scott in turn gently slapped her ass and whispered, "I know it will be hard, but try not to miss me." Beth tried another quick punch after Scott's sarcastic comment, but swung wildly in the air.

Scott joined his friends, laughing and punching each other as they walked toward Jake and the loaded airplane.

Beth walked over and stood next to Laura and Ace. Laura wrapped her arm around Beth and gave her a gentle squeeze. Scott turned around before he jumped into the plane and waved. On his face was a huge, goofy grin, and Beth couldn't help but smile back as she waved, extending a big, fat middle finger as she did.

Scott was right; he had to be right. This was the trip of a lifetime, and everything was going to be fine. The excitement she'd seen in Scott's eyes bubbled up in her and her worries faded away.

He would never regret this trip, never forget his experiences up there. It would be talked about by everyone for years to come.

Chapter Thirteen

The Ride

Scott had never been inside a float-plane before, so preparing to climb inside made this trip that much more exciting. All the other guys were already inside the plane and strapping themselves into their seats, but he paused for just a moment to take in the bright yellow fuselage with a blue stripe running the length of its side. Now that he was close up, he could tell that the plane had had its share of wear and tear. She'd probably been used for a joyride or two, and he bet if she could talk, she'd had some pretty good stories to tell. In fact, if he had more time, he may have asked Jake for some stories himself.

He turned around and gave a sarcastic salute at Beth and his parents one more time outside the door before climbing in the plane. Oh yeah, Beth was going to be sore at him for a while. Even from behind the window he gave her one final little wave, she almost never let that middle finger down, but at the last second blew him a farewell kiss.

Scott rode up front in the co-pilot's seat next to Jake. It was a small plane and felt a little cramped with the combination of six people and a full load of camping gear, but Jake had assured him it could handle the weight, so Scott didn't worry.

Scott twisted in his seat to look over their gear one last time. He'd already double and triple checked everything they needed, but he had to make sure just at first glance they weren't forgetting anything. He went over the mental checklist in his head, looking at each bag and thinking of its contents. Rope, medical supplies, flashlights, matches, blankets, yes, those basics were all there. He continued to count off things in his head.

Once he was satisfied that they were truly prepared for the expedition, he turned around to get himself situated for the flight. Jake was outside doing an inspection of the aircraft and circled around the plane as he looked over the gears. When Jake shifted in his seat to get comfortable, he was careful not to pull loose the long strip of well-worn duct tape holding the leather in place. Yes, Scott decided as he watched, the plane was well-loved.

He wasn't going to let the state of the plane dampen his spirits, though, no matter how old the aircraft was. Everything seemed to be going just as planned; Scott felt great, the supplies were packed, and all his friends were with him. Sure the float-plane wasn't exactly a shining model of the latest in avionic technology. The thing was probably older than Scott, but if his father had confidence in Jake, then Scott knew he had nothing to worry about.

When Jake jumped into the plane, Scott took the headset hanging in front of his seat, situated it over his ears and adjusted the microphone up to his lips.

Jake fired up the engines and the float-plane roared to life, cutting off the goodbyes of family and friends come to see them off on their trip. Scott felt a smile on his lips as the vibrations of the plane rumbled through his seat. He also realized just how useful the headsets would be. There was no way they'd be able to carry on any sort of conversation over the thunder of the engine. And they weren't even moving yet.

"All right, gentlemen." Jake was yelling to make himself heard over the constant rumble of the plane. "Put on your headphones and let's make sure all of them are working." He pointed to the headphones and their coordinated jacks.

"Okay, can everyone hear me?" Jake's voice now came through the headphones, clear and easy to hear. All the guys answered at once, resulting in a jumble of noise in everyone's ears.

Jake held up his hand to silence them and laughed. "All right, boys, this is going to be a little like grade school all over again. Talk when I point at ya." He pointed to each seat in turn, and after a few moments, they were sure all headsets were working fine.

"It'll take a little getting used to," Jake said, "but you'll get the hang of it. You just have to take turns."

The guys nodded, but no one spoke this time, prompting more laughter from Jake. They laughed along with him, causing a cacophony of noise through the headsets.

"Okay, let's get going. We've got about two hours of flying ahead of us." Jake pushed the throttle forward and the plane moved through the water slowly, leaving the dock behind them.

"Do you expect any problems with weather?" Scott asked, holding his mic close to his mouth.

The plane was moving forward now, angling toward the center of the lake.

"Shouldn't have much to worry about for the majority of the flight." Jake glanced over at Scott as he spoke. "I hear our destination is tricky with the winds coming in a little strong through the top of the mountains, but we shouldn't have a problem beyond a little turbulence here and there. I've flown in worse."

"So those clouds over there?" Scott pointed to what looked like a major thunderstorm. "They won't be a problem?"

"Nah," Jake said, waving his hand dismissively. "We'll just fly around it if it ends up in our path, but it looks like it'll probably blow away from us, anyway. You learn where weather's going when you fly as much as I do."

Scott wasn't sure how to feel about the casual way Jake talked about what could be dangerous weather. This man was either reckless, crazy, or he really was the best. Scott reminded himself again that his Dad had recommended Jake, so he must be the best. Still, Scott found his fingers crossing over one another.

The plane picked up speed and started skipping across the water. Jake pulled back on the stick and the nose pointed to the sky. Scott felt his stomach lurch then drop as they gained altitude and rose higher into the air, his hands tight on the armrests as they rose. His ears popped, and the ground faded away beneath them as they started to turn and then straighten.

Once they'd reached a level cruising height, far above the trees, Jake spoke again. "So as I understand it, we're headed up into uncharted territory – what do you boys plan on doing up there, anyway?"

Scott waited to see if any of the other guys would speak up, but took their silence to mean they were leaving this question to him.

"A little of everything, I suppose," he said. "We hear the fishing is fantastic up at Spider Lake, so we're planning to check that out. But I think all of us are just excited to explore the area. We want to see what's up there. We'll find a nice place to set up camp and use that as a base, then hike around, maybe take some nice pictures. After all, no one knows how much nature has to offer until someone gets up there to see."

"I think I remember hearing the fishing was good up that way," Jake replied. "But that was a long time ago, before the restrictions were in place."

"How long have you been a pilot?" Pete asked.

Jake chuckled. "Couldn't put a number on the years if I had to. Let's just say I've been flyin' longer'n you've been alive, son."

Scott thought he heard a sigh over the headphones, but it could have just been static.

"It's not really a profession anymore, though." The bravado was gone from Jake's voice now. "It's more of a hobby. I suppose I don't fly as much as I used to or as I'd like to. Don't find the time to take people where they want to go unless it really proves worth the while."

Scott glanced over his shoulder and saw the guys exchanging worried looks at that. He guessed offering Jake double payment proved worth the while to the man.

"But flying a plane is a lot like riding a bike," Jake continued calmly. "It just kind of comes back to you after not doing it for a while. So don't you young folks worry any, we'll be fine."

Pete's eyebrows went up, and Frank subtly tightened his seatbelt with a little tug. Scott kept his laugh to himself and faced forward again. They were committed now, so there was no point in worrying.

"So where did you learn to fly?" Scott hoped hearing about Jake's days in flight school would help the guys relax.

"I'm mostly self-taught, really," Jake said.

Scott winced. Not what he wanted to hear, and that probably included the guys, too.

"But I flew for the military in the Gulf War, so that's where I put in the majority of my hours. Those were the days of good ol' free style flying. Ya don't get a lot of flying like that anymore, even in the military."

Scott thought the old pilot was winding up for a story, but radio traffic cut into the conversation, and Jake turned his attention to that.

"Where was I?" Jake said after responding to the radio. "Ah, hell, never mind. Military's nothing like it used to be, that's all." He shook his head and fell silent.

Scott looked out the window and stared out over the landscape below them. The mountains were as familiar as his own home. He'd spent so much time in them that he could pick out the trails, lakes, rivers and other landmarks even from this altitude and know exactly where they were. He recognized the waterfall where he'd cracked his ribs and rubbed absently at his chest.

But the longer they flew, the less he recognized. Eventually, nothing was familiar and he was only guessing at features based on what he remembered from the maps tucked away in the back of the plane. Still, he felt pretty confident after so much studying.

With no familiar sights to pick out, Scott's mind wandered on the trip. He took in the tiny images of evergreen trees covering the ground below, noting the way the tree line changed as the elevation increased, with aspens, oaks, and maples mixing in. Large rock walls with jagged faces jutted out from the mountainside here, and a particularly tall ridge rose up in front of them.

Scott could see beyond the ridge to a large valley that stretched on for miles. A huge lake was in the middle, fed by three or four smaller streams flowing down from the surrounding mountains. One larger stream exited the lake and flowed out of the valley to lower elevations. It probably fed some of the waterfalls where he gave tours in the summer seasons.

"That's where we're landing." Jake pointed to Pepper Lake. "But we've got to go all the way around the ridge to where the mountain breaks to get a good landing point; see over there?"

"Yeah." Scott nodded when he saw the gap in the rocky cliff faces. It was easy to miss, but it was there, and it was obviously the only way to reach the lake without flying directly over the mountains.

"It might get a little bumpy here, boys," Jake said. "No telling what kind of wind currents're whipping around in there between those walls. Seat belts tight, eh?"

Scott checked his seatbelt and imagined the looks on the guys' faces as they approached the narrow pass.

The air was calm and the ride was smooth right up until the moment they entered the pass. The second the mountain walls surrounded them, a rush of air hit the wings and the plane tilted sharply to the left. Jake did his best to keep them steady, but it was impossible to compensate for the jolt completely.

In the next instant, the crosswind hit and they jerked back to the right. Scott was sure in his mind's fit of panic they were going to be dashed against the rocks.

But Jake kept them flying, increased the power, and started bringing them down. Just when it looked like the tops of the trees were about to rake the bottom of the fuselage, they vanished, replaced by the shimmering lake.

Scott had flown plenty of times before and been through his share of rough commercial landings. But he wasn't prepared at all for landing on water that was stirred and chopped by the wind.

The plane lurched downward and leveled off mere feet above the water. A fresh gust of wind pulled them sideways, and the plane's right wing tip came far too close to the water for Scott's comfort.

He opened his mouth to say something to Jake about it, but when he turned his head he saw the stress and concentration on Jake's face and decided to keep his mouth shut. He would do best to let the professional work and keep to himself.

Jake cursed under his breath and wrestled with the controls to get his plane back under control. The crosswind was still buffeting them too much for comfort, and Scott was starting to wonder if they had time to land before they ran out of lake. The shore seemed to be approaching much too quickly for his comfort.

Jake leaned forward on the yoke. "Come on, baby," he coaxed the plane, his brow furrowed to expose his wrinkles.

The plane hit the water, bounced once, twice, then settled onto the surface and skidded across the water. Jake pulled back on the throttle, and the plane slowed down to a manageable speed.

"Oh, I'm gettin' too old for this cowboy flyin'," Jake said with a laugh. "But it sure does give you a rush, don't it?"

The guys all laughed, more because they needed to release the tension than because Jake's joke was funny. It was better than screaming.

A minute later, Jake had the plane secured at a smooth area of beach where they could unload their stuff. With all of them working together, it only took a few minutes to get the pile of stuffed packs off the plane.

"All right, boys, you have a good time up here." Jake slammed the rear hatch shut as he spoke. "Be safe."

"We'll have a great time, I'm sure." Scott walked up to Jake and shook his hand firmly. "So we'll meet you back here, same spot?"

"Yep, right here, same spot, on Monday morning," Jake confirmed. "I'll be here by eleven."

Scott nodded. "That's perfect, we'll be here."

"I don't wait around, son, so I'll warn you fairly now, don't be late," Jake said as he turned back toward the plane. "Don't rightly like sticking around places like these longer than I have to."

"We'll be on time," Scott ensured. "Maybe we'll even come back here to camp on Sunday night so we don't have to do any extra hiking the day of. This seems like a nice enough spot to make camp overnight, and maybe the fishing is good here, too."

"Not a bad idea." Jake climbed into his plane and waved through the window. "See ya Monday, kids."

The plane pulled away from the shore with no more delay, and the men were left completely alone, ready to begin their adventure, cut off from the outside world.

Chapter Fourteen

The Hike

Scott stared up into the sky, watching until the tiny dot of the float-plane was completely out of sight. It was simply eerie to watch their last connection with the outside world vanish into the sea of hazy clouds. He rarely traveled without a sat phone, and even though he was confident in his abilities, he did feel naked without a method of connection to the outside world. It reminded him vaguely of Ryan's dependence on his phone and he chuckled at the similarity. Not that he would ever admit that need to anyone. Especially the guys standing around him now.

"Hey, princess," Pete called to him, "staring up at the sky isn't going to get you anywhere, unless you have telepathic powers and you want to call that pilot back. You're supposed to be in charge of this adventure, remember? We've got to get going." He picked up Scott's pack and swung it back like he was going to toss it.

"Don't throw it." Scott held up his hands. He knew of too many breakable things in that pack. He walked over to Pete and took the bag from his hands. "I got it. Sorry, you're right, we should get going."

They each pulled on their packs and adjusted the straps until they were sitting comfortably on their hips and backs. Scott waited until everyone seemed ready to head out, then waved them over to him so he could share his directions with everyone.

"All right, map boy, where are we headed?" Frank asked, asserting himself.

Scott pulled a map from an easily accessible pocket of his pack and angled it back so everyone could see the lines he'd drawn out to guide them to their first camping space. They crowded closer to get a good look at the map.

"All right, so Jake dropped us off here at Pepper Lake." He pointed to the large body of water on the left edge of the map. "And for the remainder of today, we're going to hike three miles up to this lake." Scott's finger found a much smaller blue spot, east of their current position.

"And that's Spider Lake, right?" There was a faint tremor in Pete's voice that he didn't quite manage to hide. Scott ignored it and realized that everyone else did too. Maybe the guys were more nervous about being up here than he thought.

"Yeah, that's Spider Lake," Scott agreed. "We should have no problem getting there and setting up camp before nightfall sets in and makes it too dark to see where we're going. Might even have time for some fishing, if we keep a good pace. How does fried fish for dinner sound?"

That earned him a few grins from the crowd.

"There should be a trail that will lead us there," Scott continued, "but I'm concerned it might be grown over considering it hasn't been used for a long time. It depends on what kind of trail it was beforehand. The trail moves east, so we should be able to find the trailhead in that direction, or at least the remnants of the one that used to be there."

"So what do we do if there's no trail?" Tim asked. "Supposing it's gone after all this time, or overgrown, or whatever."

Scott shrugged. "Make our own." He folded up the map and slipped it into this pack.

"Make our own?" Marcus asked, raising an eyebrow.

"Sure. We have compasses to guide our sense of direction, and we know where the lake is, so we'll use the sun and the general directions to get us there. As long as we don't lose our sense of direction, we should be fine."

Tim and Pete exchanged worried looks, but everyone else seemed fine, so Scott ignored them. They'd just deny being afraid if he asked about it, so there was no point in asking them.

Frank clapped his hands and took a step toward the trees. "Well, ladies, you heard him. Let's look for the trail and see what we can find."

Marcus started to follow him, but Scott held up a hand, working to keep from laughing.

"Not gonna find anything in that direction, Ma'am." He pointed in the opposite direction, toward the east. "Trail's that way."

Frank and Marcus turned on their heels and fell in with the others to a chorus of laughter.

Moments later, to Scott's delight, they found the trailhead marker, right where it was supposed to be. The trail itself was largely overgrown, but they could still see where it had been years ago.

"That's the trail?" Marcus blurted when Scott started to walk into the tangle of tall grass and weeds that led into the trees.

"Don't worry, Marcus, the rest of us can see over the weeds; we won't let you get lost. Just yell if you start to lose sight of us."

Marcus' protest was drowned out by laughter, and Scott smiled. This trip was going to be perfect.

*

"How many miles do we have left?" Pete asked just as they were starting mile two.

Scott glanced at his pedometer. "Well, we've gone a little over a mile so far. Can you do the math?"

"What?" Pete said, his tone exasperated. "That's it? Just a mile?"

"Well, look at it this way," Scott said with a chuckle, adapting to terms he used with tired tourists, "we've already finished a third of the hike. That's pretty good."

"Not really," Frank said from the back with a sigh. "A third of the hike doesn't sound like much. I'd much rather hear that I've finished half the hike. Or more than half." He let out a weak laugh.

Scott chuckled again. "All right, let's stop for a break."

No one argued with him. No one even bothered to respond. They just moved a few steps off the trail, found a place in the shade, and sat down.

Frank let his pack slide onto the ground and started shaking the back of his t-shirt. "Oh, that cool breeze feels good. I didn't realize how much I sweat."

"I guess we're not quite as young as we used to be, eh?" Tim said. He forced out a laugh as he leaned back against a boulder.

"Yeah, three miles felt like nothing ten years ago," Pete said, chugging half a water bottle. "I guess I must really be out of shape."

"Speak for yourself," Marcus teased as he pretended to stretch.

"It takes your body a little while to get used to the backpacks," Scott reminded them. "I think it'll get better after another mile. By then, you'll be used to the extra weight."

"Says the guy who does this for a living," Frank said.

Scott flipped him off and laughed with the rest of the group.

"We can only hope, I guess," Pete said. He stood up and pulled his pack back up around his shoulders. "I guess we don't want to waste too much time on a break or we won't make it up to the lake by nightfall. Am I the only one who doesn't want to be hiking and setting up camp in the dark?"

Scott was opening his mouth to give Pete a hard time about being such a pussy when the other guys mumbled their agreement and dragged themselves to their feet. Had they gotten so old that they were all afraid of hiking in the dark? Then again, Spider Lake was already unknown territory. Exploring it during the day was already a challenge, but night would be near impossible.

He kept the thought to himself. Pete was right. Hiking and making camp in the dark wasn't a good idea. Maybe the guys had grown up enough to realize that now. That was all. It wasn't that they were scared.

When they set off again, the group was much quieter. Scott decided they were either focusing more on the hiking or not willing to waste any precious energy on banter.

Whatever the reason for their uncharacteristic silence, Scott took the opportunity to notice the landscape in more detail. He didn't know what to expect from the area, so he wasn't sure how to tell if anything significant had changed beyond what he could discern from the maps.

The trail, or at least the parts of it that weren't covered in undergrowth, was no more than a simple, small dirt footpath, the kind millions of families march through every year. It was only about a foot across and it snaked through the landscape rather than cutting through it. The way it moved was a minute detail occasional hikers or typical tourists wouldn't notice, but Scott really appreciated trails that were made this way. Some trails felt awkward because they were cut through the land with the grace of a monster truck, driving against it for the sake of convenience. But other trails, like this one, moved and curved as the land itself did. It was more natural, more beautiful, and more real.

The canopy of trees surrounding them was mostly composed of pine, with an occasional honey locus thrown in. There were even a few types that Scott didn't know. But that wasn't too shocking to admit to himself, as they were far out of his usual territory now. Shedding their old coats, the pine trees had covered the forest floor with a thick bed of crunchy pine needles. With no visitors in the area for decades, the floor was pristine of any public residue.

Despite the layer of pine needles, plenty of vegetation had defied the piney prison layering the ground and sprouted through the undergrowth. Various flowers and tall field grass, as well as assorted sizes of mushrooms, filled the area with life and colors. The sight of so many mixed shades and textures was breathtaking, leaving him with a feeling reminiscent of seeing a painter reveal his masterpiece for the first time. It was so undisturbed, so private, that Scott almost felt a nagging guilt associated with his presence. But this kind of beauty begged to be enjoyed, so he stubbornly soaked up every drop of it. Scott wasn't really a religious man, but he felt that a forest this pure, this natural, was almost sacred.

But it wasn't all forest. The landscape was far more complex than that. At times, when one came to a clearing of pine, the trees would dissipate and the trail would widen into a large field of grass. The path disappeared in the shelter of grass much like a winding serpent seeking shelter so that they had to hike through the field with no idea where the path would pick up on the other side. The fields were never large enough for the path to entirely escape them, so picking up the trail wasn't difficult. With the five of them searching in a combined effort, they didn't lose much time.

After they had hiked about three miles on this trail, Scott noticed something up ahead that seemed out of place. He couldn't make out what it was at such a great distance, but it seemed too commercialized to be out in the woods this far from civilization, segregated from the sanctity of nature he'd seen since the beach.

"What is that?" Tim asked, squinting.

Just then Scott figured out what it was. "It's a fence," he said with a tinge of disappointment.

"I can see that it's a fence," Tim snapped. "I meant, what is it doing here?"

Scott shrugged. "Must be the fence they put up when they restricted this area. Helps keep the tourists out."

"You mean we haven't been in the restricted area yet?" Frank asked with disbelief.

"Nope." Scott shook his head. "We didn't have good enough maps, I mean, maps with current information on them, to find a place where Jake could drop us off inside the restricted area. So he had to drop us off where he did, and we had to hike in like this."

Frank stopped walking and threw up his hands. "So all this time, I thought we were hiking in the forbidden forest like badasses, and we were just walking through some random woods that anyone could go strolling through like a bunch of tourists on a picnic?"

"You're acting like a girl," Pete replied as he passed by Frank on his left. "Haven't you seen the stuff we've been hiking in?" He waved at the trail behind them. "It might as well have been restricted if it wasn't already. I don't think anyone has been up here in years."

Frank's mouth moved, but his words were robbed from him and he just gaped like a fish gasping for air.

The other guys laughed. "Oh come on, Frank," Tim said as he started walking again. "If we have to take a break hiking in it, it's wild enough for me."

Frank followed, but Scott was pretty sure he heard him mumbling under his breath.

The fence may have been more threatening when it was brand new, but it wouldn't stop anyone now, after years of rot and disrepair set in on it, aging it prematurely. Whoever had built it thirty years ago had used wood — not the best construction medium for the middle of nowhere, but they probably figured visitors would seldom arrive. By this time, the peeling, wooden boards were rotting and many had fallen to the ground to provide a new home for bugs. Some sections were completely collapsed in on themselves. It was simple to find a spot to just step over in defiance.

Once they were all successfully over the barrier, Scott looked up and down the length of the old barrier. It ran maybe a hundred yards in each direction, before bumping against two steep rock faces that would be nearly impossible to scale even with the proper equipment. Scott briefly considered the possibility that Mother Nature herself was trying to keep people out, but he shook the thought off.

"Hey guys, check this out," Marcus said.

Scott turned back to see Marcus holding up a metal sign with the rusted words "Area Restricted to All Civilians. Authorized Persons with Official Permission ONLY Beyond This Point" emblazoned in large red print across the front.

"They got these things all up and down the fence." Marcus pointed left and right. "I guess it's a good thing we have 'official permission,' eh guys?" He marked his words with air quotes.

Tim laughed. "Yeah, especially since they obviously have somebody up here patrolling the area to make sure nobody enters without it. Authorized persons only, my ass."

Pete stepped over the dilapidated fence and stopped next to Scott. "So if no one is keeping tabs on the place, how would anybody even know if you came in here without the permits?"

Scott shook his head with a shrug of his shoulders. "Probably wouldn't." He started walking away from the fence, trying to put it behind him in both the literal and figurative sense. "It doesn't seem like a place they really monitor or worry about all that much, does it?"

"So why did we go through all the hassle of getting official permission if they didn't care to keep the place maintained?" Marcus held up the sign he was still carrying with him.

"Yeah, why didn't we just come up here when you first thought of it?" Frank asked.

"Well, first of all, I didn't know it was going to be like this." Scott spread his arms and pointed at the empty wilderness all around them. "Nobody knew. And second, if we did get caught, I'd probably have to shut down my company. I'd lose all my licenses and permits to work up in the mountains, not to mention my house, my car, my fiancée and pretty much my life's work. Not worth it."

Marcus nodded and dropped the old sign where it had left an imprint in the grass after falling. "Oh yeah, I guess that's true."

"Still, it's kind of interesting," Pete said thoughtfully, still looking back at the fence. "After all the runaround they gave you about the permits and all that, you'd think there would've been a little bit more security up here – right?"

"You'd think," Scott said, his shrug a little more exaggerated.

"Well, with what's supposed to be up here…" Pete's voice trailed off and he looked up into the mountains around them. "I mean, you'd think they'd build a little bit bigger fence to keep it in."

"Seriously?" Scott said. He threw a glance at Pete without slowing down. "You don't really believe all that stuff people say about this place, do you?"

"Me?" Pete forced a laugh. "Of course not, I just meant, you know, I was talking about, well, you know…the stories we all heard as kids."

"They didn't build this fence to keep anything in." Frank shoved Pete from behind. "They built it to keep us out."

"Well yeah, I know that," Pete said after he got his feet back under him.

"Come on," Scott said, eager to put the matter to rest. "Let's keep going. We've still got a little more than a mile until we make it up to the lake, and the sun's starting to make me sweat."

"Who knows, maybe we'll see if those rumors are true while we're up here," Frank said, wiggling his eyebrows at Pete.

"Wouldn't that be fun," Pete mumbled, turning his gaze to the ground.

The final mile to the lake passed quickly. No one needed a break since their muscles and bodies had acclimated to the packs and hiking, just as Scott had predicted. He suspected the fading sunlight was also a good push.

Without warning, they rounded a bend and found themselves staring over a lake of crystal blue water dancing in the afternoon sun. It was jaw-dropping beautiful. Smooth green grass surrounded the lake on three sides like a carpet and the woods pushed up against the far bank to seclude the corner in their shadows. Scott had been nervous that the water they discovered would be stagnant, nasty, and filled with slimy moss, but this was the clearest water he'd ever laid eyes on.

Scott could have stared at the lovely sight for hours, admiring how perfect it was, but there was no time for that. "We should find a good place to set up camp."

They walked to the edge of the lake and found a nice flat spot, not too close to the water, but still close enough they could walk to it in no more than a few minutes. They all knew from experience that making camp right next to the water was a bad idea.

When they were just out of high school, young and inexperienced, they had gone camping up in the woods just outside of town and wanted to be close to the lake. They built a big bonfire at night and slept in sleeping bags right on the water's edge. They figured it was convenient to be so close to the water. They had easy access for cooking, cleaning, and swimming, of course. It just made sense, and they didn't understand why more people weren't camping at the water's edge. That is, they didn't understand until morning, when all the animals came to the water.

The boys were still sleeping after their late night escapades, but the animals were at the shore bright and early. A number of different, curious animals came over to the boys' camp to see what they had to offer in the way of breakfast.

At first it wasn't a big deal--a few hungry deer, a handful of squirrels, a rabbit or two, but then the animals spread the word, and they started to scavenge more and more. Raccoons and foxes tore through their bags of snacks searching for any bits of food they could find.

And the guys, ever heavy sleepers, remained dead through it all. They didn't have a single clue anything was going on until the grunts of a small black bear roaming through their camp jolted them awake.

The guys had exchanged worried looks, but stayed zipped up, cowering in their sleeping bags. They didn't know what else to do, so they lay there, hoping the bear would soon become bored and leave on its own. Eventually it did, of course. It was there for food, not to attack anyone.

But it didn't leave before ripping apart their bags, devouring what was left of their supply of food and wrecking their campsite, including ripping a few holes in their tent.

Everything was such a disaster on that trip that they never camped near the water again. Their packs were ruined and smelled like animal feces, their food, what scraps they could scrounge up, was wasted even to the point where the animals had denied it. Luckily, the guys hadn't been far from civilization and home. They weren't in a dire situation where they'd be stranded for days without food or ways to purify water. They walked back out in a matter of hours and went home, sulking about the situation. But by the afternoon, it was just another hilarious story for them to embellish.

Scott smiled to himself as he thought back on the experience. They had been young, foolish, and naïve when they were younger. Things were so different now. They knew better than to make mistakes like that. They were older, more experienced, and wiser. Good thing, too, because those weren't the kinds of mistakes you made on an expedition like this one. Those kinds of mistakes got you killed.

Looking around at his long-time friends, Scott felt the familiar rush of excitement knowing that they were going to have a good time together. They hadn't gone out all at once on a trip like this in a long time. It was great to be with them again in a familiar setting.

"This spot looks good; let's set up camp," Scott said.

"Yes, sir." Marcus playfully snapped to attention and gave a sharp salute.

"Shut up."

Pete bent over his backpack to pull out his tarp and groaned halfway down. "Ugh, I feel like an old man." All of this walking was making him hurt in places he didn't know could hurt.

"You are an old man." Marcus hobbled around like he was using a cane. "Need your beeper in case you fall down and can't get up?"

"I'm two months older than you." Pete rubbed his back as he stood up, glowering at his friend. "So what does that make you?"

"Younger than you," Marcus laughed, dodging a pinecone Pete used as a projectile.

Pete rummaged in his pack for something else to throw at Marcus, found a pair of socks and launched them towards him. Marcus snatched them out of the air and sent them sailing right back.

"Well us old farts," Tim said with a clearing of his throat, "we gotta take care of each other. As you'll recall, I'm older than all y'all, since they held me back a grade when I was seven." He deposited his pack on the ground next to Pete and dug out a large glass bottle. "I guess that means Pete and I will be enjoying this nice whiskey I brought up here, and you young'uns will be drinking the purified water. Can't trust the little ones with the big boy stuff."

"Ah, that's right." Pete smiled. "There's a good man." He patted Tim on the back.

"You hauled a bottle of whiskey up here?" Frank laughed and looked up from his unpacking. "Is that really part of your necessities? I can't believe you lugged that three miles."

"Neither can I," Tim said, "and I don't want to carry it a mile further, so we're gonna drink it all tonight, because my back is killing me." He held the bottle of whiskey up to the sky in a toast. "To abusing our livers and screwing the system, just like the old days."

"Here, here," Pete cheered.

"Here, here," the others piped up, laughing together.

"So what's for dinner tonight?" Marcus asked, rifling through his pack and taking out odds and ends. "I'm starving after that long hike."

"What did you plan for dinner?" Scott said without looking up.

"Seriously?" Marcus whined, sitting down on the stump of a nearby tree. "I didn't know we were all on our own for meals."

"I'm just kidding. We all carried some of the food for each of the meals. I wouldn't leave you high and dry, Marcus."

"You'd survive just fine without a couple meals, Marcus." Tim grabbed at Marcus' love handles and pinched.

"Hey!" Marcus jumped back. "That tickles." He straightened out his shirt. "And who are you to talk, anyway? You could stand to lose a few pounds yourself. Drinking a few too many beers lately? I can see a little of a beer belly poking out."

"And proud of it." Tim grabbed his own gut and pushed it out further than it hung naturally.

"You just look pregnant." Scott punched Tim in the gut, forcing him to grunt and pull his stomach back in with a lopsided grin.

Laughter erupted around the camp, and Pete decided it was a good time to find something to do before it was his turn to be the butt of the jokes again.

"I'm going to go down to the lake and get water so we can get some purified. I'm gonna be thirsty after some of that whiskey." Pete pushed himself to his feet and scooped up a few empty bottles. He headed toward the lake without waiting for anyone to offer to join him. An extra pair of hands might be useful, but he wanted a few minutes of solitude to enjoy the nature around them before being surrounded by those goons for a while.

He loved being with the guys, of course, but every once in a while, a break was in order.

Pete reached the lake and found a small stream that ran off a bank and fell a few feet to the water below. A perfect spot to fill the water bottles. As he held the first one under the tiny waterfall, he looked out across the lake and took in the beauty. A few birds flew across the water and landed somewhere in the trees on the other side, singing as they flew.

Their familiar song, a serenade to the forest life, stirred a part of Pete that hadn't been touched in years as it joined the other natural sounds of the forest. There was something comforting about the peace and tranquility of the sounds surrounding him. He took a deep breath of fresh mountain air, closed his eyes, and relished the scent of the pine in the air around them. He was lost in the purity of the moment, but all at once, like someone flipped a switch, the sounds were gone. An uncomfortable silence closed in from all sides.

Pete opened his eyes and looked around.

Everything looked exactly as it had before. The lake glistened, the trees swayed in an unfelt breeze. But the sounds were gone. The birds had stopped singing, the insects weren't buzzing; the forest was utterly and eerily silent.

For a moment, Pete thought perhaps he wasn't used to the outdoors yet. His ears hadn't adjusted from the noise of town and they were missing all the activity that was surely surrounding him.

But something just didn't feel right about this silence. Unlike the rest of the experience out here, the silence was...unnatural.

Water rushed out over the top of the water bottle and ran over Pete's hand. The chill of the water startled him and brought him to his feet. Rather than staying to finish filling the remainder of the bottles, he gathered them all clumsily into a pile in his arms and walked quickly back up to camp. In less than a minute, he could hear the sounds of camp again and the eerie silence was left behind him.

"So what's really on the menu for dinner tonight?" Frank asked the leader of their little group.

He saw Pete walking back into camp out of the corner of his eye. It looked like a few of the bottles were still empty, but Frank didn't look any closer to be sure.

"I thought we'd fish and see if we can get anything at the lake," Scott said. "Fish over a campfire sounds great to me, and even if we don't catch anything, we all have freeze-dried food in our packs to last us a while. It's lightweight, so it won't matter if we eat it tonight or carry it another day, unlike the whiskey. I've heard the fish up this way are amazing, so I would much prefer the fish to any freeze-dried food, and I think you guys would probably agree with me." He looked around at the group. "Thoughts?"

"Then what are we waiting for?" Marcus said. "I'm ready to get some dinner cooking. I've got my pole somewhere in my bag. Let's go get some fish." He started digging around in his bag for his fishing gear.

"I gotta take a leak," Frank said. "I'll be back in a minute." He stood up and wandered out of camp, not far, just enough to get some privacy to relieve himself.

Just as he was finishing, he felt the sensation that he was being watched. It wasn't a feeling that he was being watched by human eyes, either. The hairs on the back of his neck stood on edge and everything around him seemed to stand still as his senses heightened to danger. He started to zip up his pants, but his fingers fumbled to find the zipper, his eyes fixed on the forest around him. He felt like a kid learning to pee standing up all over again. His body went cold, even though he had been sweating seconds before.

His mouth was bone dry, and even if he had wanted to say something, the words wouldn't come to him. He could hear the sounds of the guys fifty feet away still talking and bantering back and forth at camp. But around him, nothing but silence. No birds, no insects, no creatures scurrying through the underbrush.

His feet were glued to the ground. His eyes scanned the trees around him, but saw nothing.

Something in his brain snapped, and like a wild animal he ran — legs churning, arms flailing, crashing through the forest like a rabid dog was biting at his heels. Twice he twisted his head back to see if something really was following him, only to see the grass and weeds disturbed by his thrashing.

Feeling foolish for his lack of control, he stopped ten feet before camp, put his hands on his knees, and tried to regain his composure. *Come on, now, Frank. Get it together, man.* He was gasping for breath, and his heart beat wildly. He stole one more glance behind him, hoping for a glimpse of something to justify the overwhelming sense of fear that was only now starting to fade.

Nothing. There was nothing there but a crazed path made by an equally crazed man.

Frank shook his head. He was a grown man, not some ten year old kid frightened by the sound of a wolf howling at night. He shouldn't be scared of things going bump in the night, asking others to check his closet.

But he couldn't shake that feeling. That raw, uncontrolled fear.

Finally, after another moment of calming himself, his breathing slowed, and he was ready to walk back into camp as if nothing happened. The guys were talking about girls and their most recent relationships or lack thereof and gathering their fishing equipment to head down to the lake.

"Come on, Frank," Tim said, casting him a precursory glance. "Aren't you coming fishing?"

"Yeah, of course," Frank replied. "Just let me get my things." He rummaged through his bag and found his fishing gear, gathering it in his arms and joining the party. They walked down to the lake together to set up their fishing poles, hoping to get a good catch for dinner.

Neither Pete nor Frank mentioned their uneasiness, and after a while of joking and tossing out their reels, forgot about their experiences entirely.

Chapter Fifteen

The Fish

Scott paused and took a deep breath when they broke through the trees into the clearing around Spider Lake. He could not imagine a more perfect way to end this day. After the long hours of hiking in the hot sun to get here, an afternoon of sitting and waiting for a bite on the end of a line was exactly what they all needed.

Scott could see the brook trout swimming just beneath the lake's sparkling surface as they got closer to the water. He was in awe of how clear the water was, but seeing their golden scales shimmering in the sun only made his desire to catch one even greater.

"Oh yeah, check those babies out," Marcus said, smirking.

Tim reached the edge and started setting up his fishing pole. "I see a few beauties with my name on them."

Marcus laughed. "You mean my name, you blind bastard. You won't catch a thing." He slapped Tim on the back amiably. "You never do."

"Fuck you. I'll catch more than you."

"Okay, tough guy." Marcus backed up with his hands in the air, surrendering to his bigger brother. "Put your money where your mouth is. Let's bet on it. Whoever catches the least fish has to clean all the fish as a consolation."

"Whoever catches the smallest fish," Scott threw in. "Less likely to have a tie that way."

"Deal." Tim nodded and held out his hand to Marcus. Everyone else nodded their agreement and got to work setting up their fishing poles, each one equally sure he was not going to lose the gamble.

The fishing was simply fabulous, even more than Scott had hoped. Whoever had started the rumor that Spider Lake had the best fishing for miles was dead on. The guys spent the rest of the afternoon together enjoying the peace and relaxation of fishing, watching the sun sink toward the trees and paint the sky in bright hues of red and orange.

By the end of the day, everyone had caught at least two fish. And, much to everyone's shock, Tim, Scott and Marcus all caught three. Frank caught the two smallest fish, so he was stuck with cleaning and preparing the fish for dinner, though he tried to excuse it by saying the sun was in his eyes.

When the sun was touching the tops of the trees across the lake, Scott stood up, calling it a day. "We've gotta pack it up for now, guys."

His announcement was met by a chorus of groans.

"I know, I know, I want to stay, too. But if we don't head back to camp soon, we won't have any light left. You want to be left out here when the night comes and you're blind as a bat?"

Tim was the first to haul himself to his feet, probably eager to quit while he was still ahead. "We'll have to do some more fishing tomorrow. This was awesome. So relaxing."

"Like our lives are so stressful and full of difficult decisions?" Marcus cocked an eyebrow at Tim.

"You're a jackass," Frank said. "Anything's better than working all day. I'd take fishing up here any day to being down in town and having my parents breathing down my back about how it's time to grow up and be responsible. As if I'm not already working my ass off most days."

"Wait, what?" Tim said. "You still live with your parents, Frank?" He shook his head. "Maybe you should think about moving out!"

"It's free rent." Frank shrugged and looked around. "Why should I?"

"Your dating life, for one. I mean how are you ever going to explain to a girl that you live with your parents?" He slung his bag over his shoulder and stepped up next to Frank. "Picture this – the date is going well, you're having a good time. You want to bang her, but then you realize that if you're going to take her home, you'll have to sneak her past your parents' bedroom and slip her down into the basement."

"Easy," Frank replied. "I bring her to your place."

Pete was the last to get his pack ready. They headed for the trees and the camp. But Tim wasn't finished.

"And then," he said, "how do you explain to your parents while your mom cooks your favorite pancakes that you've got a girl in the basement?"

Scott was following just behind the two of them, holding in his laughter.

Tim threw an arm around Frank's shoulder. "Oh, and not to mention that you'll have to convince the girl to go along with all this. You probably won't even get her in your door, much less in your bed."

Frank dropped an elbow into Tim's rib cage and ducked out from under his arm. "Fuck you. Just because you can't match how much I get laid doesn't mean you try to pass on your failure to me."

Tim laughed and stepped away, but not before pushing a little harder. "Tell us, Frankie," he said. "Exactly how many girls have you fucked in your parents' house?"

Frank didn't answer, and the rest of the guys roared with laughter. He took another swing at Tim, who danced just inches out of reach of the fist.

"I gotta admit, though, to be serious for a minute," Pete said when the laughter died down, "it is nice to get away from it all and enjoy a little relaxation. I mean, how could life get any better than this?"

Scott looked at the towering pines around them and threw another glance over his shoulder at the lake reflecting the red sky. He was about to voice his agreement with Pete when Tim spoke up again.

"Sorry, sorry, I know this is all pretty good." Tim walked out in front of the group and turned to face them. "But I can think of one thing that's a little better than this, if you know what I mean." He winked, still walking backwards out in front. "She's blonde and beautiful, a real bombshell. I met her last weekend at The Iron Pub." He pointed at Marcus. "Marcus met her and you can ask him; he was there. She's a real looker, but that's not all she's good for either. She's a wild one, she is."

Tim's heel caught on a root and he stumbled, but kept his feet under him. He turned around to walk forward again, but kept talking over his shoulder. "I'll have to introduce you guys to her when we get back to town. You'll see what I mean by wild." He laughed at his own joke.

Scott caught Frank's glance, and they both rolled their eyes.

"Let's get moving. We've gotta get back to the campsite and get these fine fish frying over the fire," Scott said.

"Whatever, jackass," Tim was still laughing. "Not all of us have a Beth to dream about while we're away and to sleep next to when we're home. Some of us are still searching for that caliber of girl."

"Maybe if you saw the inside of a gym every once a while, you'd lose a few pounds and be a little more appealing to the ladies. And if you're looking for a Beth of your own, you might want to think about not drinking so much beer every night of the week, ya jackass." Scott wrapped his arm around Tim and escorted him back toward camp. "Girls don't appreciate a gift of whiskey at night."

The other guys laughed and followed behind, driven on by the thought of fresh-caught fish frying over an open fire.

With Tim's antics silenced for the moment, Scott took the chance to soak in the scenery. It was more beautiful up here than he could have imagined. The air itself was serene and peaceful, undisturbed by anything or anyone. He would be coming back here with Beth for sure, and they would have a great time, the two of them. There was clearly no reason to keep the restriction in place anymore, and he was confident he could convince Hank to see that now.

Scott could feel the presence of animals watching them from the trees all around. But that was to be expected as they were the outsiders invading their territory, and it didn't bother him. Most of the creatures in these woods had probably never seen a human being before, so they wouldn't know what to make of the strange new animals in their space. Every animal Scott had seen was keeping its distance and watching from a safe vantage. They were curious, yes, but more cautious, and therefore, didn't present any cause for concern. As long as the guys didn't do anything to spook a dangerous predator, they had nothing to worry about.

When they reached camp, the light was already fading. Scott looked back at the group and did a quick head count to make sure everyone was there. His count came to three.

"Hey, where's Pete?"

Within minutes, all the guys were fanned out over the trail, calling Pete's name. Scott was maintaining a calm exterior, but he was starting to crack on the inside. Pete had vanished without a trace, not more than a few feet away from him.

"What do you think happened?" Frank came up behind Scott, his voice low.

Scott shrugged. "I don't know. If I was out with clients, I'd assume he'd just stepped off the trail for a few minutes and gotten confused. But Pete's smarter than that."

"You sure about that?"

Scott gave Frank a sideways look. "Not now, Frank."

"Hey, I'm just saying, we all know Pete's not the best outdoorsman around. Maybe he got lost on his own, just like you said."

Scott shook his head. "Maybe. But something doesn't quite add up here. Tim, Marcus, you guys stick together and head on back toward the lake. Maybe he doubled back."

They moved back down the trail, and Scott turned to Frank.

"We'll search farther around the trail." Scott started to move off the trail, but Frank grabbed his hand.

"Hey." Frank looked around, like he thought someone might be watching them. "Those old stories and myths, do you think—?"

Scott raised an eyebrow at him. "No. Absolutely not. They're just stories. I believe that now more than ever. We've been up here for almost a day and absolutely nothing has happened to us."

"Nothing?" Frank asked, giving him a look as if he were crazy. "Pete is missing."

"You said it yourself; he probably just got lost."

"And you said just now that explanation doesn't add up. It's a little creepy up here, that's all. I can't quite put my finger on it. Something just feels oddly different, I guess."

Scott started walking off into the woods. "It's just your imagination, Frank. Don't let it run away with you. Pete is fine, we just have to find him."

He heard Frank follow a few steps later.

"Pete!" He couldn't be far; surely he'd hear their shouting. Unless Frank was right and the stories were true.

Scott shook his head. That was absurd. There was nothing out here. Nothing but a bunch of animals and empty forest.

They spent the next two hours walking in every direction in that empty forest. Every minute they didn't find Pete made it more difficult for Scott to maintain his conviction that the stories were just stories, that there was no danger here. It was only the first day, and already someone was missing.

By the time the sun dipped below the horizon and the forest darkened, he was almost ready to admit that something must have taken Pete.

He rounded a tree, horrible thoughts building in his imagination, and saw Pete sitting by a creek at the bottom of a hill.

"Pete! Pete, what are you doing?"

"Getting a drink." He looked up. "Why do you look so freaked out?"

"Why do I look so freaked out? We've just spent over two hours looking for you, thinking you'd been dragged off by a wild animal or lost in the woods. It's getting dark." Scott looked back over his shoulder and shouted loud enough for Frank to hear. "Frank! I've got him. Go and tell Tim and Marcus!"

"Why were you looking for me?" Pete stood up and walked toward Scott, cocking an eyebrow.

Scott's mouth dropped open in a dumbfounded look. "We got back to camp and you were gone. We've been walking around screaming your name for two hours, we thought, we thought you—"

"You thought I what? You thought I couldn't handle myself in the woods? Relax, man. I just needed some alone time, that's all. Don't call out the rescue squad so quickly next time."

Scott threw up his hands. "Some alone time, what the fuck. Pete, this is serious shit out here. We're not setting up tents a mile or two outside town anymore. This is real wilderness where we have to know where everyone is. We've got to stick together, you got it?"

"All right then, let's stick together." Pete pointed back behind Scott. "Camp's that way, right?"

Scott nodded, and Pete walked past him.

Chapter Sixteen

The Bag

Marcus was busy weaving through the trees near the lake, searching for any sign of Pete. But there was nothing.

Not even a footprint. Marcus was no tracker, but a dude as big as Pete would leave some kind of trail for sure. Tim was searching the area around the lake itself, in case Pete had fallen into a small creek or something, but it was getting dark and Marcus had to admit he was starting to lose hope they would find him tonight. If they didn't find him soon, they'd have to call in some back up—forest rangers or something. Anyone who would be willing to come up here.

"Hey! Tim! Marcus!" It was Frank's voice, yelling from a distance away. "Scott found Pete, he's fine!"

Marcus yelled his acknowledgment of the message and let out a sigh of relief. Time to head back. It was a good thing, too, because he didn't like the idea of having to wander around in the middle of the night getting further and further from the safety of his camp.

Marcus started back towards his camp, feeling much better. His right foot caught on something and held fast while the rest of his body kept right on moving. His arms flew up, and his face plowed into the thick mat of pine needles and leaves on the ground.

He cursed loudly and spit dirt out of his mouth, brushing himself off as he got up. He pushed himself to his feet and looked back to see what had tripped him. But instead of the exposed tree root or rock he expected to see jutting out of the ground, he saw a large, misshapen lump. It could easily be mistaken for a rock at first glance, but when he leaned closer and gave it a little push with a foot, he realized it was a large duffel bag.

Marcus approached the duffel bag and carefully tugged at it until it loosened from the ground. Once it was free, it was clear to him it was extremely old. Years ago it had probably been blue, but the exposure and rot had turned it to a pale yellow tinged with just enough blue where it had been under ground to make it look green.

What in the world was a duffel bag doing up in the woods, especially when no one had been allowed here in a long time? Maybe it was from before the area was restricted and someone had forgotten the bag after a camping trip. It certainly looked old enough to be from that time. Still, it seemed strange.

Marcus started to unzip the bag to rummage through its contents but hesitated. It obviously contained some personal items. Whoever it belonged to might be offended by a stranger going through his stuff.

But his curiosity won out in the end coupled with the fact that he very much doubted its owner was going to come back, and he started to pull things from the bag, squinting to recognize them in the failing light. The first few things were large, bulky items, which filled most of the space, a puffy red winter coat, an oversized tacky sweatshirt, and a pair of tall, slightly stained rubber boots. The clothes weren't particularly interesting or pretty to look at, so he tossed them to the side and dug deeper.

He pulled out an old flashlight that looked ancient, nothing like what they were using today. At first, he wasn't even sure it ran on batteries, but on further inspection, it did have some, or maybe what used to be batteries. Once useful, they were now completely outdated lumps of metal covered in fuzzy white remnants of battery acid.

Marcus turned the flashlight over in his hand to inspect the outside of it. It was rusted and brown from misuse, but he thought it might have been bright silver at some point in its proud history. It had a long, skinny handle that ended in a wide circle where the bulb was. He flicked the switch on and off but nothing happened. Not that he had expected it to, honestly.

Functional or not, the thing was fascinating and dated the bag somewhat accurately. It had to be forty or fifty years old, which meant the person it belonged to had been up here before the restrictions were in place for sure.

Marcus set the flashlight aside and continued to rummage through the bag to see what else it held. He found a yellowing toothbrush, a black hairbrush with the plastic chipping away, a flaky bar of soap, a mess kit, a box of ruined matches, and some other camping supplies that had all been ruined to some degree by time or water damage.

Just when the sack was feeling empty and he was about to start stuffing everything back in like a modern Santa Clause, his hand found something familiar – a wallet. Wallets had all sorts of information about people inside them. He figured it would give him at least a little information about the bag's owner, and that might point him in a direction.

The first thing he saw when he opened the wallet up was a picture of a man standing with his wife and two kids. The picture itself, one of the only clues to who the mysterious man was, looked old and worn, despite being protected by the wallet, and had a real 1960s look to it.

There were a few more pictures, all of the same unknown people, then two slots. A credit card sat in one, a driver's license opposite. Marcus slipped the driver's license out and looked it over.

The guy's name was Tom Bower; he had been born on July 14, 1935.

Yep. Before the restrictions for sure.

The license had the normal information about the owner's eye color, hair color, height, and weight, all matching the picture on the driver's license and the pictures of the man with his family.

It must have been so inconvenient for this guy to lose his whole wallet up in the mountains. He would have had to replace his driver's license and credit card, not to mention buying a new wallet. From the look of the leather, this hadn't been a cheap one, either.

Marcus thought about his own wallet tucked away in his backpack at camp. If it were him, he would never leave that bag behind knowing his wallet was inside. It had everything he needed to function in the real world. He could barely imagine how inconvenient it would be if he lost that bag up here and had to replace everything inside.

He shook his head. How careless did this Tom Bower guy have to be to leave his bag up in the mountains?

Then he noticed the cash.

Marcus pulled out the bills one a time, counting them as he did. It was a big wad of cash – more than Marcus ever carried in his wallet. By the time he was finished, he'd counted over $100. Even more of a reason to think this guy was nuts for not coming back for the bag and his wallet. That much money was worth more a while back, but even today was worth looking for if lost.

Marcus decided he might as well take the bag and all its contents back to camp and see what the rest of the guys thought of this bad luck Tom Bower. Maybe they would want to be all noble and look this guy up to return the cash. Marcus didn't want to take that chance - he would have liked to keep the $100 dollars himself and was tempted to pocket it right then and there. But the bag and its contents were just too much of a mystery not to share with the other guys, so, grumbling, he slung the bag and its contents, money and all, over a shoulder.

He felt the straps give a little with the weight and cringed as he readjusted the weight. All he could do was hope they would hold long enough to get the bag back to camp.

He took a step toward the trail. Something flashed across his vision. He staggered back, stunned. A tree branch snapped up ahead of him. The sound was so sharp and sudden that he jumped and dropped the duffel bag with a thud.

Marcus searched the woods around him frantically, but he couldn't see a thing in the failing light. He remembered the old flashlight in the duffel, but there was no chance it would still work after so long abandoned to the wear and tear of nature. Then he realized he couldn't hear anything either. The forest was dead silent. He thought he had gone deaf for a moment, but all at once, like a switch was flicked somewhere unseen, the sounds of nature returned.

Marcus' heart was pounding after the experience, but he convinced himself after a few slow breaths that it was nothing. Besides, whatever it was, it was gone now.

He bent down and picked up the duffel, slung it over his shoulder, and headed toward camp. He was eager to share his discovery with the rest of the group and get away from the creepy area.

Scott came back into camp with an armful of firewood just before Marcus arrived, who was weighed down by a bag Scott had never seen before.

"What's that?" Frank pointed at the duffel bag, instantly curious.

"Check it out." Marcus let the bag fall off his shoulder. "I found it while we were out looking for Pete. It's some guy's old duffel bag from like the 60's or something. Cool, right?"

"Wow, what's inside?" Scott said as he knelt next to them on the ground. Tim walked away from the nearly completed fire pit and joined them as well.

"You can look through it, if you want. It's nothing too exciting, mostly camping gear that's long gone, but it's all really old stuff, so that's kind of cool – like the flashlight." He pointed to it as Frank pulled it out of the bag. "It's different than anything we have today."

"Yeah, it is different, check out these batteries." Frank carefully pulled the batteries out of the flashlight, knowledgeable enough to avoid the leaked, old battery acid, and examined them. "I don't think they even make batteries like this anymore."

"I'm sure they don't," Tim said, the name peeled off of the batteries in thin crumbles of metal. He reached inside the bag once more. "Check it out, here's a wallet."

"Yeah, I already went through it," Marcus said.

"And there's cash in here," Tim said. That got everyone's attention.

Pete ran over and stuck his head over Tim's shoulder. "How much?"

"Don't know." Tim started to pull the cash from the wallet.

"About $100," Marcus confirmed. "I counted it before I came back."

"Who leaves a hundred dollars out here in the middle of nowhere?" Pete asked, putting a hand to his chin and rubbing it.

"It's not just the hundred dollars. There's a driver's license and a credit card in here, too. I was asking myself the same thing; who leaves their wallet up here and doesn't come back for it?"

No one offered up any quick answers, and Scott reached in to check on the side pockets Frank hadn't gotten to yet.

"Hey, there's keys in here, too." He held them up for the others to see.

"Seriously?" Marcus said. "I didn't see those before. That's crazy." He shook his head. "Keys and a wallet. That just doesn't make sense. I mean, I guess I can see a bag getting left behind by accident, right? The camping supplies inside make sense. You're in a hurry to leave or something and you pack everything up and somehow this bag gets left behind. But then you get to hiking and somewhere along the way you realize this bag is gone. If you left the supplies behind, it's no big deal. But this one is a different story. You know your keys are in there, your wallet is in there, you have cash in there. I mean come on, what would you do? You don't just leave something like that behind, right?"

"I'd turn around and go back for it," Tim confirmed as if it were being put up for a vote.

"Exactly. You wouldn't leave it up here. Something just isn't adding up about this guy."

"Well, when we get back into town we can look him up," Scott said. "Maybe he's a local? We could take his duffel back to him." He looked at the beat up and faded bag again and shrugged. "Or at least what's left of his duffel and all the stuff inside it."

Pete shook his head and stood up. "Scott, you have to think about this for a second. The guy's probably dead by now. He was born in '25, that would make him well into his eighties, almost ninety. I mean really, do you think he's still alive?"

"We won't know until we ask around." Scott dropped the keys back in the pocket and stood as well. "Maybe someone knows him. Or at least knows about him. If he is dead, there must be some family around or something that maybe we can give the stuff to. Does it really matter?"

"Well no, not really," Pete said with a shrug. "I just don't want to be the one to carry his stuff. My pack is heavy enough as it is."

Frank and Tim quickly added that they didn't want the extra weight either.

"Oh, you guys are all wimps." Marcus snatched up the bag and carried it toward his own gear. "I'll carry it. I want to find out what happened to this guy. I think there's more to his story than this bag can tell us. It'd be cool to hear the story from him or maybe a family member. It's not that heavy anyway." He let the bag fall onto the ground. "And hey, maybe they'll let the person who brings it back keep the money as a reward."

"We'll see what you're saying after we've been hiking a few miles," Frank said.

"Oh Frank, will you please carry the duffel bag for me." Tim spoke in his best Marcus/Scarlett O'Hara imitation and held the back of his hand to his forehead as if he was going to faint. "I just can't handle the extra weight another step, I swear."

"Shut up." Marcus whipped the coat from the duffel bag and threw it at Tim while everyone roared with laughter, even Marcus.

"All right, we better get the fire going," Scott said. "We lost a lot of time earlier." He threw a glance at Pete. "And the sun is down. We're running out of light to work by. And besides, I'm starving. Let's get these fish cooking."

"Agreed," Marcus said.

Pete joined Tim at the fire pit to get it going. After about fifteen minutes of burning down some of the firewood, they finally had the coals ready to cook the fish. By the time they threw the first one on, the sun had set and the sky was darkening quickly, but their fire kept things bright enough for them to see.

The fire cracked and crackled, its flames dancing in the fading light. While the fish cooked, the sounds of night started to emerge all around them.

Crickets chirped in a chorus and the buzz of insects swelled to a dull roar. The occasional frog added a croak every few minutes from the direction of the lake. A couple of owls hooted nearby from overhead trees. The cacophony of calls slowly blended together into a familiar, friendly sound which made the party relaxed. As they pulled the fish off the fire and ate them, everyone lapsed into a mesmerized silence only broken by the occasional hiss of a log falling off its place and disturbing the fire. Scott stared into the swaying dance of the flames, watching the bright colors and absorbing the sounds of the night forest.

Then one by one the sounds stopped. First the frogs stopped croaking, and the owls no longer hooted. Then the buzzing of the insects fell silent.

Scott noticed sooner than the others something strange was happening. The chirping of the crickets ceased all at once, and a forest full of life sounds became as quiet as death.

Scott stood slowly, aware that everyone's eyes were on him and waiting for an explanation. But he, the leader of the pack and the great outdoorsman, had none. He spun in a cautious circle, peering into the dark to find the reason why the forest had lost its voice. He could see nothing beyond their little ring of light, of course, but he strained his ears, desperate for some sound to give him a clue.

As suddenly as it had gone, it was all back.

A rush of air moved through the forest like a silent breath, and the crickets, insects, frogs, owls, and everything else sprang back to life. After the crushing silence of the intermission, the sudden noise was almost deafening.

"What was that about?" Frank's voice was a whisper, as if he was afraid he would bring the silence back by speaking too loudly.

Scott realized they were all expecting him to offer up an explanation. But he still had no answer. So he only shrugged. He'd never experienced a situation that odd in all his years exploring the mountains. Maybe there was something unusual about this place, more than he thought.

"Now that that's over with—" Tim reached into his bag and brought out his bottle of whiskey. "—let's get down to business!"

That brought a round of cheers from the guys, and Frank started passing shot glasses around the circle, one to each man there.

Scott took one more look into the darkness before turning back to join them. When he got there, Frank had a filled glass ready to push into his hand, which he accepted.

"Tonight is a night to make some memories," Frank said, holding his glass high.

Pete thrust his glass into the air as well. "To making memories."

"To making memories," they all said in unison. Glasses clinked, shots were taken, and the eerie silence was washed from their memory.

Before long, Scott even forgot about the scare they'd had with Pete going missing. Things like that happened sometimes when someone went camping out in the wild. It was no big deal, as long as Pete was all right. Scott would move on and they'd have a great day tomorrow.

With, Scott hoped, no more complications.

Chapter Seventeen

Dawn

Scott woke up early the next morning when a pool of sunshine fell through the trees and onto his face, both warming it and making everything look brighter. It was an unconventional alarm clock, perfect for a man like him. He was a little groggy from the night before, and he couldn't remember exactly how many drinks he'd had, but his excitement for the new day ahead was more than enough to override the hangover. He stretched his arms above his head, and then climbed out of his sleeping bag, rubbing the sleep from his eyes.

It was still early for the other guys to be awake; the sun had only just peeked over the treetops to the east, so he was careful to make as little noise as possible. He was a few feet outside of camp, on his way to pee, when he noticed the same oddity as last night; there was no sound at all. The forest was usually quieter just after sunrise before all the critters started waking up, but this type of silence was odd. Dawn or not, the forest should have been alive with noises of the early risers, but the only sounds Scott could hear were his own. He zipped up his pants and glanced around the area, trying in vain to subdue a feeling of discomfort, making up excuses for it even he didn't believe.

He turned to walk back toward camp, painfully aware of the loud noise he made with every footfall. Suddenly, amongst the crunching of his feet on bits of dry leaves, he heard a low growl from somewhere behind him, and he froze. Somehow, in the pit of his stomach, he knew it wasn't a threatening growl, just a warning. It was faint – probably twenty or twenty-five feet away from him, but loud enough to set his nerves on edge.

He spun in a slow circle while his eyes darted through the trees, searching for a sign of whatever was watching him. But he found nothing.

Scott stopped looking and took a deep breath to calm himself, then started searching his mind for the animal that could make that sound. It wasn't as if he could forget it that easily, not when the very thought left him with shivers rippling down his back.

Bear? No, too low.

Mountain lion? No, not smooth enough, too full of gravel.

Coyote? Couldn't be, too small, and this is way too isolated for them to live. Not up here.

He listened for the growl again to refresh his memory, but it didn't come.

Scott didn't want to move without knowing what kind of predator he was dealing with this close to camp, but he couldn't stand around all day waiting. He had his animal identification book back at camp. He'd have a chance later on to flip through that and see what he could find by way of written descriptions. He was too on edge to come up with the answer right now.

He couldn't let whatever this was throw him off balance, not when the other guys were so impressionable. He took another deep breath, let it out slowly, and walked back to camp as steadily as possible, back straight, chest out to look more intimidating than he really was. A dozen steps later, his heart was still pounding behind the cage of his chest. He moved slowly so as not to arouse any predatory instincts. Then something crashed behind him, and he couldn't have controlled his feet even if he'd wanted to. He ran the rest of the way back to camp as if he were in an Olympic sprint with a murderer behind him and didn't take the chance of glancing back until he had camp in view.

At that instant, the forest woke up. The sounds of birds chirping, insects buzzing, and a dozen other comforting nature noises filled his ears. A rabbit scampered across the floor of the forest in front of him, and he reminded himself that these woods were like every other forest he had ever been in, stopping to catch his breath before the others could hear him.

The nagging thought that something wasn't right remained lodged in the back of his mind, but Scott dismissed it. This was their second day on the mountain, and everything was fine. Sure, there had been a strange occurrence or two, but those moments were just a product of the legends they'd grown up listening to, certainly nothing to worry about and ruin their trip in the process.

This was a forest like any other, only a bit more remote.

The incident already out of his mind, Scott thought about how they should spend the day. He considered fishing again, but had other possibilities in his mind, too. Fishing was kind of their go-to activity, but this area had a lot more to offer and the guys enjoyed other things, too. If they only had so much time to do things, it was best to start with things they knew they couldn't do any old time they wanted.

Back at camp, the rest of the guys were still sleeping. Scott concealed a chuckle under his breath. If there really were dangerous animals in the area, they would all be animal fodder. He went to his pack and opened it up, rifling through the basic necessities. The animal identification book was visible, but he dug past it and pulled out the maps. Thinking back on it now, he was sure it was just a bear, possibly only a little older than a cub, warning him not to come any closer. Nothing more.

He stretched the map out and looked it over. Even though the maps he had were old, they hadn't failed him so far. They'd led them straight to Spider Lake, so he trusted they would help him find some good places for hiking.

He found a few trails with streams and even some possible rock climbing spots. The trails looked fun, but not too tough, so they would make perfect day hikes, especially in the wake of Pete's complaining yesterday. He'd talk with the guys when they woke up and see what they felt like doing before making a final decision.

Scott stood up and rolled the map up lightly so he could bring it out easily when he needed it. Rolling the maps, as any good outdoorsman knew, kept them from getting worn out near as much as folding.

"I swear," Frank said a moment later, "Mother Nature sure doesn't let you sleep in the wilderness."

"Tell me about it." Marcus buried his head deeper into his sleeping bag.

Pete peered out from the inside of his own mummy bag at Scott. "How long have you been up, anyway?"

"An hour or so." Scott shrugged his shoulders, trying not to embellish it. "I wondered when you guys would start dragging your lazy asses out of bed."

"I'll wake up when I damn well want to wake up." Tim's voice was muffled by his still-unopened sleeping bag. "The sun can screw itself."

"You can sleep at home." Scott gave the bag a stern, firm kick. "Get your lazy ass up. Who knows when we'll have the opportunity to come up here again? We've got to make the most of this trip."

The guys continued to grumble, but they dragged themselves out of their sleeping bags as they did. After their eyes were open for a few minutes, everyone had a better attitude, and they started to get excited about the prospects of doing some hiking.

"Let me see the maps." Pete held out his hand and Scott passed over the map he'd been looking over.

"Geez," Pete said, turning the map one way and then the other, "these don't give a lot of information, do they?"

"Nope, not a lot, but they were the best I could find, and I marked it up to make it easier for us to follow."

"Adds a little to the mystery of this place, doesn't it?" Tim peeked at the map over Pete's shoulder.

"Yeah, I suppose." Scott shrugged. "I just figure nobody's been up here since it's been off limits, so it's not worth spending the government's money to make new maps and shit."

"Well, that would be the logical explanation," Frank said from his spot by his bag. "But the mystery makes it a whole lot more interesting and exciting, doesn't it?"

Scott laughed.

"So what should we do?" Marcus elbowed his way between Pete and Tim to get a look at the map. "Fishing or climbing?"

"I vote for climbing," Scott said. "We fished yesterday."

"Yeah, but climbing is so much more work." Pete held out both hands to punctuate his sentence, groaning out loud as he did. "We gotta hike all the way there and then climb and then hike all the way back, right? I'm not sure that even sounds like fun."

Frank laughed. "I think I agree with Pete on this one. And that might be the first time I agree with him – ever."

"Well if we're voting," Marcus jumped in, "I'm voting climbing, so it's two-two. Tim you get to be the deciding vote."

Everyone focused on Tim.

He folded his arms and looked back and forth. "Honestly, it's fine with me if we just stay here and sleep. So would anyone like to offer me some incentives?" He raised one eyebrow. "I'm easy to bribe."

Pete and Frank moved close to huddle up and Scott looked over at Marcus.

Marcus shrugged his shoulders. "I don't have any bribing material, don't look at me."

"Me either," Scott said. What would Tim want that they had out here in the middle of nowhere?

"Well, we may not have anything here with us, but I'm sure we can come up with something that will sway him to our side."

Scott smiled and nodded, and they both turned back to Tim.

"All right, Tim," Marcus said, "Scott and I have talked, and we've agreed we will wash your truck when we get back home."

"Hmm, enticing." Tim folded his arms, pursing his lips in thought. "Marcia could sure use a good washing. I can't remember the last time I washed her, to be honest."

"I'll bet she could." Pete slid over to put himself between Marcus and Tim, slipping his arm over his brother's shoulder as if he were the devil on one side combating the angel on the other. "But couldn't you use some more beer? I noticed last time we were over at your place that you were running low. Why don't Frank and I buy your next couple packs and restock your fridge for you?"

"Hmm, both good offers." Tim sat down on a tree stump and rubbed his chin, seemingly deep in thought, holding his hands out to measure them.

Scott knew his and Marcus' offer would win out. Tim had money for beer, but he was lazy and wouldn't pass up a chance for some free labor, especially when his truck was typically caked in mud.

Tim opened his mouth and raised a finger, ready to announce his decision, but he was cut off by a shrill cry ringing through the forest. It was close, maybe a few hundred yards away, and high pitched, almost like a human. Almost.

The sound lasted no more than five seconds, but it seemed to hang in the air long after it stopped.

Scott's mind was racing through animals again, trying to identify it, but he could not remember an animal that sounded like that. Nothing that he could think of was even close.

After a minute or two of silence, Tim mustered up the courage to speak. "What kind of animal was that?"

All eyes turned to Scott.

"I don't know," he admitted freely, keeping a calm exterior even though his pulse was pounding. "I've never heard anything like it before."

"Whatever it was," Marcus said, taking the lead, "I suggest we hike away from it. Because it did not sound happy."

Scott raised the map. "Well then, we're going fishing. The climbing trail heads that way." He pointed in the direction the strange cry had come from, leaving the party silent.

"Well that settles the argument nicely," Pete murmured with a thin smile.

"You're a jackass." Marcus shoved him and walked over toward his things. "I guess we might as well get a daypack with our fishing gear."

Everyone but Tim started moving for their own packs.

"Hey," Tim said, the wheels in his mind turning. "This means I get my beer, right? I vote for fishing."

Frank walked up to Tim and shoved a bag into his arms. "We're not going fishing because of your vote, idiot. You get nothing."

"Let's get going," Scott said. He walked past Tim, and the others followed him.

"But, we're going fishing. You said—"

"Shut up, Tim, let's go," Pete called back.

Scott didn't have to turn around to know Tim was trudging along behind. All he could do was try his best not to smile.

A couple hundred yards down the trail, Scott realized they'd left camp without eating any breakfast. He couldn't ask everyone to turn around now. That would mean admitting they were so freaked out by that animal that they had forgotten to eat.

So instead, he pulled a protein bar out of his pack and started to eat it. He wasn't halfway done when he heard wrappers crinkling behind him.

"You guys see the game last week?" Tim asked.

"What kind of question is that?" Pete said. "Did we see the game last week? Of course we saw the game last week. We all watched it at the Iron together. The question is, did you watch the game last week?"

"Well yeah, of course I watched the game," Tim huffed. "Haven't missed a Hawks game all season. They're 7-0."

"We all know they're 7-0," Frank said. "We've all been watching the games, too."

For the rest of the hike they talked football and debated whether or not the Seahawks had a shot at making it to Super Bowl and what it would take to get them there.

Scott didn't add much to the conversation, as he didn't always have time to watch football with his job the way it was, but he was grateful for the distraction from his futile attempts to identify the mysterious animal and joined in the best he could.

Marcus had fallen to the back of the group after Tim caught up. Frank and Tim carried most of the football debate, and Marcus threw in a comment every now and then.

Football had always been their favorite sport — they'd played on the team together all through high school and still found time for a pickup game every once in a while as a family.

But as the conversation went on, Marcus heard crunching leaves and rustling bushes, sounds he assumed up until now he was making himself. But when he really started to pay attention, he realized the sounds were too far back on the trail to be his own, and, with a sinking feeling, realized he was the last in the group.

Marcus kept glancing over his shoulder to see where the noises were coming from, but he couldn't see anything. After a few minutes, he'd fallen well behind the rest of the group and decided he should catch up. Scott would get super pissed if anyone wandered off today after what happened with Pete yesterday.

Then a branch snapped like a heavy foot had stepped on it. Marcus stopped in his tracks and whipped his head around, but the path was empty.

The awful shrieking noise they'd heard before leaving camp rose up in his memory, and Marcus wondered if whatever had made it could be following them now. It couldn't be. They had hiked in the opposite direction. Animals weren't that smart or fast.

Marcus broke into a quick jog to catch up with the others. He slowed down once he got close so they wouldn't notice, but his heart was racing so fast he was sure they'd hear it. He tried to shake the thought that something was following them, but he couldn't do it. Even though he hadn't seen anything and the trail behind him had fallen silent, he knew there was something back there.

He edged past Tim and Frank on the trail, skirted Pete's big frame, and caught up with Scott.

"Scott, I think there's something following us."

Scott didn't break stride. He just looked at Marcus, keeping his tone low. "What makes you think that?"

"I kept hearing things on the trail behind us—leaves rustling, branches snapping"

"Marcus, we're in the woods," Scott said, giving him a look of disbelief. "You're going to hear stuff like that all the time."

"But what about that thing we heard back at camp?" Marcus said. "It could be following us or something. Right?"

Scott shook his head. "I don't think so. Whatever that was, it was in the other direction. There's no reason for it to follow us this—"

He stopped short, and put a hand on Marcus' chest, forcing him to stop as well. Marcus was about to object when he saw the beast blocking their path.

A huge tan cat, at least 140 pounds, with pointed ears and a long tail, was crouched on the trail, blocking their way forward. Scott could tell by the shape and crop on the edge of her ear that it was a female, and probably out hunting for cubs, since it was close to that season for mountain lions. This news was not good news, because when it came to cubbing season, the females grew aggressive and nasty.

Behind them, Pete grunted when Tim bumped into him.

"Hey, what gives?" Tim said just before he got an elbow shoved into his gut to hush him.

"Quiet," Scott hissed. "Nobody make a sound."

"Why not, what's goin'— holy shit!" Frank said.

The mountain lion dropped into a hunter's crouch, her tail flicking back and forth in the air in agitation.

Marcus turned around, his scowl almost as deadly as the mountain lion. "Shut up, Frank." Frank's eyes were as wide as the big cat's paws, and it was clear he wasn't going to be saying anything else.

A low, warning rumble came from the cat's throat, and Scott dropped into a crouch. "Everybody move slowly off the trail and get behind a tree or something. Keep your eyes on the cat. If she moves, growl at her."

"Growl at her?" Tim said, his voice incredulous.

"Yes," Scott hissed. "Or make some kind of noise to scare it. Have to intimidate her to get her to retreat."

They all obeyed, backing away slowly. Marcus stayed close to Scott as they made their way off the trail's left edge and behind a large tree. They were in place first and watched as the lion feinted at Pete, kicking up a little dust. To his credit, Pete barely flinched; the others started making noises of their own.

The cat sprang back, startled by the noises coming at her from different directions, but didn't retreat. She still looked angry; she lowered her head to the ground, her tail twitching faster.

"Follow my lead," Scott said. He reached down and picked up a fist-sized rock. Marcus did the same.

Scott hurled the rock at the lion. Marcus was half a second behind him. The first rock, with Scott's decent aim, bounced off the lion's shoulder, and the second landed just in front of her right paw.

She jumped back, hissing at the flying objects and even batting at the air, but she didn't leave.

Instead, she slinked closer, low to the ground but fast, straight for Scott and Marcus, her predatory pupils sharp.

Scott shoved Marcus aside into the side of the trail and reached into his pack. The lion pounced, pinning Marcus, and the man stared up at fur, claws, and teeth. Then he heard a noise like a can of spray paint, an awful screeching, and the lion was gone.

Pete was the first one to reach them after the lion was gone, examining Scott first. "Hey man, are you all right?"

Scott nodded, still trying to catch his breath. He realized he was still clutching the pepper spray tightly in his sweaty right hand and slipped it back into his bag.

"Marcus?" Pete said.

Marcus was lying on the ground. He patted his body in search of injuries as he stood, exhaling slowly. "Yeah, yeah, I'm fine."

Frank and Tim ran up behind Pete.

"Was that the thing we heard earlier? Back at camp?" Frank said.

Scott shook his head, regretting that he couldn't say yes and put the fears to rest. "I've never heard a mountain lion make a sound like that…" The faces around looked more uncertain, so Scott tacked on, "…but I guess it could have been. Maybe if it has cubs nearby or something, I don't know."

"What do you mean you don't know?" Tim questioned. "You're the expert; you're supposed to be keeping us safe out here and you set our camp up on top of a mountain lion den?"

"I'm not saying there's a den here. I'm saying I don't know what made that sound," Scott shot back.

"I know what made the sound." Tim pointed in the direction the lion had run off. "The fucking mountain lion that just tried to eat us!"

Pete put himself between them and forced a hand to clamp on each shoulder to calm them down quickly. "Cool down, you guys, just chill out. This isn't anyone's fault."

Tim huffed and turned away, and Scott adjusted the shoulder straps on his bag.

"I think we should head back to camp," Scott said, his tone leaving it more of an order than a request.

Tim whirled around. "Back toward that thing?"

This time Scott stepped into Tim's face. "Listen, man. The mountain lion went away from camp; we don't know that's what was making the sound we—"

"Then there's something else back at camp, and it's pissed. Hell no, I'm not going to that camp."

Scott shrugged and pushed his way past Tim. "Suit yourself, then. You can hang out here with the mountain lion and whatever else might be hiding in the woods, but I'm going back to camp where I know I have what I need to live."

He moved down the trail and heard the guys start following him a few seconds later. He wasn't actually going to leave Tim out here alone. He knew the guy was all talk; he'd be following them back to camp in five minutes, max, if he wasn't in line with the others already.

This trip was starting to come apart at the seams. The incident with Pete getting lost wasn't too big of a deal and easily solved, but this mountain lion attack would have everyone on edge for a lot longer. There was no chance of them relaxing after this.

But Tim was right about one thing — Scott was supposed to be keeping them safe, and he obviously wasn't doing a good job of that.

The first thing he'd need to do once they got back to camp was calm everyone down and get their minds off the mountain lion and whatever had made the strange sound earlier that morning. It wouldn't be easy.

Back at the campsite, Scott could immediately tell something was wrong. He had been hiking at the front of the group and saw the campsite first. He stopped cold when he saw it, and Frank almost ran into him. His abrupt halt set off a chorus of objections.

But their voices all fell silent as they spread out next to Scott and looked at the wreckage that used to be their campsite.

The campsite had been ransacked. Their backpacks were overturned, the contents pulled out and strewn across the ground. A few bags had gaping tears, others had been tossed on the ground.

"That's it," Tim said, going to salvage what he could from his pack. "We've got to get out of here. I've had enough of this shit."

"What could've done this?" Marcus asked, ignoring Tim's outburst.

"Could've been a bear, maybe that mountain lion," Scott replied. "Looking for food, I'd guess. Anybody leave food in their packs? Something it could smell?"

No one replied right away, everyone thinking, trying to remember and not wanting to admit anything. Scott didn't expect anyone would admit to having food, of course. They'd all blame it on someone else if they did, but someone must've had some. Why else would an animal wander into their camp and do so much damage?

"All right, don't confess," Scott said after a minute of silence. "Doesn't matter anyway. Let's get this cleaned up or it might come back."

They found a roll of duct tape and did damage control on sleeping bags, packs, and anything else that was in need of repair, gathering the scraps of food and going in pairs to bury them a good distance away.

Not a permanent fix, but it was the best they could do for the time being.

While they worked, Scott tried to come up with something that would raise everyone's spirits. He knew Tim wasn't the only one who would be wanting to pull out early unless he found them a reason to stay, and the pressure was building.

Finally, it hit him, and he slipped away while they finished patching up the camp. By the time they were done, he'd set up a makeshift horseshoe pit out of sticks and rocks. They spent the afternoon playing, and as sparse laughter and teasing returned, leaving wasn't mentioned again.

When the sun started to fade behind the trees and the moon and stars rose into the sky, they built a fire and cooked up the rest of the fish from yesterday's catch.

Scott thought they were settling into a comfortable silence when Frank spoke up.

"I think we should try and leave early," he said. "With all of our gear damaged, we should probably hike out tomorrow and go home." He didn't sound happy about it, but he'd still said it.

A quick look around the circle confirmed that everyone else was thinking the same thing.

Scott took a deep breath. "We can't," he said. "Look, I'm not saying it's not a good idea, or that I want to stay to prove a point. It's just fact. The float plane won't be here to pick us up until Monday."

"Well, just call him and explain the situation," Frank said. "I'm sure he'll understand enough to come get us a day early."

"No service up here," Scott said. "We can't call anyone."

Frank didn't reply, only slumped his shoulders forward and stared into the fire, his expression troubled.

Scott knew the wrecked campsite was the final straw for the trip; nothing could save it now. What was supposed to be the perfect guys' weekend had turned into an endless wait for their ride home in an unknown border.

"Oh, come on," Pete said, his voice bright and peppy. "Who cares about our gear? Quit being pussies. It's a little torn up, so what?" He stood, looking at each man in turn as he walked around the circle. "It's not that cold up here. We've all dealt with worse. We got food enough to last, especially if we fish." Pete stopped behind Tim, grabbed his shoulders, and gave him a good shake. "So a mountain lion tried to make us her dinner. Who cares? We pepper sprayed that bitch so hard she forgot which way to run. We're up here to have a good time." He released Tim and walked over to Frank. "We don't want to go home early." He thumped Frank on the back. "We want to stay up here and play." He came into the center of the circle and spread his arms wide. "We've got one more good day, so let's get plastered again tonight and enjoy our time together."

Everyone laughed a little, and Tim even pulled out another unspoiled bottle of whiskey from his pack to pass around.

Only Frank kept staring at the fire, expressionless.

"Come on, Frankie. Give it up." Pete put his hands on either side of Frank's face, forcing him to smile as he pulled his cheeks back.

"Get off, you jackass." Frank pushed him away, but he was smiling now, which gave Pete the victory.

Pete stumbled backwards, laughing. "I may be the jackass, but it got you to smile, so it worked!"

Soon everyone was laughing and cracking jokes, the fish were pleasantly roasting, and the fire was roaring. The sounds of their fun soon muffled the ominous nature of the forest and the mystery within.

Chapter Eighteen

The Questions

Beth vaulted up from bed in the middle of the night drenched in sweat and shaking uncontrollably. She couldn't remember any details from the nightmare, only that Scott was in horrible danger. She hugged her pillow close to her chest and tried to settle her breathing, tried not to think about the fact that Scott was gone. God she needed a drink. She moved to the fridge and took one of Scott's beers. Nasty stuff, she'd always thought, but she needed something to calm her nerves, and there wasn't much else to choose from in the house.

She never worried about Scott's trips usually, but something felt different about this expedition. From the very beginning she'd known something was different. She'd thought the strange fear would dissipate once Scott was actually out in the woods, but she admitted now it had only grown worse since he'd left. Both nights she'd been alone, she'd had these nightmares, filled with a vague fear and sense of danger, but no concrete details each time she awoke.

By the time the sun peeked through the cracked curtains, Beth knew she had to do something to keep herself calm or she wouldn't sleep until Scott came home. She showered and threw her hair up in a messy bun to get it out of the way. She thought about breakfast, but nothing sounded good, not in her current mood. In fact, everything she thought of made her stomach turn, so she made herself a cup of tea to help settle her nerves.

Beth sat in the kitchen and stared out the back window while she sipped her tea. The mountains rose up behind the house as they always did—a sanctuary, a safe haven. But looking at them now, Beth didn't feel they were as safe as they had always been. Instead of looking peaceful and inviting, the pine covered peaks rose like threatening sentinels, warning away any one who dared to enter, enveloping the valley in their shadows.

That's when it hit Beth. It was the restricted area that was worrying her so much. She'd been worried about it before Scott ever left, and she'd dismissed those thoughts until now after he had reassured her. Seeing the mountains as sentinels, guards, made her realize the cause of her foreboding feelings — Scott was going into forbidden territory. And somehow she sensed that the restriction was imposed by something higher than man's law, something more than a simple written restriction.

She needed to talk to Hank. Now that the guys were already gone and there was nothing he could do to stop the trip, maybe he'd open up and give her more information, whatever it was he was keeping from her before now. If not, then maybe just talking would settle her nerves enough so she could sleep.

She went back into her room, threw on some presentable clothes and hurried to Hank's. She tried his house first on the off chance that he wasn't working up on the mountain today. It was the weekend after all, and she was closer to the house than the mountain place.

Sure enough, Hank's old pickup was sitting in his driveway when she pulled up. She would have made the trek all the way up to the game warden's office if she'd had to, but it was better that she'd caught Hank here in town, for both her nerves and her car.

She looked at the clock on her dashboard — 8:28. It was too early to visit someone just to talk. She hadn't noticed what time she'd gotten up, but it must have been earlier than she'd thought – definitely earlier than she usually got up.

Beth cursed out loud and leaned back in her seat. What was she going to do now? Nine-o-clock was probably okay, but that was still another half hour away and she wasn't looking forward to sitting and fretting for another half hour.

She caught movement out of the corner of her eye and looked up. Hank had stepped out on the front porch and was standing with his hands on his hips, amusement apparent in his expression.

"You gonna stay in your car all morning?" he called out.

Beth smiled, turned off the ignition, and stepped out. Thank goodness some people were earlier risers than she. "I thought it might be too early to knock," she replied politely. "I was debating about whether to leave and come back later."

Hank laughed. "I haven't slept past six-thirty in twenty years or more. I guess that's part of getting older. Or maybe it just comes with the job." He shrugged and gestured for her to come in. "In either case, you're welcome to come in now instead of waitin' to be sure."

Beth followed Hank inside. He led the way through a foyer and then into a small sitting room that didn't look like it had really ever been used. Beth had never set foot in the man's house, but she silently assessed that it could do with a woman's touch. The furniture was nicely crafted but old and passé. She was on the verge of saying something about how nice it looked when she realized it was all far too feminine for Hank. All of this furniture must have been picked out by his wife before she died.

Beth suddenly felt incredibly uncomfortable, as if she was intruding somewhere she really didn't belong. When she looked at Hank, it was clear he was even more uncomfortable.

"Do you have any coffee?" Beth asked, trying to give Hank an excuse to move to the kitchen, figuring if he was up that early, he'd probably have already started brewing a pot. "I didn't sleep real well last night, so I could really use a pick-me-up this morning. If you drink coffee."

"Yeah, I could throw a pot on," Hank said, seeming to appreciate the opportunity for an excuse to go. "Let me just go to the kitchen and see what I've got in the pantry."

"I'll come with you," Beth offered. "It'll make it easier."

"Sure." Hank almost ran out of the sitting room at the pace he set and ended up in the kitchen, where he got a pot of coffee started.

With the coffee going and Beth sitting at the bar, Hank visibly relaxed and Beth felt herself settling down as well.

"So Beth, to what do I owe the pleasure of your mighty early visit this morning?" Hank said with a hint of friendly sarcasm in his voice.

Beth tried for a weak smile before explaining. "I'm not entirely sure how to ask you about this, Hank. But I need answers, because I'm getting desperate. This is the first time I've ever really been nervous about Scott. He's competent in the mountains, and I keep trying to reassure myself that he's fine up there, but something's just eating away at me this time. I'm having a hard couple of days with him gone and trying to deal with it, but I guess I just was hoping you could ease my apprehension a little, even if it's just talking."

Hank took a deep breath and turned away from Beth to look out the window. "Scott is a very competent man, Beth. We both know that. He's spent most of his adult life up in those mountains – and many years in his youth, too. He knows what to steer clear of and how to handle just about any emergency." Hank paused and took a deep breath.

"I'm sensing a 'but' coming." Beth could feel the tension leaking back into her body; she was getting a headache beating around the bush so much.

"It's a restricted area, Beth. I consider myself pretty competent, and it's like I told Scott, I wouldn't risk going up in those mountains. It's restricted for a reason, lots of reasons, and I wouldn't push my luck. It's dangerous up there. I don't rightly know what you expect me to say to comfort you."

"Don't spoon-feed me the facts like I'm a baby, Hank. I already know it's restricted. I know you didn't want Scott and the guys to go up there. I want to know why."

The coffee maker beeped, and Hank moved to the machine. He poured two cups and offered one to Beth, taking a long sip of his own mug, long since stained with a coffee color. "Cream and sugar are right there."

"Thanks." Beth didn't reach for cream or sugar. She wasn't really here for coffee anyway.

"I already told you and Scott—it's dangerous. The area got closed down years ago and there's been nothing to convince me that the restriction should be lifted." Hank set his coffee on the counter, untouched, and his gaze went to the window again.

"There's more you're not telling me."

Hank rubbed his temples for a few moments before saying anything. "Let me try and explain it a different way. It comes down to knowledge, experience, and wisdom. Scott has the first two; I think we can both agree on that. He knows probably everything there is to know about survival in the mountains. He's well equipped with experience, too. He's been out in the woods in sticky situations plenty of times and has done the right thing instinctively. Being an outdoorsman is just in his blood as pure and right as it is in mine, I'll give him that."

Beth nodded. The 'but' was coming again.

"But Scott doesn't have the wisdom of somebody that's been around a long time and seen the mistakes of others. It's like the old saying that says knowledge is knowing that a tomato is a fruit, but wisdom tells you not to put it in a fruit salad. Scott has all the knowledge he needs, but lacks the wisdom that only time can give him. He's too full-on hardy to believe I know what I'm talking about, and that means he should ignore his own drive. I wish that he would have listened to the wisdom of those who understand and know more about things rather than putting himself and his friends in danger."

"So they are in danger?"

Hank sighed and looked at Beth again. "I've said that from the beginning, but no one takes any notice."

"What are they in danger from, specifically? What's up there, Hank?" Her voice was louder than she'd meant it to be in her passion, so she lowered it and continued. "I know this isn't about mudslides. There's something up there that you haven't told me about, or Scott, or Ace, or anyone else. What is it?"

"Now, Beth." Hank's voice was calm, but stern. "I've told you and the others everything you need to know, which is to steer clear of that area. Scott and Ace both decided not to listen to me." He held his hands up. "I'm washing my hands of the whole mess and hoping everyone comes back just fine."

"You're hoping they come back fine? That's bullshit, Hank." Beth regretted the outburst for only a split second before her anger drove her on. "They're already up there, so there's no reason to keep quiet about anything now. There's nothing any of us can do about it except hope they all come back home safely."

"Well then, you might as well stop asking questions, Beth." The cool authority in Hank's voice was enough to send her over the edge.

"Thanks for the coffee." She stood from the bar and left the mug sitting there without a sip missing, the liquid inside still steaming.

"I know you came over for comfort and reassurance, Beth, but I can't give it to you, no matter how much you want it. I'm just as uneasy as you are about this trip. I've said so from the beginning."

"I know, Hank, I know. You think it's all a horrible idea. You've made that plenty clear." She walked past him, heading for the door.

"Beth. Wait."

She stopped, but didn't turn around.

"I'm sure they'll be fine. You've got nothing to worry about. Just stop asking questions, and wait for Scott to come home."

Beth turned to leave without looking at Hank. Stop asking questions? No chance that was going to happen, not when Scott needed her.

*

Beth left Hank's with a lead ball in the pit of her stomach. Hank had done nothing to make her feel better. Instead, he'd only made her feel worse, even though he'd told her nothing pointing either way. That was twice now he had completely avoided her questions about Spider Lake and why it was restricted, and that in itself made Beth feel nervous.

But she wasn't going to stop now. Somebody in town had to know about it, and she was determined to do more digging until she was satisfied with this ditch. A place that big couldn't just be closed off to the outside world with no record left anywhere, not if it was as dangerous as Hank seemed to think. She just needed to apply herself in the right places to find out more, and that place wasn't Hank's house. If nothing else, her ongoing investigation would distract her from worrying about Scott.

The library was her first stop. The Redwood Public Library wasn't anything to gawk at, but it got the job done. There was no sweeping staircase in front or grand pillars flanking the entrance, just a plain brick building with a sign out front. Beth had only spent time in the children's section of the library gathering resources for school, so she wasn't too familiar with the rest, but that was about to change.

Luckily, the library wasn't the most popular place in town; it was nearly empty on a Saturday morning now that people had movies, stores, and other treats to entertain them. Beth approached the bored-looking librarian named Kate leaning her elbow on the desk and enlisted her help.

That mission seemed to perk up Kate, who went straight to work to find what Beth needed. In less than two hours, Beth had a stack of newspaper articles, editorials, even court records, all about the restricted area around Spider Lake.

"You want me to help you sort through all these?"

Beth looked at Kate and almost said no. This was a personal mission for her. But then she looked at the pile of documents before her, reluctantly calculating how much time it would take her to look through them alone, and nodded. "Sure."

It didn't take long for them to realize there was a lot more to this story than anything they had ever heard. There were several articles dated before the area had been closed off about people going up to Spider Lake and disappearing. Faded headlines with cracked lettering would read, "Another Hiker Goes Missing at Spider Lake," or "Two Campers Missing after Fishing at Spider Lake."

Beth tried to keep track of the stories to remember differential details, but they were all the same in the end. Hikers and campers who went to Spider Lake and never came home.

"This is so weird." Beth dropped a newspaper to the table, calculating how many people were missing during the last few decades "Why would so many people go missing in that area? What could be up there?"

"I don't know," Kate replied, not nearly as bored as she had been before then. "Let's read some of the editorials. I bet people had ideas about what was going on and that'd show up in old editorials."

"Yeah, good idea," Beth agreed.

Together they worked through several editorials. Most weren't helpful, they expressed little more than outrage at the Warden's Office. All the blame was laid at the feet of the warden, Allan Morrison, for not doing everything he could to recover bodies and take care of whatever was causing the problem. The most popular opinion was that the killer was an out of control bear the warden could put down easily if he cared enough to try. Beth felt saddened reading the interviews with the warden in which he expressed what seemed to be profound sadness for the losses of the families.

But a few claimed there was something more out there. They spread odd rumors about a man, or something like a man, that lived in the mountains alone. Other sources said he wasn't a man at all, more like a beast. But none of the writers who made such claims had anything more than rumors to back up their stories, and it was obvious they were ridiculed by others in town.

Beth looked up from the editorials and tried to let everything sink in. The stories of some beast in the mountains weren't new to her. They wouldn't be new to anyone in town. She'd heard them growing up; she just couldn't remember exactly when or where. Everyone knew the legends of why Spider Lake was off limits. But no one seemed to know the real reason for the restrictions; it certainly had nothing to do with a legendary monster.

As a teenager, Beth had assumed those legends and myths had been created by somebody to keep local kids from trying to get into the restricted area. She'd never taken them seriously before, but seeing the articles about the area, back at the time before the restriction even existed, gave her pause. Could there be something or someone up there killing people for food? Or worse, for fun? Something like that couldn't be completely covered up if it was true. Beth shuffled through the papers and found the court documents that declared Spider Lake and the surrounding area off limits. She scanned through the entire document, looking for the specific reasons why the area had been restricted to the public. Over and over again she found the phrase, "area deemed unsafe for public use." She scanned a second time, then read it through more slowly, but there was no elaboration.

Beth tossed the court documents aside and found a newspaper article that talked about the area becoming restricted. She read through it carefully.

Local Officials Finally Restrict Spider Lake Permanently from Public

After what seems like decades of public outcries, local officials have finally decided to close off and restrict all access to Spider Lake and the surrounding area. Gates and fences will be built to remind residents of the restrictions in the next month. Game Warden Allan Morrison spoke of the restriction as a win for the community. "I believe that having the restrictions in place will mean we no longer need to worry about our campers, hikers, and fishermen going missing."

There has been a lot of speculation about what exists in the now restricted area of the mountains, and when asked, the Mayor said, "We know the area is unsafe for the public. We've seen a lot of tragedy up there due to a variety of reasons, which is why we are restricting access. Hopefully this will help to keep us all safe."

Many local outdoor advocates are concerned about the restrictions because the area is regarded as one of the best locations in the state for fishing and rock climbing. It attracts people from around the country every year. They worry that the restrictions will lead to a decline in our local economy as well as disappointment for local outdoorsman. Warden Morrison commented on this as well, "There are plenty of other great fishing and camping spots in the mountains that aren't restricted and won't be. Just stick to those places and you'll be satisfied with your fishing and your camping trips."

Beth skimmed the rest of the article and saw nothing useful, so she set it down on the table in front of her.

"Seems like there's a little bit of back story here somebody's trying to cover up," Kate said. She put down an editorial she'd been reading and looked at Beth curiously.

"Yeah, I think you're right." Beth leaned back in her chair. She wasn't learning anything new. Except now she was more certain than ever that Hank was hiding something.

"From what I've read in the editorials," Kate continued, "it sounds like the warden – this Morrison guy – and the Mayor, Dave Muir, were trying to get the restrictions pushed through really fast and without a lot of questions. People wanted answers, and they wanted to know what happened to their friends and family members, but Morrison and Muir just kind of swept everything under the rug and made everyone move on by putting up a restriction and a lot of flashy explanations."

"Yeah." That was a familiar story to Beth. "I think there are some people still trying to hide the truth." She thought of Hank and his refusal to answer a single question about Spider Lake.

"So what do you think was up there?" Kate asked.

"I don't know." Beth was overwhelmed. This quest for information was not helping her relax at all. "I've never heard of a bear killing so many people, but I guess it's not impossible. I'll have to ask Scott." Just saying his name brought the sickening feeling back to her stomach. She was sitting down here reading stories of missing campers and mysterious restrictions while Scott was in the very area where so much tragedy had occurred.

She reassured herself that whatever was causing all the terror back in the '70s couldn't possibly still be alive now. A bear was the most likely explanation after all, and they didn't live that long.

"Well, I think I've learned everything I can with these articles," Beth said. She pushed back from the table and stood up. "Can I help you put this stuff away?"

"Nah," Kate said. "I need something to help fill my eight hour shift. This will help the time go by faster. Thanks for coming in and giving me something to do." She smiled. "Otherwise it's just sitting here at the desk."

"Thanks again," Beth said as she turned to leave.

She walked out of the double glass doors with new feelings swirling inside her. If it was nothing more than an out of control bear, like most people seemed to think, why didn't Hank just tell her that? Was he around when Allan Morrison was the game warden? Had Morrison told him the truth before he took the job?

Before now, Beth hadn't really thought there was any danger, at least not life-threatening danger. She'd just had an uneasy feeling. But now, she wasn't sure what to think. The last time people had been allowed to go to Spider Lake, they had gone missing. What did that mean? What if there was some truth to those old legends? No monsters, of course, but something else, something wild and vicious, that was responsible for those missing people. Was it still up there with Scott and the others?

Beth tried to calm all the questions dancing around in her mind on the drive home. She turned up her music and did her best to get lost in it, but it wasn't working. She still wanted to *do* something, now even more than when she'd woken up this morning. But she knew that she couldn't do anything yet. She had to process all of this and figure out the right course of action.

Chapter Nineteen

The Silent Night

The forest was alive and full of noise. Owls hooted and swooped through trees that swayed in the gentle wind. The branches of those trees creaked, their leaves rustling. A tiny pair of eyes stared out into the night from the cover of brush and darkness. Something scurried through the leaves, over a tree root, and deep into an unseen burrow. The moon lit up the night sky, but its luminescent light didn't penetrate the canopy of trees to reach the forest floor.

A man walking through these trees at night would be lost within minutes. The grey trees, tall as skyscrapers, all looked alike in the blackness. And many men had disappeared here. A single wrong turn and a person could disappear forever, swallowed by the forest, never to be seen again.

But there was a glimmer of civilization within the vast wilderness.

Through a gap in the trees that was just large enough to allow some moonlight down to the forest floor, sat a small cluster of meager, zipped tents. Strewn about the campsite was an empty whiskey bottle accompanied by a handful of used cigarettes and a few sagging camping chairs. The fire in the center, previously crackling pleasantly, was now nothing but a faint glow. A puff of wind blew between the tents, and cold ash spread around, extinguishing the last trace of the blazing fire. The same breeze, blowing from the northwest, rattled the tent fly and sent dead and broken pine needles dancing harmlessly across the forest floor.

Then everything stopped.

The crickets chirping fell silent.

The scuffle of creatures scurrying under the brush ceased.

Pete was jerked awake by a flying sock colliding with the side of his face.

He jerked up in his sleeping bag. "Hey, what the hell are you doing?"

"Stopping your goddamned snoring!" Tim snapped. "It's 3 A.M., and if I don't get to sleep soon, I'm going to stuff this sock in your mouth to knock you out!"

"Sorry, princess, I didn't realize how important your beauty sleep was." Pete unzipped his warm sleeping bag and rolled out. He was damp with sweat and his bladder was full, so going back to sleep was not possible. He shuffled to the tent opening, pulled down the zipper with a fast flick, and stepped out into the cool night air.

"Where are you going?" Tim asked, sounding like a bear who'd gone too long without hibernation.

"Need to take a leak," Pete mumbled in reply.

"Just stay out there, will you? Maybe I can finally get some sleep without your thunderous snoring in my ear." Tim rolled over.

Pete lumbered to the edge of the clearing, stopping just before the nearly invisible wall of trees. The thin moonbeam that had illuminated his walk winked out, sliding behind a cloud.

Any other time, the slow shift into darkness might have freaked Pete out. But he was still more than half asleep and revelling in the simple gratification of emptying his bladder.

He was only halfway done when he realized that he hadn't heard a single noise since coming out of the tent. Not the chirp of a cricket, an owl hooting, or even a squirrel. His chest tightened with dread and he looked behind him, sure there had to be something there.

He couldn't see anything, but it was pitch black. Anything could be there.

Pete pulled up his pants and took a step backwards, away from the trees, his eyes searching for any hint of movement.

A stick cracked to his left, and he jumped out of his skin.

He forced a laugh to cover his fear. "All right, Tim, you got me," he said into the darkness, faking his way to a grin. "You made me jump, very funny. Now quit it."

Another stick broke, closer this time. Pete froze, dread draining away the color of his skin, leaving him pale.

"It's not funny anymore, Tim. I know I don't snore that loud."

A guttural growl came from the darkness. Pete felt the dinner from last night rising up from his stomach. He looked left, then right, then spun around to face the tents, wondering if he could make it in time if he ran. He heard heavy breathing from the trees behind him and spun again to face the trees.

Pete's muscles coiled with fear, and his reflexes launched him into action at the same moment a huge shape leapt out of the forest, barreling straight at him like a bullet from a gun. His feet tangled underneath him, and he fell to the ground.

He tried to scramble away, clawing at the grass and dirt for a hold on something to use as a weapon. Something clenched around his neck and lifted his body off the ground.

Pete kicked his legs and lashed out with his fists at whatever had taken hold of him. But the more he struggled, the tighter the grip on his neck became. In seconds, the air was squeezed from his lungs. Pete could feel his eyes bulging out of their sockets like balloons. He made one last, futile attempt to free himself, digging his fingers into whatever had a hold on him. A blinding light filled his vision. Everything then faded to a black, even darker than the forest.

Chapter Twenty

The Awakening

Tim lay flat on his back in the tent, enjoying the peace that was found between waking and sleeping. He could feel the rays of the morning sun warming the tent through the fabric and hear the soft whistling of birds singing, all of the chirps sounds he didn't recognize. A gentle breeze shook the tent just enough to push him all the way into consciousness.

He stretched his arms above his head, twisting from side to side in an attempt to loosen the muscles in his back. But they remained stiff. After a night on the cold ground, he shouldn't have expected anything else, especially after getting such little undisturbed sleep. Scott's adventures were always a blast, but they made him so sore that he couldn't manage more than a couple a year.

Tim rolled out of his warm sleeping bag and got ready to punch Pete in the stomach to wake him up, but he was suddenly aware that the sleeping bag next to him was empty.

Pete might have been a hard worker, but he was not an early riser. Maybe the fresh air up in the unspoiled mountains was doing the big man some good.

Tim crawled out of the tent and stood, still trying in vain to get the knots out of his back. Next time, he was bringing an air mattress and sneaking it in his brother's pack.

Despite the sun, it was still cold once he got outside, and the ground was covered in beads of dew. Tim reached back into the tent to grab his boots before his feet got any wetter. Shoving his feet inside them, he walked around the campsite looking for Pete.

Frank climbed out of his tent, shielding his eyes against the sun's light. "Morning!" he called out to Tim. He stretched his arms up above his head and groaned. "How'd you sleep?"

"Better the second half of the night! Pete was rumbling like a freight train most of the time," Tim said. "Next time he's your roommate."

Frank laughed. "Where is that prick, anyway? Still sound asleep this early?"

"I'm not sure where he is. He was already up and gone when I woke up. I was actually hoping he would have breakfast started," Tim said with a wry smile. "I thought if anything, that's what he'd be doing."

"Pete, cook?" Frank said. "Yeah right. Maybe if we want burnt oatmeal."

Scott and Marcus stepped out from between the trees, carrying two large jugs of water respectively.

"Hey guys," Scott said. "Got fresh water ready, if you want to clean up." He set his jug down next to the fire pit.

"Clean up?" Tim looked around at the empty woods. "I don't see any women around here. Who the hell are we cleaning ourselves up for?"

"Scott just wants to see us all naked," Marcus said as he set down his own load. "Makes him feel more confident he's not so inadequate." Scott elbowed Marcus in the gut, and the shorter man grunted. "Oh, sorry, didn't realize that was supposed to be a secret."

"Where's Pete?" Frank said. "He bringing another jug?"

Scott bent down to pick up a log from the wood pile. "I don't know where he is, don't you?"

Tim sat down in his camping chair, ready for Scott to get breakfast going. "You mean he's not with you?"

Scott and Marcus exchanged a glance as Scott threw a log onto the fire pit, sending ash flying into the air.

"Does it look like he's with us?" Marcus said, taking his own survey of the campsite just in case he'd missed Pete somehow.

Tim rolled his eyes. "I can see he's not with you, idiot, but he's not here either, and no one has seen him all morning."

Scott stood up from lighting the kindling and tossed another log on the fire as it sprang to life. "Don't worry," Scott told Tim, "he'll turn up soon, once he smells breakfast cooking. I'm not going to be wandering off looking for him again just to find him taking a piss in the woods like last time."

The fire was blazing with the slightest of prodding. It added its own heat to the rising sun, and the cool of the morning was pushed back. Scott broke out some dehydrated eggs and began cooking them over the fire. He also made some coffee to help all the guys with their whiskey hangovers, himself included.

Tim's stomach rumbled as the smells drifted to his nose. No way would Pete be able to resist that. Scott was right; he'd be back within minutes.

"I'm thinking we should head farther north today," Scott said once breakfast was under way.

"Farther?" Tim said. "I don't think I can carry Marcus much farther than we walked yesterday, especially after he's eaten."

Marcus reached out to punch him, but Tim danced away.

"Tim does kind of have a point," Frank said through a mouthful of eggs. "Why do you want to go farther?"

Scott shrugged. "Why not? We're up here to see the area, I want to see as much we can. It won't be hard to get back to camp, either, if we head in one direction. We can come back the same way."

"Plus," Tim said, "he caught less fish than anybody yesterday, and he thinks he'll have a better chance in a different spot."

The group broke out into laughter that drowned out Scott's protests.

"I'm starting to get a little worried about Pete," Marcus said when breakfast was nothing but a few scraps of egg saved for him. "He wouldn't miss breakfast unless something was wrong. You don't think he might have wandered off and really gotten lost, do you? He's not exactly a top-notch outdoorsman like some of us."

Tim swallowed his last bite and let out a loud belch. "Well, the last time I saw him was about 3:30 or so when he left the tent to take a leak."

The other men looked at him with wide eyes.

"What?" Tim said. "The burp wasn't that loud."

"We don't care about your belch, you moron. 3:30 was almost four hours ago! There's no reason he would be gone for that long unless he's gotten lost."

"Jesus Christ, Tim, did you not think that was odd when you woke up and he wasn't there?" Frank said.

"This is deep wilderness out here. It's not a place to fuck around!" Scott stood up. "We've got to start searching now. Marcus, you go east, I'll take west. Frank you go north, and Tim—"

"South, I get the idea," Tim said, still not confident Pete was truly missing.

"Don't go out too far yet. We'll start with a small radius and slowly expand it. He could be hurt or unconscious right outside of camp," Scott said. "Keep your ears peeled and shout if you get wind of anything."

They all moved off in their designated directions.

Tim didn't know why everyone was freaking out so much. Pete was a sharp guy and would find his way back even if he was indeed lost. The guy was big enough to defend himself from most of the stuff in this forest. They'd find him. Besides, it wasn't like it was Tim's job to babysit the snoring prick.

Tim scanned the ground as he walked, looking for anything that might mark Pete's trail. The guy was so big, it shouldn't be hard to find something if he came this way.

"You find anything over there?" Tim called out over his shoulder. A chorus of negative responses came back.

Tim kept going, hunched over close to the ground to make sure he didn't miss anything. But there was nothing. No sticks broken, no obvious disturbances in the leaves that covered the forest floor. Nothing.

Then, as his gaze swept the floor of the forest, he suddenly saw a little puddle of dark color near a tree. Tim looked up and froze.

"Help! Help, everybody get over here!" he screamed. "Get over here now!"

Scott turned at the sound of Tim's scream, and then sprinted back toward camp. He reached the campsite seconds after Frank.

"What? What is it?" Frank was yelling.

Marcus rushed up a moment later. They looked at each other with wide eyes, and then turned to go after Tim.

Scott was half a pace behind Frank when the man slid to a sudden, screeching stop. Scott crashed into his back, and they both fell to the ground.

"My God," Frank said, a shudder in his breath. "Is that Pete?"

Scott pushed himself to his knees and choked back bile that rose in his throat at what he saw.

Pete's body was leaning against a tree that towered up into the sky; it was unrecognizable. His eyes were red blisters, no whites, no irises. Only red. His left arm was crushed. Not just broken, or even snapped, but shattered. The bone shards and muscle strewn on the ground were all that was left of it.

But that wasn't the worst part.

Pete's chest was completely caved into itself. Every rib was broken and the organs underneath it were no more than a bloody, pulpy mess of mush. His body had been shattered by brute strength. There was no animal Scott knew of that could do this to a human body.

Frank climbed to his feet, turning his gaze away, his hands shaking. "What could have done this?"

"It had to have been a monstrous grizzly," Scott said. He stood as well, avoiding the body as best he could.

"A grizzly?" Frank exclaimed wildly, throwing an arm back towards what was left of the body. "Look at him! Look at what's left of him. I've never heard of a grizzly attacking like this."

He was right, of course. But what else could it be? Scott crouched down. He scanned the ground, looking for any sign of the animal that had done this. "What else do you think could've done so much damage to a person?" he said to Frank. "I've never seen a grizzly do this either, but there is nothing else capable of this."

"But why didn't we hear anything? How could this happen with us sleeping so close? Why didn't the bear continue his rampage in our campsite?" Frank shouted. "Why—?"

"Shut up!" Scott yelled. "Just shut up for a minute and let me think." He paced back and forth in front of the body, doing his best not to look at it for long periods.

Scott broadened his search area, looking for tracks, broken twigs, anything that would give a clue about what happened. While he looked, Marcus came back with a sleeping bag, and Tim helped him cover Pete's body. With that task done, they all went back to the campsite, where they felt the safest, to sit and talk.

Scott joined them a few minutes later. "No bite marks, no flesh wounds. It just doesn't make sense."

The others didn't even look up as he walked into the circle.

"What are we going to do? Can we get the hell out of here and contact the game warden somehow?" Marcus demanded.

"Boys, listen, we have to stay focused," Scott said. "There is no reasonable way out except by plane. Our ride doesn't come for another two days; we're stuck here until then."

"What the hell are you talking about, Scott?" Tim said. "Let's pack up and move now. I'm not staying another goddamned minute, even if I have to walk until my feet bleed!"

"Listen," Scott barked. "I know we're all freaked out, but we need to take a deep breath and stay calm. Panic is not our friend right now, keeps us from thinking straight. We're thirty miles from the closest road. Our plane is not scheduled to pick us up for forty-eight hours. We have to stay here for another twelve hours, minimum."

They fell into silence after that.

Scott tried to keep some conversation going. He knew everyone was in shock after what they'd seen, himself included. Interacting with each other would be the only way to keep their heads on straight. But as the minutes crept into hours, the half-hearted attempts at conversation became non-existent. What were they supposed to talk about? Fishing? Playing horseshoes? There was nothing to do but talk about the death, and no one wanted that.

Finally, Scott offered a plan, something to give the guys some hope.

"Listen," he said. "I think I have an idea. Say we spend the night and leave at first light. We can take shifts staying awake, so if the animal does return, hopefully it will stay clear when we see it. We can survive this if we work together and be smart." He paused and tried to make eye contact with each of them. "We can live through this; we aren't going to die."

No one looked at him, but they all nodded.

Hours passed, and they watched the sun fall until it sank beneath the trees. As darkness encroached on the campsite, a chill filled the air. Scott wasn't sure how much of the cold was natural and how much was in his head after what they'd seen. Hard as he tried, he couldn't get the image of Pete's smashed body out of his head. And he still had no idea how it could have happened.

So he stoked the fire in a vain attempt to distract himself. He got it blazing four feet high, sparks flying up into the night, but he didn't feel any better.

When darkness had fully settled over them, he broke the silence again. "So, who wants the first shift, and who wants to sleep?"

"Are you nuts?" Frank said. "Who the hell is going to sleep after what happened? I can't stop seeing Pete every time I close my damn eyes. I can't stop seeing him, his body, thinking about whatever the hell it was that just...broke him like that. I can't stop wondering why we never heard screams. If I fall asleep, I'll just see him there, too. What's the point in trying?"

The others nodded, and nobody moved towards a tent.

"I know," Scott said. "Look, I can't stop seeing it, either. It's just as hard for me. But we have to get at least some sleep, or we'll never make it to the pickup site tomorrow, and then what? Don't you get it? We'll all be dead on our feet."

"Better than being dead like Pete," Frank muttered.

Hours later, Frank's eyes were growing heavy. Despite what he'd said to Scott about having no intention of sleeping, he didn't think he'd stay awake much longer.

But no one else had moved from the comforting crackle of the fire, so he wouldn't budge either. The fire got darker and smaller as the supply of wood ran out. It was obvious that no one was going to venture out into the darkness for more firewood to keep it going. So, slowly, almost painfully so, it faded to embers.

Frank felt his eyelids drooping and tried to force them open, but he was losing the fight. Sleep washed over him.

Then Marcus heaved himself out of his chair with a gasp. Frank's eyes snapped open, adrenaline jerking his body from sleep to full alert in a fraction of a heartbeat.

"What? Did you hear something?"

"No, that's the problem," Marcus murmured. He stood next to the fire, not moving a muscle, his head tilted to the right. "I don't hear anything at all. Something's not right, and it's not the first time it's happened."

He was right. The sounds of owls, crickets, and other creatures of the night that had lulled Frank to sleep were all gone. Total silence reigned in their place. The hairs on the back of Frank's neck stood on end, and he could swear he was being watched.

He scratched his neck to drive the sensation away. "What time is it?" he whispered, praying that dawn was close.

"6 A.M.," Scott replied.

"An hour until dawn? Jesus Christ, this is a nightmare." Frank rubbed his neck again, but he still felt like something was staring at the back of his skull. He wanted to look behind him, but fear paralyzed him. It was just his imagination. There was nothing there.

"Why is the forest so freakin' quiet?" Scott said. His voice was harsh and tense, stiff as a board. Frank knew Scott always liked to be in control on trips like this, but this situation was way out of his hands.

Marcus took a few steps away from the campfire, towards the darkness. "We need to get this fire going again, boys. We could all die from hypothermia before we die of...something else." He passed Frank, and Frank still couldn't bring himself to turn and watch Marcus as he headed outside the camp borders. "I think it's pretty safe to assume that whatever's out there, it won't be a fan of flames. Let's try to—"

The sentence ended in a ragged scream that was choked off an instant after it began.

"Marcus? Marcus!" Frank bellowed. "Answer me!"

But the silence was back. For the briefest of moments, Frank wondered if he had imagined Marcus' scream.

A crack like a branch being snapped off a tree came from behind Frank, and he jumped along with the rest of the group, scrambling to join them and huddle together. He turned in the direction of the sound before he remembered that he didn't want to see what was behind him.

A savage roar came from the darkness, followed by pounding footsteps that shook the Earth beneath Frank's feet. Tree branches snapped and the rumbling grew louder, then something came hurtling through the air and landed in what was left of the fire.

Frank couldn't hold back the shriek of terror when he saw Marcus' body lying among the ashes. Scott and Tim screamed in horror. Another deafening roar drowned out their cries.

The side of Marcus' face was crushed, his legs were twisted and buckled, snapped like twigs.

Frank scrambled away from the sound of the creature still charging closer. He huddled up closer against Scott and Tim in a desperate attempt to escape.

"What is it? Is it a grizzly?" Scott yelled over the roaring.

Then it stopped. The Earth stopped shaking, the roars fell silent, and deathly quiet descended on the forest again.

Frank's heartbeat echoed in his head like a rapid pulse of an African drum, his breathing heavy and ragged.

He looked up and could see the first hints of dawn in the sky. The stars still ruled, but they hung against a deep blue sea rather than an obsidian slate. When he directed his gaze back downward again, everything was still in shades of black and grey. He was cursing even the fire they'd had burning most of the night. Without it, maybe his eyes would see more than shapeless grey masses in the trees.

One of the masses moved. Not much, no more than a fraction of an inch. If Frank had blinked, he would have missed it, but once he saw it, he couldn't convince himself it was in his mind. Whatever had attacked and murdered Marcus was right there.

A huge, hulking beast stood between two trees, silhouetted against the dull glow of the moonlight. Two dark red eyes were staring right at him, swallowing him in their gaze.

"You're not a grizzly," Frank whispered.

In a flash, the beast was on him.

Frank screamed and threw up his left arm to ward off the creature.

He heard Scott and Tim's screams join his own. A blinding pain consumed his arm. Frank fell to the ground. He tried to focus his eyes, but something was wrong. He couldn't see his arm anymore, only a mangled mess of flesh at his shoulder.

The creature roared again, the sound rattling his brain inside his skull. It stood over him, holding his severed left arm high in the air. It raised one giant foot over his head. Frank shut his eyes to block out the image. The foot crashed down over him.

His last thoughts were focused on the image of his wife and little girl, running along the lakeshore, jumping from the rocks, screaming with delight.

Scott took off the moment he saw Frank's arm ripped off. There was nothing he could do for his old friend now. Tim was right on his heels as he crashed through the tree line.

The rational part of his brain was screaming at him, telling him that he needed to slow down, get his bearings, and decide which way to go. Running blindly through the woods was as likely to get him killed as to get him to safety. But the rational part of his brain was drowned out over the constant crashing waves of terror and panic that were consuming him.

So he ran on like a dumb wild animal, closing his eyes against the stinging of the branches that slapped and stung as he tore through the undergrowth and stumbled on every unseen rock that crossed his path.

Scott could hear the creature gaining; he knew it wasn't a grizzly now by its speed, crashing through the trees behind them. It sounded like it was tearing whole trees from the ground and snapping them like toothpicks as it moved.

"Scott!" Tim cried in desperation. "Wait for me!"

Scott glanced over his shoulder and saw that Tim was falling behind, too far behind. He could hardly see his friend through the dense forest as anything more than a fleeting dark shadow. He shouted back so loudly his voice cracked.

"Hurry up, Tim! Move it!"

He strained to hear Tim's reply over the pounding of his pulse, but all he could focus on was the thunderous footsteps of whatever beast was chasing them.

Scott's heart pounded harder in his chest, so hard he thought it may escape from behind his rib cage. His lungs ached from the exertion of sucking in dry, short breaths. He felt his legs starting to slow, each step sending a throb of pain through his muscles, but he pushed himself to keep running with only the fear of death to encourage him.

When Tim's horrified cry filled the air, Scott stopped. He turned around and placed his hands on his knees, breathing out hard, shaking exhales. He swore under his breath and straightened as Tim screamed again, but he couldn't see where the sound was coming from now.

A sickening crunch came from the trees, silencing Tim's scream. Scott was sure he would've thrown up in the middle of the forest if he'd eaten anything since yesterday's breakfast.

He bolted again, crashing blindly through the trees.

His conscience told him he had to do something to help Tim and try to keep his friend alive, but his brain told him there was nothing he could do and Tim was long gone. Since his brain had priority when it came to the terror coursing through his veins, he ran on.

Tim's haunting screams continued to echo in Scott's head, almost as loud as the pounding feet of the behemoth bearing down on him.

Scott had no idea how long he'd been running. He gasped for breath to give his body strength. Sweat beaded on his forehead and ran into his eyes despite the cold stinging them. His lungs burned. But he kept running.

"Please, please let there be a way out," he panted. "Oh God, please let there be a way out."

It was his survival mantra, and it was the only thought circling in his head as consistently as his breathing. There was always a way out if you looked hard enough. How many times had he said that to a customer on a trek when they felt lost?

There was a way out of this.

He just had to find it.

Fifty yards ahead of him, Scott saw it.

There was a clearing, brighter than the rest of the forest, where soft green undergrowth covered the ground. He could see tiny drops of morning dew shining on the blades of grass like diamonds.

Somehow, his panicked mind had taken him in the right direction. Thank God for his instincts. He must have been running for even longer than he thought to get this far. He didn't know he had pushed himself so hard.

But that didn't matter. He was safe.

His strides got faster, it was easier to pull air into his lungs, and his legs no longer felt like Jell-O as hope flooded his body. He was going to make it.

Scott broke through the tree line, legs pumping through the grass.

Then skidded to sudden stop.

This wasn't the clearing he was hoping for.

Scott stood on the edge of a cliff, looking out over a valley he'd never seen before.

His heart sank in his chest like a piece of lead. The cliff was high, at least five hundred feet above the canopy of trees below. He had no chance of surviving a jump, and he had no tools.

As the reality hit him, his whole body started to shake.

"There is no way out," he whispered, his eyes widening. Then his voice rose to an agonized shriek. "My God, there is no way out!"

His scream echoed in the silence.

Silence? He paused in a moment of realization. Had he lost his pursuer?

The hair on the back of his neck stood on end. He knew he wasn't so lucky. He turned around, slowly…and came face to face with the killing machine.

The beast was standing no more than forty feet away from him, just inside the clearing, breathing hard. It had to be over nine feet tall and as wide as a pair of silver-back gorillas. Its body was covered in thick, wiry, black hair from head to toe, its face the only bald spot.

As frightening as everything about the monster was, it was the face that froze Scott with terror.

The features were huge and ape-like, with a nose spread out wide across the cheeks. Its mouth curled back into a snarl to reveal huge, yellowing, sharp teeth that curved over its thick, grisly lips like scimitars.

Scott couldn't tear his gaze away from the narrow, searing eyes. They were red and savage, but he'd never seen such a cold, calculating stare before. The creature was thinking. Deciding.

And then its mind was made up.

The monstrosity took a step towards him.

Scott's mind turned to all the people he'd never see again.

His beautiful fiancée, Beth, and the wedding that he wouldn't attend, were the first images in his mind, followed by the children they would never have and the dream house they would never build.

Then he thought of his mother, the woman who had birthed him, raised him, and taught him what real love was.

And his father, the man he admired more than any other. The man he'd looked up to all his life. The man who'd taught him how to hunt, how to survive in the woods.

Scott laughed aloud at that thought.

Survive.

All the survival knowledge he had, all the experience he'd gained, was useless here. There was no guidebook on how to escape nature's ultimate killing machine. No worst case scenario this bad.

The towering beast flared its nostrils. A rumbling, ominous growl came from deep in its throat. Its face expressed a fury Scott had never seen in humans or animals.

It moved closer, walking slowly now, clearly not worried about losing its prey. As it approached, its eyes never wavered from Scott's.

When it was ten feet away, Scott blinked.

Those eyes weren't animal at all.

They were shockingly human in nature.

Scott whimpered, and a tear rolled down his cheek. He knew this was the end for him, and he was scared. This wild creature, whatever it was, was far too ferocious, far too intelligent to escape from now.

There was only one way to elude it. One thing it wouldn't see coming.

Scott turned around, his toes poking over the edge of the cliff. He stared across the valley, trying not to look down, staring at the view of the sun that was finally beginning to peek over the mountains, and he smiled.

A fitting final view for a real outdoorsman.

The monster roared as if in defiance. It charged across the clearing towards him, almost as if it could sense what Scott was planning to do to best it.

The ground shook so hard, it was difficult to stand. Scott could hear the beast's panting, the thick mucus popping in its throat, its teeth snapping in anticipation, grinding together.

Scott took a deep breath, spread his arms, and leaned out far over the cliff.

He felt a huge hand swipe at the back of his shirt, but he was inches out of reach, falling off the cliff, away from the monster, away from life, and into the dark abyss that promised peace.

As Scott fell towards the floor of the bottomless valley, the monster roared with rage. Scott's body turned in the air to face upward, and the last thing he saw was the beast leaning over the cliff edge as it roared. He smiled.

Then all was black.

Chapter Twenty-One

No Return

The shrill bell rang through the hallways of the school. Beth closed the book in front of her.

"You're dismissed," she told her students as they rose and gathered their backpacks. "Have a good afternoon. See you tomorrow."

She didn't know about the kids, but she knew she'd have a good afternoon. Scott was due back from his trip today. It had been four long, grueling days since she'd seen him last and bade him a loving good bye, and she'd been counting the seconds to that final bell all day.

Beth took her place on the stone steps of the school to monitor all the students as they streamed out of the building. Though she usually didn't mind the job, today she found herself tapping her foot and glancing at her watch every thirty seconds or so, mentally urging the kids to hurry themselves out the doors.

The students were noisier than normal, caught up in the excitement of a warm fall afternoon. Beth chewed on her thumbnail, anxious for the students to be on their way so she could be on hers. Scott was probably already home waiting for her by now.

Unless, of course, something had gone wrong. Accidents weren't uncommon in the mountains around Redwood. It was a wild, rugged place.

Beth shook her head. She had nothing to worry about. Scott was an experienced woodsman, and he'd never come across any serious issues on his trips. But this trip was different, and she still couldn't push the questions about Spider Lake and what was up there out of her mind.

Scott knew Beth was inclined to worry about him, and he always sent a text, made a call, or something to let her know that he was okay during a trip. She'd known before he left on this trip that the territory Scott was in was so remote that he wouldn't be able to communicate at all, so she hadn't expected any contact.

But knowing that didn't make it any easier, only made it simpler to worry.

Faster than normal, but not fast enough for Beth, all the students were out of the school, either on buses or picked up by parents. She cast a perfunctory eye down the hallway to confirm that there were no stragglers, and then pulled the heavy wooden door shut. She locked it tight, slipped the keys into her pocket, and skipped down the steps two at a time.

Beth jumped into her car, shoved the keys into the ignition and brought the engine roaring to life. She slammed it into gear and screeched out of the staff parking lot, ignoring the skid marks of the car. Good thing most of the other teachers were already gone, or she'd probably get a lecture about responsible driving the next morning.

Scott and Beth lived just a few miles outside of town on a piece of land surrounded by woods. Even though Redwood was a small town, it was nice to have some distance from the hustle and bustle at the end of the day. Plus, Beth was trying to convince Scott to get a dog, and having a house outside of town made arguing for that a lot easier. They'd bought the house just three months ago, in preparation for their marriage. It was their first investment as a couple, and they were proud of it.

Beth flew down their quiet street, breaking every speed limit possible. The closer she got, the more butterflies filled her stomach at the thought of seeing the man she loved once again. She slammed on the brakes and banked hard into the driveway, heart racing in anticipation.

But her smile faded as she saw the driveway was empty.

She felt a flash of alarm and pushed it down. Scott always tried to be home before Beth finished her school day when a trip ended. He loved to be there to greet her. But she convinced herself of the fact that he wasn't home yet didn't mean something was wrong. He hadn't told her exactly when they'd be back from Spider Lake; they might not return until after dark, wanting to enjoy another full day of daylight.

Satisfied with that explanation, Beth hopped out of her truck and walked up the porch steps. The old wooden front door creaked as she opened it and dashed into the single-level house. She headed down the hallway, eyes looking for the flashing light of the answering machine. Since Scott hadn't gotten home yet, she was sure he would've called to leave a message and at least tell her he was back down from the mountain.

She rounded the corner into the kitchen and saw that the light on the answering machine was a steady green. No messages.

"Damn it," Beth muttered under her breath.

She was disappointed but still willing herself to remain unconcerned. Scott was a great man, but he wasn't the most punctual. It was highly likely that he'd been fishing, reeling in a big one, bantering with the boys and lost track of time.

Beth knew she wouldn't be able to stop thinking about when Scott would return, so she busied herself with preparing dinner. Without something to occupy her mind, she'd be checking out the window every time she heard a car driving down the road.

Beth walked to the counter and pulled out her recipe book. What should she cook to welcome him back home? She flipped through the book, but she was barely even seeing the words as she debated.

A car door slammed outside and her heart jumped in excitement. She fought the temptation to run towards the window and start waving to Scott. Instead, she just smiled and waited to hear the sounds of his footsteps on the porch floor.

Inspiration for dinner struck, and she flipped through page after page of recipes, looking for grilled salmon with a honey glaze, Scott's favorite. She'd bought some salmon this week just for the occasion. Her smile got bigger and bigger as the seconds passed, each moment bringing her closer to seeing her fiancé.

But the seconds kept passing, and time kept dragging out with no sign of Scott. No sounds of him heaving his bags and gear out of the truck, of him crossing over to the front door, or of the inevitable swearing that occurred when he struggled to find his keys and get them into the lock without dropping them.

Beth slammed the recipe book shut and ran a hand through her hair, pulling when she came to the tangles out of frustration. Why was he taking his sweet time to get inside and see her? Was it really so important to spend more time with the guys than with her? Couldn't he at least have left her a message?

She crossed over to the window and knelt on the couch to peer through the curtains at an empty driveway, resting her chin on her arms.

Scott still wasn't home.

She rested her forehead against the window and sighed. A hint of anxiousness tried to worm its way into her stomach, but she pushed it aside. Scott was fine.

The sun was going down as Beth attempted to busy herself around the house. But everywhere she turned, there was another reminder that Scott still hadn't returned, and a greater return of the doubt she felt without him beside her.

Her half-hearted attempt at Scott's favorite meal sat unfinished on the cold stove. The salmon filets were half-frozen and the glaze still a loose mixture of honey and vinegar in her mixing bowl. She had been halfway through cooking when she noticed that the carpet was filthy and had to be vacuumed right away, anything to keep her mind off of Scott.

She was vacuuming the living room when she noticed the television screen was far too dusty. So the Hoover sat in the middle of the floor, still plugged in and running, as Beth frantically wiped her duster over the screen.

Every two or three minutes, she would cross over to the phone and lift the receiver to ensure that she could still hear a dial-tone and be sure her phone was working. Then she'd slam it back down, just in case Scott was trying to call at that exact moment.

Beth sent carefully worded texts to his cell phone. She had to ask where he was but didn't want to sound too worried for fear of ruining his time out with the guys. She called him twice and left chirpy voice messages, playfully asking if he was avoiding her or had fallen in love with the woods. He'd tease her if he knew how worried she was, but she knew for a fact that if it were the other way around, and it was Scott waiting for her, he'd be sick with concern and calling her every other minute.

She was dusting along the mantel when her eyes fell on a picture of the two of them taken just after Scott had proposed to her. She smiled, enjoying her first real somewhat pleasant distraction from her worries over Scott.

The day that Scott proposed was the happiest day of her life. She'd had no idea that he was planning to do it, and it came as a total, wonderful surprise.

Beth didn't know a thing about the weeks he'd spent preparing, stressing about it, and asking for opinions on every little detail from all his friends and family, until afterwards. He'd asked all of them for input on which ring to pick, the way he should propose, whether or not she'd say yes.

"Of course she'll say yes!" Frank would shout in exasperation, before taking a long gulp of his beer, shaking his head, his eyes wide with frustration. He'd told Beth that Scott had asked him if she'd say yes at least fifty times and was tired of the postponement. And that didn't count all the other questions.

Beth had always loved the mountains around Redwood, and they took romantic drives on the mountain roads whenever possible. So when Scott suggested that they go up to the mountains for a picnic, she hadn't suspected at all that this drive would prove to be one which changed her life.

They drove up on a Sunday morning with a picnic blanket, a packed lunch, and some hidden wine in the trunk. And, the most unbeknownst to Beth, a diamond engagement ring with a rock the size of a raindrop tucked away safely in Scott's jacket pocket.

Scott told her later that he had spent days rehearsing romantic lines to say as he proposed. In fact, he'd spent most of the previous evening going over various lines at the pub. Frank eventually stormed out of his dad's pub midway through his beer, commenting that his dad might as well convert it into a chapel.

In the end, though, Scott had decided to go with the simplest proposal, the truth.

After their lunch, while they were sipping their wine, Scott pulled Beth over to him and kissed her cheek.

"Beth, you know you mean the world to me, right?" he said in her ear.

She turned her head toward him and laughed. "Of course," she said. "Of course I know that. Do you know that you're my world, too?"

He smiled and kissed her nose, his lips warm against her cold skin. "Yeah, I know. But do you know that I want to spend the rest of my life with you? That you're the first thing I think of when I wake up, the last thing I see before I close my eyes, and that I think about you all day long in between?"

Beth looked up at him, still smiling, her eyes searching his as he held both her hands in his.

"And," he continued, "do you know that I can't imagine being with anyone else, that I know there's no one else for me, that you're my soul mate, and the one that was made for me?"

Beth's eyes started to fill with tears at his words, and she whispered, "I know."

"Good," Scott said. He reached into his coat pocket and pulled out a small box. "So, since you know all that, you should be able to figure out that I want to marry you."

Beth had gasped, her tears building, and squeezed his hand, sitting up and turning around so she could look straight at him.

"Beth," Scott said, "will you marry me?"

She'd squealed and threw her arms around his neck. Then she remembered she hadn't actually said anything yet, pulled back, and said, "Yes, of course I will!"

They both broke into laughter, giddy with excitement and intoxicated with love. He held her face between his hands and kissed her deeply. She felt him smile against her lips; he'd leapt up and grabbed the camera.

"We have to document this moment." He pressed a series of buttons to set up the self-timer and balanced the camera on the hood of the pickup truck. He ran back to Beth and sat behind her on the picnic blanket, pulling her close against him once more.

They smiled towards the camera as the green light blinked three times and flashed, capturing their perfect moment forever.

Beth put her favorite framed picture back down on the mantel and looked at the phone. She was tired of waiting at this point. Her patience was gone. It had been too long, and she was going to get through to him no matter what.

She dialed his cell phone number again, her fingers flying over the well-known sequence of buttons. She pressed the phone to her ear and gritted her teeth when it started ringing. No more nice voicemails; it was time to find out what was going on.

Beth could feel her heart pounding its way out of her chest, and when the phone clicked, it leapt up into her throat for the briefest of moments.

"Hi, you've reached Scott, can't take your call right now, but leave a message and I'll get back to you," Scott's voice said to her for the fifth time.

"Scott, where are you?" Beth's hand clenched the phone tightly, sweat making the plastic slick. "You need to call me right away, just call me and tell me where you are. Are you okay? You had better be on your way home. Call me. Please, just call me and let me know." She paused. "I love you."

She ended the call and pressed the phone to her lips for the closest kiss she could manage.

Maybe something was wrong with Scott's phone. One of the other guys would answer their phone, surely. Why hadn't she thought of it before?

She punched in another number and listened to another series of unfeeling rings.

"Hey you've reached Frank, I'm not avail—" Beth hung up.

Who else was with him? She didn't know any other numbers by heart, so she grabbed her address book and found Tim's name first. She got an odd ring and then a click from Tim, some weird song she'd never heard before came on. It was better than the endless ringing she'd been listening to all afternoon, but it still led to another voicemail, which in turn led nowhere.

She tried the other guys, Pete and Marcus, then Scott one more time, in hopes that her constant calling would be rewarded. They all went to the same voicemails, and her knuckles turned whiter with each invitation to leave a message as her hands tightened over the receiver.

Beth flicked through her address book again to find one more number.

She pounded out the number and leaned her back against the wall, her foot tapping out a frantic rhythm against the floor, holding back tears she could no longer keep down completely.

After a few rings, she was relieved to finally hear a real voice on the line. "Good evening," a brusque female voice said. "Huntington Construction, this is Marcy."

"Hey Marcy, this is Beth, Scott's fiancée. I was hoping to speak with Ace. Is he still there?"

"Oh, hi love. Sure, hold one moment."

Hold music filled the earpiece, and the moments passed even slower than they had been. Beth's foot tapped faster and faster in a futile effort to speed the seconds along until she was forced to pace.

"Huntington Construction, Ace speaking." The connection was bad, full of crackles and static, but that was typical, and Beth knew to raise her voice in order for him to hear her.

"Ace? Hi. It's Beth." Her voice was wavering despite her best efforts to hold it steady. "Have you heard from Scott? He was due back today but he isn't home, and I haven't heard from him yet. He always calls me on his way home, always. He would've called me; it's not like him to not call me."

"No, sorry," Ace said, his voice still covered by a layer of static. "I haven't heard from him since the day he took off up there. Don't worry, though. You know what he's like, probably just caught up fishing with the guys. If they're still up where they were headed, there's no chance he'd get any reception and if not, hey, he probably got them to turn off their phones for a last day of peace and quiet."

Beth willed herself to listen to Ace and believe that Scott was okay, that she was overreacting. She desperately wanted to believe that was true.

"I know you're concerned," Ace was saying. "I'll let you know if I hear from him."

"Yes, please let me know." Tears started to overflow her eyes, and she knew she had to hang up before her voice gave her away. "Please, the minute you hear anything."

She dropped the phone into its cradle, and a tear escaped her left eye and ran down her cheek. She sniffed and wiped it away, blinking rapidly to keep the others back. She was being foolish, getting upset like this.

"It's nothing," she whispered to herself. "He's fine. He's just late, but he's fine."

Beth slid down the wall, biting her lip to keep from crying any more, and pulled her knees up to her chest. There was all the time in the world... to wait.

The moon was high in the sky by the time Beth looked again at the clock on the wall.

11:14 pm.

Beth was still sitting on the floor, staring at the wall. She hadn't bothered turning on any lights; she could see well enough by the moonlight.

Her eyes remained fixed, and her body didn't move, but her head was a battleground. Her fear and paranoia would fight their way to the surface every ten or fifteen minutes, only to be beaten down again by a more reasonable voice. She would talk herself into believing that everything was fine, that she'd hear Scott's pickup truck rolling up the driveway any minute now. She played games with herself, counting to ten, sure that once she reached the end of her count, Scott would unlock the front door and walk in with an armload of roses and apologies respectively.

But he didn't.

And it was never long before she was reaching to lift the phone from its cradle, pressing it to her ear to hear the dial tone once more.

The clock continued to tick the seconds, every one slower than the last, each thunderous click of the second hand screaming at her that everything was not fine. She ignored it as long as she could, staring at the silhouette of the mountains against the dark sky, the mountains that had always brought her joy and comfort. But tonight, they were an unconquerable force and they were keeping Scott from her.

It was 11:54 pm when she decided to call Ace again.

Beth had reached the pinnacle of her patience. Something had happened to him and she had to find out what.

She pulled the phone down to the floor with her and started to dial the number for Ace's business. Then she remembered it was midnight, cleared the number, and started over with Ace's cell. She braced her back hard against the wall and stared out the window again, waiting for Ace to pick up with baited breath.

*

Across town, Ace jerked awake at the sound of a shrill ring. He sat up and looked back and forth, searching for the source of the sound for a few seconds before he realized it was his phone. He glanced at his wife and saw that she was still asleep. She could sleep through anything, thank God.

Ace grabbed the phone from his nightstand where it was plugged into its charger and lifted the receiver to his ear. His already gruff voice was even more so at night, and he had to clear his throat a few times as he answered.

"Hello?" he tried to say. But all that came out was a rough grunt. He cleared his throat and tried again. "Hello?" That was better, as least it resembled hello.

"Ace, it's Beth again. I'm sorry to bother you so late, but something has happened to Scott. I'm sure of it now."

"What?" Ace said. He was fully upright now, all thoughts of sleep driven from his mind. "What happened? How do you know?" He switched on his lamp so he could see to move out of the darkened room and heard Beth sigh on the other end of the line.

"I don't know how I know, Ace. But I know it's midnight, and he's not home. He's still not home. He hasn't answered his phone for ten calls and neither have any of the others."

Ace could tell she was trying to sound calm, but the tears were coming through loud and clear now.

Ace rubbed his eyes with one hand as he walked into the hall and closed the door behind him. "Beth, calm down, okay?"

"Calm down? How can I calm down? My fiancé, your son, has not been heard from for days. He's up in an area that we both know is dangerous, an area where people have disappeared! You know he would've called me, he would've radioed you, he would've done something to keep us from worrying. He always gets in touch. Always! Have you heard from him? Did he radio you?"

Ace winced and held the phone away from his ear. When Beth had called earlier today, he'd been sure she was overreacting, but now that he thought about it, she had a good point. There had been a lot of rain the past few days, so it was possible that a mudslide or flash flood had held them up on their way down the mountain. But if that was the case, Scott definitely would've attempted to radio him. He'd taken great care to raise a smart son. "Hold on a sec, Beth."

He heard his wife stir in the room, probably reacting to the light he'd left on when he slipped outside to talk.

She sat up in bed and turned towards her husband's voice after discovering his spot empty. "Ace?" she murmured, "What's wrong?"

He placed his hand over the mouthpiece and cracked the door to call to his wife. "It's Beth, sweetheart. There's no problem, just turn off the lamp and go back to sleep."

She lowered her head to the pillow, clicked the light off, and was out again without another word.

"Beth?" he asked once he was sure he wouldn't disturb his wife anymore. "Are you still there?"

"Yes, Ace, of course I'm still here." Beth sniffed.

He sat down at his desk, switched the phone to speaker, and set it down. "Well, to be honest with you, I'm not sure of our options right now. It's too dark to attempt any kind of search, and we don't know where he is. For all we know, he may have come back into town late and just stayed at one of his friends' houses. They're always exhausted after their trips."

Beth let out a long exhale into the phone. "I know that's possible, Ace," she said. "But I've called everyone. No one has answered. I know you think I'm overreacting, but I really think something has happened to them. I can't shake the feeling. I know something's gone wrong and I don't know what to do."

Ace paused. Beth was not a stupid girl, and he had always admired her for that. She had her head screwed on straight, she was a very strong woman and knew his son even better than he did. If she was this worried, then there really was something to worry about. "All right, you just sit tight. I'll be over in a few minutes and we'll see what we can do."

Twenty minutes later, Ace pulled up to Scott and Beth's house. Beth was waiting on the front porch, wrapped in a thick winter coat.

Ace climbed out of his truck and walked toward Beth. It was a cool night, but not cold enough for that heavy coat. The poor girl must be driving herself insane.

"Hi, Ace." Beth stepped off the porch to meet him. "Thank you for coming. I'm so sorry to drag you out of bed like this, but I just didn't know what else to do."

He put his arm around her shoulders to hustle her back into the house. "Beth, you're family," he said. "We'll always be here for you, and I know your concern isn't unfounded."

They sat down at the kitchen table.

"So what happened, Beth? Why are you sure that something's gone wrong?"

"There's nothing to explain, Ace. He's just not home. He comes home when he says he's coming home, and if he knows he won't be home, he calls. I've tried his cell a dozen times, I tried Frank, I tried all the guys, but none of them picked up."

Ace rubbed his hand over his face. "Now, I'm not dismissing your concerns, but there's really not much we can do until daylight. A search party would do no good now, it's too dark. Once the sun rises, I'll go to Hank and we'll organize —"

"The sun won't rise for another six hours! That's too long; anything could happen to them within that time. We have to go see Hank now!"

"There's no point going now, Beth; he'll be asleep, and we still won't be able to conduct the search until —"

Beth banged her fist against the table. "Don't you understand, Ace? I don't care how late it is right now. I mean no disrespect, but we need to go now. I cannot sit around thinking about him for six hours and wait. I can't do that."

She buried her face in her hands, drained by the hours she'd already spent waiting and exhausted by her last outburst.

Ace grabbed the keys to his pickup. "Come on," he said, pulling Beth up by her hand. "Let's go."

*

Hank woke to the sound of raucous banging on his front door. He roused himself quickly. This wasn't the first time a lost hiker or distraught dog owner had come to him for help in the middle of the night, and he knew it wouldn't be the last, either. You got used to it after a while. But when he swung upon the door to see Ace and Beth on his porch, his eyes widened.

"Beth? Ace? What the hell is going on? Do you know what time it is?"

Beth pushed past him into his hallway before he could object, and he had to turn to face her.

"Scott's missing, Hank. Him and the other guys, they're missing. They were due back from Spider Lake today but they haven't shown up. We need to form a search party right now." She stared at him, her arms crossed over her chest.

Hank ran his hand through his hair and closed the front door behind Ace with a great sigh. "Are you sure he's missing, Beth? Is it possible that he just came back tired, and stayed at-?"

"No!" Beth shouted, cutting his words off. "Do you think I haven't already thought of that? Do you think I wouldn't have called everyone to see if he was there? He's not anywhere! None of them are home yet! And no one has heard a damn thing about them!"

She began gasping for air, and Ace wrapped his arm around her shoulder, doing his best to calm her down.

Ace looked at Hank and nodded toward the kitchen.

Once Beth was seated at the table, Hank looked at Ace.

"Beth's been waiting for hours, Hank," Ace said, his hand resting on Beth's forearm. "Since this afternoon, when she called me worried and I told her to calm down, not to worry. We wouldn't have come to you unless it was serious, and unfortunately, it's reached that point. You know where the boys went."

Hank nodded. He did know where they went. And he knew they shouldn't have gone there in the first place.

"They've been there for half a week. That long in a place that remote, any number of things could've gone wrong."

"Exactly," Hank said, lifting his chin as he faced Ace. "And most of those things are no big deal for an experienced outdoorsman like Scott. He's the one who insisted that he could handle himself up there."

Ace removed his hand from Beth's arm and leaned into Hank's face, his eyes narrowed. "This is not the time to say I told you so, Hank. They were coming back today and no one's heard from them. That's not like Scott. We have to get a search party together. Now. And when my son is back safe with all those other boys, then you can rub your victory in my face all you Goddamn well please."

"Have either of you called Jake?" Hank asked thoughtfully. "He would have been scheduled to fly up and pick the guys up this afternoon sometime. Best to hear what he saw."

Beth shook her head. "I don't have his number."

Hank stood and walked over to the phone, mentally sighing. The woman's soon-to-be-husband takes a trip up to a dangerous territory and no one bothers to get the contact info of the pilot. It was almost as bad as tourists. If anyone would know anything about the guys, Jake would be the first one to contact. He would know if they came down from the mountain or not. He had known Jake for some time, and had the number in his list, dialing himself because he knew that waking Jake in the middle of the night was not going to be a nice phone call.

The phone rang several times before a groggy voice answered with what could vaguely be recognized as a mix between a hello and a bear growl.

"Jake?" Hank asked.

"Who the hell is calling me in the middle of the night?" Jake replied.

"Sorry, Jake, it's Hank. I know it's late," but before he could continue, Jake interrupted him.

"Late, hell, Hank, it ain't late, it's goddamn early. Do you know what time it is?"

"Yes," Hank sighed, looking over at Beth and Ace. "Look Jake, you know I wouldn't call you unless it was important. I've got some people here and we're wondering about those boys you were supposed to pick up in the restricted area. Did you go up there and get them?"

"You're damn right I flew up there to pick those boys up," Jake replied. "And they never showed. I told 'em when I dropped 'em off on Friday clear as day that I don't wait around in areas like that for anyone who's late. But of course I waited for 'em when exits are few and far between. I waited around for two hours, Hank, but they never came, not a one. Storm was coming in, so eventually I had to pull out and come home rather than risk being stranded myself. I figured I would head back up tomorrow and see if they decided they was ready to come home yet. They best be ready to pay a little extra for my time and effort, though."

"Yeah, okay," Hank said. "Well, don't worry about being compensated for your time, Jake. We'll make sure that all gets taken care of after the boys are back home. But I think I better go up with you in the morning and take a look around, all right?"

"You think something happened to 'em?" Jake asked.

"Well, we don't know, but we're just going to make sure. It could just be that they missed their ride and will be waiting on the beach for us when we get there. I want to go with you just in case."

"Sounds good."

"Can we head up around seven?" Hank asked, knowing that was only a few hours away and hoping it would appease Beth.

"Seven?!" Jake was obviously not planning to head up that early by the explosion on the other end.

"Yeah, seven," Hank replied, knowing that pushing it any later would have Beth boiling over.

"Well, you're the boss," Jake replied, obviously unhappy about the time but willing to accept it nonetheless. "I'll be ready. Now let me get some more sleep."

"Great, see you in a few hours," Hank said, hanging up the phone.

Chapter Twenty-Two

The Search

The jagged mountains loomed in the distance, a serrated knife blade cutting into the bright sky and slicing through layers of puffy clouds. The Cessna flew high above the tree tops, creaking and shaking with every gust of wind. And today, there were lots of strong gusts.

But Hank wasn't worried. Not about that.

Jake Blaylock had fifteen years' experience flying this old bush plane, and Hank knew he could handle anything Mother Nature threw at him.

Hank had done a lot of thinking after his phone call with Jake. He'd spent a fair amount of time in the mountains around the restricted area growing up. Most of the area was unexplored now, but he knew the area well enough, better than most people even though it wasn't frequented by travelers.

Since he knew the area, he knew that Jake had dropped off Scott at one drop off location close to Spider Lake, but not the closest. Hank knew of a closer lake, Meadowlark Lake, which would put them very close to where he assumed Scott and his friends had camped. It was unfortunate that they couldn't land on Spider Lake itself, but the surroundings made it impossible.

Meadowlark Lake, on the other hand, was doable even though it would be tricky, even for a great pilot like Jake. The uncooperative weather wasn't helping.

But Hank didn't want to make the five mile hike up to Spider Lake that Scott and his group had made on their first day, especially if he found someone injured. Without radio or sat phone service, he was worried about what kind of condition he might find the men in. A five mile trek to call for additional help would not be a good idea.

However, convincing Jake to land on Meadowlark wasn't an easy task. Jake wasn't an idiot and knew the risks he was taking when Hank proposed the idea. But after much coaxing and convincing him that it was a much better idea for their search and rescue, Jake gave in.

So now they were flying in the direction of Meadowlark Lake. They had circled above the first drop off point, and Hank wasn't surprised the guys weren't there flagging the plane down. It wasn't like Scott to miss the ride back, much less twice in a row.

Hank stared out the small window of the plane down into the dense forest. A knot of apprehension had curled itself up in his stomach, but he wasn't sure what it was about this rescue trip that had him so on edge.

Maybe it was the realization he hadn't been up this far into the woods for a long time.

Back when he'd been a kid, before the area was restricted, his father would bring him out here to hunt. This deep in the woods, this far from civilization, it was easy to track the animals.

Hank closed his eyes against the memory of the last hunting trip he'd been on with his father. That was not a trip he wanted to remember, but the thoughts came anyway, hitting him as hard as the winds were whipping the plane.

The snow was covered over by a layer of fresh ice that crunched under his heavy hiking boots with every step. Hank hefted his rifle up over his shoulder and tried to find a comfortable place for it to rest. He was really still too small for such a big gun, but his father believed that he could use it, and Hank always wanted to make his father proud regardless of what facts might argue.

"Not long now, buddy!" Hank's father called back to him. "We're almost to the spot."

Hank smiled and nodded at his father. He loved the hunting trips, just him and his hero, out in the wilderness. There was nothing better, no matter how it ended, kill or not.

Before they reached the spot where they would camouflage themselves from the animals, Hank's father did his usual sweep of the land to make sure things were safe. He looked for any indication that there might be larger predators nearby, like fresh wolf or bear tracks, or any sign of an injured and bleeding animal that could draw a scavenging predator in to finish the job. Hank's father was smart enough to know.

Hank squatted down on the ground to wait out his father's sweep. He picked up a stick and traced lines through the snow. At first, he drew random shapes and squiggles, not paying attention to what he was doing. His eyes followed his father through a large circle around the area.

When his father went out of sight, Hank turned his eyes to the snow in front of him and started drawing the shape of a bear. He was never very good at drawing, but that didn't matter when you were using a stick in the snow and when your only goal was to entertain yourself, not others. He hummed a song he'd just learned in school as he finished the pointy fangs on the mouth, and then looked up when he realized he couldn't hear his father's boots crunching through the snow anymore.

He must have been making a big sweep. Before he could call out against his better judgment, his stick hit something under the snow.

Hank leaned over to get a better look at whatever it was and smacked at the thing with the end of the stick. Snow fell away, revealing something dark brown beneath the white surface. He reached down and pushed it with a gloved finger. It was solid.

He dropped the stick and brushed more snow away with his hands until the sole of a boot was sticking out from the ground. Hank sat back on his haunches, wondering in bewildered awe how someone could leave their shoe out in the cold in the middle of the wilderness. He brushed back a little more snow and realized the boot was connected to something; it still had a frozen foot inside. A foot that was still attached to a leg.

Hank opened his mouth to scream for his father, but the older man dashed out from behind a tree a little ways away, running towards him.

Hank stood, visibly scared now and trembling; he'd never seen his father run so hard before. Not with a look like that on his face.

His father ran past him, grabbing his hand as he went and yanking him alongside. "Run, Hank!"

Hank obeyed, stumbling behind, doing all he could to keep up with his father. A terrible roar filled the air behind them, and Hank tried to turn around to pinpoint the sound with an image, but his father tugged his hand and forced him to run faster.

"Don't look behind you! Just go! Run! We're almost there! Almost there!"

"Almost there! I'll take you up to the lake," Jake yelled above the roar of the engine, pulling Hank out of his memory with those words. He was grateful. He gave Jake a thumbs-up.

"I'm happy to wait for you there, but I don't want to wander on any further into the forest." Jake looked at Hank out of the corner of his eye. "And I don't think you should either."

Hank looked away, pretending that Jake's last few words were drowned out by the engines and the wind, though the words still echoed in his head louder than both.

It wasn't a hard ruse to pull off. He could see storm clouds rolling in off to the east, Jake's attention was fully on them now.

An unexpected gust of wind caught the left wing of the plane and tilted them dangerously to the side.

Hank used his arms to brace himself against the roof, but his stomach was doing flips. When the plane hit an air pocket and dropped a few feet down, Hank was sure he would've thrown up if he'd had any time to eat breakfast before leaving.

He could see Jake wrestling with the controls, but things didn't seem to be getting any better. Any pilot other than Jake and Hank would have been worried about getting himself there, much less bringing anyone back with them. They tilted to the other side and lost a few more feet of altitude; check that, Hank was still worried.

Then they leveled off, and Hank laughed in relief.

"Picked a hell of a day to come up here, Hank," Jake said through grit teeth. Then he laughed as well.

Both men echoed sighs of relief as they saw the lake coming into view.

The clouds hadn't gotten close enough to cover it yet, and the surface was still shimmering with the reflection of a thousand rays of sunlight. But the wind had whipped up the usually calm lake into a churning cauldron, white froth capping the tiny waves as they sloshed back and forth ravenously.

"Can you land on that?" Hank shouted over the engine.

Jake looked wounded, clicking his tongue though Hank couldn't hear. "Watch me."

He began to descend, the wind whistling steady warnings through any holes that it could find in the body of the plane.

Hank's ears popped when they were a few hundred feet above the ground. He forcefully yawned to help them along should they need a second time and rubbed his hands together, trying to create some warmth as the temperature dropped. It would probably be a warm day once he got outside and into the open woods, but the sun hadn't chased away the night chill yet, and it was freezing in Jake's plane.

The lake grew darker as it rose up to meet them, and the sun disappeared behind an ominous grey cloud.

When he looked down again, the plane was mere feet above the water. It set down with a soft plop, and the waves began to rock them back and forth. The propeller slowed, and Jake steered towards the edge of the lake. A minute later, the twin pontoons under the plane bumped up against the sandy bottom.

Jake shut down the engine and looked at Hank. "Can I land on that, he says?"

Hank slapped him on the shoulder amiably. "How could I ever doubt you?" He opened his door with a groan of metal and swung out of the plane into waist deep water. Hank waded out of the cold lake as fast as he could, already surveying the area for signs of a campsite or, more importantly, campers.

Nothing out of place that he could see. The sunlight filtered down through the trees, as it always did. The air felt crisp, cold, as it always had. Everything looked ordinary.

Everything he could see.

There was something off, though. A feeling Hank couldn't shake or identify.

Jake stopped next to Hank on the bank and shivered. "It's quiet up here. Too quiet. How long do you suppose it's been since anyone has been up this far?" he muttered. "Other than Scott and the boys? Feels almost sinister, don't it? You think they're alright?"

Hank let out a long breath. Jake had voiced his thoughts exactly, but Hank didn't want to show his nervousness.

"Ha! Sinister?" Hank laughed. "You've been watching too many of those damned horror movies, Jake. They've gone to your head. I'm sure the boys are just stuck up a tree somewhere with no radio and an angry bear on their butts."

Jake shook his head and sat down on a rock. "Off you go then." He waved towards the woods. "I'll give you a few hours, at most. But if you hear my engine hollering that means I'm leaving soon, Hank, with or without ya'. You better get yourself back here quick smart, because I won't wait." Jake pulled out a pipe and lit it.

Hank nodded and walked towards the woods. He wasn't afraid of them. He knew these woods like the back of his hand, and there was no chance he would get lost. But that feeling, that tickling sensation of dread that some undefinable thing was wrong up here wouldn't leave him.

To the untrained ear, the forest would have sounded silent as Hank's heavy boots tramped through the underbrush. But there was plenty to hear for a man who lived and breathed the outdoors. He could pick up the faint roar of the river in the distance, the shuffling and scratching of tiny feet running along tree limbs, and the rustle of fallen leaves being blown along by the wind. Hank kicked fallen branches aside as he walked, his eyes scanning the ground for...what?

Some sign of Scott and his friends, that much he knew. But all he could say for sure was that they were in the restricted area, which didn't narrow things down much. He didn't know where they were among these miles of land. His odds of finding them were slim, but he had to try. For Ace. For Beth.

The sound of the river grew louder as he followed the sound, his vague sense of dread swelling with the increase of the sound. It wasn't as easy to ignore that tingle at the back of his neck now that he was alone as it had been with someone else around.

The wind picked up, and Hank had to lean against it to keep moving forward. It felt like an unseen hand pushing him back, trying to turn him away from the path he was on before it was too late. They were in for some wild weather on the return trip, that was for sure, and Hank didn't fancy being caught out in the woods once the storm center hit. He hoped he'd find something, check that, someone, quick.

Hank was suddenly aware of a scent on the wind that didn't belong in the line of smells contained in the forest, and he froze. Mixed in with the standard smells of pine trees, dirt, animal musk, and other fresh forest scents, was something else completely out of place. He sniffed the air, the smell triggering a blurred image of something vaguely familiar. But just like the elusive sense of fear preying at the back of his mind, he couldn't isolate the reclusive memory.

He climbed up onto a large fallen log with a grunt of effort to steady himself, still searching his mind for the last time he'd smelled that undeniably familiar scent. Hank jumped down onto the ground with a thud and a small explosion of dust, bending his knees to absorb both impact and noise.

He didn't straighten right away, but scanned the small clearing from a crouch to keep himself hidden.

He'd found something not far-off. And what he found didn't look good.

The bedraggled remains of a tent sat on the far side of the large clearing. Vicious gnashing of the wind had folded the material over and collapsed it inward on itself. A few yards away, an almost unrecognizable second tent lay broken and torn to shreds, nothing but a pile of blue material and some twisted support rods. Camp chairs were strewn across the clearing, lying broken in pieces and tangled on the ground. Swirls of hazy ash and charred logs sat in a forgotten fire-pit.

Hank stood up, the dread no longer confined to a prickle on the back of his neck but running up and down his spine; his heart began to pound in his chest. No way had the wind caused all of this damage, not when the supports were torn in half and the metal was snapped.

He walked through the wasteland of debris, kicking his feet through the stray piles of leaves to uncover thermal vests, pants, a single shoe, and a few pieces of what once were fishing rods. Scott and the boys had been here once, but they'd either left in a hell of a hurry or weren't able to leave at all. Hank paused and ran a hand through his hair, unsure of what his next move should be.

He could go back now and organize a bigger search party to make locating the boys easier. But he didn't have any answers for Ace and Beth, and they would not be happy about that. If there was anything he didn't need right now, it was the hysterical pair of a father and fiancée on his tail. He'd better look a little more to see what else he could figure out. The boys could be hurt or unconscious within yards of their abandoned camp.

Hank didn't consider the other options.

A flash of red at the edge of the clearing caught his eye, and he walked over to it. As he got closer, he identified it as the remains of a flannel hunting shirt, the red checker pattern a stark contrast against the browns and greens of the forest floor.

As he stopped in front of it, Hank saw that something was strange about the pattern on the shirt. He didn't want to look, didn't want to confirm his fears, but he had to follow through. He scuffed at the ground with his boot, digging it slightly out from under the dirt. It moved stiffly, not free-flowing and loose as cloth should have been. Hank crouched down and saw that the shirt was drenched in a dark color different from the red of the shirt...blood. The blood had hardened and dried to a dark brown, explaining why he hadn't seen it at first.

Hank looked out into the trees to see if the blood had come from above him and covered his mouth with his hand to swallow the bitterness rising in his throat. A severed leg, still attached to a boot, sat a few feet away from him among the branches. Hank felt his eyes widen as he took in the carnage. The body part had been hidden by trees when he was in the clearing, but here, at the edge of the trees, it dangled in plain sight.

He walked towards the leg with careful steps, glancing left and right as he went in case the predator was still around the clearing. He froze when his eyes fell on the body of a man, propped up against a tree trunk. He couldn't tear his eyes away. It was Marcus, and he seemed to be staring right at him, his eyes wide, open but unseeing.

Hank almost ran to the young man, but then his face contorted in terror as he took in the full scope of the devastation before him. Marcus' body had been torn apart. His chest was ripped open as if it had been pried by a vice, and the only thing left intact was the face, twisted in horror.

Hank staggered back a step and felt his boot bump up against something buried in the leaves. He kicked aside the debris to reveal an arm ripped off at the shoulder. The frozen hand was palm up, the fingers locked in a clawed position thanks to rigor mortis, as though the man had been trying to defend himself at the end.

Hank stared at the snapped shard of bone protruding from the shredded limb, and a wave of nausea swept over him. He had to get out of these woods soon. He'd figure out a way to tell Ace what he saw once he was gone. He was turning to head back toward the lake when a twig snapped.

His head whipped around toward the source of the noise. His eyes narrowed, and he stared hard into the trees. The storm clouds were rolling in now faster than before, and the forest was getting darker every second. He couldn't see more than twenty yards away from him.

Something rustled behind him. He shut his eyes and listened to the forest, picking out sounds and isolating their directions. Gradually, he was able to pick out rustling leaves and soft footsteps all around him.

A long, eerie howl split the air, and Hank's eyes snapped open with certainty.

Wolves.

Hank swore under his breath. He must have wandered too close to their den during his inspection, distracted by the destruction around the campsite.

A large stone-grey wolf with tattered fur, dark eyes, and swishing tail slowly stepped out from between the tree line, its eyes fixed on Hank. Dark, congealed blood covered its snout, and it bared its long, sharp, yellowing teeth in a silent snarl to protect its scavenging.

Hank caught sight of another wolf, probably a mate, coming up behind it to flank him. He turned his head, trying not to make any sudden movements, and watched as more and more wolves appeared from out of the wood surroundings. Their paws made whispered, graceful movements over the forest floor, and all of them were covered in blood.

Hank doubted these creatures were responsible for tearing Marcus to pieces, but they'd likely been scavenging off his body, and now he was threatening to steal it.

The wolves moved closer, somehow signaled by the alpha male to close in on Hank. Those closest to him lowered their bodies to the ground and slid forward with ears flattened against their heads, muscles tensing. A chorus of low growls went up, and Hank raised his hands in a show of submission.

He found the alpha again, the big grey one he'd seen first, and locked eyes with it. The growls were getting louder, and a couple of the wolves were snapping their jaws at him, snarling. He fought the urge to step back from the one in front of him, knowing that would only take him closer to the ones behind.

Hank's fingers brushed over the sidearm holstered at his hip, an M&P 9mm from Smith & Wesson. He was too smart to come into a situation without protection. It came with reinforced polymer chassis, superior ergonomics, ambidextrous controls, and was loaded with a seventeen-round clip of 9mm bullets, bullets he would not hesitate to use if he could only get it in hand. He had a carbine rifle slung across his back that had more stopping power. That was his best chance to fend off an attack by the wolves, but by the time he pulled the rifle into position, it'd be too late.

Hank calmed his mind and spun in a slow circle, hand on the 9mm, counting the wolves surrounding him. Ten. If they did attack, and it was all but certain that they would if he waited much longer, he knew he could take down a few before the rest of the pack was on him.

His eyes landed on the alpha again and narrowed in concentration. If he took that big beast down, it might make the others hesitate long enough for him to get away.

Hank scanned his surroundings, looking for an escape route. There was a large tree nearby, with a thick, sturdy trunk and plenty of low, thick branches perfect for supporting a human's weight. Two wolves were pacing on either side of it, but if Hank could get a shot or two off, take one down or at least distract them, he could make it up there. Once he was in the tree, he'd be safe until Jake came looking for him.

A light rain started to fall, and Hank knew it wouldn't be long before those dark clouds unleashed a downpour. Not the best time to be stuck up a tree, but it would be better than being gnawed on by a pack of wolves.

He eyed the alpha; it was still staring at him, not growling or snarling like the others, just staring. He seemed to know that Hank had no chance of outrunning their pack.

And Hank knew that he didn't have any choice but to try.

He lowered himself into a crouch and steeled his nerves, getting his legs ready to run faster than they'd ever run before now. He tugged on his sidearm, pulling it halfway out of the holster.

The large grey wolf slid closer in a movement so quick Hank almost didn't see it. The wolf lowered its head and snapped its jaws, saliva flying from its fangs. Hank took a deep breath and let it out slowly, then sprang forward, ripping his gun out of the holster and dashing for the tree as if he were in an Olympic race for his life. He brought his pistol up to fire at the alpha, but before he could get off a round, the wolves yelped and scurried away from him.

Hank stopped and watched the wolf pack scatter through the trees. Had they given up their hunt so easily? He'd never seen such behavior in wolves before. They were nefarious animals, relentless when they were onto their prey.

He craned his neck to watch the last few stragglers darting away with tails between their legs.

"Wow." Hank shook his head and slid the pistol back into its place. "What the fuck was that about?"

He waited until he could no longer hear the wolves thrashing through the bushes. Then he waited a bit longer to be sure they weren't going to return. Hank wouldn't put it past the wolves to pull back and wait until he was in a more vulnerable position before reassembling.

But he'd never be much more vulnerable than standing in the center of a wolf pack, all alone. He should be dead right now. This didn't make sense.

The sound of a crackle nearby spooked him, so he drew his pistol again. Hank quieted his breathing to listen for the direction of the sound that had startled him.

Then it hit him. No sound could have startled him. The forest was silent. There were no sounds at all.

Birds were no longer chirping even in the distant trees, the shrill calls of insects no longer filled the air, even the breeze had stopped moving through the trees.

Fuck. He's here.

A deep dread drenched Hank's body, the hairs on the back of his neck standing on end, chills crawling up and down his spine. He felt a quaver coming into his hands and forced them to be still.

The wolves were gone, but he knew that he was still being watched, and the predator was far more dangerous this time.

He turned in a slow circle, eyes alert for danger, trigger finger tense. His gaze fell on what was left of Marcus. Had Marcus and the others felt this same sensation before—

He cut the thought short. Thinking like that wasn't going to get him out of here.

Hank closed his eyes and took a deep breath. After a few moments, he managed to slow his breathing to something approaching a normal rate. He searched the forest with his eyes and ears, but found nothing.

Part of him wanted to bolt, to sprint back to Jake's plane as fast as his legs would carry him. But he couldn't move. Not with the forest quiet as death, when the slightest crunch of dirt beneath his feet could be his undoing. He had to identify the threat, select the best escape route, and proceed with caution.

Still not a sound.

Angry rumbles of thunder rolled in the distance, echoing through the trees. The rain fell harder. More than a shower now, but not a downpour. Yet.

Hank let the sound of the rain and the thunder wash over him. He listened past those sounds, into the silence.

And then it wasn't silent. There was breathing close by him. Heavy, ragged breathing, no more than a dozen yards behind him, shuddered beyond the noise of the rain. For a brief instant, he thought it could be another of the boys, maybe even Scott, wounded and in need of help.

But a wounded man would attract wolves to him, not send them scattering in a fit of fear.

Another chill swept over him, and a wave of nausea hit his stomach. Hank opened his eyes and turned his head to look behind him, dreading what he would find.

Nothing.

The storm clouds were closer now, and the rain was falling hard, hard enough to sting his bare skin. If he didn't get back to Jake soon, they'd have a hard time taking off and getting back in one piece.

Hank lifted his foot from where it had been attached like a construction beam to the ground and took a step. His eyes were focused on his surroundings like an eagle hunting for prey, his ears finely tuned to every sound. But even so, there was still nothing.

Thunder crashed overhead and Hank jumped out of his concentrated state, spinning around and aiming his gun at nothing.

He shook his head and kept moving, finger unwinding from the trigger as the gun returned to its holster. He'd lost the sound of the breathing among the rainfall and was beginning to doubt if he'd really heard it at all. Maybe it was just his terrified mind playing tricks on him out here in the wilderness. He had to get out of these woods now, while things were safe for them to take off in the plane. When he couldn't trust his own ears on his own, he was in trouble.

Then he heard it again.

Thick, laden breathing, like a huge dog panting. Right behind him, so close he could almost feel the warmth on his neck.

He spun around and saw nothing. This time his finger stayed on the trigger.

The rain was pouring now, the thunder crashing again and again. The wind was back, whipping through the trees and tugging at his clothes in every direction.

He convinced himself that the sound was only the wind, scanning the woods around him, when he froze at the sight of two red eyes staring out at him from the sheets of rain.

Hank blinked away rain drops spattering his vision, but the eyes were still there, nine feet above the wet earth. He wanted to close his eyes, make the image go away, but the fierce eyes held him in an invisible grip.

Every muscle in Hank's body was taut to the point of pain. He remembered the pistol in his hand and started to raise it, finger quivering on the trigger. A flash of lightening lit up the woods, and Hank saw the beast in that split instant. It was huge, covered in thick fur, and judging by the spark in its eyes, angry.

Unbidden, the pistol fell from his quaking hand and hit the ground at the same moment a deafening crash of thunder shook the world, making the resulting shot silent.

Hank took off. Every bit of training that told him not to show fear, to stand his ground in the face of an attacking wild animal, was overruled by an overwhelming desire to get the hell away from that thing.

Branches scratched at his face, his legs ached, his lungs burned, but he plowed ahead. He flew through the clearing that held the shattered campsite and heard a roar behind him, gaining volume. Or was it another crash of thunder? No, the roar came again, and there was no mistaking the fury in it. Not thunder.

Just on the other side of the clearing, Hank's boot caught on something in mid-sprint and he fell headlong into the dirt, his arms not able to come up in time to soften the fall.

He lifted his head and looked behind him, ignoring the pain from his scrapes. No sign of the creature, but he couldn't see more than seven or eight yards in this rain. He lowered his gaze and saw another pair of hiking boots, a nail head in the heel, lying next to his own with the toes pointed at the dark sky.

Hank scrambled to his feet, gaping at a second body in a condition just as bad as the first. The man's face had been crushed beyond recognition, but Hank knew it was Frank because of his boots. The boy wore those boots everywhere, and the nail was his trademark.

He couldn't tear his eyes away from Frank's pulverized head, much as he wanted to look anywhere else. What could do that to a man?

Another roar reached his ears, and Hank had his answer.

He ran on without looking back; there was nothing he could do for Frank, and he held out little hope that any of the others could have escaped the thing chasing him through the trees. Or, for that matter, that he could escape it.

Hank crashed out of the woods and onto the beach of the lake to see Jake already in the plane, engine running.

He waved his arms, screaming as he ran, "I'm here, I'm here! Let's go!"

The passenger side door slid open, and Hank threw himself inside, scrambling to slam the door behind him.

Jake was already turning the plane away from the beach and getting ready for take-off. "Bear?" he shouted over the engine.

Hank nodded, deciding that was as good an explanation as any until they were airborne and he had more time to talk. He looked out the window, squinting into the rain. He couldn't see anything, but the thing could be anywhere. "Go, just go!" Hank yelled, saving explanations for later when he had the time.

He leaned his head back against the seat and shut his eyes until he could tell the plane was in the air, above the trees. Then he opened his eyes and forced his shoulders to relax.

Hank felt Jake's glances as he flew, but the pilot didn't say anything. Hank knew he must look half dead and conversation was probably not the first item on his agenda.

Jake got them clear of the storm and leaned back for contact. "Hank, what the hell happened back there? Your face is all cut up. And is that blood on your boots? What had you so goddamn in a hurry?"

Hank put his face in his hands and felt his whole body begin to shake.

"I found the boys," Hank said, massaging his scalp, the images flashing before him. "What's left of them."

Jake inhaled sharply. "What happened to them? They're all dead?"

Hank nodded, still hiding his face in his hands. "I found two, but from the looks of their campsite, I don't think any of them made it. And God help me, I have to tell everyone."

Chapter Twenty-Three

The Cover-up

The storm that had drenched Hank while he was in the woods was now following him back to Redwood like an omen of the news he had to deliver to everyone.

Jake, as Hank expected, hadn't said a word after Hank delivered the news to him. That was fine with Hank at first, but the torn limbs and smashed skulls from the woods were piling higher and higher in Hank's mind, and by the time they'd been in the air for half an hour, he couldn't take the silence anymore.

He shouted to the pilot. "Bear attack," but his voice was lost in the relentless buzz of the engine.

Jake brought the plane lower without having a clue Hank had said anything. The silence stretched on, and Hank was desperate for Jake to say something, anything, that would take his mind off what he'd seen back there and the conversation he'd have to have after they landed. He had to talk to someone.

Maybe he should have been practicing what he would say. He didn't want to be standing in front of Ace mumbling like an idiot. He needed to break the news gracefully.

But no words came.

What words existed to tell your oldest friend that his only son had died in such a horrific way? His mind was filled with the images of those poor boys ripped to pieces. The fact that he hadn't found all five bodies meant nothing. He knew what they were up against, and no one could have survived that attack, it was impossible.

Hank felt constrained inside the body of the plane for the whole ride back, so much so he readjusted the seatbelt until his hands were sore. It was as though he was stuck up in limbo, trapped in the air and unable to go forward or backward.

By the time Redwood came into view, a tremor shook Hank's hands.

The front edge of the storm was just reaching the town when they landed, so when Hank got his feet back on the ground, he stood in the rain for a few seconds. The cold water didn't do anything for the shaking in his hands, but it did remind him that all of this was real. As much as he might want to, he couldn't avoid the responsibility before him. Jake offered to accompany him to Ace's, but Hank knew this was something he needed to do alone. He wasn't even sure why Jake had offered. Maybe it was more out of respect than a true willingness.

So, thanking Jake again for his help, he said goodbye to the man and took refuge in his truck.

He was still sitting there, the radio static fizzing, his hands gripping the shaking steering wheel, ten minutes after Jake had pulled away.

Hank banged his hands against the steering wheel. Hard. When that didn't make him feel any better, he did it again. And again. But the images of the dead boys were still in his head, and nothing would shake them loose. So he threw the truck in gear and drove off.

The drive to Ace's house was even more cramped than the plane ride. With each mile, his hands shook worse, and a knot grew in his throat until he wasn't sure he'd be able to speak at all. It got so bad that he had to pull over halfway there, dry heave for a minute, and get a hold of himself to avoid driving off the road.

When his hands were finally back under control and his breathing was at a rate that approached normal, he pulled back onto the road.

The storm had arrived in force by then, and he could barely see the road even with his wipers on full speed. With every flash of lightning he shut his eyes, afraid to see those glowing red eyes staring at him from the trees along the road. In every crash of thunder, he heard massive footsteps or rumbling growls.

Despite driving well under the speed limit to compensate for the storm, he reached Ace's neighborhood too quickly to find the right words. Then the realization that it was still only late afternoon had hit him. Ace wouldn't be here; he'd be at work. But then Ace's driveway came into sight, and his red Dodge pickup sat there.

Hank wanted to be relieved that Ace was home, but he wasn't. Maybe a small part of him had been hoping Ace would be at work now. That would at least give him a few more hours to decide what to say, to make up excuses about why he hadn't come to visit his friend at work to tell him the news. He sat in the truck trying to compile his thoughts, but torn limbs and crushed faces were still all his mind could see. After wasting a few more minutes with no success, he gave up trying to prepare a speech. There were no right words for a situation like this. He'd just go in and trust his instincts to kick in when the moment was right.

The front door swung open when Hank stepped onto the porch. Ace's wide frame filled the doorway and stepped aside as Hank got closer.

No words were exchanged. Ace moved to the kitchen, and Hank followed.

A few steps in, Hank remembered he was soaking wet from standing outside. He mumbled an apology for his wet clothes and muddy shoes, but Ace waved it off.

They stopped at opposite ends of the kitchen table. Hank couldn't bring himself to sit, and Ace didn't offer him a chair, anyway. Hank looked around the room in a panic when he realized that Laura and Beth might be here waiting for news as well. But there was no sign of them, and he was grateful for that. Talking to a friend who was a man seemed easier than talking to a fiancée or mother. This wasn't the kind of conversation he wanted to have with either of them present.

"I should be the one to tell you this," Hank said. He rubbed the back of his neck and tried to force himself to make eye contact across the table, but found himself looking past Ace instead. His eyes found a family picture hanging on the wall, and the knot returned to his throat. Seeing Scott standing next to his father, smiling, his arm tucked tightly around Beth's waist, intensified his heartache. The young man in that picture looked so happy, so confident. Hank silently hoped his death had been quick.

Ace turned and followed Hank's eyes to the picture. He leaned over and put a palm to his forehead, forming a brace between the table and his head.

"Scott's not okay," Ace whispered, his voice choked. "Is he?"

Hank wanted to say yes, to get it over with, but he couldn't reduce the reality of it all to that one word. Hank exhaled. He should have known that Ace would guess his son's fate before he even said anything. He made uneasy fists that searched for a comfortable position, loosening and tightening like pulsing hearts. Should he sit down at the table or continue standing? Would he look like an ass if he decided to sit now?

"A bear." The words tumbled out of his mouth like an echo from the plane just now catching up with him. Too many things were catching up with him lately.

No more words would come. He suddenly wished he had rehearsed at least a few lines and desperately wished that it had been a bear that killed Scott and his friends.

"Bullshit." Ace's hand fell to the table like a hammer. A ceramic candle holder shook, causing the candle within to tumble down to the table.

Hank stared at the fallen candle to avoid the man's gaze and waited for him to continue.

Ace's voice was furious, but there were tears welling up in his eyes, reflecting the light coming from the ceiling. "He was too experienced for that, Hank. Scott would never—" He choked up, either in anger or pain, Hank couldn't tell.

Hank shook his head at himself for what he was about to say. He didn't want to do this, but it was his job. It was the only way to keep more people from going back up there. He swallowed the bile that was trying to rise up his throat.

"You're in denial." He tried to say it softly, in a whisper, but it came out sounding like a growl.

Ace's mouth moved, like he was trying to speak but couldn't form the words. His jaw quivered, and his eyes started to bulge.

Hank braced himself for the outburst that he knew was coming. His lie had undoubtedly killed their friendship, but it had to be done.

Then Ace's face went flat and his eyes cold. Not a muscle on his body moved.

"Get out of my house, Hank." Ace didn't make eye contact, but he spoke with a finality that left no room for discussion.

Hank hesitated. He couldn't bring Scott back but he could give his friend the dignity of knowing the truth about how his son died. He could save the only true friendship he had left, if he could only speak now.

He opened his mouth.

But shut it again a heartbeat later.

Ace's chest rose in a deep breath and Hank took a step back from the table, both hands up.

"Okay, Ace. I'm going."

*

Hank sat on his porch and watched Beth's car come over the horizon. The sun was behind him, and it would be shining straight into her eyes now.

He'd been waiting for her ever since leaving Ace's house. He'd drained his drink hours ago, the empty cup still in his hand because he couldn't bring himself to go inside until this was done. He didn't know when she would come, but he knew she would, and he was determined to be right here, ready to meet her.

Her car eased to a stop, too carefully, too smoothly. Through the windshield he could see her with both hands on the wheel and her head high to keep the glaring sunlight from falling directly on her face.

She got out of the car with clear control over herself, every motion careful and deliberate. It pained Hank to see the usually lively girl so contained. There was no bounce in her step; even her long auburn hair was plastered flat by the pounding rain. But he was proud of her for having the strength to come and hear Scott's fate for herself. Even though he would give anything to avoid this talk.

"Good for you, Beth," he whispered under his breath.

"Hank," she said as she stepped onto the porch.

He stood, set his glass on the railing, and stepped forward from the porch to meet her.

"I'm sorry."

She didn't flinch or acknowledge his apology. "I want to know the truth."

He wrung his hands and sighed. "You heard it from Ace."

"Ace says you're wrong."

Hank broke eye contact for a moment but forced himself to look back at her. "I know what he says."

He wanted to take a few steps closer and hug the poor girl, but he tried to match her strength and remain steady. She reminded him of how he had acted at his wife's visitation so many years ago. Stoic. Feet flat and bolted to the ground. Actually, she was probably doing a better job of remaining under control than he had. The thought made him disgusted with himself. How could he deny her the truth when he knew this tragedy to be his own as well?

"What was out there, Hank? And don't tell me a bear. I know it wasn't a bear."

Something they don't even whisper about anymore. A force of nature that works in obscurity and can't be reasoned with. Something I swore I'd never think of again.

Everything from the woods flashed through his mind again. The angry red eyes boring into his soul, the thick, humid breathing, the deafening roar. A chill ran down his spine as lightning flashed and, for a brief moment, he realized how lucky he was to be standing in front of Beth and talking to her at all.

The thought brought a fresh wave of unpleasantness to his throat. Why was he the one standing here instead of Scott? What did his good intentions matter when those young men were dead?

"It was a bear." He injected all the confidence he could muster into the words. "I know you don't want to hear it, because you don't want to believe it, but it was a bear. I know you don't believe bears can act like that, but that's just because we don't have bears like that down here."

Beth rolled her eyes and leveled a detached stare at Hank.

He sighed heavily, his shoulders rising and falling with the weight of the necessary lie. "Beth, those animals up there are uncivilized. They aren't used to being around humans. Not like the ones down here. Down here, all the animals have seen humans before. They know how to steer clear and keep to themselves so we can share the land with each other. Up there it's different. Those animals are fiercely territorial when someone shows up where they aren't supposed to be. They haven't interacted with humans in half a century or more, and they're savages. Most animals down here would never attack a human because they see us as the highest predators on the food chain, but up there, we're fair game."

"I don't buy that." Beth's voice was smooth, not a hint of emotion to crack it. "Scott would have been aware of that and he'd take the precautions to make sure they were safe."

"Maybe, maybe not." Hank swallowed again. Who was he to put Scott down when he knew the boy had done nothing wrong? "When I was up there looking for them, I was almost attacked by a pack of wolves. I couldn't tell you the last time there was a wolf attack down here. It just doesn't happen. But they will attack an unfamiliar presence that invades their territory. I'm afraid that's what happened with the guys. They must have invaded the territory of a bear, even if they didn't realize."

She nodded and, for a split second, Hank thought he'd won her over and everything would go away.

But she wasn't finished.

"This won't end until you talk to someone, Hank." Beth turned towards her car but didn't leave. "It doesn't have to be me. But you have to tell the truth to someone. The truth is going to come out, because I won't stop pushing until I get it."

She tilted her head up again, and Hank knew he would be a fool to doubt her. She would keep fighting him for the rest of her life if she had to. Beth stared into his eyes for another moment, and then got into her car.

Hank understood now that she hadn't been keeping her chin up in the car to hide her eyes from the sun. She had been stopping any tears from escaping, fighting gravity itself, and he saw, as she got into the car, that she'd eventually lose that battle.

Hank waited until Beth drove away, and then, wondering how he was going to recover from this tragedy, went inside, wishing that he wouldn't hear from her again but knowing this was far from over.

The empty glass on the banister caught the reflection of Beth driving off on one side and Hank slinking behind a screen door on the other, the images stretching, wrapping around the cup until they collided at both ends.

Hank tried to shut his eyes and make everything go away, but every time he shut his eyes the creature was there. The red eyes, the contorted faces, the torn limbs – everything about his visit to the forest was lodged so deeply in his mind, he doubted he'd ever sleep again. His mind was replaying every detail of his search over and over without pause. And with every repetition, the chills ran through his spine and the hairs on the back of his neck stood on end. The creature's eyes burned in his brain, eyes more human than animal. Eyes of a predator, hunting its prey and killing for –

For what?

Hank didn't know why the creature killed. Every detail of Frank and Marcus' bodies was burned into his mind, so he analyzed them.

Was the creature killing for fun? For sport?

It wasn't killing for food because it hadn't eaten the bodies, merely left them pulverized.

Hank stopped himself and shook his head. This wasn't a puzzle or some crime show on television. These were real people, friends of his, he was talking about. His chest and the cold reality sunk in even deeper.

He let his body slide slowly to the floor and sat with his head between his knees. Tears wouldn't come, but his chest heaved in powerful sobs like he was hyperventilating.

"Damn it, I'm too old for this shit," Hank said aloud. He got control of his body, but the weight of the situation continued to push down on his chest. Hank stared through the blurred window, up at the dark sky, which was still dumping buckets of rain down to the Earth. He wished a mudslide would sweep him and his whole house away. He wanted to be done with this horrifying reality.

But he knew it was far from over.

Chapter Twenty-Four

The Recruit

Ace pushed open the door to Rudy's Bar, crowding the dim room with the intruding wash of daylight from outside. He let the door shut behind him and paused to let his eyes adjust to both the light and the customer base currently in the bar. Ace saw nothing but a bunch of sideways glances and dirty looks.

Ace knew he belonged in the Iron Pub, not Rudy's. It was an old quirk of the town, older than Ace himself, and the intangibility of the fact didn't make it any less real. Some folks drank at the Iron Pub, others drank at Rudy's, and if you were a customer of one, venturing into the other was like a betrayal for your home away from home.

So when Ace Huntington of all people, the most loyal customer of the Iron Pub anyone knew, stepped into Rudy's, it attracted more than a little attention.

Ace's instincts kicked in without him even having to try; he almost turned around and walked out of the unfamiliar place. But his political connections and network of favor-trading couldn't help Scott now. So he swallowed his pride and stepped further into the bar, driven by a desperate and unfamiliar feeling of helplessness.

He looked around the bar, but it was too dark to see any faces clearly. Besides, he'd never met the man he was looking for.

All he knew was that Scott's main competitor in the wilderness guide business did most of his business here. But he didn't know the man's name or even the name of his company, so it wasn't much to go on as far as leads. As far as he knew, the organization didn't even have a proper name or phone number. It wasn't even something you could look up online. It was Ace's understanding that he worked on a cash-only basis. Everything was done under the table, which was strictly against Ace's business sense.

Normally, leaning with his own instincts, he might want to report business practices like that, but today he didn't care how the business was done. Today he was only concerned about one thing – finding the guy who ran it.

But that wouldn't be as easy as it sounded. He was pretty sure the guy's name was Gabe. Or maybe Jacob, something like that.

The only things Ace knew about the guy were random facts Scott had mentioned in passing comments. He was older than Scott by five or six years, which was probably a sore spot since Scott was more financially successful. But according to Scott, the guy had survived several encounters with bears and at least one run-in with a pack of wolves. Ace didn't remember all the details of the story, but he knew Scott had been impressed that he'd made it out alive — and with his whole crew.

The only reason that story stood out in Ace's mind now was because he knew this Gabe character had two long scars running from his forehead to his chin, probably from one of those encounters. Those scars were the only chance he had of finding him in here.

And finding him was the only chance he had of finding Scott.

Ace knew that Gabe's underhanded business tactics annoyed Scott, but he'd never tried to shut his rival down. Ace had always been secretly proud of Scott for not being petty or cutthroat, but he couldn't say he wouldn't have done the opposite. Now that Ace needed Gabe, he was thankful Scott hadn't inherited his less merciful business strategies.

Ace thought about shouting Gabe's name out, but since he wasn't even sure that was his name, he decided for a slightly more subtle approach.

"I'm looking for someone who can take me up to Spider Lake, into the restricted area. Anyone here that can do that?" Ace spoke loud enough for his voice to carry over the conversations and music filling the bar.

He'd imagined conversations pausing mid-sentence, music falling silent, and heads turning towards him. But all he got was a few more irritated glances. Ace was used to people giving him their full attention, whether he asked for it or not. It wasn't that he expected it; that was just the way it was. Being flat out ignored like this was making him feel even more unwelcome and making him understand how little natural rules applied here.

No one stood up to respond to his question, so Ace moved farther inside to grab a seat at the bar, feeling defeated and trying to reason out the next best course of action.

Scott had told him once or twice that Gabe secured most of his clients through chatting with strangers here, so Ace had assumed it would be fairly easy to rope him into a conversation. He sat down at the bar. He'd give it a few minutes and see if someone, anyone, approached him with some information. If not, well, he'd have to find another way.

The bartender came over. "What'll you have?"

"Scotch on the rocks." Ace threw a glance over his shoulder to see if anyone was coming.

The bartender nodded, but he was just as cold as the patrons filling his bar. Ace had been hoping that if no one else was willing to talk to him, then at least he could chat with the bartender, but the man was as unwelcoming as his patrons, offering no conversation besides asking what people wanted and telling them their bill amount. He stared blankly at his hands. What would his next move be if this didn't work?

He couldn't just go up there on his own; he needed someone with more experience and knowledge of the outdoors than he had if he was going to find Scott.

A few more minutes passed, and the bartender brought him his scotch. He drank it too quickly; it hadn't been in the ice long enough to get cold, but he didn't care. He wasn't going to stay somewhere he felt uncomfortable if it was getting him nowhere.

Ace stood and tossed a few bills down on the bar to cover the scotch and walked for the door. This wasn't working, and he couldn't sit here all day knowing that his son needed him.

Just as he was pushing the door open, a hand grabbed his arm. Ace spun around to see a bald man with two long scars on his face leaning close and smiling.

"Let's chat."

The man, who could only be Gabe, turned and walked toward a particularly dark corner of the bar.

Ace hesitated for a beat, then followed, steps feeling lighter than they had all morning.

The table Gabe stopped at was separated from the bar's other customers by a few empty ones. Gabe put his elbows on the table and pressed his hands together in front of his face. He snorted and tilted his hands toward Ace. "You need to leave." He laid his hands flat on the tabletop and leaned forward. "You're not being funny."

Gabe obviously knew exactly who he was talking to.

Ace fought back an urge to roll his eyes or snap back at the ignorant kid.

He leaned in, stopping inches from Gabe's face, eyes narrowed so the boy knew he was serious.

"Does it look like I'm trying to be funny? I need to hire you. To help me save my son. Two confirmed dead, three others still unaccounted for, my son among them. I've got good odds."

*

Ace stood on his porch and addressed his rescue party. It hadn't taken more than a few minutes to convince Gabe to help. In fact, he'd agreed to do it for free, though Ace couldn't pinpoint why.

"We don't know what happened up there, but we know there are men up there who need our help, and we will not abandon them."

Standing next to Gabe Batstone were John Leonard and James Positano, two of Gabe's best trackers. It wasn't a big group, but it would be enough. They had every man they needed.

Every man but Hank. Ace pushed the thought from his mind.

"We know where Scott and the others were planning to go, so all we have to do is get up there and follow their trail. We will find them, and we will bring them home."

There were no cheers from the group in front of him, just unemotional nods and determined faces.

For another fleeting moment, Ace caught himself wishing that Hank's face was among them. But he hadn't even invited Hank to come on the rescue mission, not that he would have gone. Still, Hank's expertise would have been valuable. There was no one more skilled and experienced than Hank when it came to the mountains — those mountains in particular.

But no matter how nice it would have been to have him there to help, Ace wasn't about to ask his friend to go with them to look. He could still feel the burning I told you so in Hank's eyes the night he'd told him that Scott had been killed by a bear.

Ace turned his attention back to the men before him.

"My son may be dead. A young man who was too smart to end up in that situation. He always made it out alive. And now the game warden doesn't want us going up there, not even to find the bodies. You tell me — does that sound right?" He made a point of meeting the eyes of each and every man so that they could all see his determination and feed on it. "We're going to bring my son home, alive…or not."

Ace stepped down from the porch, and the men parted before him as cleanly as if he were Moses parting the Red Sea. Someone patted him on the back as he walked past, but no one said anything. He kept his face hard and his emotions stuffed deep. As he reached his truck, he heard the front door open. He knew that Laura and Beth had stepped out onto the porch.

The others were marching to their own trucks now, and Ace paused with his foot on the running board.

He wanted to look up at the house and promise Laura and Beth that he would bring Scott home to them. He wanted to tell them that everything was going to be okay. But he knew that if he did, his thin shell of emotionless determination would crumble under the baseless claim. He would break down into sobs and curl up on the ground. There was no time for such self-indulgence. So he swallowed hard, swung his body into the truck, and slammed the door shut.

Single-file, they poured over the road—traps, firearms, and survivalist tools neatly organized in the beds of their trucks. All that was left was their pilgrimage to a sea of wilderness where bodies lay under the canopy like abandoned beacons.

Chapter Twenty-Five

Back to Hell

"Ace, you can't do this." Hank had positioned himself between Ace and the plane sitting at the dock with propellers already spinning. "You're smarter than this; I know you are."

"I can do whatever the hell I want, and you aren't going to do anything to get in my way." Ace's fists were clenched, his anger barely restrained.

The men with Ace had backed up a few steps to give them some space, but Hank doubted their voices would stay low enough to keep anything they said between the two of them.

Not that anything of what had passed between the two old friends over the last twenty-four hours was a secret.

"Please, Ace." Hank groped for anything that might turn Ace back. "Don't do this to Laura. She needs you, especially now."

"My son needs me," Ace snapped. "He needs to be rescued from whatever is endangering him and the rest of those boys on that mountain. And being the good father that I am, I'm going to go up there and save him." His voice was cold, devoid of all feeling. "You might not care about him enough to bring his body back, but I do."

Hank took a deep breath. There had to be something that could keep Ace from going up there. He couldn't let any more people die.

"The whole town knows you're a lying coward now," Ace said, "or else I'd ask you to do the right thing and come with us."

The words struck Hank like a physical blow hard enough to shatter bone.

He hadn't been the one to deliver the news to the families of the other men because he was so caught up in dealing with Ace and Beth. He knew some people were upset about that, but if there was any truth to Ace's words, the hostility ran far deeper than he'd thought.

Hank ran his fingers through his hair, searching for something to say, anything to say that might stop Ace. To try and think of something that might save Ace's life and the lives of the men with him.

He finally settled on the only option left to him, though it was the one route he wanted to take the least of all.

"I assume all the registration and paperwork is current on the plane you're taking with you?" he asked.

"What the hell are you talking about?" Ace's voice was harsh, but a hint of confusion had crept into his eyes.

Hank cleared his throat. "As I recall, the pilot of that plane has failed to pay his registration fees and licensing. Therefore, he's operating illegally." Hank felt full of pettiness and dirty dealing using this tactic. He'd thought of it just before leaving this morning and, knowing Jake, figured the taxes were late. He'd looked it up in the database, and sure enough, his fees were over a year past due. "I'll call it in to the sheriff and have him arrested for operating illegally, especially with paying customers."

"That's bullshit, and you know it." The confusion was spreading now, making Ace's voice less strong than it was before. "You just flew with him yesterday and didn't seem to care."

"I wasn't aware of the situation until this morning," Hank said defensively.

"It don't matter, anyway," Ace shifted his weight forward, determination subduing the confusion. "The sheriff won't do anything about it now. He knows that Jake is the best pilot around here and our only hope of getting up there. He won't arrest him over something stupid and put our boys at even more risk while he sorts out some traffic ticket."

It wasn't a traffic ticket, but Hank knew it wasn't worth arguing. Ace was right anyway; the sheriff wouldn't arrest Jake and jeopardize the rescue mission for something so minute. Hank was only making himself look like a bigger asshole for trying to stop it.

And now he was truly desperate because his last ditch effort had fallen flat.

"Have you really talked Jake into going back up there?" Hank asked. "I'm sure after our last trip, he isn't too keen to fly back again."

Ace settled back into a more relaxed stance. He knew he'd won. "We've made arrangements that seemed to settle his nerves."

"And by that you mean you paid him enough money that he couldn't refuse." Hank shook his head and looked down at the dock.

"You're just full of accusations today," Ace snapped. "I'm not going to sit here and listen to this." He turned and started to walk away.

"It's not safe up there." He was out of logical arguments but still not ready to give up. "I've been up there, and I'm telling you, it's not safe. It wasn't safe for the boys, and it's not safe for you or these men you're taking with you." He pointed at the men behind Ace and raised his voice to be sure they could hear him. "You'll be putting the lives of all these men in danger if you go up on that mountain."

A few of the rescue party members were fidgeting, but that was a small victory. None of them would turn back now unless Ace gave the word.

"I know it's not safe up there, Hank." Ace stomped back, leaning into Hank's face with jaw clenched and eyes blazing. "And that's exactly why I'm going up there. My son, who thinks of you as a second father, by the way, is probably up in those mountains scrambling for his life, and I won't stand down here for another minute letting him face the elements alone."

Hank just shook his head.

"You should be the first in line to lead this search party, Hank." Ace's voice wasn't angry now — it was disgusted. "You should have volunteered to be by my side the moment those boys didn't return home. You're a coward, Hank. You don't deserve to be the game warden. You're a disgrace to the position, and I'm embarrassed to have ever called you my friend."

Ace's words stung harder than Hank's healing wounds, but they roused Hank's anger as well. "I warned you about those mountains, Ace. I warned Scott, too." Hank stepped even closer so that his nose was barely an inch from Ace's. "I never sanctioned their trip up to Spider Lake because I was afraid of what might happen. I was the first one up there, Ace, and I saw what happened. Now you're trying to tell me that I'm a coward for not putting my life, and the lives of an entire search team, on the line to go and confirm what I already know?"

Ace's breath came in short heaves, and his fists clenched tight. "You didn't come to try and stop me from going." He shook his head, disgust dripping from every movement. "You came here to gloat. You came here to say, 'I told you so.' Is that it? Is that why you're here?"

"You stubborn old man. Why can't you see reason? Why can't you see the truth when it's staring you in the face?" Hank spoke louder with each word until he was shouting. "For God's sake, Ace! Listen to reason!"

Ace paused only long enough to suck in a deep breath. "Go!" Ace shouted, vehemently swinging an arm, which, if not for Hank stepping back, would have smacked right into his face. "Get out of here before I do something I'll regret. I never want to see your lying, cowardly ass again, or God Himself won't be able to hold me back."

Hank replied in a whisper, "Go fuck yourself" He turned and stormed off the dock with anger lodged in his throat and weighing his heart down like lead.

But even as he slammed the door of his truck and drove away from the dock, he couldn't ignore the growing fear in the pit of his stomach.

What would they find up there? Or more importantly, what might find them?

Chapter Twenty-Six

The Perimeter

The first dusting of snow of the season was falling in the mountain altitudes, muting every sound but the crunch of cold soil underfoot as the search team trekked through the forest. Ace reached an arm up to wipe the sweat from his forehead, musing silently on how odd it felt to be sweating among snow. The sun had set over an hour ago, and the air was bitter cold, but the exertion of the hike still had Ace perspiring.

He stopped and pulled a map out from his jacket pocket. Plumes of condensation burst from his mouth and dispersed in the night air as he exhaled. Ace squinted at the map he'd found at Scott's. Scott had roughly marked out a trail on the worn paper. It was filled with scribbled notes and marks for sites where he wanted to camp, but Scott's chicken scratch was hard enough to read at the best of times.

"John," Ace called back behind him. "Let me use your flashlight."

John came forward, and Ace heard Gabe and James groan and drop their packs to the ground for a break. John slapped the flashlight into Ace's outstretched palm. Ace nodded his thanks and flicked on the light.

Scott's penciled line went high up the mountain, past the border of the restricted area, and ended at a big 'X'. Ace examined the map for the hundredth time and pulled out his compass as backup. He checked their location, glancing up at the stars and muttering under his breath.

Jake had dropped them off at Meadowlark Lake just like he'd dropped off Hank the day before, but it had been much later in the day and the plane ride had been longer because they'd had to fly around a brewing fall storm. They had arrived almost at nightfall, and it was hard to see much of anything. Even though they figured Scott probably had camped close to Spider Lake, which wasn't too far from where they'd been dropped off, they'd had a hard time finding where exactly in between the two lakes their camp had been.

John went back to join the others on the ground. They did this every mile or so. Ace would stop and stare at the map while they caught their breath. He wouldn't have stopped at all except that he had to make sure they stayed on the right path. Any time lost wandering in the wrong direction was more time Scott was out here alone.

He found what he needed and stuffed the flashlight and map into his jacket. "This way." Ace was already moving.

He heard the long, tired sighs of the others as they dragged themselves back to their feet, but he knew they wouldn't complain. They understood the situation as well as he did, and they were willing to tough it out a bit longer.

In any other situation where someone's life was not in immediate danger, Ace would give them more breaks. They were all completely exhausted from hiking, not to mention lugging heavy rescue equipment after them. Ace had the food and tents in his pack, Gabe had the ropes and the safety harnesses, James carried all the medical equipment, and John had drawn the short straw and gotten stuck with the majority of the steel bear traps, which meant he was always last in the group train.

The trails were completely overgrown, even worse than Gabe had told them to expect. Gabe had been at the front of the line for the first couple of miles to hack a path for them, but it had opened up naturally after a while, to his relief.

Ace trudged forward, blinking the flakes of snow out of his eyes. It wasn't falling hard, and nothing was sticking to the ground yet, but Ace was still worried it could wipe out their only chance of finding Scott on time.

He closed his eyes to shield them from a bone-chilling gust of wind, and when he opened them again, he saw something up ahead.

"Hurry! Quick!" Ace's voice cut through the still night air. "I've found something!"

When the others caught up with him, Ace was standing in the middle of a clearing, staring down at a fragment of clothing in his hands.

"What the—?" Gabe stopped next to Ace. "What the hell happened here?" He carefully lowered the bear traps to the ground.

To say the clearing was a mess would have been kind. There had obviously been a campsite here once, but there wasn't much left of it now. Large blue tents were ripped to shreds and scattered across the ground, the material flapping eerily in the night breeze. Fallen leaves dusted with snow, covered half of the fire pit, obscuring the charred logs underneath. Metal camping chairs lay twisted on the ground, legs broken off and scattered in pieces nearby. The site looked as though a tornado had ripped through it.

"Ace?" John questioned when he and James caught up.

Ace turned around to face them, still clutching the material.

"Scott's hunting shirt." His voice was softer than it had been since news of Scott's situation had reached him. Holding the red, checkered sleeve of the shirt in his hands was breaking him.

"Ace, we don't know what that could mean. He could've ripped it while running away from..." John looked around the clearing as if trying to spot it, "whatever happened here. It doesn't mean anything."

John spoke with confidence, but Ace could feel desperation crowding out his determination.

"Hey, look at this." James was holding something black and dull. "This was a cast iron frying pan, but look at it now."

There was a huge dent in the base of the thick metal.

"You tell me what animal could've done that? This is tough stuff, strong metal, built to last. But something crushed it like paper." James shook his head and lowered the pan. "I don't know what happened here guys, but I think the sooner we get back to town and raise the alarm, the better."

"Not until I know what happened to my son!" The mere suggestion of giving up snapped Ace back into gear. "We set up camp for the night here. With the storm coming in fast, and the darkness, there's no point in going back now."

He walked over to the bear traps and hefted them up onto his shoulder. John rushed forward to help him carry the load, but Ace waved him away.

"I'm going to set up a perimeter. Nothing will get past without setting off one of these."

He stalked off into the trees, leaving the rest of the rescue team staring after him.

Ace paused just outside the clearing after laying the traps.

"Poor guy is cracking up." James was saying to the others. "What makes him think it's safe to stay out here? I don't want to be the one to say it, but someone has to. What hope is there of finding Scott alive? Or any of the other men?"

"Hey," Gabe said, his voice low and stern. "Don't talk bullshit like that. Stay positive for fuck sakes. You have to, for Ace. I know it doesn't look good now, but we have to keep our spirits up for him, if for nothing else. We'll camp here tonight and figure out what happened here in the morning. The snow might cover all the tracks of whatever attacked them, but there will be other clues, you'll see."

Ace strode into camp and cleared his throat, clapping his arms around himself. "Got a fire ready? I'm freezing."

"Just about," James said, still squatting over the old fire pit. He may have considered using the kid's shirt as a part of the kindle, but after that talk, he couldn't have done it.

Ace decided to let the comments about Scott slide. He needed to save his energy anyway.

A few minutes and some stoking later, a small fire was crackling pleasantly despite the cold surrounding it, and the tents were pitched. Not long after that, the weather worsened, bringing with it stronger winds and heavier snow billowing through the campsite mercilessly. There probably wouldn't be any trail left by morning from their arrival to guide them back. But there was nothing Ace could do about now. At least they were surrounded by towering trees on all sides that would shield them from the worst of the storm. Ace just had to hope that, wherever Scott was, he was sheltered as well.

Ace stood hunkered in front of the fire, hands extended to absorb more warmth.

"You set up those traps all right?" James asked, rubbing his hands together as he came up behind him.

"Of course I did." Ace didn't bother to turn and look at the younger man. "I've been setting those traps since before you were born."

He moved away from James and sat down on one of the chairs, a bad taste lingering in his mouth. He spread Scott's map out over his lap and studied it in the flickering light of the fire for any clues about where his son might have gone, but the lines remained nothing but lines, the scribbling as cold and lifeless as the paper itself.

One by one, the other men retired to their tents, but Ace stayed by the fire, staring into its empty flames until there was nothing left but a pile of glowing embers.

*

Ace's eyes snapped open to see the darkness, his body jerking. Something had woken him, but there was no sound now. Not even the wind.

He realized that the snow had stopped falling while he'd slept, leaving only a light, dusty layer of white over the brown of the leaves and pine needles.

Ace looked around to see if one of the other men was the source of the noise, but they were all sound asleep in the tent. He leaned forward in his chair, grabbed a branch, and poked at the fire, stirring among the ashes. The embers glowed a bit brighter as he jabbed at them as if they'd been angered, and he tossed on a few fresh twigs to get it going again. A few moments later, a tiny flame flickered underneath the kindling.

The flames crackled and popped softly as they were stirred further, and Ace felt his eyelids start to droop again. But then he heard footsteps in the forest.

Or he thought he did. Maybe it was just the sound of the fire playing tricks on his tired and desperate mind. He looked at the other men again to see if they had heard anything even remotely suspicious, but no one stirred.

Wide awake now, Ace focused all his attention on searching for the sounds he had heard. He realized then that the crackle of the fire was the only sound in the forest. Fresh snow or not, there should be some kind of noise out here.

John suddenly let out a loud snort and bolted upright in his tent.

"Quiet," Ace hissed. "Something's out there."

John stuck his head outside of the tent flaps, a frown on his face. "What the fuck is it?"

"I said—"

A sharp crack resounded through the trees and brought Ace to his feet.

John scrambled out of the tent, Gabe and James hot on his heels, all the men grabbing for their weapons.

"What the hell was that?" John's rifle was already on his shoulder as he went to Ace's side.

"The traps." Ace scooped up his own rifle and headed for the source of the sound. "Something set the traps off."

The others were right behind him, rifles up, moving quickly through the trees.

"We got something!" Ace couldn't see the trap clearly yet, but there was something there within it. Something big.

A fierce cry of intense pain and rage split the silence and was abruptly cut short.

Ace chambered a round in his rifle and moved towards the trap.

"Ace, wait!" John called. "We don't know what's out there."

Ace heard him but ignored him, jumping over a fallen log and making a tight turn around a tree.

He came to a stop at the trap. The huge trap was closed tight around the leg of an enormous brown bear. Ace crept towards the animal, keeping his gun trained carefully on it in case it moved.

The others came crashing up behind him.

"Ace, careful," Gabe said, putting a hand on his shoulder.

"It's dead," Ace announced, brushing the hand away as he approached it.

"How?" Gabe asked.

As they moved closer, James and Gabe pulled out their flashlights and shined them on the animal. Gabe and Ace crouched down beside the beast.

"Neck's broken. See?" The grizzly bear's head was tilted at an unnatural angle and twisted past ninety degrees to the left.

Gabe turned the beam of his flashlight towards the bear trap, brow furrowing.

"But the trap caught its leg, not its neck."

James flicked his light around the area, but it fell on nothing but trees and snow. "Probably broke its neck when it fell. That animal must be over 800 pounds. That much weight behind it would've snapped a bone in a second if it didn't realize."

Ace stood up, reasoning silently. James' explanation didn't quite seem to fit, but he couldn't put his finger on why. Gabe was still inspecting the animal, looking for an explanation when another crack broke the silence of the forest.

"That's the second trap!" Ace shouted, already sprinting for it.

The others were right behind him, their breath filling the air with clouds of vapor as they ran through the trees. When they reached the trap, its metallic jaws were closed firmly on nothing at all.

"What set it off?" James said. "What the hell is out here?"

A fear deeper than any Ace had felt before settled somewhere deep in his gut like a lead fist. He brought his rifle to his shoulder and swept the area for movement.

Something unknown shifted to their left. Four muzzles swiveled to the spot, but nothing was there.

"You all saw that, right?" Gabe said, staring into the forest without blinking.

"Shh," Ace whispered. His finger tightened around the trigger.

Wind whistled through the trees, branches brushed against each other, and leaves rustled. A twig snapped to their right, and James' rifle went off, the shot echoing through the air and sending a flock of birds screeching into the night sky.

"Hey," Ace yelled over his shoulder. "Calm it down."

James glared at him. "Sorry. I'm a little tense, I'm sure you can imagine. I know I'm not the only one hearing whatever the hell is out there."

"Well, you've just let whatever it is know exactly where we are," Ace snapped.

James opened his mouth to retort, but Gabe cut him off.

"Shh." Gabe pointed into the trees. "Look."

Ace and James stopped arguing and turned to follow Gabe's finger.

"What?" James said.

Ace searched the trees, but he didn't see anything.

"There," John whispered, his voice shaking.

Ace saw it at the same moment John spoke. Between two massive trees, at least nine feet up in the air, two narrow, red eyes were staring at them.

Ace's mouth opened slowly, his eyes widening in fear. "What the—?"

The eyes blinked once, and then vanished into nothing.

Heavy footsteps crashed through the trees surrounding them, tracing a wide circle around the spot where they stood as if it were stalking them. The group spun around wildly, searching for a glimpse of whatever was making those noises. Flashlight beams crisscrossed the air and bounced off the tree trunks before illuminating something black and hairy for half an instant.

"Jesus Christ," Gabe yelled. "What the fuck is that?"

"Cover each other!" John shouted.

They formed a rough circle, back to back, guns trained out in four directions now with flashlights held steady along the barrels.

But there was no more movement. No more sound.

Ace narrowed his eyes, willing the darkness to peel back and show him what was out there, but his will, no matter how strong, did not defy nature. The fear was still sitting in his stomach, but his determination was back now, displacing it, strengthening him. A certainty as deep as his fear told him that whatever was out there was responsible for the bodies Hank had found, and his old friend must have known that.

Movement erupted behind Ace, and an enormous, dark figure raced passed him.

The ground shook. Ace swung his light back and forth trying to find the figure, but it was always an inch ahead of the circle of light.

Someone screamed, and Ace spun around just in time to see John being dragged off into the darkness. His legs were kicking frantically, his hands clawing at a thick, fur covered arm wrapped around his neck.

Ace broke and ran. There was nothing he could do for John now, but the man's sacrifice gave them opportunity to escape.

"Come on," he heard Gabe yelling at James.

Someone vomited violently, but when Ace cast a glance over his shoulder there were two flashlights bouncing through the trees behind him.

Ace rounded a wide tree and flattened his back against it. Gabe and James joined him a moment later.

"Help!"

John's agonized cry reached them through the woods, and James stepped out from behind the tree, but Gabe yanked him back.

James shook off his hand, teeth grit. "He needs our help!"

"And how in the fuck do you think you're going to help him?"

Another wordless scream echoed through the blackness.

"We have to do something! Listen to him scream!"

Gabe looked back at Ace.

Ace took a deep breath and let his head fall back against the tree trunk. He'd come up here to save lives, not let more get killed. "James is right. We have to try."

Gabe shook his head, but chambered a round regardless.

"Let's move," Ace said. "But stay close."

They edged around the tree together, moving toward the sound of John's cries for help.

Then a scream so long and ragged it hardly sounded human shook the woods. The wail that may have once been John was cut off sharply; the silence that followed was loud enough to hurt Ace's ears.

A long, deep, reverberating howl filled the woods, savage and clear both at the same time.

Ace looked at Gabe, then James, and saw his own fear mirrored in their eyes.

Gabe's eyes slowly narrowed, and the fear leaked out, replaced by a steely anger. He turned toward the direction of the howl, raised his gun, and opened fire.

Ace and James were only a split second behind him.

The night sky lit up with muzzle flashes, and the air was saturated with staccato explosions, a chaotic series of sounds among what should have been peaceful in the woods.

Ace pulled the trigger again and again, emptying his chamber of bullets a little at a time. Branches fell to the ground, small trees burst into sprays of splinters as bullets ricocheted. A part of him knew he wasn't going to hit anything. But a bigger part of him didn't care. He poured all of his outrage, all of his fear, all of his pain through the barrel of that rifle until a dull click announced that he was out of ammunition. He didn't even hear the click until he realized the guns beside him had gone silent, too.

The rifles of the other two men lowered to their sides. Ace reached into the pouch at his hip for more bullets. He reloaded and pulled the gun up to his shoulder again.

He squeezed off three more rounds before Gabe's voice brought him back to reality. "Shut it down, Ace."

He lowered his gun but kept his eyes fixed on the darkness ahead. "Do you think we got it?" He might have been speaking too loudly; it was difficult to tell with the echo of the gunshots still ringing in his ears.

Gabe shook his head. "Not a chance. We were too far away." He swept his flashlight in a wide arc. "But I think we're safe for now."

Ace turned to face the guide. "What makes you so sure?"

"When there's a top-level predator nearby, something above all the rest in the food chain, all the other wildlife goes quiet, hides away until its safe." He pointed at the trees. "Have a listen for yourself."

The ringing was finally fading from Ace's ears, and he tuned in to the sounds around him. The forest was bustling with activity. Night birds resumed their evening calling, animals moved through the underbrush. He remembered the eerie silence when he'd awoken and nodded. "So now the question is, how do we take down a predator like that?"

Gabe only stared off into the dark trees.

Chapter Twenty-Seven

The Last Stand

"What the hell was that?" Ace whispered when they were back at their camp, sweat still beading down his forehead.

"I think we all know what it was." Gabe looked around the clearing. "What we need to do is figure out how we plan to get out of here alive now that we know it's here."

James nodded in fervent agreement, his eyes nervously scanning the dark forest behind him and around him. It was apparent he realized that creature could come hurling into the campsite at any moment, and his finger rested on the trigger.

"Well, as I see it we have two options." Ace held up a finger. "Option one, we try and hike far away from this area and hope he doesn't follow us. The plane isn't scheduled to be back until the day after tomorrow, and we don't have any communication up here, so we can't call him to come sooner. If we want to go back, that's our only way." He lifted a second finger. "Two, we stay and fight the thing until Jake gets back. We've got the traps and the guns, we can kill this thing, or at least keep it at bay."

331

James shook his head, his voice shaking as he spoke. "We already know he can outsmart the traps. He's proved that damn well. Might as well be setting traps for us. And we don't know if these guns can even harm him, since nobody got a clean shot." He held up his rifle. "The thing is huge; for all we know, these are nothing but BB guns to him, barely enough to make him mad."

Ace shrugged his shoulders. "Maybe you're right. Either way, that's the choice we have to make. Fight or run. His brute strength seems to be the only weapon he's using, so he can't be that advanced, not if we all work together. He doesn't have tools or real weapons. If we all keep calm and think hard enough, we'll be able to outsmart him. Somehow."

James wasn't convinced by Ace's speech, not at all. "As far as I'm concerned, we have to make a run for it while we have a chance. The thing is gone now, which gives us a small window of opportunity. If we leave right now, I bet we can make it back to town before it even knows we're gone."

"And let the monster follow us back just to put everyone in town in danger?" Gabe said.

"Don't you think he'll make it there eventually either way?" James argued.

"No," Ace said, firmly enough to cause both men to look at him. "It was perfectly happy up here, and still is. It's probably been here for years and never bothered to come down because it never needed to explore. Gabe is right, if we lead it back to town and give it a whole new perspective, there's no telling what havoc it might cause down there."

James looked from Ace to Gabe, defeated. It was clear they had already made up their minds, and there was no way he'd be taking off through the forest alone with that beast out there. He lifted his hands and let them fall back to his sides in a show of his forfeit. "I guess we try and make a stand then."

Ace gave a curt nod. "We'd better get ready. Let's get some sleep and start building our defense first thing in the morning. We just have to hold it off for one more night, and then we're out of here."

The remainder of the night was a cycle of restless sleeping in turns and sudden waking, particularly for James. Just as he drifted off into an uneasy slumber, a noise would snap him back awake. After listening for a moment to assure himself that the sounds of the forest were not silenced by the presence of the creature, he'd slow his breathing and struggle to fall asleep again.

*

"All right, boys, let's get to it."

James felt like he hadn't gotten a bit of useful sleep, but he was still relieved to hear Ace's announcement, because the sooner the barricade was started, the sooner he'd be able to take some solace in their spot. He pushed himself up with a groan and stretched his back.

Ace wasted no time getting down to business. "Gabe, you set up the traps, everything we've got. Take your time and pick the best places, we already know he can avoid them so we want what we have to count. Move the ones that we laid earlier to new spots so he won't remember where they are."

"On it." Gabe slipped into the woods, traps clinking from being slung over his back.

"James, you get to work digging some pits on the outside of the camp. Deep enough to keep that thing stuck for at least a few minutes. Try for two or three to start."

Ace moved off into the gray light of the dawn before James had a chance to object, but he was still incredulous. Pits? Was he serious? That thing had ripped John to shreds, and Ace wanted him to dig some holes to stop it?

But as much as James disliked the idea, it was the only sensible one, so he didn't have any other choice. He grabbed a shovel and started digging, making each plow count. After he'd gotten the first pit dug, careful not to fall in himself as he observed the depth, he decided it might not be such a bad idea after all. He'd dug close to four feet deep, probably enough to hopefully slow the monster down while they got clear.

Before starting the second one, he decided to add some smaller holes as well. Nothing that would trap the Bigfoot, but just some potholes that might trip him up and buy them a few more precious seconds. By the time he'd dug a network of holes sprinkled with several good-sized pits, he was almost sure these things would save their lives.

When the digging was done, he went to each hole and covered them all with blankets of leaves and branches to conceal the openings. He was amazed, and secretly somewhat proud at the end results. The forest floor looked perfectly undisturbed. If he hadn't dug the holes himself, he wouldn't have known they were there. He headed back for camp feeling impressed with himself.

While James was digging, Gabe was laying the traps and having similar feelings of success. They had brought six bear traps in all, so his supplies were limited and his choices for location had to be perfect. Three of them had been set the night before, and the creature had triggered two of them. Gabe moved and reset those two and repositioned the third as well, making careful note of their location for himself. Then he set up the other three to complete a full circle around their campsite.

Last night, Ace had set the traps in a hurry, leaving them out in the open and easy to see, but that was understandable, as the typical dangers in the woods would not have thought twice about the locations of the traps. Whatever was hunting them now was too clever for that, so Gabe did his best to conceal them with leaves and branches so they couldn't be seen until it was too late. When he was done, he was satisfied that no animal would be smart enough to detect them. Hell, most humans wouldn't be able to detect them.

Just to make sure that none of them triggered the traps by accident, Gabe noted a specific landmark next to each trap, be it a stray boulder, a certain pine tree, or even, in one case, a small group of pinecones. He'd tell Ace and James about all of them once they were finished with the preparations.

Gabe was the first one back to camp. He wasn't sure what Ace and James were up to, but the forest was still bustling with its usual noise, so he knew they were fine.

The creature's howl echoed through his brain, and he squeezed his eyes shut to block it out. If he let thoughts of last night linger for too long, John's screams would come up as well and he couldn't handle that reality right now. Not if he was going to get through this alive.

Gabe remembered then that they had more traps. They were designed for much smaller animals, but having them set up couldn't hurt if in the worst case the creature avoided all the large ones. Plus, Ace had said to set everything they had, and the little ones were part of that supply.

He laid them all around the campsite as a final perimeter and scattered a few in camp as well. They wouldn't be nearly as effective as the bear traps, but they'd at least slow that monster down. As with the bear traps, he disguised them with leaves and brush from nearby growth. They'd have to be extra careful walking around camp, now that they were all concealed from human sight.

When Gabe was finished, the campsite looked like a war zone – a minefield long since abandoned. He stood back to admire his handiwork and counted the traps. Ten small traps in and around their campsite, the ones meant to slow the creature down in a chase. His mental count of the bear traps came to six, and that made sixteen total. Perfect. That was every trap they'd brought along.

He picked up his rifle and sat down to wait for the others to come back.

With the other two guys occupied, Ace was building vine nets, a skill he'd learned as a boy and kept handy in case he ever needed it, and placing them at strategic spots around camp and along the beginning of a potential escape route. They were designed to spring up from the ground when triggered and entangle whatever was standing on them. Ace set them up so that he could release them on the run. The timing would be tricky to perfect, but if he got it just right, he could buy them some time. The Bigfoot, being so big, would probably break free from the nets with very little effort, but it would slow him down a bit. And that might be all they could hope for.

Ace had learned to build these nets with precision and a steady hand, but he was grateful now that he'd never lost the skill as it was coming in handy. Most of them were on the forest floor, waiting to be snapped up to the trees, but he wove a few between limbs at various heights. Some were close to the creature's head level and others were near the ground, intended to trip him up.

They were simple and didn't look like much, but Ace was confident that the nets would help them in their moments of need against the beast.

The terror of exactly what they were preparing to fight nagged at the back of his mind while he worked, but Ace refused to dwell on it. There was no time to think of anything but survival, to make sure he, Gabe, and James made it out alive.

He wanted to think about Scott, but that simply wasn't logical anymore, not when his own life was hanging in the balance. He'd come up here to find out what had happened to his son and, as far as he knew, he'd done that. This thing, this creature, hadn't left Scott or any of the other guys alive; he was sure of that now. If Scott and his friends had survived even a single night up here with that creature, it would have come back the next night to finish them off. Just like Ace was sure it would try to do to them tonight. This wasn't the kind of beast that left anything alive in its wake.

Ace didn't want to imagine how his son had died. In fact, he consciously blocked out any speculation. He only hoped that it had been fast. That he hadn't screamed in agony like John had last night.

He pulled the final vine tight, too tightly, as the truth hit him harder than any beast ever could. The rough material cut into his hands, calloused as they were, and spotted the vine in blood. He would have given up all of it if it meant bringing Scott back alive. He planted his hands on his hips, taking a breather and wiping the blood off on his pants. No one would question it, he was sure, not now. His breath was coming in thick heaves similar to how the beast breathed, a desire for revenge washing away the pain of losing Scott.

That beast had taken his son from him. Now it was going to die, and if Ace had anything to do with it, he'd hope the beast suffered. If anyone deserved to die, it was that monster.

The sun was well past its peak when James walked back into camp. Gabe and Ace stood to meet him and go over the hazards placed around their stronghold.

"Any sign of him?" Ace asked, rifle cradled in his hands but ready for action.

"No, nothing yet," James said with a slight shake of his head. "But I'm sure he'll be back. A beast like that doesn't leave survivors, not when he knows where they are."

The bluntness of James' words caught Gabe short. But he couldn't deny the truth in them.

"Okay." He rubbed his hands together as he faced the silent Gabe. "Where are the traps, and if we're running how do we lead him to them?" The question was practical, but Gabe really just wanted to talk about something other than the monster they all knew was lurking just out of sight. He fumbled for an answer and sufficed to point towards the closest one.

Fortunately, James got what he wanted; they spent the next half hour showing the others the traps they'd each laid out. It was a complex web of razor sharp steel traps, treacherous pits, and hidden nets, so it was important for them all to know it well. All combined, the setup would certainly slow the creature down, and it might even help them trap and kill it in the long run.

Not that Gabe had such lofty ambitions, no sir. His only goal was to make it through the night and get to the plane in the morning. Monster be damned, he was going to give up the woods after this.

Once they were all comfortable with their mental map of the maze of traps and snares, they moved onto creating hiding places for themselves. Some were up in the trees and others were buried in the earth.

The fading light in the sky above the trees was blood red when they sat down at the end of the day. Gabe decided to take the color of the sky as a good sign. He'd heard somewhere that a sunset like this was a good omen or something like that. The deep red color unnerved him more than he wanted to admit, but he ignored the feeling.

The mood around the camp was far from light, but it lacked the impending sense of doom that swallowed them earlier in the day. Still, as the light crept from the sky and the color drained from the forest, the fear returned full-swing.

"Let's get a fire going," Ace said.

Gabe nodded and stood up. "A roaring fire."

They all ventured out for firewood and had a massive fire blazing in no time. The fire sat in the center of the camp and cast its dancing light all around them. No one spoke, because speaking left them less open to listening for silence. One look at Ace and it was clear he was deep in his own thoughts. Gabe did his best to keep his mind blank, filled only by the sharp crackling of the fire. He let its warmth seep into his bones and drive out the encroaching chill of the night.

Then his eyes snapped open.

The sounds of the fire popping were the only noises in the night. The rest of the forest was silent as death. He sprang to his feet, snatched up his rifle, pulling it to his shoulder and taking aim at nothing in particular.

James and Ace were right behind him.

"What is it?" Ace hissed.

"I don't know yet," Gabe whispered back, "but something is out there. Listen. No sound."

The three of them looked out into the darkness, straining to see or hear something, anything, but true to Gabe's word, there was nothing but stillness and silence. The minutes stretched on and still there was nothing. After ten minutes, James took his seat without a word, his finger still on his gun's trigger. A few minutes later, Ace joined him. Gabe lowered his gun after that but didn't sit. He knew better than to ignore the feeling in his gut that told him he was being watched by someone or something.

Nearly an hour later, the sounds of the forest returned, and Gabe was satisfied that the threat was gone again.

"What do you think happened?" James said.

"He was here," Gabe said. He sat down again but still couldn't wrench his eyes away from the darkness beyond their ring of light. "Maybe he sensed our traps and didn't want to push forward, not until he got a better idea of how to attack."

"That's a good sign," Ace said. "They're holding him off, he can't get through."

"I wouldn't be so sure," Gabe said warily. "He'll be back. He'll keep studying them until he figures out how to get around them."

"How long do you think that'll take?" James' voice cracked as it turned upward to form his question.

Gabe shook his head. "He's probably found a way past some of them already."

"Way to rain on the parade," Ace said. "Here, we might as well keep our strength up." He tossed around some trail mix and jerky. "Still got a long night ahead of us before we can hike out of here."

The night passed without a visit from the Bigfoot or a wink of sleep. It was long and cold, but Ace was warmed by the fire in front of him and the need for revenge deep in his gut.

They kept the fire roaring all night, as much for the sense of safety it brought as for the warmth, though both were appreciated when the snow began falling again just before dawn.

"I'm worried I won't remember where everything is with all this snow on the ground," James said, ever the captain obvious in the group.

"Just go with your instincts," Gabe told him. "You were born with good instincts. You'll be fine."

Ace couldn't tell if Gabe was being sincere or just trying to calm his troubled friend.

"Besides," Gabe continued. "This will make it even harder for that thing to find the traps now."

That was true, but Ace wasn't sure he was going to be able to find anything anymore either. And that made him more than a little nervous. Everything would look different with the fresh blanket of snow, and Ace wasn't completely sure which way to hike to meet the plane.

But that didn't matter yet because their pickup wasn't until mid-morning. Light from the rising sun hadn't even penetrated the trees yet, leaving them in a murky, pre-dawn gray. They still had to survive at least five more hours before they had a chance at making it out of this situation alive.

Despite the slowly brightening skies, Ace wasn't feeling particularly optimistic about the situation. A glance at his companions told him that they felt the same apprehension. He tuned in to the sounds of the forest. As long as they were surrounded by those, they were okay.

Birds singing, insects humming, crickets chirping, bees buzzing – Ace sighed, trying to force himself to relax.

Snap.

The metallic twang of a steel trap rang out through the suddenly silent woods.

Ace swung his head and made eye contact with Gabe.

Gabe nodded.

Snap.

The bear traps were springing, but there were no howls of pain, so he wasn't stepping on them as they'd intended.

How had he found them? He'd have to be testing the ground, prodding it with a stick as he walked to detect them so easily or throwing things to make them spring, rocks, heavy ones.

This creature was smarter than they were giving it credit for.

Ace was dumbfounded.

Snap.

His feet were glued to the ground. He knew he had to run while the creature was busy. The traps weren't working, their defenses were crumbling. But he couldn't move.

Then a deafening roar shook the forest with the fourth snap. Finally, it had stepped in one of the traps.

The ground-shaking roar snapped them all back to their senses, and they turned to run. The carefully laid gauntlet of traps was forgotten in the face of an overwhelming desire to survive.

Ace expected that he'd fall behind the two younger men quickly, but James had a nasty smoking habit he'd cleverly chosen to ignore while they were faced with such an advanced predator. The effects, however, lingered. He was wheezing in seconds and struggling to keep up.

"Guys! Help! Don't leave me!"

Ace pushed forward, refusing to look back, because he knew the moment he looked back, he would be pressed to help the man. Just like with John last night, there was nothing they could do. If they went back or slowed down, the creature would catch them all.

He saw Gabe throw a glance over his shoulder, but he knew the stakes as well as Ace did and wouldn't be turning around.

A scream of unimaginable terror almost made Ace stop, but he shook off the need to help. Then the terror turned to terrible pain, and he knew that scream would haunt him for the rest of his life.

Even if that was only a few minutes.

Chapter Twenty-Eight

The Final Farewell

Gabe forced all thoughts of James from his mind in the face of fear and pushed forward. James wasn't just an employee to him as he would be to Ace, he was a friend, and his agonized screams were ripping Gabe apart just as savagely as the Bigfoot attack.

"Gabe! Help!"

At the sound of his name garbled so desperately, Gabe hesitated and started to turn back toward James, but Ace grabbed him by the shoulder, the proverbial devil to the angel on his opposite.

"There's nothing you can do for him, son. We have to keep moving or he'll catch us, too."

So they ran on, Gabe hating himself more with every step.

Gabe was knocking branches aside and swatting sticks out of his eyes to save time. He could hear Ace panting heavily behind him, but there was no time to slow down. Finally, when Gabe was soaked in sweat despite the cold temperatures, and his lungs were burning from the effort of each gasp, he stopped in place and put his hands on his knees to try and ease his pain.

"We have to go back," Gabe said in between labored breaths. "We don't have any supplies close enough to use. Even if we get away from the Bigfoot now, we'll die from the cold out here without help. We have to get our things back if we have any chance. And besides that, the pickup point is back that way."

Ace grunted. "Might as well go back then, and try to use those traps we laid out."

Gabe nodded. That was small consolation, at least. The traps hadn't done much to stop him from getting into the camp, not when he could set them off one by one. But maybe if the creature was on the run, the remaining ones would cause him to get tripped up more easily.

Gabe took the lead again on the way back, going much slower this time, slow enough to distinguish each crack of a leaf he stepped on from the sounds around them. He picked out their path carefully, constantly listening for any signs of danger. They had to make sure they didn't run into that thing until they were back in range of their traps.

The eerie silence invoked by the creature's presence was still smothering them. After all the times he'd wished for silence during a hunt to better hear the soft footfalls of his prey, Gabe now found it almost funny how he longed for the comforting sounds of the forest. The quiet should have made it easier to detect a threat, but he doubted it would make much difference with this beast, and it made him feel the prey all the more.

They hiked back to the campsite with their guns drawn and ready. Gabe knew the Bigfoot was doing one of two things, stalking them through the forest or sitting at the campsite waiting for them to return. Either way, he could only pray.

With any other predator, Gabe would assume the former. A predator out here wouldn't have enough experience with humans to predict their behavior and would have to stay close enough to keep tabs on them. But with the thing hunting them now, he wasn't so sure it behaved like a typical wild animal at all. It had demonstrated an uncanny intelligence so far, and somehow Gabe knew it would anticipate their return and would lay in wait for them, patiently planning its attack.

Gabe shook his head. What was he thinking? Could this creature really be that smart, on par with human beings?

A tree branch snapped to their right.

He and Ace both whirled to the sound, shooting blindly into the forest, hoping to buy themselves some time, but after hearing nothing but rounds emptying, it was apparent there was nothing there. When his gun clicked on an empty clip, Gabe reached over and stopped Ace from shooting.

"There's nothing there." He slapped a fresh clip into his gun and looked around slowly. "At least not anymore."

Ace grunted, and they started moving again.

Ace listened to the forest as he trudged through the fallen leaves, each step crunching, his ears straining to hear even a whisper of the woodland creatures that normally roamed the woods.

There was nothing.

The sun was fully up now, but it hadn't brought much warmth with it, certainly not enough to save them from freezing to death with time. His clothes were drenched and beginning to freeze as the wind added a further temperature drop.

Their scheduled pickup time wasn't far off now, but the creature was somewhere between them and the lake. And knowing that would make getting there far more difficult.

Ace was turning all of that over in his mind when he heard Gabe go down.

"Fuck," Gabe yelled, crumpling to the ground and disappearing from sight.

Ace ran forward to help him. He'd fallen into one of the pits James had dug yesterday morning. The fresh dusting of snow had hidden it from view, and even though it wasn't very deep, it was deep enough to break Gabe's ankle at the odd angle he fell, which was better than what one of the bear traps would have done to him had he tread on that.

Ace reached down and helped pull Gabe from the pit, having to get on his stomach to get the leverage he needed. "We've got to keep moving," he said urgently.

As soon as he put any weight on his ankle, Gabe was right back on the ground again, biting his lip hard to keep from expressing his pain.

"I need something to brace it," Gabe said through gritted teeth. "A stick or something, anything we can find."

Ace dug through the dismembered leaves on the ground and found a stick he thought could handle the man's weight, which he handed to Gabe. He then tore a few strips off of his shirt and tied them around his ankle to hold the stick in place.

Once the makeshift brace was completed, Ace handed Gabe a larger stick to use as a crutch to help support his weight. Once they were ready to move again, Ace scanned the forest. The hair on the back of his neck stood on end. He could sense that the creature was close.

"Come on, let's go."

They had to be close to camp now that they had found one of the pits. At least they had some protection from the traps, assuming Gabe didn't step on one of them next.

With Gabe on his feet, they got moving again. Much slower now, but Ace was glad they were still moving at all after the break. Every few seconds he threw a glance backwards, sure that something was behind them. But each time, after seeing nothing, he quickly turned his gaze forward, afraid of ending up in another pit.

Or the steel jaws of a bear trap.

It was getting brighter and brighter, and Ace felt his hopes rising with the sun. The higher the sun got, the closer they were to making it home. But the unyielding and unnatural quiet all around them seemed to slow the minutes to a crawl.

Suddenly a chillingly familiar howl pierced the silence.

Ace jumped, and Gabe dropped to one knee to draw his gun.

The howl came from up ahead of them, but it was close.

Ace fought the instinctual urge to turn and run in the opposite direction; there was no point in running. They still needed to get their gear, and the pickup site was in front of them, not behind.

He looked to Gabe, fretting his lip as he debated over whether the man would be able to make it.

Gabe had his walking stick under him again and motioned for them to move on with a wave. They made their way through the forest carefully, looking for any signs of movement.

They had only been walking for five minutes or so when Gabe stopped in place. "There," he whispered.

Ace was about to ask where and when he saw it.

Two red eyes were looking directly at them, no more than thirty yards ahead. The eyes blinked once, and then disappeared.

Ace shot his rifle once in the direction of the eyes, a warning shot, but there was nothing there.

"He's already gone," Gabe said.

"How? I didn't even hear him move."

Gabe didn't answer. He just limped forward silently. Ace followed, gun propped up on his shoulder.

The camp was in sight when they heard rustling in the trees above them. Ace aimed his gun at the branches but didn't shoot, following Gabe's lead, and waited until he saw something concrete to shoot at. That thing couldn't have supported weight in the trees overhead. It must have been shaking the trees around it.

"He's taunting us," Gabe whispered. "The bastard's taunting us."

Ace's hands were shaking and slick with sweat at this point. He wiped them on his jeans to try and dry them, but they were wet again an instant later, so it was futile. He wasn't sure he'd be able to pull the trigger even if he needed to.

They entered the campsite; it was clear of any sign of the beast. Ace let out a sigh of relief. One obstacle was down. Now they were in the center of their web of traps and pits. All that was left now was to make it to the plane alive.

"What time is it?" Gabe asked, his tone hushed.

Ace glanced at his watch. "9:15."

"Pickup's at 11, right?"

Ace nodded.

"Close enough," Gabe said. "Go. Make it to the plane while you can. I'll hold him here."

Ace stood, staring at Gabe with his mouth hanging open. He looked off in the distance where the plane would be landing on the lake soon, then back at Gabe. Leaving someone behind that he knew would not make it less difficult, but leaving behind a man who was still capable seemed impossible.

Gabe met his baffled stare with a cool, but false, confidence. "Go. Someone needs to get back down there and warn them about what's up here." He pointed at his foot. "And we both know it's not gonna be me."

"No," Ace stammered. "We can get out of this hell together. I can help you." He moved closer to help support Gabe's broken ankle. "You can't give up."

"Go!" Gabe roughly pushed him away. "You have a wife, a daughter-in-law, and the town needs your leadership more than they ever will mine. Go for them. I'll only slow you down."

Ace continued to stand there.

Gabe gritted his teeth. This was the way it had to be. He knew that. But if Ace didn't move soon, his resolve might give out.

"No one will miss me when I'm gone." He waved a final farewell to Ace and turned back toward the trees. He faced the hidden menace lurking behind them.

After a few more moments of silence, Gabe heard Ace's footsteps running away. Towards safety.

He closed his eyes, willing himself to stay strong, exhaling a breath of immense relief. This was his moment. The time when he proved to the world what he was made of and, more importantly, proved it to himself. He stayed like that, still and quiet, for what felt like a long time. Eyes closed, listening to the silence of the forest around him, gathering his courage for when he knew he would need it most, thinking about Ace and the life he would have.

A stick snapped ahead of him, and his eyes popped instinctually open.

The Bigfoot was there, screeching and smashing its way out of its hiding place just behind the tree line.

The sound was deafening, the sight almost paralyzing, but regardless of his terror, Gabe managed to pull his gun to his shoulder and open fire. With his hands violently shaking, he unloaded a whole clip into the direction of the Bigfoot. He watched as the bullets pounded into trees and rocks around the raging creature. A few bullets nicked and ricocheted into the muscled torso without inflicting damage more serious than scratches.

The creature roared at him and reached to grab him with an enormous hand, but Gabe rolled away at the last possible second, avoiding the fate similar to his friends. *I don't think so, asshole.* As he dove, he released one of Ace's unsprung nets. The web of vines closed around the Bigfoot and carried it five feet into the air.

Gabe took the opportunity to reload his gun and get off another few shots at it. But the net didn't hold the enraged, thrashing Bigfoot for long. The sheer weight of the beast snapped the vines, and it crashed to the ground.

Gabe hobbled through the maze of pits James had dug, dodging the small steel traps he'd laid at the same time. The Bigfoot was right behind him, its footsteps rocking the Earth. He could hear the smaller traps springing as they ran, but they weren't big enough to draw a reaction from the creature, much less slow him down.

Then the ground shook so violently that Gabe was almost knocked off his feet. He looked back to see the Bigfoot stuck in a deep pit, roaring with fury and frothing at the mouth.

Gabe caught his balance and scampered up a tree. Fifteen feet off the ground, he put too much weight on his injured ankle and nearly fell.

But he hauled himself back up and kept climbing until he was high enough that he felt safe.

The Bigfoot was out of the pit in less than twenty seconds and spotted Gabe right away. It rushed to the tree and began shaking the thick trunk so that the whole thing swung back and forth like a flag in the wind.

At fifteen feet up, he was being flung in a wide arc, and he clung desperately to the branches around him for a solid hold, fingernails digging against the bark and ignoring the pain from digging too deep. But his grip slipped, his fingernail broke, and he plummeted to the earth.

Something cracked when he hit the ground. Maybe a rib, maybe his back. It didn't matter either way. He knew he didn't stand a chance on the ground.

The Bigfoot stomped on both his legs so hard they were crushed instantly. Gabe cried out in agony.

The creature pulled both arms from Gabe's torso in a single motion, turning his scream into a strangled gurgle for air.

He blacked out for a moment then, but his sight came back just in time to see the massive jaws coming down to finally end his life.

With blood still dripping from its teeth, the Bigfoot turned and sniffed the air. A low, rumbling growl thundered in its chest. There was still one human in its territory.

Chapter Twenty-Nine

Answers

Beth accepted the steaming cup of vanilla chai from the barista with a forced smile. "Thanks." They'd forgotten to add the whipped cream, but she didn't have the strength to return it.

She trudged across the coffee shop and pushed open the door, causing the friendly chime to ding on the way out. It was cold outside, too cold for fall in Beth's opinion, but the temperature would help to wake her up a little bit. Coffee wasn't even helping with that anymore, so she had to do something.

There had been snow up on the taller mountains yesterday, but nothing in Redwood yet, just the bite of cold and chilling wind rushing down from the peaks.

She plopped down at an abandoned metal table outside the coffee shop, the see-through underside dotted with a wad of chewed gum from an earlier, careless patron, and decided she should organize her thoughts. Maybe if she could just put them all in some kind of reasonable order, it would calm her anxiety.

She started by putting everything into a timeline. Scott had been missing since Monday when he hadn't returned home as planned, the same day she'd gone to Hank for help in rescuing him. Hank had gone up to Spider Lake on Tuesday and returned home the same day with nothing but a lame, falsified story about a bear. She and Scott had encountered a bear together before on one of her first trips out to the woods, and he'd known exactly what to do and how to handle the situation. There was little chance that a bear, no matter how wild, had killed Scott and all his friends to boot.

Ace had gathered his rescue team on Wednesday and left early the next morning, on Thursday. Now it was Friday, and Beth felt completely helpless without news. Scott had been missing for over five days by now, and all she was doing was sitting around drinking watered-down, lukewarm tea with no whipped cream. She knew she should be doing more as his fiancée, but what?

Beth hadn't been to work all week, either. She had debated about going in on Tuesday to keep her mind occupied on other things, but she knew she couldn't do it when her mind was elsewhere, when one of the children in her class shared the same name as Scott. She had called in and let her principal know she wouldn't be in for at least the rest of the week.

She'd tried to convince Ace to take her along with the rescue team, but he'd said no without even pausing to consider it. Not that she had expected anything different from Ace, but she'd had to try.

Ace had told her that her place was here in town. She had to be here in case Scott came home, he said. Laura even backed him up, but Beth had expected that from Laura. Though she couldn't deny that she desperately wanted to be home when Scott came back, there wasn't much chance of him wandering into town on his own at this point, and Beth didn't like being treated like she couldn't handle something.

Now Ace was in the mountains doing the real rescue work while she sat, frazzled and jittery, sipping now-tasteless tea and checking her phone every five minutes just in case she'd missed something.

A puff of vapor escaped from Beth's nose at the blank background of her phone. She belonged up in those mountains looking for the man she loved. She could handle anything they ran into just as well as Ace and his band of searchers. If only she'd gone with them.

Logically, she knew that something had gone terribly wrong with the guys after none of them returned, but she kept the knowledge suppressed. Beyond all reason, her heart held on to the hope that Scott would walk up behind her and startle her, making her spill the cooling tea all over herself. She'd be angry with him for scaring her so badly, but then everything would go back to the way it was before and she'd be kissing him too quickly to catch her breath.

She looked up at the mountain range that loomed over the city. Their jagged peaks had always looked so beautiful, so majestic to her. But looking at them now, Beth felt only sick to her stomach. There was something up there – something that had been kept a secret from the town for so long that no one dared talked about it anymore, except in whispered legends. She'd heard the stories as a kid, everyone had, but they were just stories people told, like the fairy tales and bedtime stories parents whispered to keep their kids from wandering too far from home when they played outdoors.

But nobody thought those stories had even a shred of truth to them. It was unfathomable.

She thought back to the stories and articles she'd read in the library. Back then, people had disagreed about exactly what was up there, but they all agreed that there was something there. No matter how crazy it sounded, there had to be some kernel of truth in the legends she'd heard as a girl.

But that just couldn't be true. There was no giant monster there, no Bigfoot beast stomping around Spider Lake, waiting to devour any hikers foolish enough to wander past. Sure, something dangerous was up there, it had to be for the area to be sealed off completely, but it was something rational, something science could explain.

Beth slammed her cup down on the table so hard that some tea splashed onto her hand, but she ignored the feeling of the wet, sticky drink dripping down her wrist. Normally when she had a question about something in the mountains, she'd ask Scott. But he couldn't give her any answers now.

There was only one person who knew more about those mountains than Scott – Hank.

He'd been against them going up into the restricted area from the beginning, but he refused to say why. Beth had suspected the entire time that Hank knew more than he was saying, that he was hiding something.

Now, with the absence of Ace and his story about as stable as a sandcastle, she was convinced.

Hank knew what was going on up there, and it was time that he talked about it. Beth wasn't going to leave him alone until he did.

*

Hank sat in his house, staring out the window at the mountains, thinking about his workplace. He hadn't been up to the game warden's office since bringing the news about Scott and the others back to town. For all he knew, the folks who were so furious about the way he was handling things, they had burned it down by now.

Part of him, a big part of him, knew they were right to be angry. Hell, if his girls ended up dead after something like this, he didn't know what he'd do. He should be doing something, anything. But what could he do? He knew what that creature was capable of.

The crunch of tires rolling over gravel turned his head toward the driveway. For a moment he thought the angry people of Redwood had come for him at his house, but then he caught a glimpse of Beth's car through his window and he sighed audibly.

Hank pushed himself to his feet. He might prefer to deal with an armed mob rather than talk with Beth again, but he couldn't ignore her, not when this whole thing involved her so deeply.

She was coming up the steps to the front porch when he swung open the door.

"Beth, let's talk on the porch." He knew his voice was ragged, but he didn't care. He was tired of hiding things, too tired to even try.

She followed him to the two worn wicker chairs that looked out over his driveway and the pine-filled mountains beyond.

Once she sat down in one and leaned back to conform to the shape, Beth didn't say anything for a long time, and Hank was content to wait. Hell, he would have waited forever.

Finally, she took a deep breath and began. "Hank, what's really up there? I don't want the bullshit, either. Don't tell me about a bear or a crazy mudslide or anything else you make up on the spot. I want the truth."

Hank didn't even spare a sidelong look at her. "I don't get a good morning?"

"I didn't come to exchange pleasantries, Hank. You know that."

So he did. Hank closed his eyes and rubbed them. He'd been fighting to hide the truth from the world for so long that he hardly knew what the truth really was any more. He opened his eyes and found Beth staring at him, awaiting her answer. She was so strong, yet so innocent. And she deserved to know the truth, God, she deserved to know what had really happened to Scott and the others.

"Beth, I, I want to tell you; it's just—"

"I said no bullshit, Hank. I know there's something you haven't been telling me. Something you wouldn't tell Scott or Ace, though I don't know why." Her voice was firm, solid, but not angry.

Hank broke eye contact and rubbed the rough stubble on his face. He wasn't sure he could even bring himself to talk about it after forcing himself to forget for so long. And if he did get it out, would she believe him afterwards? Would she think he'd gone mad?

He looked at Beth again, considering. She was still drilling him with the same determined stare. She wasn't going to leave his porch without the truth. That much was obvious.

He shut his eyes one more time to give himself a boost of concentration and strength, pulling in a big breath. There was no reason to hide the truth anymore, not when it was facing him dead-on.

"All right, Beth," Hank started, keeping his eyes on her. "I don't expect that you'll believe what I'm about to tell you, but this is the truth, by God in heaven and my Sarah's life, I swear that what I'm about to tell you is the truth."

Beth leaned forward, now convinced.

"When I was younger, much younger, I was the assistant game warden under a man named Allan Morrison. You probably don't recognize the name."

"The warden who put the restrictions in place."

Hank's head tilted to the side. "How do you know that?"

Beth waved the question off, not willing to talk about her endless pouring through articles and books. "Doesn't matter. Go on."

Hank blinked, but then resumed his story. "It was the late 1970's and we had some kids go missing up near Spider Lake."

Hank shook his head. That funeral with the empty caskets open for public viewing still haunted his dreams.

"It was a real tragedy, young kids disappearing out of nowhere, no warning. They weren't the first to go missing either," Hank continued. "We'd had others just like them. They'd go up to Spider Lake and never come home. It was a mystery for a while. Morrison and the mayor at the time, Dave Muir, went up themselves looking for the missing kids in a sort of political stunt, they found nothing on the first trip. But the families of those kids were so devastated that Morrison made it his personal mission to find those kids and bring closure to their families. So he left me in charge of day to day stuff in the office and went up in those mountains, searching himself."

Beth's eyes were locked on Hank's, like a kid hanging on every word of a story. "Did he find them?"

Hank shook his head. "Tragically, he didn't. But he found out what happened to them. He was only gone two days. I can remember the afternoon he came back like it was yesterday. I was a bored young man, sitting in the game warden's office, filing some paperwork for a family to take an extended camping trip, when he came tearing through the door, almost ripped it right off the hinges in his hurry. His eyes were wild and all the color was drained from his face, more ghost than man. He was dripping with sweat and looked like he'd seen the souls of those missing kids – or worse."

Telling the story, Hank felt like he was experiencing it all over again.

"Warden?" Hank bolted up from his chair so fast it toppled backwards, fearing the man had been bitten by a snake or something and needed medical attention quick. "What's going on?"

"Tomkins." Morrison put his hands on his knees and gasped to catch his breath. "We've got to do something. There's a creature, a beast, a man, something, God it's a monster." He'd straightened and looked at Hank with eyes too wide for his face.

"There's what, Warden?"

Morrison had swallowed and continued, slower. "There's something up there. I saw him. He's not a man but it's not really an animal either. He's something in between."

"What, like the missing link or something?" Hank had thought it was some weird joke, an initiation for the new assistant warden.

"No, I don't know, it doesn't matter what he is. He's hunting humans, Hank. The humans that come into his territory are his prey, and he hunts them for sport, like animals hunt animals. He almost killed me, but I got away. I made it out." His voice got softer as he finished, and he'd stared at a blank spot on the wall as if he were afraid it would hear him and come charging through the side of the office. His voice was thick again, and Hank knew a part of him was back in the mountains, reliving whatever nightmare he'd been through up there.

"You didn't kill it?" Hank had asked, puzzling at how seriously Morrison was taking this joke.

"Kill it?" Morrison erupted, his eyes coming back to Hank. "That thing can't be killed, not by anything I had with me. No gun, sword, weapon made by man can kill it. I didn't go up there prepared to hunt Bigfoot. You don't understand, boy, this creature, this monster, he's taller than any man, shakes the ground when he runs. But, when he wants to, he can slip through the forest without making a sound."

"Well, we have to go after it." Hank took a step toward the gun case. "We can't let something like that go on living in the forest when tourists are still heading up there every day. It's our responsibility to keep the town safe."

"Sit your ass down, kid," Morrison snapped. "Now you listen to me and you listen good. This is going to stay between you and me for now. You don't go running off and telling people about what's up there, not before we're ready for the repercussions. We don't need panic in town.

We're going to handle this, and it's going to be done in a way that's best for everyone."

Hank's eyes focused on Beth again. "And that's when the restrictions were created. Morrison told the mayor about what he'd seen, and they worked together to get the restrictions set up. They pushed it all through quickly and quietly. Fences were built and signs were put up and that was the end of it. There were plenty of whispered rumors about what really was up there, conspiracy theories about the government, maybe a thing or two about aliens. But no one really took them seriously, and after a year or two, the whole thing was already legend, myth. When people asked about the restrictions, we told 'em mudslides and that was the end of it. Morrison, Dave Muir, and I were the only three who ever knew the truth."

"So you never saw the Bigfoot, or whatever it was?" Beth asked.

Hank met her gaze, surprised to see that she really did seem to believe his story. "I never saw it, and never thought I would. Not until this week."

Beth gasped, recoiling slightly.

"But I believed Morrison from the start. I saw the terror on that man's face when he came into the office. He wasn't lying."

Beth nodded soberly. No doubt there was something in his face that made it apparent he really was telling the truth as he knew it.

"I saw him take on a mountain lion with a stick in hand. Nothing scared that man, Beth, nothing. But whatever was up at Spider Lake scared the shit out of him. I wasn't about to argue or go up there myself just to prove a point." He sighed and stared up into the mountains. "But all that changed when Scott decided he needed to explore up there."

Beth was quiet for a few minutes, and Hank gave her the time she needed. Any sane person would need a breath or two to process the kind of story she'd just been told.

"Why didn't you just tell him?" Beth finally said. It wasn't meant as an accusation, just a question.

"Tell him what?" Hank said, a chuff of breath coming from him. "That the myths he grew up hearing about Spider Lake are true? That there's some kind of Bigfoot up there wandering in the woods?" Hank snorted. "He'd have thought I was lying, grasping at straws to keep him here. Nothing I could have said could change that boy's mind, Beth. And even if he did believe me, what do you think Scott would have done if he thought it was true?"

Beth nodded in understanding. "He would've wanted to go even more. He would have wanted to see it for himself. Or kill it, if he got the chance."

"I was young once, and I felt the same way about challenges. I was a lot like Scott. I wanted to be the hero in everyone's eyes. For years I dreamed of it. I wanted to know how it felt, going up there, armed to the teeth and taking on the beast. What people would say when I came back into town with its pelt in my truck as the hero who had protected everyone. But that was a fool's dream, and some part of me knew it. Not every bully in the playground needs to be provoked. Sometimes if you just leave things be, everything will work out."

Some of the fire came back into Beth's eyes. "If you had at least warned them, they could have gone better prepared." Tears welled up behind her eyes, but she choked them back. "You let them go up there with no idea what they'd be facing."

"I had hoped that maybe the creature had moved on or died. Maybe he wasn't there anymore. It's been decades, a lot can happen in that amount of time. But I was wrong." Hank hung his head. Hearing the words come out of his mouth, they sounded pitiful. Beth was right.

How could he have let those boys go up there without the slightest clue what they were getting into?

"So he is still there," Beth said.

"Yes," Hank said. "I saw him on Tuesday when I went looking for the guys. He was still near their campsite, and still as ferocious as ever. I escaped and made it back to the plane in time to get away, but," he looked at Beth, then back down at the porch. "Scott and the others weren't so lucky."

"You saw Scott's body?" Beth's voice was perfectly calm, not a hint of emotion in it.

"No," Hank admitted. "But I saw what was left of some of the others, and it wasn't pretty." The images rose up in Hank's mind again, and he did his best to block them out. "Beth, no one could have survived an attack like that."

"You did, and Morrison did, so why couldn't Scott?" Beth tilted her chin up, defying Hank's bleak evaluation.

"We both went up there knowing there might be trouble. We were ready for it, on guard. Those guys were just camping, completely unaware. They weren't expecting any kind of an attack like that. I was on edge the entire time I was up there, ready to run at a moment's notice. I was lucky because I had the plane to run to. If I hadn't had that, I wouldn't have made it." Admitting the fact out loud sent a shiver down Hank's spine. "Scott didn't have anywhere to run. He would have had to outrun that thing for miles. I barely made it a few hundred yards with a good head start. I wish I could believe that Scott had a chance, but now that I've seen this thing..." Hank's voice trailed off. He couldn't bring himself to look up into Beth's eyes, but he saw her nod.

"It's like nothing I could have imagined even after hearing Morrison's description." Hank groped for words, but there wasn't anything else he could say. He wanted to comfort Beth, but he didn't know how. He wanted to tell her everything was going to be okay, but it wasn't.

So he fell into silence.

Every few seconds, he stole a glance at Beth. It seemed like she believed him, but she hadn't really said as much to bring her heart to do the same. Maybe she was preparing to yell at him again, to accuse him of lying. Or maybe she did believe him and held him more responsible for Scott's death now than before.

"I know it's hard to accept." He had to break the silence. "But it's the truth."

Hank finally looked up into Beth's eyes and saw neither disbelief nor anger.

Only determination.

"I believe you," she said. "Now the question is, what are we going to do about it?"

Chapter Thirty

The Decision

The question hung in the air between them like a deep, thick fog.

Beth's eyes bored into Hank's until he couldn't hold her stare any longer.

Hank looked at the wooden boards of his porch, focusing on the nicks and the holes they'd garnered over the years. "We aren't going to do anything, Beth."

"Hank, there are still men up there in those mountains." Beth pointed up in the direction of Spider Lake. "Ace is up there."

"I tried to stop them." Hank ran his fingers through his thinning hair. "I tried to warn Ace, but the stubborn bastard wouldn't listen to me no matter what I said. Grief was too much for him."

"Maybe if you'd told him the truth about what happened to his son, he would have listened to you." There was a sharper edge to Beth's voice in that statement. She wasn't angry yet, but she was close. Hank needed to be careful how he went on explaining.

"You know Ace, Beth. He would have been up there doing the same thing he is now, no matter what I'd told him. I couldn't have stopped him, though I sure as hell tried. He'd be tracking down the creature and bringing home its head on a stick to parade through town if he could. Ace is the hero of the town, and nothing I could say was ever going to change his mind here." Hank shook his head and set his jaw.

"So you're just going to leave your old friend and a whole team of men up there to die?"

Hank looked up, but still couldn't meet the cold accusation in Beth's eyes.

"What else can I do?" Hank shrugged his shoulders to try and rid himself of the pang of guilt he felt. He'd gone up there and narrowly escaped once.

Beth rose to her feet and planted her hands on her hips. "We can go up there and get them out before they all die at the hands of that monster."

Hank didn't bother standing, immediately shaking his head. "And put your life in danger as well as my own?" He waved his hand to dismiss the idea. "I think enough people have been put in harm's way in the last few days; there's no need to continue tempting fate."

"Screw fate. This is about doing what's right, not what seems smart. And that's going up there to warn those men," Beth said. "If they haven't already met the beast, they deserve to know what is up there."

"Oh, I'm sure they've already crossed paths," Hank scoffed. "He wouldn't wait this long before dealing with intruders."

"Then what are we sitting around here talking for?" Beth was just short of shouting now. "We should be grabbing Jake, getting in his plane, and heading up there now. We may already be too late."

"That's exactly the point," Hank shot back.

"What?" Beth asked.

Now Hank met her eyes. "Have you even considered that we may already be too late for Ace and the others?" Hank heard his tone rising; he stood up to walk off his growing frustration.

"What do you mean?" she murmured, her tone fallen and quieter.

"Beth, we're not rushing up there to warn anybody," Hank shouted, whirling around to face her. "They're dead! They're all fucking dead, Beth. I was up there before, remember? I saw the bodies – what that thing is capable of, and what it did to those boys." Hank threw his arms up and turned away.

Beth didn't say anything, and Hank didn't look to see if she was shocked by his outburst or just too angry to speak.

Hank plowed on. He knew he should lower his voice at this point, but he'd cracked under the pressure of years living with this burden. "I should have died up there the other day, Beth. I'm still shocked every fucking minute that I'm alive. There's nothing we can do for those men now. They made the decision to go up there, and they've got to deal with the consequences."

"They didn't know about those consequences before they left," Beth snapped. "Because someone wasn't honest with them about what they were going to find when they got there."

"Beth, it's not—"

"You're really willing to just sit here on your porch, never knowing if you could have rescued them?"

Hank stuck his finger in Beth's face. "Now you know it is not that simple. I tried to warn them. I tried to tell them what they would find up there, and you—"

"It really is just that simple." Beth wasn't backing down an inch. "There are men up there, Hank, and we know they're in danger. It's in your job description to do the best you can to rescue those men. Do you want me to go to Laura and tell her we've got to do it on our own?" she threatened.

Hank's eyes narrowed at her. He didn't need anyone telling him how to do his job with his record of saved lives, and he didn't appreciate being threatened by anyone, particularly if they didn't understand the situation. "I don't need you telling me what's in my job description. I've been doing this job and saving the lives of people too stubborn to listen to reason for longer than you've been alive. And I don't need you starting rumors about how I'm handling the situation."

"Then don't give me a reason to." Beth lowered her voice but her brow was furrowed and her eyes were hard. "At this point I really don't care if you're going up or not. I'm not waiting for you any longer. I'm going up there with or without you."

Hank scoffed and got to his feet, walking to the porch railing and leaning over it, contemplating everything Beth had said. He knew she was probably right in the end. But it didn't matter whether she was right or wrong.

What else could he have said to stop Scott? What else could he have done to keep Ace home? He couldn't think of a single thing he could have said differently to make Scott see, or make Ace understand.

It was too late. It had been too late from the minute Scott got the idea in his head to go up to that damn area.

Shame and disgrace washed over him as he sat in silence, ruminating on the loss of the men.

Hank heard Beth start walking down the steps, heading for her car, and he gripped his hands into tight fists.

He had to do something before the guilt ate him up. Beth was right, and as infuriatingly childish as her threats were, he cared too much about his conscience to let another innocent die.

"Beth."

She stopped and turned around to look at him.

"I'll call and get us a plane," Hank said gruffly. "Meet me at the dock in half an hour, ready to go."

Beth only nodded at him before getting in her car and driving away.

Hank watched her leave and sighed the instant her car disappeared into the distance. He knew she was resilient; hell, she was one of the strongest women he'd ever known, but he didn't know if she was strong enough for what was up there and what they might find. He doubted anyone was.

Hank went inside to call Jake, moving almost instinctively. He'd have to come up with a good way to explain the need to fly up early after how petrified he'd been the last time they'd returned. Best thing would be to keep the conversation brief. It would be better to leave Jake out of it entirely, but he didn't know how else they could get up to the restricted area. Jake was the only pilot who could make the flight.

Hank dialed Jake's number and closed his eyes.

"'Ello?"

"Jake?" Hank asked.

"You're talking to 'im."

"It's Hank. I've got a favor to ask. I know you aren't scheduled to pick up Ace and his men for another few hours, but we've got to get up there a bit sooner. Actually, now, as soon as you can make it. I don't care what we've got to pay you to make it happen sooner. We've got lives at stake, and I'm taking charge." Hank took a deep breath and waited for the response.

There was silence on the other end for an agonizing moment, and Hank was frantically searching for alternate options until he heard Jake's voice.

"Well, you're a lucky man, Hank," Jake finally said amiably. "Must be somebody's looking out for ya, because I'm sitting here in the Iron Pub and I just ordered myself a beer. Lucky for you, I haven't touched it yet. Had I drank it, I couldn't have flown until their pick up time, but seeing as I haven't, I can still fly ya up there now for a price."

"Thank you so much, I—"

"Slow down, Hank. I'll fly ya up there on two conditions."

"What's that?" Hank asked.

"Number one," Jake elaborated, talking louder over the sound of someone shouting in the background, "you fill me in on what the hell is going on up there."

Hank pulled in a deep breath. How many people were going to find out about this before it was all over? They'd fought so hard to keep it a secret for so long, but now it seemed to come full circle. But because he could think of no other way, he let it out with a sigh of regret. "All right, Jake, I'll fill you in on the flight up. And what's number two?" He was braced for something worse.

"You buy me a beer when we get back since I'm wasting this one."

Hank smiled for what felt like the first time in days. He even almost laughed, relief flooding his chest and making him feel light. "You got it. I'll buy you a beer when we get home, any damn brand you want."

"I'll meet you at the plane in twenty minutes," Jake said; then the line went dead.

"If we make it back home," Hank added quietly, the dial tone resounding in his ear.

He began making preparations. He needed to be out the door in fifteen minutes to make it to the dock on time. But that shouldn't be a problem; he wouldn't need much.

They wouldn't be spending the night, that was for certain. If they didn't find anyone within the first few hours, they'd turn around and come home. The last thing Hank needed was to have Beth's death on his conscience as well. So camping gear was out of the question. But he would need weapons. He just wasn't sure which ones. How could they protect themselves against something so savage, so inhumane?

He walked over to his wall of weapons and looked over the guns. He pulled down his Kimber 84M Classic and ran his fingers over the trigger and the worn wood on the butt of the gun. It had saved him a few times before against some unfriendly animals. Plus, it was the biggest gun he had available. If this thing couldn't stop the Bigfoot, nothing would.

On a last second impulse, he grabbed a few hunting knives. Just in case things got close and he needed a quick out, they could come in handy. He also picked up two handguns, one for himself and one for Beth. They wouldn't do much damage, but they might slow the creature down if they were running, or at least do for distractions.

Then he walked into his bedroom and changed into both his thermals and hunting clothes combined. He knew it would be cold up there, maybe even snowing since it had just started raining in town. The two of them wouldn't do anyone any good if they froze to death shortly after arrival. He hoped Beth would have good, warm clothes to wear same as him. She'd been brought up in the shadow of the mountains, spending plenty of time up there, so he assumed she knew what they were heading into and would be ready to dress accordingly.

And he assumed that Scott would never date a prissy girl who didn't know how to hold her own in the wild if she needed to survive.

Before he headed out the door, Hank snatched up his first aid kit, the large one they could leave in the plane to handle major injuries. He already had a smaller one ready to go in the truck that they could carry with them to take care of minor things if, best case scenario, they found someone hurt along the way, rather than dead.

Hank glanced at his watch as he jumped in the truck and turned the ignition. He had just enough time to get to the dock and meet Beth and Jake.

Chapter Thirty-One

Final Push

Ace stumbled through the slog of muddy earth, gasping for breath and struggling to keep his bearings as he ran. He thought he was heading towards the lake where the plane would be landing, but it was difficult to be sure with the snow covering the ground and the unfamiliar trees blocking the view to any distant landmarks.

The sound of that thing behind him and the smell of its rancid breath didn't help him keep his head clear. Even the trees themselves seemed to be trying to halt his escape, their roots snaring him, the thorny, overgrown brush blockading every clear path he tried to take. The forest itself was working against him.

Ace pulled up to somewhat of a clearing, forced to stop and grope for his sense of direction among the several paths. The camp was behind him, up the hill. So the lake had to be downhill. It made sense. Right? Did they hike uphill to get to camp? How long had they hiked? Shouldn't he be there by now?

A roar ripped through the trees, and Ace broke into a blind, panicked run without thinking about his direction any more.

Just when he was convinced he'd gotten turned around somehow he heard the sound of a plane's propellers churning just ahead. His body surged with renewed energy. He was almost there!

The realization of his close safety gave him fresh hope. He smashed his way through a thicket and ran towards the sound of the plane. The sound of escape, which doubled as the sound of salvation. He must have been wandering in the woods longer than he thought if it was already time for the pickup.

Sticks arched into his line of sight, tore at his clothes, and scratched his face, but he ran on through the blockade. More and more familiar landmarks were appearing in his path now, ones he recognized, and he knew he was close. A splash told him that the plane had touched down on the lake, but a snarl from behind told him the creature was closing in on him.

His mind jumped back to Gabe, but he didn't allow it to linger there. Gabe was gone now. His sacrifice had bought Ace the precious few minutes that would allow him to make it to the plane. He could now make it home and warn the town about the evil in the woods.

In the midst of the chaos, the struggle for escape and survival, it dawned on Ace for the first time that Hank must have known about this thing the whole time. That monster was the reason he didn't want to allow anyone up here. The stories about rock slides and savage bears were the bullshit Ace had always known them to be.

But why had Hank never wanted to do anything about this threat? How many lives had been lost because of Hank's cowardice?

Ace resolved again to get home, but he also decided he'd be coming back himself. Eventually, he'd come back with more men and bigger guns. Together they would hunt this thing down and destroy it for good.

The whirring of the plane's engine was getting louder with every step. He had survived this long; all he had to do now was make it out of the woods to the safety of the plane.

The sight of a clearing up ahead was an answer to Ace's prayers, and he found a strength reserve buried deep in his muscles to put on a fresh burst of speed and bolt for the tree line. He knew that adrenaline was the only thing keeping him from collapsing to the forest floor, and he could only hope there was enough left in his system to get him to that lake.

He burst out of the trees and found the limits of his endurance. His body failed him and left him standing there motionless.

The plane was there on the lake, right where it was supposed to be. But standing in the fifty or so yards of open space between the trees and the lake stood a towering behemoth.

The Bigfoot wasn't even panting or breathing heavily from the trip to catch up with Ace, just standing there in the open, looking almost bored as it waited for Ace to come.

Ace put his hands on his knees and gasped for breath, but it wasn't filling up his lungs, not as fast as he needed it to.

The trees rose up behind him like walls and the sky, clear of clouds now, appeared like an iron ceiling. The lake glistened on the opposite side of the creature, promising safety, but unreachable. He imagined Scott and his friends running through the woods just like him, desperate to navigate their way out of their own circles of hell. He realized then that he'd brought this on himself. He had put himself in the path of a monster and death was all he could expect. He was the architect of his own fate.

He'd had no other options but to come up here. Even if he had known the truth, he would've still come.

The creature still wasn't moving. He knew Ace had nowhere to go and was content to wait him out.

"Ace! Holy shit, Ace, what is that thing?" Jake shouted from the plane.

Ace didn't answer, and the Bigfoot didn't turn. Jake might have been no more than two hundred yards away, but he wasn't in their world. There was no one here except him and the Bigfoot.

"Ace!"

The new voice slammed into Ace's consciousness and snapped him from his trance.

"Hank?"

Now the creature moved. Not to acknowledge the voices behind him but to charge Ace.

Ace tensed and prepared to sidestep the creature.

But it was even faster than he imagined. His jaw unhinged and he blacked out for a moment. When he opened his eyes, the hard ground was supporting his head like a pillar, and he saw the world tilted on its side. His breathing was suddenly calmed, no longer ragged and exhausted as it had been. The rush of escape was gone.

With the fight for survival now over, he could relax.

Ace tried to say something, anything. He wanted to shout his relief at no longer being hunted, except, for some reason, he couldn't push any words out at all. It wasn't until his lungs pushed against his chest and forced him to gasp for a sharp breath of forest air that he realized the wind had been knocked out of him; the beast had caught him.

Hank's voice reached him again, but it was faint and distant. There was a third voice as well. A woman's. Had Laura come all the way out here after him?

It didn't matter. Whoever was calling for him, they were in another world.

He swung an arm through the space behind him, but the blow was caught. Then his feet lifted off the ground, and his body followed them up, turning on an axis beyond the restraints of physics. His life had been spent building testaments to human ingenuity and engineering, and now, in the woods, he had transcended all of that in the grip of this otherworldly thing. His will fell out of him with the next exhalation, his lungs aching inside him as though his ribs had collapsed on them.

The beast seized Ace by the collar, shattering his bones until they molded to his gargantuan hands. He could feel one hand shaking violently but couldn't feel the other at all. It was numb, lifeless, cut off from the rest of his body.

Ace wanted the shaking to stop, so, unable to control himself, he closed his eyes. But his eyelids refused to cooperate any more than his hand, flitting uncontrollably as if they wanted him to watch, to face reality and die with eyes wide open, pupils flooded with light.

His vision filled with the snarling face of his nemesis. Still operating outside of his own volition, he sucked in air one last time to scream a pain too deep to be expressed by words.

In his final moments, Ace's thoughts were of Laura. At least Laura would be well taken care of by the rest of the town. She was a strong woman and the friends they'd made here would help her get through the loss of her husband and son.

Then he thought of Scott.

Had Scott's final minutes been similar to his own? Had his survival training and instincts helped him at all against such a savage and unforgiving animal? Ace had never been one for religion, but in his final seconds he hoped and prayed that there was an afterlife and he would have the chance to see Scott soon if it was true.

A final release of oxygen flooded his body, and the pain seemed to subside for a moment. The creature had been crushing him, holding him tight against its chest, but then he hit the ground. The impact sent sharp pains shooting through his body. Raspy sounds bubbled up from Ace's throat, despite his efforts to keep them silent. Perhaps the creature was gone, not realizing he was still alive.

He risked opening his eyes a crack to see if the creature was still there.

It was still towering over him, but its eyes were pointed toward the lake now. Ace tried to stretch and see what could be drawing the creature's attention but couldn't see or hear anything beyond the sounds of his own struggles to breathe.

His battered and broken body wouldn't move even as he demanded his limbs to work. In a final effort to escape, he tried to haul himself to his knees, but his shattered bones couldn't support the weight. He collapsed again in a heap on the ground. The sudden movement and noise brought the creature's attention back to Ace. If only he'd remained still.

He made eye contact with the beast as it stared down at him.

It growled angrily, and in that moment, Ace gave up his final hopes for survival. Whatever this thing was, it did not allow for survivors.

Ace surrendered to his fate and let the fight drain from his body. He no longer had the will to run or escape. He was ready to die.

"Finish me," Ace gurgled, a mixture of blood and spit spewing from his mouth, obscuring the words behind it.

But the creature understood. A sharpened, talon-like claw pierced Ace through the chest as easily as if his skin were paper. It felt like a balloon had been punctured and was deflating inside his chest as the air and blood streamed from his wounds. With his lungs no longer capable of working and his heart bleeding out, Ace knew it was finally over.

He closed his eyes and let the darkness, now only comforting, wash over him.

*

A violent scream ripped its way from Beth's throat when she saw Ace's body drop like a ragdoll from the monster's clutches. He fell without a sound, and Beth raced forward from the edge of the lake, stumbling over logs and rocks as she went.

The stories Hank had told her were simply unbelievable. Her mind told her it couldn't be possible, but the horror that filled Hank's eyes as he spoke told her heart that they were true.

Still, when she stepped out of the plane to see that creature towering over Ace, dwarfing the large man, shock had frozen her. Somehow believing that such a thing existed and actually seeing it with her own eyes were two very different things.

She ran full speed toward Ace, ignoring Hank's cries for her to wait. She had no idea what she would do when she reached Ace, only that she had to get to him, she had to save him before that unearthly creature smashed him for good.

If he wasn't dead already.

Beth crashed through a thick bush and pulled up short. The vision of what was lying before her was not of this world. Ace was lying on the ground, still breathing, but barely.

She struggled to think straight, to find a way out of this inescapable situation. Her eyes moved from Ace to the beast, and her mind went blank at the sight of creature's almost human-like eyes. There was something more than animal rage in them, and, for a moment, Beth wanted to step toward it slowly, hand extended in peace.

But then the beast's nostril's flared angrily, and he growled a warning at her. This was the monster that had killed Scott and was now threatening Ace's life. There was nothing human about it, and similarly, no way to reason with it.

Seeing Ace up close, Beth knew she didn't stand a chance of survival. She knew she should turn and run while she still had a chance of making it back to the plane. But her feet were glued to the forest floor, and she couldn't tear her eyes away from the scene before her.

Ace made a rough, gurgling sound that pulled Beth's attention away from the beast and back to him. It sounded like he was trying to speak, but she couldn't distinguish his words.

Beth gasped in horror as the beast finished him; she watched the blood drain from Ace's heart. The smell of his insides, now part of the outside, hit her nose, and the reality of the horror she'd just witnessed suddenly made her sick to her stomach. She turned away, bracing herself to puke into the grass.

But another low growl drew her attention back to the beast.

It took three giant steps and grabbed Beth by the throat. Beth didn't waste her energy trying to struggle. She was lifted off the ground, gasping for air, staring straight into the eyes of the beast. The rage was undeniable.

Hank was sprinting full speed after Beth, but she had disappeared behind a large bush before he could catch up with her. As he got close to the bush, he heard a low warning growl and slowed.

He was close.

Hank worked his way carefully around the thick thorn bush, gun raised to his shoulder, finger tight on the trigger. As he came around the edge, his eyes were filled with the most frightening image he'd ever seen in his life: Beth four feet off the ground, her legs swinging back and forth as she struggled for air against the grip of the creature's colossal hand around her throat. And Ace's lifeless body, still bleeding out at the monster's feet.

Hank expected the creature to turn to him instantly, but, somehow, his presence had not yet been detected. He guessed that two victims caused too much excitement for the moment. That gave him a few extra seconds to evaluate the situation and get an advantage over the beast for the first time.

He had the drop on him now. That skull had to be too thick, even for the high caliber rifle in Hank's hands, so he'd only have one shot to put a bullet straight through the monster's heart. That should be easy at a mere ten feet away. The only problem was that Beth was dangling between him and his target and moving to a better vantage point risked revealing his presence and losing the opportunity.

Hank pulled back the bolt on the 84M. The metallic ring of the bolt sliding home startled the Bigfoot, and he turned to face Hank directly, Beth still hanging from his powerful fist.

Time slowed as Hank waited for the Bigfoot's next move. Beth was still blocking his shot, but just barely. Hank could move a step to his right and be clear. But Beth's neck could be snapped like a twig before he finished the move.

The creature appeared to be analyzing the situation, taking into account the same factors as Hank. Then he released Beth, letting her fall to the ground. Hank's relief lasted less than a heartbeat as he realized the beast's full attention was now on him and his rifle.

Beth was on the ground gasping for air, but she didn't seem hurt. The minute he knew she wasn't hurt, Hank focused on the Bigfoot. He had a clear shot now, but something kept him from taking it. His instincts told him there was something going on here that he didn't quite understand.

Hank looked up into its eyes and saw rage and anger. But there was more there, things Hank had never seen or even imagined possible until now. There was pain, frustration, desperation. Fear.

Hank's trigger finger loosened a fraction of an inch as he struggled to understand what he was seeing. What drove this creature to such bloodlust? Why was it killing so many people?

Hank heard the expression, the eyes are the window to the soul. Goddamn, whoever'd said those words was right. The eyes held the answer. Hank stared into them, as if transfixed in time, and he saw it all. Understanding washed over him like a gentle rain after a long drought.

The Bigfoot wasn't killing for sport or for fun. He felt threatened. He was only protecting what he considered to be his own. Spider Lake, and the area surrounding it, was his, and had been for some time.

The world around Hank faded away until nothing was left but him and the creature. Though a good chunk of brain insisted he was going insane, Hank listened to the tiny part that felt a pang of sympathy for the creature. He took his finger from the trigger. He lowered his rifle from his shoulder and placed it gently on his side, maintaining eye contact with the Bigfoot the whole time. He hoped his eyes could communicate his understanding as well as the Bigfoot's had communicated his message.

Heartbeats were the only track of time as Hank continued staring into the eyes of what he could no longer call a monster. It was an amazing and surreal feeling, but an utterly terrifying one as well. He was totally vulnerable and completely at the mercy of the Bigfoot.

The Bigfoot lowered his eyes, looked at the rifle resting harmlessly at Hank's side, and turned its head to one side, just like a human would. His eyes found Hank's again, and Hank felt his heart stop.

The rage, the anger, the malice, were all gone. The fear, too. Hank was still trying to put his finger on exactly what he did see in those eyes when the Bigfoot turned away and walked into the forest, away from the lake, away from civilization, towards a new and unknown border where he wouldn't be disturbed again.

Gratitude, Hank decided after a moment of thought. It was gratitude that he'd seen. Gratitude and respect, shared alike.

In the distance, a long final howl echoed through the forest. Beth, still lying on the ground, let out a whimper.

"They are all dead." She looked at Hank, eyes filling with tears and flicking to and away from Ace's body. "God, Hank, they're all dead."

"I know, Beth." Hank's voice was soft. He walked to Beth and helped her up, keeping his own eyes averted from his dead friend, doing the same for her as he brought her into a secure hug. "I know."

"What about us?" she whimpered, fear still quaking her body.

"We're safe now, sweetheart." He squeezed her tighter against him. "We are safe."

THE END

ISBN: 978-1-77084-583-1